BIRD WATCHING
FOR BOOZERS

To my friend
Toni –
Hope you enjoy!

Stephen Molineux

To order additional copies of this book, contact:
Xlibris Corporation
1-888-795-4274
www.Xlibris.com
Orders@Xlibris.com
77625

Table of Contents

Dedication

In memory of my parents Mary Louise and Stephen Molineux. I thank my father for the book's title, his drawings and notes and some of Mole's field notes.

My dad always wanted to write novels, instead he lived one.

Acknowledgements

I'd like to thank my wife Reen for being a patient listener during the writing process. Her kind words and encouragement are appreciated. To my son Christopher, thanks for all the help with the word processing and all that computer stuff.

This is a story. It is fiction. Although based on my life, it is **fiction**. Some characters are real, some composites of many people and some made up. None of the names are real. The events, again, are the product of my mind. Some from memory, some from imagination, and some from my father and mother's stories told to me over the years.

Thanks also to my friend and wonderful artist Paul Cosgrove for his fantastic cover art.

Thanks lastly to my uncle Danny Kelso for letting me pick his memory, and to my many friends and family who took the time to read the drafts and encourage me to continue, especially Steve Condon at 10/10 Films. Thanks brother for making it happen.

Chapter 1

On an early morning wake up

I guess I didn't know what to expect. Mole did call me; five a.m. on a Sunday morning. My dad could be worse than a pack of Jehovah Witnesses with the way he would wake you early on a weekend. At least the Jehovah Witnesses would knock on your door. You could just ignore them and they would go away. On the other hand, if you felt like messing with them, you could invite them in for a cocktail or a blood transfusion. Since their religion did not allow either one, it was a sure way to run them off. I saw Mole do that once and they never bothered us again.

I was not going to be so lucky.

I reached over and fumbled for the phone. Half expecting the 'Come get me your mom had me locked up' call, I wearily answered.

"Steve, it's me Mole."

"No shit!" I said, now expecting the drunken 'I'm here if you need me' speech.

No, this was different.

"What are you up to?" he began.

"I'm sleeping asshole. What do you want?" I answered.

"Early to bed, early to rise makes a man healthy, wealthy and wise. Good ole Ben Franklin said that. He also wrote an essay called 'Fart Proudly.' Did you know that?"

I was in no mood for his call, let alone his rambling digressions. Mole had the attention span of a crack baby with ADD.

"Dad its five o'clock in the morning, what's up?"

"A little trip," he slurred.

"Call me later, you know I've got no time for you when you're banged up." I answered, as I had a million times before.

"Listen son I'm not drinkin." He lied. "Suitcase and I are planning a little R n R; an ornithological outing."

"What?" I barked.

This was getting old.

"Birding!" He slurred in a combination alcohol/ methamphetamine/ weed drawl that can only be replicated in the wee hours of the morning. You know the time, when the only people who should be awake are fishermen and paperboys.

Mole was neither.

I promptly hung up and returned to the land of slumber.

I woke up at eleven am. So much for the discipline of college.

I glanced over at the phone and realized I had two messages blinking on the answering machine. I stretched as far as I could but could not reach it. I gave up.

The remote was much easier.

I turned on the T.V.

No matter what I do I always seem to gravitate to the animal channels. As a kid it was *Mutual of Omaha's Wild Kingdom*. I was fascinated by the dangerous situations they always threw at the lackey Jim. The host, Marlin Perkins would dryly recite the scene—usually Jim in some sort of mortal danger.

"While Jim wrestles the giant anaconda we note that you can never have enough life insurance."

Who says product placement is something new?

Today, it is *Animal Planet*. The show I turned on that morning was about the rare animals of Madagascar. I was intrigued, in a slow, getting my thoughts together, starting the day kind of way. A bird was building an elaborate house to impress a potential mate.

I looked out the window at the McMansions being built across the street from my apartment and laughed. Boy, we really have evolved, I thought.

I remembered Mole's call. I got up and hit the answering machine.

The first message was my mom.

"Stevie, it's me mommy." As though I couldn't tell.

Why do mothers feel the need to identify themselves to their issue?

"Your lovely asshole father is on the warpath. He's been on a two-day tear since he got paid in scotch by the Gambinos for a carpet job. I have not seen him, but he has made his presence known. He chopped down the neighbor's tree, pissed on the Zook's back deck and stole your little sister's coin collection again. If he calls, don't help him out. Just avoid him. He hopefully will . . ."

She was on a roll, it was a shame the machine cut her off.

So, he was back to stealing coin collections. I still hadn't gotten over his theft of ten liberty head silver dollars from me years back. I didn't mind the theft as much as the use of them to buy vodka and Gallo vin rose—at face value no less, that I found unforgivable.

What was this pissing on Zook's deck and chopping down their tree?

It was common knowledge that he hated Otis Zook—Bud to his friends, ever since Bud had shot the pigeons that roosted in the eaves of our home. I couldn't blame Mole either. I mean it was comical.

Bud had warned Mole for months.

The birds were shittin up the driveway we shared and they were shittin up Bud's roof too. When Mole dismissed the idea of hiring an exterminator, at a fifty fifty split, Bud had generously offered, I knew it was headed for a showdown.

Weeks went by and the pigeon controversy died down.

One night, Bud came home from work early. He went right up the driveway to his latest toy, a candy apple vintage pickup. Now I didn't get the fascination; it looked like Fred Sanford's old junkyard truck, minus Lamont. To Bud it was the world. He had left the cover off to air it out. In the twenty-four hours since the truck had seen daylight, the birds had done a number. Two to be exact. The whole truck looked like it was in a paintball tournament.

I heard Bud scream, "Boids dirty, stinkin boids!" he choked. I was reminded of the concierge in Mel Brook's, "The Producers".

He quickly got control of his anger and his pronunciation.

"Jerry, get me the gun! These birds are history." Zook screamed.

His petrified son Jerry dutifully brought the Crossman 760 pellet gun to his now deranged stepfather.

Bud immediately began to pump the gun for what seemed like an eternity.

He aimed at my house.

Psst! He shot into the crevice.

Nothing happened at first. Then, after a brief pause, out crawled a pigeon.

Like some trapped outlaw flushed from his hideout, the bird tried a winged escape. It came tumbling down and with a disgusting thud hit our driveway.

It lay petrified and bleeding. It's one black eye moving frantically around in it's head, looking for death.

While Jerry and I sat gazing in wonder at death's pending arrival so close to us, my dad pounced on the BB gun.

"Give me that fuckin gun Zook, you murderer!" Mole bellowed.

Bud snapped back. "It's a stupid pigeon and it is a BB rifle, asshole."

He snatched the gun back. A tug of war ensued.

Before the neighbors could call the cops, my mother came out.

"Marylou, has he been drinking?" Bud asked.

"What do you think?" My mother tiredly answered.

My dad would have none of it.

"Birds are human too," he blurted out.

We laughed.

"You know what I mean, you sons of bitches," he clarified, trying to appear sober.

Just then, a pigeon flew out of the cubby. We all looked up, except Mole, who continued his drunken defense of the birds.

"They are just trying to raise a family up there like you and me Otis. They are God's creatures . . . they got a right to live like anything else."

He folded his arms in debate victory.

At the exact moment of his spirited defense of the common house pigeon's right to life, the escaping bird, perhaps from fear, or maybe in some feeble attempt at revenge, let forth a shit that cascaded to earth and landed directly on Mole's bald spot.

We exploded.

Bud, my mother, Jerry and I began a laugh that felt like it would never end. Just when we would get control, it would start again.

This was followed by a round of cheesy puns that kept the laughs going and further stoked the Mole.

"Crappy toupee," my mom blurted out.

We howled.

"Shitty weather," was my lame follow up.

Even Bud tried. "Ha ha, the yokes on you." He slapped his knee as we stopped laughing and looked at each other.

When the laughs had died down, my father reached over, and calmly took the gun from Bud.

He then began to shoot wildly at the pigeons and my house. He might even have shot out a window. I can't remember.

What I do remember is that the bad blood with Otis Zook as a result of the 'Pigeon Incident' as my mom named it, had not gone away.

What was up with Mole? I wondered, as I turned off the machine and stepped into the shower. Whatever it was, it no doubt involved alcohol.

When I was done and toweled off, my thoughts turned to food.

I picked up the phone to order a pizza. I noticed the message machine blinking. I still had a second message. I ordered, then hit the play button.

"Stephen Dean my boy, it's me Mole again."

Oddly, he sounded somewhat composed.

"By now you no doubt have heard from your mom. I'm sure Larose has told you lurid tales of strange doings to our neighbor Otis. I assure you it WAS me. The eagle has landed, as it were, on Mr. Zook."

I had no idea what he meant.

The message continued to ramble.

"The feathered friends have got their revenge. What a great way to start our journey. Please pay no mind to Larose and join us as we embark on a little sojourn into the great outdoors. We will drink some beers, smoke some giggle, eyeball some eagles, befriend the falcon, hang with hawks and debate with an owl."

He had lost his mind years ago, but this was whacked!

"That's it! He's high!" I said out loud. "Smoke some giggle," he had said.

He's stoned. I was now very interested.

Just then the machine ran out.

Every college kid dabbles in marijuana. Every other dorm has a bong secreted away in the closet or a 'one hitter' or a dugout in a desk drawer. On any given weekend, some resident assistant somewhere across the college dorms of America is following their nose, looking for the source of that familiar smell emanating from under a dormitory door.

Even now as we speak thousands of under-grads are 'waking and baking'.

It is the American way.

I however, didn't just dabble. I SMOKED ACRES OF WEED whenever and however I could.

At that particular time no one on campus had as much as a seed. It was the beginning of the dreaded dry summer.

If Mole or his cronies had weed, well that was another matter.

Where was he?

My mother's message didn't say. Neither did Mole's. At least not before the tape ran out.

I would need to see my mom. She would have an idea, although she didn't like me around him when he was hammered. I had to see him.

I called my buddy Triangle Head to drive me to my mother's.

Chapter 2

How my mother got fit, got some new duds, got country, and got a nickname

Everyone's mother is a Saint. My mother is a Saints' Fan. Even though we lived outside Philly and were in Eagle country (the team),my mother loved the Saints. Really she just loved the team colors and their helmets.

Women. Go figure.

Anyway, one year, for their anniversary, Mole took her to New Orleans to see a game. Of course, in typical Mole fashion he also took me, his friend John or Suitcase as he was called, and his friend Beans Walsh. My mother wasn't thrilled to be on her anniversary with Mole's drinking buddies, but if this is how she got to New Orleans and her beloved Saints, than so be it.

The trip started like every road trip of my youth— with a trip to buy beer and smokes. Looking back, it is amazing that I don't have lung cancer or that I did not die in a fiery drunk driving crash. My parents, ok, my **dad** and his friends, did not go anywhere without the old Styrofoam cooler filled with the High Life and a carton of Kools or Marlboro.

It was as a result of a stop in Nashville to re-up on beer and smokes that my Mother's life took a change.

We had stopped into a roadside bar. My dad and Suitcase went in. My mother and I waited in the car. Beans was passed out. When they were gone a few minutes my mother said she had to go to the bathroom. Since she didn't want to leave me unattended and Beans was worthless when he was on a load, she took me in with her.

I will never forget the look on her face when we walked into that honkytonk. Country music was blaring from an old tinny sounding jukebox. I forget what the song was, but I like to remember that it was Jimmy Rogers. Everyone was decked out in jeans, cowboy hats and rhinestone shirts. They were hootin' and hollerin' and sort of line dancing even though it wasn't called line dancing then.

It was love at first sight for my mother.

The next day she bought the whole get up. White pants made to look like chaps, with elaborate stitching around the pockets. A white vest with fringe. It was supposed to be leather, but it was definitely NOT leather. Suitcase called it pleather and my mom got pissed. The outfit was capped off with a Ten gallon white cowboy hat. It had black and gold feathers to match the Saints team colors.

I heard her on the payphone with her friend Heffie ravin' about the whole thing. How she couldn't wait to get home to try it out.

I saw Beans roll his eyes then roll over and go back to sleep.

The rest of the trip it was all she talked about.

Her friend Heffie was puttin' on a few L.B.s so the country dancing was going to whip them both into shape. "And the outfits! Well they are just too cute," she said as she stepped out of the car to model her all white cowgirl outfit.

Now it was Mole's turn to roll his eyes.

"Mary if you get all fit and trim from country dancing you'll look like the Lone Ranger on Steroids!" My dad joked.

Suitcase quickly shortened it to LaRose and a nickname was born.

For the rest of the trip my mom insisted on playing a country eight track she picked up at a gas station. Mole and his buddies insisted on calling her Larose.

To this day if I hear 'Southern Nights' I find myself singing along until my friends pummel me and change the station.

I don't remember too much else about the trip. Can't tell you who the Saints played or who won.

Oh yea, I do remember Mole threw up on Bourbon Street from too many Hurricanes and I remember LaRose getting furious at Beans for trying to bring a whore into our hotel room.

Great trip.

To this day my mom goes country dancing every Thursday night. Her friend Heffie doesn't. Something about her bunions. I think it's because of her weight. LaRose gets pissed if we joke about it.

Neither Mole nor Suitcase will drink Hurricanes. Although they will drink almost anything else.

Beans? As you will find out, Beans would drink anything.

Chapter 3

On the Invisible man
and the Shape of things to come

Triangle Head's real name was Kevin Broderick. Like everyone who grows up in the Philly area he went by a nickname. The only rule for a nickname was, you couldn't give yourself the nickname and you couldn't like your nickname.

Oh, you could grow to tolerate it, maybe even come to grow comfortable being called it, but you could never like it. As a result, my dad was Mole, short for Molineux. I was Mo, or Little Mole. We had Suitcase, my dad's best friend, and Beans—short for Bernard, Mole's other best friend. He was a merchant marine, who also worked six month's of every year on the oil rigs in Saudi Arabia.

Of my friends, there was Gub, and his brother Glob. Schmo Hallihan, Moon-dog Mooney, Marty-O, Smeg McCain, who because of bad hygiene, was named after dick cheese, which by the way became his other nickname when the punk rock craze hit. Then there was Quad Ed—he had multiple personalities, and lets not forget Chuckie Floppo, who was named for the sound the soles of his sneakers made when he walked down the street.

The list went on and on.

Then there was Triangle Head. Poor Kevin Triangle Head. His head was indeed shaped as his name implied.

Mole himself had named him.

The first day he walked into our house my drunken father had remarked, "Son your head is shaped like a pool rack!"

Kevin, taken aback said, "Excuse me sir?"

Mole replied, "No, it's not really a triangle shape it is more like a sperm whale head."

Kevin was beside himself.

Unfortunately, Mole was just warming up. "Son, have you seen those old Triumph sports car commercials? You know, the ones with the TR7 car shaped like a wedge? With the tag line 'The shape of things to come'? Well son, your wedge head is the shape of things to come." Mole finished. He was obviously pleased by his humor.

Triangle Head, because in truth, during this tirade he had become forever Triangle Head, Kevin Broderick the name, was gone, stood dumbfounded.

To this day, he is Triangle Head. Believe it or not, not only is he comfortable with the name, he also is quite fond of the Mole.

It is because Kevin likes my dad and his misfit toys that he calls friends, that he gladly offered to take me to my mom's to pick up the Mole's trail.

He pulled up in the white Gran Torino. To my dismay, it was being driven by Triangle's dad.

Shit!

Mr. Broderick was a nice enough guy, all things considered. But he chained smoked Lucky Strikes no filters. This was a habit he picked up in the Navy. If this wasn't bad enough, he had also apparently become allergic to the sun from all that time on a carrier flight deck. This caused him to wear long sleeve shirts in summer, a big straw hat, sunglasses, and work gloves. As a result of this getup, and with the cloud of cigarette smoke filling the car, Triangle head looked like he was being driven by the Invisible man on a foggy night.

Triangle head was not happy.

He was probably a little embarrassed too. His old man was quite a sight. In addition to his get up, he was also a recovering alcoholic. Now, all he drank was cheap cola. Between the caffeine and the nicotine he was one helluva' dry drunk. He could be a bastard.

As soon as I got in, Triangle could see my smirk from the side view mirror. I immediately began to make exaggerated choking signals to him. Despite my academy award performance in the back seat, Triangle head would not say a word or even roll down a window.

I began to poke him in the side between the passenger seat and the door. He mouthed in the side view mirror that his dad controlled the windows.

Sure enough, when I tried the automatic window next to my seat, it wouldn't move.

It was getting desperate! The smoke was so bad I was in danger of becoming a ham or at the least a piece of lox or something. I started to feel sick.

Finally, I jabbed Triangle head so hard he grunted. He looked over at his invisible man father and blurted out, "Could you at least crack a window?"

His old man didn't miss a beat. With a flick of his hand he cracked his son instead. "Shut up! Until you get your own car, don't be telling me what to do."

Triangle head's lip began to quiver, but he wouldn't cry.

We rode on in silence.

Amazing, even when booze is no longer in the picture it can still leave a nasty snapshot.

Fuck it if my shirt reeked. It sure beat my buddy getting clocked again for nothing.

We drove the rest of the way home. He dropped us off at my folks' house.

Chapter 4

How Triangle Head
and I went to a Garden Party

Mole wasn't there. I didn't expect him to be. My mom wasn't either, although Triangle noted that the door wasn't locked. "No shit Columbo." I muttered as I quickly slid by him after picking up what seemed to be three days of the *Philadelphia Inquirer* at my parent's door.

I will let you in on a little known fact about the working poor—they don't have locks on their doors. Oh yea, at one time they might have, but once something happens, and something always happens—they don't get replaced.

It might be that they don't replace them because the cops keep busting the door open answering one too many domestic calls. Or it might be that your alcoholic father busted in to get into his own house too many times, leading to the police being called to answer a domestic. Or it just might be that since no one has any money to go anywhere, there is always someone home. If someone is always home, why do you need a lock? Where I grew up, no one had a working lock on their door.

Pick your reason.

We entered the house. The first thing you noticed in my parents' house were the worn out carpets. Despite the fact that Mole was a carpet installer, we never had our carpets replaced during my youth. It was not until the house was sold years after college that new carpet was installed. Even then, only at the insistence of the realtor.

That's another fact of the working class. Whatever the breadwinner did for a living you could guarantee they did not do it for their own family. Auto mechanic Bud? His cars didn't run. Bill the painter down the street? His house looked like the Bates Motel. Tom the air conditioner man used a fan. Even Steve the Florist, never got his wife flowers and his mom's grave was bare.

There was only one exception to this rule in blue collar land.

The electric utility man.

We called them Peco men. Short for Philadelphia Electric Company.

The Peco man was guaranteed to insure that his family's home had the best in electrical service. He had the biggest display of Christmas lights well after New Year's Day. The rest of the year he had the multiple spotlights flooding his ten foot yard. Why, he even went as far as to convert to electric heat when the rest of us used oil or even coal.

Because another truism of the have—nots is, it's OK to screw the man.

The man was the law, the rich, or any corporation.

The electric company worker was THE ONLY employee that brought his work home. Of course, what this meant was that the Peco man managed to doctor the meter so it didn't run. A well placed matchbook in the meter gummed up the works. Once in a while they were forced to take it out so they had some token bill to pay each month. They used a special key they were issued to open the meter. I guess this qualified as bringing your job home.

But in our house like a lot of others in my neighborhood growing up, work was NOT brought home.

As I got us something to drink, I next noticed the couch. It was quite obvious Larose was sleeping on it. It had a folded sheet and a comforter. To the untrained eye it would just look like the homeowner was insuring that the couch could be covered quickly if someone wanted, to say, sit down in their work clothes.

I knew better.

My family were couch people. Not couch potatoes, which is a cute name for a lazy person. No, COUCH PEOPLE, is something entirely different. It is a group of people who go through life without a bed. They have a bed and certain times during the year they may sleep in that bed. Most of the time either because poverty prevents them from having enough beds to go around, or because of broken relations, fear, or hatred they never get to sleep in that bed. Still others never slept in the bed for more mundane reasons—their spouses snored loudly or had chronic gas.

Others were worried about a promiscuous daughter and believed if they stayed downstairs they would prevent a pregnancy. Some couldn't sleep until their late night sons were safely in the house. By the time the bar closed they were already passed out in the living room-waiting.

Whatever the reason, for them, the place where they laid their head at night was where others sit. The living room couch.

My mother had joined the ranks.

Things must be really screwed up I thought.

Just then I heard the backdoor slam. "Stevie is that you?"

My mother walked in, taking off her gardening gloves.

"I wondered where you were," I said.

"Your dad planted his usual huge vegetable garden, then of course lost interest," she sighed. Of course we both knew what she really meant.

Drunks make bad gardeners.

"Why are you here? Oh hello Kevin, I didn't see you there," she said.

Mom didn't call anyone a nickname and constantly ragged Mole for teasing my friend.

"Can I fix you boys some lunch?"

"No thanks mom, where's dad?"

"Stevie didn't I tell you not to worry about him?"

I went to the back door and looked out. Sure enough, mom had been trying to clean up and weed what looked like quite an ambitious backyard garden. Despite the weeds, I could still make out rows of tomatoes, plenty of peppers, enormous zucchini, some bad excuse for cucumbers, and of course some pot plants badly hidden in the middle. Although everything was overgrown, the plants themselves looked healthy and well tended.

Some things never change, I thought, as I turned back to the kitchen and Larose.

"Mom, he said he needed to see me. He didn't tell me why," I lied. But if he is out and about I don't want him to get a drunk driving charge."

I gave her a look that suggested that I might be able to rein him in.

"I don't want you two fighting again," she said. Although I could tell she was mulling over my suggestion. "I am definitely worried. I mean Christ, he cut down the neighbor's tree! Why would he do a thing like that? He must be bombed!"

You could tell she was at wits end.

"When did you last see him Mrs. M?" It was Triangle now back in full Columbo mode.

"Kevin, he was here yesterday with Suitcase and Beans," she answered, allowing Triangle to warm to the role.

"Did they say where they were going?" Triangle followed up.

Was he actually starting to take notes? Where did he get a pad of paper?

"Shut up you tool," I said as I pulled the note paper away from Triangle head.

It was my mom's shopping list.

"I assume they were drinking ma'am, but who was driving," I said.

The Colombo act was contagious.

"Suitcase as always," she answered.

I should have known. Suitcase could POUND beers, yet he never appeared to be tanked. The only indication of intoxication was that he started to sound like Rod Steger in *On The Waterfront*. Of course, he would tell you he was doing Brando, but it was Steger all the way.

"They were here all day drinking in the backyard. They were shooting your old bow and arrow set at a target by the O'Hanlon's garage. Beans had passed out on a blanket and pissed himself," my mother said disgustedly. "The O'Hanlon's were having a backyard barbeque. Just having a nice time in their own yard. But Noo!"

Now my mom was doing her best Belushi.

"Mole had to keep raising hell. Mr. O'Hanlon came over two times to nicely ask them to quiet down. Still they kept it up. Finally, Mole shot wide and the arrow knocked Mr. O'Hanlon's highball out of his hand. He was furious!"

My mother looked at me embarrassed because she realized my friend was taking all this in.

"What happened next?" I said.

"Guess what he tells your father?" My mother paused, allowing the set up. Even when she was telling a mortifyingly embarrassing story, she could still find the humor.

"You know, it's all fun and games until someone loses an eye!" She delivered like a stand-up.

"Mr. O'Hanlon. Always the dad." She tried to laugh. "Your father and his friends stuck around a little while longer. At least they stopped target practice.

When Beans woke up, he wanted to shower and get changed, so they left. I guess that would be a good place to look for them."

She sighed, and took a tea kettle off the stove.

"By the way Kevin, why don't you take some tomatoes and zucchini. We have a ton."

She lent me her car keys and forced a bag of produce on Triangle as we headed out the door.

Chapter 5

Beans, Beans he's good for your heart

Bernard Walsh was my father's oldest childhood friend. They met in kindergarten, and Beans was Beans even then. By far, he was the biggest character of all of my father's friends.

He started drinking with Mole in the sixth grade.

What chance do you have of not becoming an alcoholic when you start drinking in the sixth grade?

The truth is, that's when he started my dad to drinking. Beans had been drinking well before that. He may have been the one who started Mole on the sauce, but it was Mole that kept himself there.

Like people attract like people, I guess.

Mole told me that Beans had tried to get him to drink even before sixth grade, but, according to Mole, he had successfully fended off those attempts.

It was only when tragedy struck, that Mole finally succumbed to Beans and the sauce.

My dad had a dog when he was a kid. The dog's name was Brownie. Mole loved Brownie although in actuality it was his little brother's dog.

My uncle Paul, my dad's little brother, was responsible for taking care of the dog. It was my grand parent's way of giving him some responsibility Each day he was to give the dog food and water and let him out.

According to my dad, Brownie, like most dogs, would chase any animal that moved. One day when Paul let the dog out, Brownie took off after a rabbit or another dog or something. The point is—Brownie ran off.

In hind sight, it was probably Mole who let the dog loose. He always felt animals should be free. Further, he never accepted blame, and come to think of it, he always was blaming things on Paul. I'm pretty sure then that despite Mole's version of who was to blame for what happened, Mole and Beans certainly played a big part.

After the dog ran away, the boys were heartbroken. Uncle Paul told me he searched every day, even skipping school to look.

After a week the boys gave up hope.

That weekend, Beans invited Mole down the woods to his fort.

The fort was really just a thrown together shack. Beans and his friend Josh Keenan built it out of some stolen lumber from the old Harris school, some parking barriers as foundations, and some tar paper left over from when Josh's dad redid his garage roof. The thing wasn't pretty, but it was pretty much water tight. It was as good a place as any to share the sixteen ounce Gibbons Beer Josh stole from his old man.

The fort was located behind an old cemetery, next to an old deserted army base. The base was used as a staging ground for new recruits during World War Two. Beans and Josh were therefore able to outfit the fort with all sorts of obsolete army gear. Besides the expected empty fuel canisters they turned into tables and chairs, they also had a canvas tent they used for the floor, assorted ammo boxes stacked up as end tables, an old recruitment poster with Uncle Sam pointing and proclaiming, "I want You" and their prized possession, an old dilapidated canvas and metal gas mask. You know, the kind you see in those old war movies, where the Germans are using mustard gas on our boys.

All in all, the place wasn't a bad hang out. It had served them well. The cops never bothered to hump all the way back through the woods, not with all the sticker bushes and brambles. The nearest road was over a mile away. Not many people went back there. Even the funerals were few and far between, and when they took place they were over a half a mile away in the cemetery.

Beans and Mole were almost through the grave yard when they met up with Josh. "Yo!" Josh yelled to them from across the cemetery. He was leaning against a huge tombstone that read SWARTZ.

This was the Jewish cemetery. Next to it, was the African American cemetery, and down the road was the white cemetery. They are all still there. I walk my dog—Pirate back there once in a while.

It's amazing.

We are segregated in life and we are segregated in death. What chance does this country have of ever getting over racism when we can't even be buried together?

"Mole come over here. I'm afraid you are not going to like what you see," Josh said.

Mole told me at the moment Josh said those words he knew immediately it was Brownie.

He and Beans ran over.

Sure enough, it was the poor old hound. He was in bad shape. He had cuts all over and his fur was matted with dried blood and dirt. But it was the huge gaping wound on his belly that shocked the boys the most. Some how the dog had ripped open his stomach. Brownie must have caught it on some barbwire at the old base. The wound had festered and now was filled with pus and maggots. The dog whimpered in pain. Mole claimed the poor thing still managed to wag his tail at the sight of his master.

Beans took one look and took off running. Mole turned his head and began to cry. Only Josh kept it together. He yelled for Beans to come back, then he bent over and gently stroked the dying animal behind the ears.

Brownie whimpered.

"Mole what should we do? The dog needs a vet," Josh calmly stated.

My dad knew the dog was dying and was suffering badly on the way.

"No, Josh, Brownie is a goner," Mole said, as he got himself together. "We gotta' put him out of his misery."

Just then Beans reappeared. He had not run off in fear after all.

Now, he carried the old gas mask. With it he carried an old fuel can. He calmly walked up to them. Mole knew from Bean's eyes what he intended to do.

"No fuckin way!" Mole pleaded. Although inside he knew it was the only way.

"Mole, I love that dog as much as you, but he's suffering," Beans said sympathetically.

"I can't kill my own dog!" Mole said, and turned away.

"I'll take care of him," Beans said as he gently placed the ancient gas mask over Brownie's head. The dog didn't even flinch. Beans then poured the gas into the vent slots.

The dog's breathing was steady and measured.

As the dog inhaled the fumes, his breathing became slower and not as regular. After what seemed like hours, the dog shuddered and at last, the breathing stopped.

"Sorry Mole," Beans said.

Josh and Beans buried the dog there in the cemetery.

Years later Mole tried to make light of it. He joked that Beans seemed calm as Kevorkian the whole time. Mole also claimed that since Josh was an anti-Semite and Beans hated blacks they had to carry Brownie to the 'white' cemetery up the road before they could lay him to rest.

I know Mole is full of shit.

Leave it to him to joke about what must have been a terrible thing for a boy, or anyone, for that matter to endure.

Beans was there that day, as he was for most of the major events of Mole's life.

That was the day Mole started to drink.

It was a bad day but not his worst.

Beans was always there for the Mole. Always willing to do the dirty work, or anything his friends asked of him.

Semper Fi.

Always faithful, like the marines they both went on to be.

Chapter 6

On Cars

We took my mom's car and headed to Bean's apartment to track down the Mole.

My mom's car warrants some comment, if only to explain that my father impacted everything. The car was a Dodge Dart. It was once a new car. This was probably at least three owners before my mom. Now Larose called it the Dodge Dent. It's color could only be described as Factory Rustoleum. That, and a purple door. Oh, and did I mention the holes in the floor?

Thank God for Bud, next door, who felt sorry for my mom. He constantly 'borrowed' inspection stickers from his employer's auto repair business to smack on the wind shield of the Dent to keep my mom's car legal.

I was always given the keys with the warning to make sure I kept my feet up. To do otherwise, was to risk losing your legs through the floor.

Triangle laughingly called it the Flintstone mobile.

I said earlier that Mole impacted everything. Well, this car had not always been that way. Mole had smashed it so many times we had lost count, and that's just getting out of the driveway!

Mole often used the car because his carpet truck—The Ting Mobile, was always out of commission. I could of taken my dad's truck that day. I remember it was running because I remember my mom strongly urging me to take the Ting Thing.

I did not bite.

The Ting Mobile was not exactly something you could tool around in. It was, shall we say, a little conspicuous. It had originally said 'Painting and

Contracting' on the side when Mole bought it. He had started to compound out the old sign, but had given up before he was finished. As a result, the last four letters of the sign remained. Thus the 'Ting Mobile' was born.

If that was the only thing about the truck I would have taken it, but as I said, it was a tad over the top. Mole, during a prolonged bender had written the first chapter of his novel on two sides of the Ting in day-glow paint no less. He had filled out the remaining side with assorted day-glow flowers, psychedelic animals, eyeballs and semi-clad women. If that wasn't bad enough, the Ting Mobile was stick shift. Three on the tree. Anyone who knows what I'm talking about, knows that this type of manual transmission has a tendency to get jammed. When I was forced to drive with him, I would hunker down in the passenger side so no one would see me. Everything would be bearable, until that goddamn linkage would jam. And it always jammed. Mole would pull me up out of hiding in the passenger seat, pull off the carpet remnant I used to hide myself, hand me a hammer and bark, "Get out and hit the linkage!"

I would slink out of the truck like a college girl leaving the boys dorm the morning of parent's day, and slip under the Ting. I would be expected to hit the gear box or whatever it was called until it unjammed. This happened at least once a trip, sometimes more. Usually this took place on the road at a red light, so time was of the essence.

Could you imagine the spectacle of the day-glo Ting Mobile backing up traffic while your's truly crawled underneath to fix it?

Is it any surprise Triangle and I took the Dodge Dent that day?

Looking back, all my friend's cars had problems, "small annoyances" as my mother called them. My high school girlfriend's parent's car always had a light on—on the inside. Beans, had a car that needed two people to operate. One to drive and one to sit in the backseat and prop up the driver's seat with their legs because the reclining lever was broken.

These small annoyances were never embarrassing to anyone. Further, no one took notice, no one said anything and no one ever corrected them. They never got fixed. They were part of the package—the working poor package. No one ever complained and no one felt they were poor.

As my grandmother who survived the depression said, "Your lucky you have a car, I had to walk ten miles each day just to get to the store and it was uphill both ways."

We drove down South Avenue and turned onto Chester Pike. Wherever Mole was, I felt sure that Beans and Suitcase were still with him.

Chapter 7

In Seconds Flat

Triangle popped two Miller High Lifes'. I laughed. High Life? What a joke.

The car I was in was purple and rust, my other transportation option was a bad excuse for Scooby Doo's Mystery Machine—when it was running. Supposedly, I was on a mission to find my drunk father and keep him from hurting himself or others.

A high life?

You had to be high just to deal with it.

In actuality, what **was** I doing?

Looking for weed?

Killing time with Triangle?

Going bird watching?

Trying to get closer to my old man, or at least finally figure him out?

What was I doing?

As pondered my next move, I drove up Chester Pike.

Both sides of the Pike were showing their age.

This stretch of the county used to be called the 'Golden Mile.' Thriving automobile dealerships, banks and small family run businesses once lined the street. The place used to have a homey, main street feel to it.

Not anymore. Now it looked more like the rust mile. It seemed, like the rest of America, to have morphed into one never ending decrepit strip mall.

Dirty and closed store fronts. Drycleaners. Liquor stores. Cheap takeout Chinese restaurants. A seafood and chicken joint. Gun shops and check cashing operations advertising 'Payday Loans' on cheap computer printout signs.

Talk about depressing. I quickly decided to try and live at the Jersey shore when school let out in a few weeks.

"Look at this shit Steve," Triangle said disgustedly.

It was hard not to notice.

"One stop shopping for the black man." He laughed.

"It's a fucking economic issue not a race issue," I fired back, spouting my parent's party line I had over-heard on many nights when they used to sit around the kitchen table drinking, smoking and debating.

Back then it was not uncommon to find college professors, contractors, lawyers, plumbers, and my dad's childhood friends all 'mixing it up' as Mole used to say. He had a way of attracting people to him. White, black, Jewish. White collar, blue collar, it didn't matter. They all flocked to my parent's house.

My neighbors hated it.

This was long before the drinking took real discussion from our home. Never to return.

Now the only ones around were the serious drinkers. They debated too, but it wasn't the same.

"I know, I know. There are white niggers too," Triangle said, trying desperately to win me back.

"Save that fuckin bullshit chestnut for someone else," I fired back.

"Hey, I agree with you. It is economic. The haves and the have nots. blues don't have any dough. They are one segment of the have nots," Triangle reasoned, trying to reconcile our positions. "It's just that there ain't no affirmative action for my family. It seems the blues get all the government hand outs," Triangle laughed bitterly.

"What the fuck is a blue?" I asked turning into Beans' driveway.

"A blue is what my dad calls the blacks," Triangle answered as though I was from another planet. "You never heard that one? Its like the Italians calling them moulons; eggplants, because they are purple."

I was through with this talk.

"Blacks, Blues, Purples, enough of your bullshit, Broderick you fuckin Vicks cough drop dome."

Race discussions. All they cause are bruises.

We parked the Dent and walked up to the house

Beans' house was, to use Joe Strummer's phrase, a 'Ramshackle Day Parade'. At any given time it housed Beans' girlfriends, his mother, assorted parolees, and other hanger's on.

As I said earlier, Beans worked on the oil rigs in Saudi Arabia for six months out of the year. When he did, he made a shit load of money. He had nothing to spend it on except booze and gold. And most of the time he could not get either in the Muslim country.

He would therefore hit the states with a ton of cash.

The whole town would know his arrival date. The so called 'friends' that flopped at his place while he was gone would be sure to tell the ones who didn't what time the ship came in.

They would descend on the place like white trash zombies looking for booze or drugs or women.

Most got all three.

Beans would welcome them all. He would finance them all as well.

There was one exception to this rule, Beans would not pay for drugs.

"Only booze and broads!" he'd rail long into the night to any one who would listen. He was serious, but it didn't matter much.

Meanwhile, his friends would be snorting coke or meth and popping ludes in his bedroom. Bought with money stolen from his pockets when he passed out.

My father hated to see Beans exploited like that, but no matter how much he and Suitcase and Josh tried, they couldn't get the drunken tiger to change his stripes. The only way it would stop was when he ran out of money. Most times that did not take long.

Since the place was a twenty-four seven non stop party, things were always getting broken or stolen or at least saturated in booze.

Because of this, Beans had outfitted the place in nothing but junk store, second hand furniture. A sort of middle—aged frat—house décor. Definitely shabby, not too chic.

There was always an assortment of beat up couches. They were constantly being replaced because Beans would always end up pissing on them. There were milk crate bookshelves and broken lamps. Moldy newspapers, and beer cans everywhere. An ashtray that always looked like it had worked overtime at an AA meeting. There was even the interior of a 1968 Volkswagen Beetle in the living room. Mole and Suitcase and Beans' suffering mother would try to tidy up when they were sober. But since no one was usually sober the place didn't get spruced up much.

Mole would occasionally bring over a carpet remnant or two when the old throw rug needed to be thrown away. He would also use the place to display his artworks. These might consist of something as crazy as a collage of laundry detergent labels, or a painting of fish displayed in an old ten gallon aquarium rigged from the ceiling. Other times it might be a serious charcoal drawing of Kennedy or Brendan Behan, or his favorites Dylan Thomas and Henry Miller. He even did a water color of Suitcase's dog R.P. McMurphy smoking.

It all depended on Mole's mood.

Beans would let the guests destroy the house, but they better not touch Mole's art. Even the off the wall shit that should have been taken off the wall, none of it could be touched. Usually it was Mole himself who would end up tearing it down or ripping it up. Beans and Suitcase couldn't stop him. Sometimes they took the more interesting ones and hid them. I still have a couple somewhere around my house. They aren't bad.

Between the beat-up used second hand furniture and the beat up, using friends, Mole took to calling the house 'Seconds Flat'.

From the moment you walked past the huge stuffed animal clutching a pitchfork on the front lawn, to the time you made your way to the backyard that looked like a junkyard with bird feeders, you realized, you were in 'Seconds Flat.' It was the perfect name for Beans' place.

It was a mystery as to whether he owned the place. Rumor had it he rented the place from the owners of the Darby Inn, who bought it with drug money. Others said Beans was on the deed but he was a straw owner for the shady bar owners. Whatever the case, Bean's called it home.

I walked up the drive way and listened for signs of life. At first I didn't hear anything. Triangle and I walked up the steps past the overgrown front yard with its huge stuffed teddy bear sentry. Fittingly, one lone crutch leaned against a faded green front door. The house's window panes were chipped and flaking and were obscured by a tree that had grown too big for its birches, as it were. It's roots no doubt being nourished by the water pipes in the basement. Old books borrowed from the local library stacked on the steps like they were waiting for someone to answer the door.

We knocked, then entered.

We could hear a dull moaning in the backroom.

"Beans?" I yelled.

"We're back here, is that you Stevie?" It was Mole and he sounded okay.

"Come on back. The fireworks are over. We have struck while the iron was hot," he said, as others laughed at his comment. "Come on back. Doctor Suitcase, the famous Doctor Suitcase Sampson and his trusty assistants, Dr. Josh and Mr. Mole are just finishing up."

"Steve, what's up?" Triangle said, a look of bewildered fear on his face.

"I don't know Kevin," I answered, confused to the point of calling him by his real name. We walked back toward the voices.

The place hadn't changed much since the last time I saw it. Still your basic path through the ruins. The only thing missing were the party'ers. We reached the back room. Mole greeted me with a big hug and a wet boozy kiss. I pushed him away in disgust. He smelled like booze and cigarettes, like my pop-pop and probably his pop-pop before him.

Suitcase lined up for his turn. "Well if it isn't the Marjean Gumbody!" he chuckled laughing at his joke I didn't get. "With the Shape of things to come, his trusty sidekick," Mole roared.

Triangle fidgeted from the attention.

Josh, who was usually shy, slapped my back as he walked out of the room. "Beers, fellas?" he said.

It was then that I noticed Beans. He was lying on an old single bed. The mattress was beat so his head and feet were elevated and his ass drooped in the middle. The workingman's Craftmatic Adjustable Bed. He was semiconscious and bleeding from his shoulder. He had an icepack on the wound. The place reeked like burnt hair. He was mumbling and occasionally he let out a low groan. Strangely, he had a bizarre smile on his face.

"What the hell happened to him," I asked, not really wanting an answer.

"He caught Caroline cheating on him, so he made us do it," Suitcase explained.

Caroline was his ex-wife, they had been divorced for three years. I was now thoroughly confused.

"Made you do what?" I inquired as I made my way to the bed. Mole reached out and blocked me. "Unless you are family then visiting hours are over," he said in his best Nurse Ratched voice. He motioned for us to leave the room.

Suitcase put a bottle of Jack Daniels and a glass of water on the night stand. We left the room and went out to the backyard.

"Mole what the hell are you guys up to?" I asked, not really knowing where to start.

Mole poured himself a big glass of Gallo red and sat down in a lawn chair. He was in no hurry to start.

"First of all could you tuck in your balls?" I asked, disgustedly pointing out what should have been obvious to him but somehow wasn't.

He didn't wear underwear and now his testicles hung down through the webbing of the cheap fraying lawn chair.

"Sure enough!" he enthusiastically agreed. "You are an observant lad, that you are. Why it looks like my nuts could be used as a speed bag for an assortment of small animals, or perhaps a wandering pugilistic leprechaun if you believe in that sort of thing. No doubt, if you had not been so kind as to point out my dangling scrotum, I might have had it irreparably damaged. It is quite obvious that my pair could have been mistaken for a hanging chew toy by Beans' cat, Brunswick," he babbled on.

"Just put the fuckers back in your shorts," I yelled.

"What about Beans?" I asked again.

"Yes Beans." He returned to his story. "Well, he went over Caroline's to do some laundry. Despite being told repeatedly to call first, he showed up unannounced." He looked over at Suitcase to see if he wanted to add anything. Suitcase merely took a sip of his beer. Mole continued. "Despite the divorce Beans believed she still loved him."

Suitcase chimed in, "And she does, its just with the drinking and all . . ." he tailed off. Mole nodded knowingly.

"As he approached the laundry room he heard, shall we say, amorous sounds emanating from the bedroom. You know the rest of the story," Mole said. He took another drink of wine and lit a cigarette.

"Okay, but what did you do to him?" I asked, getting impatient.

"He made us," Suitcase pleaded.

"What!" I screamed.

"We removed her name from the record book, as it were. Took Caroline off his shoulders."

"His Tattoo of her?" I blurted out.

"How?" Triangle asked.

"He made us burn it off with an iron." Josh said as he stepped out of the kitchen into the back yard. He handed us the beers.

Suitcase mumbled, "He made us," then looked down and played with the label on his High Life.

"He'll be fine. He still has the sharks on his chest and the social security number tattooed on his forearm," Josh said.

Never mind that it wasn't his correct social security number, it was someone else's.

"And don't forget the Marine Corps Bulldog on his other shoulder," Suitcase added, now warming up to the bright picture being painted by Mole and Josh.

"Gentleman, lest we forget that the man still has a cock that hangs below his knee," Mole triumphantly stated.

It was true.

Beans' oldest barroom joke was that he had a cock that hung below his knee. When enough drinks were bet he would proudly roll up his pant leg to reveal a tattooed rooster dangling from a noose colorfully splashed on his calf in bright red and green.

No one would pay up on the drinks, but it was always good for a laugh.

"Do you think we should take him to the hospital?" I asked, still not believing they were being so nonchalant.

"Shit it's only a small burn. Once he sleeps off his anesthesiologist Jack Daniels, he will be fine," Josh said.

"It's his head that I'm worried about," Mole said as he flicked his cigarette into the yard. "Although he and Caroline are divorced, he still thought of her as his wife. I know it sounds funny but he never saw this coming. I worry for him."

"Enough of Beansy and his tale of woe. That bitch has been a pain in the ass longer than I can remember. Now she will be a pain in the neck until the burn heals," Josh said obviously tired of talking about Beans.

"A pain in his shoulder," Suitcase corrected.

"You get my drift. Mole lets hear from your boy," Josh said pulling up another chair. This one was from the mix and match kitchen set, and the chair immediately sunk partially down into the muddy yard. Josh adjusted himself so as to not tip over.

"Yes, grand idea Josh," Suitcase boomed.

His Steger voice would be coming soon I thought.

"Triangle go grab some more beers and there is a bag of chips too."

"How is the college boy doing?" Mole asked, as he tried to tousel my hair. I instinctively flinched. His friends noticed but didn't say anything. If Mole noticed he didn't let on.

"I'm fine. School is good. Classes are over in a couple weeks."

I rattled out the stock statements all kids use when answering adult questions they weren't interested in. It is amazing how much of your daily conversation is done on automatic pilot.

"Bullshit! I mean how are you DOING?" Suitcase grabbed me from behind as Josh playfully rose from the chair. "Mole I'm going to get the iron again if this little prick doesn't start telling us about all the sweet coed pussy he's getting and all the that ecstasy love drug he's smoking." Josh laughed and pretended he was branding me.

"OK OK, let me go and I'll give you the skinny. First of all Pop-Pop, you don't smoke ecstasy, it's a pill. And no, I haven't got my hands on any, yet."

"Don't let Beans hear you talk like that," Mole warned. "You know how he gets about drugs."

I continued on, ignoring the warning.

"I'm afraid you are going to be disappointed. You guys are probably getting more women than me, and I know you are definitely smoking more weed."

Suitcase let me go and returned to sitting on the backstep. Triangle moved over, then gave up and stood up. Suitcase was a big guy. He took up most of the back step.

"I'm still seeing that girl from high school she's at Widener too."

"Yea, but unfortunately she's screwing everyone else behind your back," Triangle said. He then retreated to the safety of the step behind Suitcase.

"Triangle head is right," I went on. "I have to stop tagging that slut. On a lighter note, I think I got Dean's List wrapped up," I said reaching out and clinked beer bottles with Suitcase.

"You HAVE the Dean's List wrapped up." Mole corrected.

Mole always corrected.

"Whatever. What about you guys? What's with all the crazy messages and what did you do to Zooks?" I drained my beer and opened another.

"To hell with Zook! We have bigger and more important plans to discuss. I am glad you could join us."

Mole sounded like some crazed drunk field marshall about to unveil his battle plans.

"Until this tattoo distraction, Suitcase and I had been planning a little trip. Actually, it was Suitcase's idea." Mole raised his glass to Suitcase.

"I just said let's go to the Jersey shore. We had such a good time the last time and your dad couldn't make it. Since I got some time now . . ." he paused then continued, "Your father came up with the bird watching part. You know how much he and Beans dig the birds. Shit, as long as there is drinking and perhaps a couple of other types of Birds, if you know what I mean, I'm in," Suitcase said. He practically glowed.

"Of course, if you are going, we will wait until your classes are done. Triangle you are welcome as well," Mole nodded toward the steps.

"I don't know. What beach? Where will we stay? How long are you going? What car are you taking brcause I don't think the Ting thing will make it. Does mom know?"

Once I started, the questions just poured out.

"Details, details don't bother me with details. The great outdoors beckons," Mole impatiently answered. "Did I mention I was able to procure two ounces of thai stick and some blond hash from Roads. You know the guy who was a body bagger in Nam?"

Mole knew my Achilles heel—The smoke.

I reconsidered.

"I might be able to swing it. I wanted to see about living down the shore this summer anyway. If mom's ok with it, I might be able to kill two birds with one stone."

"Bad choice of cliché for this trip. We **watch** and **record**. We **don't** hunt. We shoot only cameras," Mole lectured. "We are recreational drinkers and serious birders."

He looked over at Josh draining his beer. When he finished, Josh responded "Mole you are mistaken. We are recreational birders and serious drinkers."

To further illustrate, he began to chug a new beer.

"That reminds me, did you know that our patron saint of birding Audubon himself killed and ate song birds?" Mole began to lecture. "It is true. How do you think he was able to make such detailed paintings of the various species? Have you ever seen a Crested Grebe or a Hummingbird pose for a portrait? In the bird world a still life meant no life in Audubon's time. At least the old goat had the decency to eat his models. I wonder if DeVinci did the same with the Mona Lisa?"

Mole was on a roll.

I rolled my eyes at Triangle Head, and interrupting Mole's rant, I raised my beer "Bird watching for boozers!" I toasted.

"Bird watching for boozers," they replied in unison. Bird watching for boozers.

Chapter 8

Mole's Field notes #1
On Crows and Blue jays

Blue Jays and Crows are the Brinks security guards of Birdom. The crows guard the fields, the blue-jays patrol the forests. These lousiest of song birds have burglar alarms for voices. They are the super cops of ornithological law enforcement. They will bitch indiscriminately at almost anything. They will complain about chipmunks jaywalking, and snails speeding. While they may seem to just be loud obnoxious pain in the asses, they provide a valuable service in the animal world. They notify the animal world of trouble.

If you come across either of these loudmouths on your birding trips, make sure they don't start bitching about you. Otherwise, you won't get the opportunity to see any other birds. Best to move to another spot and leave these two species to complain about something else.

Chapter 9

How Suitcase didn't spell check and trouble ensued

Suitcase wasn't always Suitcase. In high school he was 'The Ox'. He never liked the name, but being the big quiet kid, he didn't get much say about it.

He was a gentle giant. Because of this, he was sometimes picked on. Mole told me he used to stick up for him. Mole said he was always drawn to John's dry sense of humor. Because everyone mistook the Ox's shyness for being ignorant, most people didn't even know he was a very funny man.

John Sampson had a rough childhood. His father ditched the family when John was only six.

His mother did the best she could to keep a roof over John and his sister Bobby's heads. Unfortunately, this meant frequent moves to keep the family one step ahead of the landlords.

Thankfully, his mother was able to keep John in the same school. He was Mole's second longest friend.

Earlier, I said you could not give yourself your own nickname.

I stand corrected.

John Sampson was the exception to this rule.

One day, long after the Brownie incident the boys were drinking at the fort. The Ox was complaining about his looks. Specifically, he was bitching about being the size of Frankenstein at the age of fifteen. He complained that it was hard enough to get a girlfriend without the added difficulty of carrying the handle of "The Ox".

Already John was six-foot two and two hundred twenty pounds. He had thin dirty blond hair and a high hairline that gave the appearance that he was going bald. In truth he was.

He wore boxy ill fitting men's clothes, having long outgrown the boy's husky department. Mostly flannel shirts and Wrangler Jeans. He wore work boots or occasionally black Chuck Taylors when his mom was working and had a few extra bucks.

Despite his loyalty and his dry wit he carried a sense of melancholia with him his whole life. You didn't feel sorry for him. You were just sorry **with** him, even when he had you laughing.

My father loved him.

On this particular day the boys were drinking sloe gin to go with Josh's filched beer. They were stuck inside the fort because it was raining. When they did venture out, it was only to pee.

Maybe because of the added booze or maybe because they were stuck inside, the boys were in a particularly talkative mood. As usual, Mole took over the conversation.

"Nicknames are always tricky, John. Most people have them and they serve a multitude of functions. A nickname may be nothing more than a shortened version of one's own Christian God given name, as mine is—Mole," he said the name and paused allowing the example to settle in on his student. He continued, "Although some would claim that Mole describes the particular traits of the animal that I happen to possess; namely extreme fierceness and tenacity despite my small stature."

"That would be the shrew," Josh corrected. "A Mole lives in dirt and eats worms. It is neither fierce nor tenacious. It is considered a pest," he continued.

Mole flashed him a look.

Mole not allowing Josh to sidetrack him went on.

"As you can see MY illustration describes the second function of the nickname, to draw attention to a particular trait of its namesake. Pay no mind to Josh," Mole said regaining his rhythm.

"Still others have no rational explanation as to their attachment to their owner. The name may merely be an inside joke. It may have been given randomly and over time just happened to stick. Others may be ironic. Calling someone 'Shorty', who is in fact very tall. Ironic may not be the term that fits this description but I digress."

He took a pull from the sloe gin.

"You always digress asshole." It was Josh again.

"I apologize. Heaven help us if I attempt to educate our dear friend on the whys and the hows of his current predicament."

Mole took a deep breath, prepared to return to his discourse.

"Yea what about me? Why don't I have a nickname? You claim that all people do," Josh challenged. He always got aggressive when he drank.

"Then there are people like Josh here. They may not think they have a nickname but in fact, they are called many things behind their back," Mole went on.

Suitcase punched Josh in the arm. He was obviously enjoying this.

"Who calls me shit! I'll kick their ass!"

Josh was now bordering on belligerent the country next to his home state—obnoxious.

"I am only Joshing with you Mr. Keenan. You have allowed me to illustrate my last category of nickname. People who's name itself is a nickname. 'Josh' already fits so many of the previously described examples that no additional tinkering is needed," Mole finished.

Josh looked confused. Was this a compliment, or a cut?

Mole just smiled and turned to his friend John Sampson. "The time has come to re-christen you with a name of your own choosing."

Mole spread his arms wide as though he were an evangelist.

"What will it be?" he boomed. When no one answered he said, "Perhaps we should continue to enjoy our rainy afternoon and allow the name to birth itself, on it's own over the course of this wonderful lazy day."

As the rainy day progressed, the boys talked about everything. Beans talked about the sea. Mole talked about Kerouac and the Beatniks. Josh probably talked about blowing things up. Mole told me Josh was always starting fires or sticking firecrackers in frogs' mouths, crazy shit like that.

Eventually after exhausting all the teenage topics, the talk turned to another of John's pending moves. They were in high school now and the constant uprooting was getting old. When John complained he was living out of a suitcase, a name was born.

It had stuck.

He was fifteen when he became Suitcase. He was forty-two now and though he hadn't moved in ten years he was still Suitcase. He had grown into a combination of Jonathon Winters, Jackie Gleason and Lenny from the *Grapes Of Wrath*. Even though his birth certificate said John, his paycheck was made out to Suitcase Sampson.

Like most of them he bounced around a number of jobs since high school. Soda jerk. Oil delivery man. Custodian. House painter.

He finally settled on sign painting. He liked it. It was good honest work that put him in contact with many types of people. It also allowed him to be in different locations most of the time.

He had worked the job for ten years now.

Unfortunately, now it was time for Suitcase to look for another job. The reason Suitcase had the time to plan a trip was because of his "grand mistake" as Mole put it. "Details, details don't bother me with the details" Mole had said. Perhaps if Suitcase had paid attention to details he would still have a job.

Suitcase painted signs on almost everything. Buildings, windows, storefronts, even the side of a house that overlooked Interstate 95 'Roma Window Replacement—We Doctor Your Panes,' he had painted on the side of the house. The bricks soaked up a ton of paint, and the truck exhausts quickly dulled the finish, but it was still there, and Suitcase had done it.

"Diego Rivera I'm not, but it looks pretty good, if I do say so myself," he told Mole at the time.

Recently, a home supply company had hired him to do their fleet of delivery trucks. Suitcase was thrilled. Not only would he have months of work, he would also have free transportation. He had cut a deal that allowed him to pick up and use the trucks as he worked on them. Plus, the owner was a friend, so he could work at his own pace whenever and more importantly wherever he pleased.

This last fact should have caused him some concern. Suitcase didn't give it another thought. When the day came for the job to start he went and picked up the first truck. As he carefully eased the big rig through the gates of the mill, the boss smiled and yelled to him over the din of the mill's saws and the truck's engines "Take your time, there's plenty more where that came from."

He waved him out of the lot.

Suitcase drove the truck directly to Seconds Flat and parked in the driveway. The driveway was smooth and flat. Aside from an old beat up wooden boat disintegrating quietly at the far end of the drive, the driveway had plenty of space for him to work. He could relax, shoot the shit with Beans or Josh, have a few beers and ply his trade

Life was good.

The sign was as basic as they come. Paint the outfit's name on the side of the box truck in black and white block lettering.

No problem. That first day he started by toasting his good fortune with his friends.

Shots of Jack Daniels and a couple of Bloody Marys. This was followed up with morning beers.

Then came talk of various other tasks they could perform with the use of the truck. At first the men were reserved and guarded. "We could help Mole with a load of carpet since the Ting Thing is broken down," Josh finally suggested.

This seemed to break the ice. The ideas flowed.

"Yea, and we can get rid of that old couch in my living room. You know the one that fat crack whore busted when she sat down too fast." Beans followed up.

Suitcase was happy. He felt good. He wanted to really raise the bar on what they could do with the trucks. He found himself blurting out, "Maybe we can take a day and drive to the shore. You guys could catch a few rays while I work." Suitcase continued, "Let me get this one done and next time we'll take the truck to the beach."

They continued to drink. Around One o'clock work began in earnest.

Suitcase was shit faced. With the help of Beans they set up the scaffolding. Josh was on a beer run.

When he returned the boys took a much needed break.

"Scaffolding looks top shelf," Josh slurred. "Thanks," Suitcase replied, obviously pleased.

He climbed the ladder and began to shimmy out on the plank paralleling the side of the truck. Despite the alcohol and the hot sun he began to expertly block out the lettering. When he was finished with the blocking he turned to ask his friends how it looked.

They were gone.

Napping no doubt, Suitcase thought.

He began to trace the lettering. Easy as pie. He was happy. The booze made him sleepy but he would have plenty of time for a nap later. Now he had sign painting to do.

DARBY HOME SUPPLY. No that wasn't it.

This truck was part of the mill supply of the store. It would deliver wood. Plus the owner said due to some credit problems he was changing back to the old name. DARBY LUBMER. Yes, that was it—Darby Lubmer.

Suitcase began to paint. He started slowly, but once he found his groove he picked up speed. After another hour and a half he began the detail work. The booze was beginning to wear off. Now he had the start of a headache. Something else bothered him but he shrugged it off as a side effect of the drinking and the sun. At about four thirty he finished up.

He got down and went to get the guys to help him clean up. He would keep the truck while it dried. He would put another coat on it in a few days.

Beans and Josh were awake and watching a soap opera.

Since Josh was collecting workman's compensation, and he didn't want his employer's insurance company to know what he was up to, he hid out during the day at Seconds Flat. Beans was two months away from either the oil rigs or catching another ship with the merchant marines.

They reluctantly went out to help Suitcase.

"Looks good Suitcase," Josh said as he glanced at the truck. "Yea, you got a lot done," added Beans, who didn't even look at the truck.

"Another coat in a couple of days, then a sealer and first one will be done." Suitcase beamed.

The next day Suitcase worked alone. Beans had gone down to the union house to see about his medical benefits. Josh had taken a day job with Mole. Suitcase took his time today. All in all he was pleased with the product. Not bad considering I was drinking he thought.

Still something didn't feel right. Just Catholic guilt at my good fortune, he thought dismissing his uneasiness. Ten trucks, my own schedule and no boss. 'No worries mate', he said to himself as he started back in on the job.

He took the finished truck back a few days later. The boss wasn't in, so he left it in the lot and took another. The keys were in it.

He was proud of his work. He knew he did a good job because on the way over a couple of people stopped and pointed at the truck. No doubt they admired his work. The new sign would announce the business. The company would garner more business as a result of the signs. Suitcase would get more work too. Everyone would know who was responsible for the DARBY LUBMER trucks.

The next one they did take to the shore. Suitcase, Josh and Beans. Mole couldn't make it because he had a carpet job. They would take him next time.

The second job went even more smoothly than the first. The salt air and the sight of the ocean made the time fly. Even Beans and Josh complimented Suitcase on the idea and the sign.

They returned to Delaware County, sunburned, drunk and happy.

He slept like a baby that night in Seconds Flat.

The next day he finished up the truck. Late in the day while the clear coat was drying, he drove back to the yard. As he approached, he noticed a large number of the workers gathering at the entrance when he pulled in. They were smiling and laughing. Some pointed at Suitcase's truck. Suitcase happily waved back. A hero's welcome Suitcase thought.

As he parked, he noticed the owner.

Tony Macientonio did not look happy. He had a look on his face like he was cleaning a cat's litterbox. Odd, thought Suitcase. Tony must be having a bad day. New construction was down. It was a bad economy. Tony will cheer up when he sees the second truck. Suitcase thought.

He parked and got out.

"You fuckin retard. You dumb Fuck!" Tony roared. He wound up and hit Suitcase in the head with a book. Suitcase bent down and picked it up—a dictionary. That's weird he thought.

"What's wrong with you Tony? Settle down for Christ's sake," Suitcase said as he handed the dictionary back to Tony.

Tony promptly threw it down. "I'm the laughing stock, you big dumb asshole. Who do you think your making fun of? I ain't no dumb Dago, you fuckin wise ass!"

"What are you talkin about Tony?" Suitcase stammered.

"Maybe he don't know boss," one of the workers said as they stepped forward to get in between the two men. "Maybe he is that dumb," said another.

"Spell Darby Lumber, asshole," Tony said trying to regain his composure.

"D-A-R" Suitcase began, Tony lost it again "Not Darby. Spell fuckin Lumber!" He screamed.

Suitcase began again. "Lumber. L-U-B-M-E-R . . . lumber", he repeated as though it were a spelling bee.

"That's it. Get this stupid ass off my property before I put a bullet in his knee cap!" Tony barked as he spit on the side of the freshly painted truck. "I wash my hands of him." He disappeared into a trailer parked next to the storage area.

Suitcase was humiliated. He realized his mistake. What was I thinking? He thought. He didn't dare ask for his pay. With all the men looking at him and laughing, he just wished that he could hide. He quickly left the mill.

He walked back to Seconds Flat.

His friends were there. They quickly gave him a drink. He didn't want any pot so he passed on the joint Josh tried to hand him. He tried to collect himself. Why was everyone so cheerful? I'm ruined, he thought. He wanted to get drunk—Rip roaring drunk.

Beans thought it was hysterical. He tried to pay Suitcase.

"Here take the money it is definitely worth it. It is priceless. Besides that old goomba is a prick. Do you know how many people he has screwed over in his day? Plus he's so fuckin cheap, I bet you he doesn't even fix the stinkin things," Beans laughed.

"Anyone can have a Lumber truck but few can have a Lubmer truck. Remember that," Mole reminded Suitcase as he handed him a beer and gave him a hit of weed. Suitcase gave in. "What the fuck, so I flipped a letter, so sue me!" Suitcase joked. Silently he prayed Tony didn't sue him. He crossed himself.

The boys drank for the rest of the afternoon. Their conversations punctuated only by the sound of the pop of the beer tops and the striking of matches as they lit their cigarettes.

Josh had the last word. "Who the fuck will notice? I still think it's spelled right. Besides no one in Darby can spell anyway."

They all laughed.

In the morning Suitcase would need to look for new work.

Maybe house painting again. At least there is nothing to spell. He fell asleep on the couch. Beans put a blanket over him.

Chapter 10

How we spent an enjoyable afternoon at Seconds Flat and Beans revived, briefly

I spent the day with the Mole. I have to admit it was fun. When my dad was with his friends and there were no distractions it could be a good time. We drank and smoked and told stories. We teased the hell out of Suitcase. After every story someone would spell it out to Suitcase. Finally, after Josh demanded that Suitcase get him another B-E-E-R. Suitcase blew up. "Josh knock it off, I have put up with enough of your shit. You saw the god damned truck, you thought it was spelled right. I am not the only dumb ass in this backyard."

He stood up from the step. Josh got up to meet him.

Just like that, it had gone in the shitter. That was the problem with these guys, it always started out great but most of the time it ended up in the shitter.

Mole got up and got between them both. "Gentlemen, we are all friends here. Josh, you know Suitcase here is 'good people' and Suitcase you know Josh is also 'good people'. Now why don't you both sniff each other's asses like two dogs getting reacquainted and knock this shit off," Mole joked. "If you don't settle down you are going to wake the patient," he continued.

Just then came a loud roar from inside the house. "Ahhhhh! What the hell have you bastards done to me?" It was Beans and he was fully awake.

"Shit, piss, and corruption! I knew you would wake him," Mole railed.

Triangle got off the steps and started toward the car.

"Relax Triangle he's all noise," said Suitcase who had now put his hand out to Josh who took it and said "I'm sorry Suitcase." He then proceeded to slowly spell it out "S-O-R-R-Y."

Josh could be an asshole.

Beans came to the backdoor. "Lads, me shoulder is on fire. What the devil have ye done to me?" he said.

When he was drunk he often reverted to what Mole called 'Piratese'.

"You old sea dog, what have you done, scuttled your remaining brain cells? Do you not recall your request to remove your ex from your pecks?" Mole played along. "Well not exactly your pecks for they already house your tattoo sharks. More like your delts." Mole said.

Mole always had to be exact with language.

"In any event we were acting on the captain's orders himself," he continued.

"For foak sake, who listens to a raving drunk man?" Beans raved.

"If we didn't do it you would have been even more pissed off at us. Here, let me give you a Percocet," Josh offered.

"No fuckin way with the drugs, man!" Beans countered.

"Then take a Tylenol, wash it down with some Jack and shut the hell up," Mole said.

"We were just discussing a little trip we are planning. Do you remember? Or did our little operation remove your memory as well," Josh finished.

Mole handed Beans a Tylenol he had in his pocket. Beans took it and washed it down just as Josh had told him.

"Mole, twenty years of kickin carpet and the man always has to have the Tylenol on hand." Beans smiled and playfully punched Mole. "Ow! You assholes have to stop listening to me," he said as he grimaced from the pain of moving his arm. He sat down gingerly and tried to get comfortable.

It wasn't happening.

Mole began. "First of all, on behalf of all us, we are truly sorry for what you are going through. We have all suffered both burns and the sting of infidelity."

"Infidelity? They weren't even married," Josh complained.

"Shut up Josh!" Suitcase glared over.

Josh shrugged and made an exaggerated motion with his hand like he was locking his lips.

He sat.

Mole went on. "We would all agree that the sting of a lover's unfaithfulness is a much more painful wound to bear than a burn on one's shoulder. But we would also all agree that with time and the companionship of good friends, both will be bound up and forever healed." Mole finished and took a long drink.

"Well said man." Josh patted Mole on the back.

I couldn't resist. I gave it my best Slim Picken's.

"Why Mole you use your tongue prettier than a twenty dollar whore."

Every one laughed.

"*Blazing Saddles*" Triangle said as he pretended to buzz in like he was on a game show.

"Wrong. **What** is *Blazing Saddles*? You didn't phrase it as a question. You lost on Jeopardy, Triangle," I joked.

"Mel Brooks is the best. Although I am partial to '*The Producers*,'" Mole added.

"What is this shit about a trip? I do recall some talk of perhaps a Cape May jaunt. Yes?" Beans said.

"Thank you Bernard for bringing us back on point. The trip. Yes, the trip. We were discussing a short sojourn to the sea. Cape May is in fact our destination or at least one of them. Of course, this is a democratic ornithological group and Cape May is certainly up for discussion," Mole said looking around the group for input.

Suitcase cleared his throat then spoke up. "We could start in Atlantic City then work our way down the coast until we hit the cape. That way we could gamble a little, and I could dip my wick with a few professional birds I know in AC." He elbowed Triangle who had returned to the stoop next to Suitcase.

It was Josh who spoke next. "I shan't care the least about games of chance but I know the female birds of which Suitcase speaks," Josh said trying to sound like Mole. "I too would enjoy a little dipping of thine wicketh into these female birdiths," he lisped, and took a flamboyant dramatic bow.

Despite the theatrics, there was only one Mole.

"Beans what about you? You are the only one who has not weighed in on this discussion," Suitcase said, handing Beans a beer.

"As long as I don't have to drive and we don't rush I'm in. Oh, and one more thing, we take the back roads. No Atlantic City Expressway. I hate the tolls."

He got up.

"Now if you will excuse me I need to change my dressing and lie down again, I mean this is my whackin off arm and all." He laughed and pretended to masturbate. He immediately cringed in pain from the effort.

"By the way, good to see you Stevie. Sorry I'm not to much for conversation I'm a little under the weather. I apologize. I would like to meet your friend too. Maybe next time. Better yet lad, just come on the trip," Beans said to Triangle. He then went into the house.

A trip to the shore, even if we were supposedly bird watching, might just be what the doctor ordered.

Shit, three out of four guys were unemployed. So we had the time.

Who was I kidding ? Four out of four—I didn't have a job either.

Where would we get the money? Where would we stay?

We had two weeks to figure it out. Until then I still had to finish up school.

SCHOOL!

I had completely forgot, I still had finals. I still had two papers to complete. I had to get back.

"Mole, I would love to stay here at the flat and shoot the shit but I need to get back to school.

I need to get Mom's car back too." I said glancing at my watch. "Yea, and I need to get home. I have work tomorrow." Triangle added.

"Mole why don't I run us home. Mom is a little worried about us." I lied. She was only worried about him. "Then after dinner she can run me back. Triangle, I will drop you off on the way."

Suitcase spoke up. "You know, I have to drop off some money to my sister. She lives in Chester."

"I could follow you to your house and after you drop off Mole and the car I could run you back to school."

"No way," Mole protested. "I can drive Stevie back. Just let me go to the bathroom and then we will get going."

He got up slowly and went into the house.

Suitcase leaned into me. "Look, I know he is in no shape to drive. Besides, when Larose sees him she is going to flip. If I'm there she will be on her best behavior and so will Mole. When he goes to sleep, I'll run you back to school on the way to Bobby's," he finished, then peeked through the back door to see if Mole was on his way. "You know it's the best thing," he added.

Josh nodded in agreement.

Leave it to Suitcase. No matter how much he drank he always kept it together.

It was the best way.

I yelled in a good by to Beans then headed for the car. Mole didn't even try for the keys. He rarely gave me shit anymore. Even though I had not been afraid of him for years and he knew it, he still was known to act up when he was drinking. He was just very unpredictable.

Still, I felt sure he wouldn't act up with his friends around. To his friends, Mole was always a victim, even from his son.

He didn't make a peep when he saw that I was doing the driving. He quietly got in the passenger seat of the Dent.

Triangle went with Suitcase.

Suitcase rolled down the window and yelled that he would meet us at my house after he dropped off Triangle.

We backed out.

//

Seconds Flat was in Darby. Chester Pike was the main artery that passed through the town. It did the same for a series of small towns all up and down its length. To people unaccustomed to the county the towns all looked the same. To the residents of the county, each town was different and distinct. Each had its own police department and local government. Most of the towns contained working class row homes and some big singles that had been converted to apartments long ago. I guess at one time these converted singles were summer homes for well to do families from Philadelphia. Those days were long gone.

Despite their similarities in appearance, the towns all looked down on each other. Collingdale was 'better' than Darby. Glenolden was 'nicer' than Collingdale. It went on like this throughout the county. When you don't have much you at least can have the feeling of superiority over some one else. Why do we need to take sand out of other people's buckets to fill our own, when we are all sitting on the same sandy beach?

The next town up the pike was Collingdale. As we worked our way home to Glenolden, we had to pass through it. It was both my mother and father's home town. Driving through it with Mole was always interesting.

Sometimes he would be sentimental. He would point out where an old bar used to stand or Sue's Malt shop, the local teen hang out that now housed an heating oil outfit.

Other times he would mock the place, calling the people ignorant or backwards, and thanking his creator for getting him out. Even though he only moved one town over and two miles away.

That night…that night he was different. He started out by commenting on the old high school. Although both my parents had graduated from it, the school had closed up years ago due to declining enrollment. It was now converted into a district court house and the town hall.

"Do you believe that Tom Narkin is the Judge in this town?" he said sarcastically. "Laroses' uncle has got as much business being Judge in this town as I have of being a brain surgeon," he continued.

I knew he was drunk because he liked his uncle in law.

Tom was a prominent local lawyer. He did not drink or smoke. He looked like Mark Twain, with a bushy mane of white hair and a wild mustache that hid his upper lip and always looked like it was ready to escape from it's home beneath Tom's distinguished nose. He had a crazy laugh that often accomplished what the mustache could not. Namely, it escaped from Tom's lips frequently.

Over the years he had acted as a referee to the various domestic incidents my parents regularly got into. Like a good boxing referee, he knew his fighters well, and he called them as he saw them. He told Mole the truth.

It was Mole's fault and he should stop drinking.

Mole no longer talked to Uncle Tom.

Now that Tom Narkin had been elected District Judge, my old man thought Tom had it in for him. He was probably right. Uncle Tom now had the power to 'help' Mole save himself from himself.

As we passed the old school turned court, Mole rolled down the window and spit "Narkin kiss my ass in Gimbels' window," he yelled.

As I said earlier, Collingdale is where my folks grew up. In fact, both sets of grandparents lived five blocks from each other. The cemetery is filled with many of my relatives from both sides. The phone book is also filled with tons of Molineux's, Kelso's, Battista's, and McGarry's. Micks and Italians and that crazy French name that no one knows much about. With all the living and dying my family has done in this five mile radius it is hard to believe the whole lot is only three generations from Ellis Island and the boats that brought Europe's tired and hungry to these shores. My family and countless others like them have been the endless scraps poured into the American meat grinder to feed this country's insatiable growth.

Workers for the factories. Westinghouse, Boeing, Scott Paper, Baldwin Locomotive, Penn Ship. Most now closed up. Others gobbled up in mergers, or acquired as part of the country's need to be bigger and better.

Soldiers for the wars. WW One, World War Two, Korea, Vietnam, Iraq. Like Lieutenant Dan in the movie Forest Gump, there have been members of my family in every war our country has been involved in since my ancestors' arrival as immigrants. Whereas Lieutenant Dan's family had someone killed in every war, in my family, while some died in combat, most made up part of the countless millions who served as truck drivers or mess hall workers or laborers.

In the rear with the gear.

Why is it that everyone who served in a war is remembered as a hero? My family were the workers of this country, why should their service to their country in war be any different than their civilian lives?

Not everyone in a war is a hero. Americans toss that word around entirely too much. Watered down is an understatement.

My family didn't go far. If America is a fabric weaved together from many different threads, then to my family, and the working class they represented, that fabric was one big, dirty wife beater tee shirt, stained in one little spot with the blood and sweat of three generations of my family.

That stain is Collingdale.

Don't get me wrong, I'm not knocking Collingdale. The people are hard working dedicated Americans. My family are part of the town and its history too.

I am not ashamed of this, I am proud of it. It just sucks being smart enough to know and understand your heritage.

Not everyone is descended from kings. And you know, there is a reason why dreams are only in black and white.

Mole knew too. He also knew he was fooling himself if he thought he had got out. I was his proof. A kid, hell, a grown man looking at you with your own eyes staring back, reminding you why you had to stay.

It must be hard on Mole, not able to ever chase his dreams, I thought. Having a kid at nineteen will do that to you.

My mind drifted, as I thought of my parents, younger than me, playing house, complete with a mortgage, a car payment, and an out of wedlock baby.

"Stevie, Steve!" Mole shook my leg. "Where the hell were you?" he said looking at me hard. "I knew I should have drove. Are you alright?"

"Yea Mole I'm alright. Are you?"

We passed through town towards home. I tried to leave those thoughts behind, as we turned the corner to my house.

Chapter 11

How I told Suitcase about the beach and he told me about Mole's phone call

Suitcase was right. My mother was pissed at my dad but she didn't scream at him. She just ignored him. Endured him is probably more accurate.

Larose had dinner already made. Because she never knew when to expect her husband or her kids she always made stuff that could sit around. Spaghetti, soup and sandwiches, macaroni and cheese, and the old breakfast for dinner were among the staples.

Tonight it was chili.

Mole and Suitcase dove right in. They quickly junked their bowls up with whatever was at hand. Hot peppers, Tabasco and cayenne pepper were passed around the table and liberally applied. My mom and I looked on in amazement. As quickly as she could tear bread from the Italian loaf she bought to accompany the chili, it was gobbled up. I was just as guilty. They washed the chili down with still more Millers.

After dinner, true to form, Mole passed out on the couch.

Mom would get a bed tonight.

As we cleaned up, she put together a care package to bring back to school. Larose always took care of me. The usual—a twenty in an envelope with a note urging me to work hard and behave.

There were all the college necessities, P and J, Ramen noodles, ice tea mix, a loaf of bread, big bags of pretzels and one of chips and my favorite to this day, Oreos.

Larose got my sister and I through it.

My mother knew the deal. She always knew the deal. But knowing the deal and doing something about the deal was another matter.

Today they call it enabling. It was enabling all right. Back then, her staying in the house and dealing with my old man enabled my sister and I to have a roof over our heads and food in our stomachs. It enabled me to see where I was and what I was so that I could make the changes down the road to steer clear of it—or at least narrowly avoid the collisions from booze and drugs and bad marriages that had plagued my parents. Back then the only domestic abuse shelter around, was maybe your grandparent's house. But that never lasted long. Women went back. That's just the way it was.

Hey, my mother may have sacrificed her life, but she sure as hell saved mine.

After packing up my stuff, she walked me out to the car. My sister Maddie wasn't home. She was over at a friends. She spent a lot of time at friends. Her friends didn't spend much time at our house.

Suitcase thanked my mother for dinner and got in the car. I put my gear in the back of Suitcase's car then turned to my mom. "He didn't seem too bad today." I started. "If he gives you any shit this week, you call me and I'll get here." I hugged her. "Thanks for everything."

I got in the car. We started up the pike toward Chester and my school.

Suitcase was the first to break the silence.

"I couldn't help but notice you were a little ahh . . ." Suitcase searched for the right word, "apprehensive, is that the word college boy?" he laughed.

"I don't know, what are you trying to say Suitcase?" I asked, not really wanting to talk.

"You know, today, when we were talking about the shore, I could tell you were a little apprehensive about going. Worried about banging heads with your old man?" He looked over with real concern. "Well don't worry. I will make sure he doesn't act up. But you have to promise me that you won't act up with him. He's your father. He deserves your respect."

I knew Suitcase meant well but he really had no clue.

"My respect! Suitcase look, I appreciate the ride but please skip the lecture. You really don't know what your talking about. You only see the funny nice Mole, not the one we have to live with."

Now it was me giving the lecture.

"The one who beats the shit out of my mom. The one that tries to beat me." I turned and glared at him. "The one who isn't beating me anymore."

I wanted the conversation to stop or at least change direction. I was afraid to get too close to the truth. Because the truth was, since I found out I could win the fights with Mole, I seemed to get into them a little too often. And to be real honest, they weren't always about his drinking or the way he treated my mom or my sister. Sometimes it was just because of me. Sometimes I just wanted to beat the shit out of him.

I changed the subject.

When you are mad or want to get your mind off of something, make em laugh.

"Suitcase you know why I'm apprehensive about the shore? Well, I'll tell you. Mole has given me some bad trips and some funky memories about the beach," I began.

"Yea, like for instance," Suitcase asked.

"Mole down the shore, I've got a million of them. Did I ever tell you the Ventnor drawbridge jumping incident?" I asked.

Suitcase smiled and shook his head.

"Remember Holly my mom's friend? Well she had a place in Ventnor, you know just south of A.C. It was really her mom's but no one used it but Holly. She invited us down for a couple of days, years ago. I must have been like ten. My sister was just a baby. Anyway, we went down.

Holly and her family were there, so my mom automatically was on eggshells, hoping that Mole wouldn't get that shit faced and embarrass us."

I looked over at Suitcase to see if he remembered the story. Maybe my mom had already told him. I know Mole probably never did. Either he was too drunk to remember or he just chose to forget.

I wish I could forget.

"Anyway, as soon as we get situated, me and my sister Maddie on the floor, Mole and my mom in the bed, one room, Mole starts drinking. Stingers. One after another," I continued.

Suitcase let out a little whistle at my mention of Stingers. I made a mental note to ask him about that at a later date.

"My mother started to panic. She got very uncomfortable when Mole started to get loud. She asked him to quiet down, but that just made him louder. Then he got on his ex-Marine kick and that's when trouble really started. You know the Marine shtick?" I asked shaking my head.

Suitcase laughed and yelled, "I am a U.S. Maureen!"

We both laughed.

Yea he knew the shtick. The drunker my dad got the more it sounded like he is saying 'Maureen.' By the end of the night he would be a full blown Irish Lass.

I continued. "My father got drunker and drunker. He got louder and louder. At one point he drops to the ground and starts doing push ups. He's yelling 'A Maureen can do push ups all night long!' Meanwhile the only part of his body that's moving is his head. He's doing head ups," I said warming up to the story.

Well, now my mother and Holly are beside themselves. Someone is gonna call the cops. Finally, my mom gets him to go into the bedroom. She knows its still daylight but she's hoping he might fall asleep.

The room overlooked the bay and the Ventnor Drawbridge. The house was actually on stilts out onto the bay. A balcony ran the length of the house. Obviously, Mole could see the bay and the bridge.

At first we could hear him in the room continuing his drunken 'Maureen' workout. He had taken off his shirt and wrapped it around his head like some demented drunk pirate as he switched back and forth between his 'head ups' and jumping jacks or as he called them 'side strattle hops'. Holly had to regret her hospitality. My mother would not stop apologizing and nervously she went around the house cleaning everything in a mad attempt to make up for Mole's behavior."

I paused to look over at Suitcase.

He was still smiling but you could tell it was a mask.

I continued. "After what seemed like hours he grew quiet. My mom sighed deeply and lit a cigarette. She and Holly let out a nervous laugh and Holly poured them both a drink.

I actually felt comfortable enough to venture out and check out the bay.

I didn't notice him at first. It was summer so it didn't get dark til after nine. It was just starting to get dark. The first thing I notice is that the bedroom window is open, I quietly looked in to see what he was doing. He wasn't there. The next thing I hear is this little old lady yell out 'I wouldn't do that if I were you, Mister'. I looked over to the sound of her voice and I see him. He's standing in the middle of the bridge in his boxers. He is up on the railing and he is warming up like he is an Alcapulco cliff diver. He stops his warm up. Then he looks over at the old lady walking her dog and he yells, 'I am a Maureen. I can jump off anything! I am not afraid to jump from any height.'

The old lady shakes her head and says 'Well Maureen or whatever your name is, I wouldn't do that if I were you.' Mole glares back at her and says 'Well you are not me and I am . . . ' The old lady cut him off and shouted back 'I know you are Maureen; suit yourself. But remember, I warned you.' She then continued to walk her dog over the bridge.

At that Mole started to hesitate. It was after all at least a twenty five foot drop. He resumed his stretching but I could tell he was second guessing himself.

When he saw me, he quickly regained his bluster. 'Stevie', he shouted, although I couldn't have been more than twenty feet from the bridge. 'Watch how a Maureen does it'. He cupped a hand over his crotch and over his face 'Balls and nose!' he yelled. 'Balls and nose'.

Just then my mother came flying out of the house holding my sister. When Maddie saw the Mole she got scared and started to cry. 'Steve please come down, someone is going to call the cops!' my mom yelled. Holly told Mole she was calling her husband who was coming down after work. 'That won't do any good' my mom said, trying to quiet my sister.

A small crowd had gathered, no doubt because of the nosy old lady's big mouth," I paused, "Suitcase, I was fuckin mortified."

I looked around Suitcase's car for a beer. I sure could use one.

"You got any beers Suitcase?"

Suddenly I needed one.

"No. What the hell happened next?" Suitcase asked.

"At that very moment he jumped. The crowd let out a gasp as they pointed at the now nude man jumping off the bridge. He hung in the air in slow motion, or at least that's how I remember it. SMACK! He hit. There was hardly a splash. All I could see was his head. He was stuck."

"Stuck? What do you mean? Stuck?" Suitcase asked.

"The tide had gone out. There was only a foot of water in the bay. He sunk up to his neck in mud." I laughed. "He began to struggle but he couldn't move much more than his head." I added.

"Thank God he had done all those 'head ups' before he jumped," Suitcase said. He laughed and smacked my thigh.

"No wonder the old lady warned him," Suitcase continued.

"Yea, she was a local. She knew the tide was out" I explained.

"It's a wonder he didn't get paralyzed," Suitcase said as the stupidity of the act began to sink in on him.

I went on.

"That's not the worst of it. As they watched him struggle the crowd got bigger and bigger.

My mom and Holly got out a little inflatable boat from the shed. As soon as I saw it I knew what she had in mind. They took turns blowing it up. With each breath I got more and more worked up. Woosh! Woosh! They blew. I started complaining. 'No way Mom I won't do it. I tell you I won't!' I begged. Woosh! Woosh! Slowly the boat took shape. I knew my fate.

'Go get your father' she said. 'I won't do it' I stood firm. There was no way I was going to let him embarrass me any more. 'I won't do it.' I stamped my feet on the porch floor. This went on for some time. Then my mother, in desperation smacked me and threw me in the dinghy."

"So you went and got him?" Suitcase asked.

"Fuck no." I said, again starting to laugh. "I paddled under the house and I wouldn't come out.

It was only after I heard my mother crying, that I came out.

I still wouldn't get him until she promised to get me a hermit crab from the boardwalk the next night." I laughed.

"You know that stubborn bastard acted like it was nothing? He even claimed that he knew the tide was out and that it was shallow before he jumped. He said that his feat had shown that a Maureen could not only jump from any height but that he could land on almost anything. He even yelled to the crowd that he had not even ruptured himself!

It took two days for him to get off that oily shit off him. We threw out his underwear." I said and shook my head.

"Shit. No wonder you don't want to go with us. But look, I promise this time I will make sure he's on good behavior." Suitcase said.

"I'm not done yet. That was only the first day," I said.

"Jesus. There's more?" Suitcase said in disbelief.

"Shit yea, there's more. This is Mole we are talking about. He is a multi-level fuck-up" I crowed.

Suitcase was going to hear the full catastrophe.

"Well don't just sit there, lets hear it. Widener University ain't that far away," Suitcase said as we drove out of Prospect Park and into Ridley.

"Well, the next day, we got up. The whole house smelled like bacon. Mole was busy in the kitchen cooking up a storm. That was another of Mole's tricks. No matter how terribly he acted the night before, it was all supposed to be excused by his kick ass breakfasts. And you know what?

A whole lotta problems do seem to go away with the smell of bacon, eggs and coffee in the morning. Not to mention we were at the beach," I said.

Suitcase nodded in agreement.

"If only it could be like that all the time," I added.

"Everyone sat down to eat. Mole acted like nothing had happened. We all made small talk. Even Holly's husband who had come down late. I guess he didn't know. If he did he wasn't saying anything. Anyway, everything was ok, until my sister innocently asked why Mole's skin was dirty and why he smelled like the bay? He still wasn't able to get himself completely clean. Everyone got real quiet. You could feel the tension. Then Mole said to Maddie 'Daddy fell in the bay last night. He will get a shower after breakfast.' So, he had fallen in. At least he didn't say he was pushed," I sarcastically added.

"Well, this doesn't sound too bad," Suitcase cautiously offered.

"This was just the calm before the storm, the calm before the storm," I said.

"I should have known," Suitcase added.

"My mom must have figured that she needed some time away from him to cool off. After breakfast she told Mole she was taking Maddie and going shopping in Cape May with Holly and her husband. She made it clear Mole was not welcome. I couldn't believe she was dumping him on me. But I figured, hey, he was sober and he was always fun at the beach."

Again Suitcase nodded in agreement.

It was true. Sober, Mole was always eighteen years old. He was the only father in the neighborhood who would join in the kid's touch football games, he would play kick the can, and have a mean snowball fight. At the beach, he would let me bury him in the sand or build big elaborate sand castles. He would openly ignore the life guards and take me really far out, and most importantly, he would give me freedom to do what I wanted.

"So, I was going to the beach with Mole. Looking back, I was kind of excited. Just me and my dad. Suitcase, I should have known."

"What happened? You didn't almost drown did you? Did he get in a fight with the lifeguards?" Suitcase guessed.

"Nothing so dramatic. I'll tell you," I continued.

"So my mom leaves and it's just me and Mole. I put on my bathing suit and as I am getting a beach towel, I notice him getting high on the porch. He tried to act like it was a cigarette but I could smell it. Then he shuffles me off to the car. That's when I notice he's got a gallon of wine that he is hiding in a towel. Keep in mind he already has a cooler of beers with exactly one soda in it for me.

My mom is already gone and this is before the age of the cell phone, so there is no one to tell anyway. I found a wagon in the shed, so I was at least able to convince him to walk to the beach instead of driving.

We loaded up the wagon with the towels, the cooler, the wine, some shovels and buckets and a football that was also in the shed. We were off. He must have felt bad for his bridge jumping act because he let me ride in the wagon the whole six blocks to the ocean.

It was a great day for the beach. Sunny and hot. Not too windy, but there was a little breeze. The breeze not only cooled you off, but it also kept the greenheads from biting too.

The beach was already pretty filled by the time we got there. Mole was not much of an early riser after the night he had. We found a spot pretty close to the water, next to a whole crew of teenage girls. They must have been from a couple different summer houses. They ranged in age from a couple years older than me, thirteen or so to some college age, I guess. Older sisters who got stuck with their little sisters or cousins or something like that. The point is, there was something for Mole too look at and something for me too. I may have only been ten or eleven, but I remember that I was definitely interested, although I was too shy to talk to them.

The day was going great. Mole was being 'Super dad' in order to impress the girls. Shit, I didn't care, I was having a ball. We made a giant sand sculpture. It was a very detailed mermaid with a trident. The girls even pitched in. After that, we went out past the sand bar to the deep water. As always, he ignored the lifeguards. It was great. I rode on his back as he swam parallel to the beach while the guards whistled and shouted for him to come in.

After he got tired, we went back to the blanket. That's when the trouble started.

First he started smoking a joint. Everyone on the beach could smell it. He could care less. Rebel without a cause. Then, when he was good and high, he started in on the wine. I tried to get him to eat but he wouldn't touch a thing. And remember, this was before sunscreen. We both didn't have anything but tee shirts to protect us from the sun, and both of us had taken them off as soon as we hit the sand.

By early afternoon the combination of the pot, the Gallo Vin Rose and the sun had done a number on the Mole. Before I knew it he was passed out on his back on the beach blanket. Actually, I was relieved. He was 'out' before he could make an ass of himself.

Now it was just me and the girls. The older ones made a big fuss over me at first. They made big overtures to play with me. They even brought the young girls over and tried to get them to play with me. I guess they were trying to get a break from entertaining them.

That's when I heard them.

At first the little girls giggled and pointed. I thought they were laughing at me, but as I looked over I could see they were pointing to the Mole who was now spread eagled on the blanket snoring loudly. That's when I saw them."

"Saw what? The girls?" Suitcase asked.

"His balls" I said.

"His balls?" Suitcase laughed.

"Yea, he didn't have underwear on under his bathing suit. The liner had ripped, and his whole package was hanging out for all to see. I was mortified.

The little girls told the other girls, and the next thing I know, everyone was parading back and forth in front of our spot giggling and pointing at Mole's Johnson.

I quickly called to Mole to wake up, but he was out cold. Then, I frantically tried to shake him awake. He grumbled something and took a semi-conscious swipe at me, like I was a bothersome Greenhead fly.

Fuck it, I thought, I'm outta here. I got up and went to the board walk.

When I was safely away, I turned and looked. The older teenage girls were now involved. They were laughing and pointing at Mole's balls.

On a dare, I guess, a couple of them had even started to throw candy at them. They were laughing and joking. I wanted to die."

As I sat in Suitcase's car I cringed at the memory.

Suitcase didn't say anything.

"After the novelty of the Mole's exposed testicles wore off, the girls went back to sunbathing and gossiping. I casually snuck back to the blanket.

To my horror, his balls were getting baked from the sun. Christ, they were turning purple. They might of even been throbbing and had their own pulse for all I knew.

He had no clue, he was that out of it."

Suitcase laughed out loud. "Shit, its making my balls hurt just thinking about it. What did you do?" he asked.

"I tried to wake him, of course. The harder I tried, the madder he got. I said, 'Mole, wake up your balls are getting fried' . . . before I could even get it out he would scream 'I don't want to play ball, God damnit! Leave me alone.' I tried again, but Mole, your nuts are getting cooked . . .

'I know I'm nuts! Let me sleep,' he roared.

Mole your testicles are getting sunburned, I pleaded.

'If you are getting sunburned put on a shirt,' he mumbled.

This went on for some time. All the while his balls were getting redder and redder. Shit, they were on fire!

In desperation, I pulled a towel out from under him to cover his now smoldering wedding tackle. This woke him, and get this, he smacks me!

He said, 'Let me sleep, you little puss gut. I played with you all fuckin day. Do you think I could get a moments peace?' Then he went back to sleep.

I tried one last time. I said, 'Mole your stuff is hanging out. Your balls are sunburned.' It was no use. He was out.

To prove it, I whispered in his ear, 'you're a drunk loser and I fucking hate you.'

Suitcase, he didn't even move an inch.

Later, when almost everyone had packed up and left, he woke up. At first, as he laid on his back, he stretched his arms and yawned. As he got acclimated to his surroundings, he sat up. Immedietly, he screamed in pain. 'What the hell, my fuckin balls. Sweet Jesus, they're fried.' His eyes fell on mine and I could see the anger building up in them as his drunken brain quickly assessed blame. 'Why didn't you wake me up? Didn't you see my . . . ' he stammered 'didn't you see me getting sunburned? Why didn't you wake me up?'

I must have been smiling Suitcase, because the next thing I know he screams, 'You think this is funny? You left me sleeping on purpose! You wanted my balls to get toasted.'

NO, Dad, I tried to . . . before I could finish he punches me in the stomach. 'You little punk, you let this happen. You did it on purpose.'

I swear I tried to wake you,' I choked out, crying.

He says, 'Get your shit together we are leaving. And get me the fuckin Noxcema.'

I say, the Noxcema is in Mom's bag . . . Don't you know he hits me again? Like it was my fault the Noxcema was with my Mother.

That bastard made me pull him and his fuckin throbbing nuts all the way home in the wagon. The whole six blocks he alternated between dramatically fanning his crotch, then putting a cold can of beer on his balls. All the while he's cursing me for his misfortune." I said, still not believing it all these years later.

"I guess I was lucky, at least he didn't make me put the Noxcema on em," I finished.

Suitcase and I laughed.

"All right, you have a point. I wouldn't want to go Birdwatching with that track record either," Suitcase said laughing, but I could tell he felt bad. There was something else too. What was it, sympathy?

Screw that, I didn't need sympathy. Didn't want it either.

"Don't feel bad for me Suitcase. I don't want your sympathy."

"I know that, Stevie," he paused, searching for what he wanted to say. "Even though he has put you through some rough times you shouldn't be so hard on him. You know he loves you," he began.

"I know, but he is still an asshole and the drinking is the root of it," I said.

We pulled into my dormitory parking lot.

"Thanks for the ride Suitcase, my dorm is over there," I said and pointed to the far corner of the quad toward the plain cinder block buildings that housed the undergrads.

"Just drop me off here."

"Stevie, don't get out yet," Suitcase pleaded.

"Suitcase, I'm tired and I really don't want to talk about my old man any more," I said reaching for my bag in the back.

Suitcase grabbed my arm.

"I listened to you, now you have to listen to me," he said seriously. Then as though alarmed at his tone, he added, "Consider it the price of the ride."

He tried to smile.

I let go of the bag and turned around in the seat.

"I'm all ears."

"Did he ever tell you about his sister?" Suitcase asked.

"Marcia. Yea I know all about it. His sister who died when she was twenty-one. Gonna tell me he's all fucked up cause he lost his sister?

Let me go and get the Widener band so we can play a pity party. Save it Suitcase, I ain't buying it," I said, reaching for the car door.

"Shut up, and stop being a punk!" Suitcase said angrily. He grabbed my arm and squeezed. I stopped trying to get out and turned to him. He had never so much as raised his voice to me since I was a baby.

He had my full attention.

"Easy John, I'm right here," I said, just a little scared.

He let go of my arm and nervously looked away out the driver's side window.

"I'm sorry. It's just that you need to listen." He paused then said, "Sure everyone loses loved ones and usually they get over it. But most times, we know its coming. We can get prepared for it, you know, brace ourselves.

Even when it's sudden, we usually have family or friends to support us and get us through the rough patches," Suitcase said and turned back to look at me. He wasn't imitating Brando or Rod Steger this time.

"When Marcia died Mole was only fourteen. His brother Paul was only seven. She was killed the night after she she graduated from Bryn Mawr College. Do you know she graduated in three years? Mole worshipped her. She was his bright, pretty, big sister and he looked up to her. Anyway she was killed in a car wreck in upstate New York. She was killed instantly. She was the only one of six in the car that died," Suitcase said.

None of this was new to me, my mom had told me when I was around twelve, when I asked if my dad had any other siblings. I was still a little skeptical about Suitcase's point, so politely I said, "I'm sure it was a shock, but my Mom-Mom and Pop-Pop were great people. I'm sure they sheltered the boys and helped them through it."

"Listen for once!" Suitcase said firmly.

"When it happened, your grandparents were shocked. One day their firstborn child graduates top of her class. The NEXT DAY! Literally, the next day, some sheriff from upstate bumblefuck calls and tells them their baby is dead. Just like that. Well, would you believe that? What would you do? You would go to your child. That's what you would do and that's what they did.

They threw some shit in a bag and they left. Just took off. They left your dad and Paul to fend for themselves at the house," Suitcase said.

"They didn't call anyone? A relative, a sitter, a neighbor?" I asked unbelievingly.

"Who would they have called? The family didn't really talk. Besides they weren't thinking clearly. They were in shock," he continued.

"The point is, your dad sees them get a call, then his parents become unglued, then he's alone with the responsibility of a watching his seven year old brother as well. He has no idea what has happened. He's just scared, and worried and by himself. He can't even act his age because he doesn't want to upset your uncle Paul.

It is like that for a whole day.

Finally, the phone rings. The boys are so scared and worried they leap for the phone, sure that mom and dad are calling to tell them everything is OK and they are on the way home," Suitcase said as he choked up.

"Your dad answered. A fourteen year old boy just wanting to talk to his parents. Instead, it was a reporter from the *Philadelphia Inquirer*. He had no idea he was talking to a child, or maybe he just had a story to write. Anyway that son of a bitch blurts out to your dad, 'Was it true that Marcia Molineux was killed in a car wreck in upstate New York last night?' . . . When he realizes your dad is just a kid and can't help him with his story, he hangs up.

Your dad and Paul stayed in that house alone for another day before your grandparents came back. Even when they got back they weren't much of a help."

Suitcase finished and wiped his eye with a Wendy's napkin he had fished out of the console. He blew his nose into it and threw it out the window.

"Didn't know that one did you?" he said try trying badly to lighten the mood.

"Thanks Suitcase, I think I will go and kill off myself now. You are such an uplifting guy to be around," I tried to joke.

Inside, I was torn up. Who wouldn't be?

It explained a lot but it still didn't excuse anything.

"Suicide?" Suitcase feigned disbelief.

"As long as you use a butter knife to slice your wrists, it's ok," he joked.

"Or, I could put my head in an electric oven?" I played along, warming to the joke. "No need to. Just over dose on a placebo lad!" Suitcase fired back.

"I could hang myself by a thread," I tried to keep up.

Suitcase had enough. He stopped with the puns, and said, "Just remember, Stevie, he's your father. It hasn't been a walk in the park for him either. He tries, and he loves you. Now back to school. I will see you in two weeks. Take care lad. I love you."

He handed me my bag and gave me a kiss on the cheek. I got out, and walked slowly back to my dorm room.

Chapter 12

How I financed the trip, finished finals and embarrassed myself in class

The last two weeks of school went by pretty quickly. I don't remember all the details, but I do remember that I put the trip out of my head and got back to the business or should I say pleasure of college.

I didn't hear from Mole at all. My mother, when she called, told me all was well. She said Mole was working steadily, and had even put away some money for the trip. I could tell when she was lying about my dad, and if she was, she was now much better in the fibbing department.

Suitcase called once. It was a few days after dropping me off. He sounded kinda' embarrassed. Like a stranger on a plane, who tells you their life story and later sees you in the airport bar. Suitcase quickly tried to make light of our talk and what he said.

"Sorry that I went all Phil Donahue on ya," he joked. Today, he would have said Oprah. It didn't matter, I knew what he meant. He was embarrassed about getting all touchy feely, I suppose. I guess Suitcase wasn't used to such serious talk, or maybe he just felt like he over stepped his bounds. How are you supposed to feel when telling someone else's secrets?

In any event, I told him that I appreciated what he had told me. I said that it gave me some insight into my old man's behavior.

We both quickly changed the subject.

"So how are classes going? We won't let you go with us unless you make Dean's list," he joked.

"Classes are fine. I finished one paper and have one left. Then its finals. Oh yea, I have a ton of student advisor sessions for next semester's classes. At least I should have some extra cash for the trip. And, if my roomate picks up some extra finals, he will hopefully pay me back some of the money he owes me," I explained.

"All right then, hit the books and I'll see you in a couple." Suitcase hung up.

Perhaps a word about my roomate and our college employment methods would be appropriate at this time.

Dan Barley was my roomate for most of my college years. He is the smartest guy I know. Today he runs a successful hedge fund, but lets just say, back then—he was still trying to work out his business practices. Looking back, he was always the budding capitalist. He was adept at finding a need, then supplying the product or service to fulfill the need.

He had two businesses. The first was taking classes or taking finals for other students. The second was stealing bikes and then reselling them. The first business he went after. The second fell in his lap.

As I mentioned, he is a smart guy. Believe it or not, at college, there are not that many smart guys. Because of this, Dan was a commodity, and a hot one at that.

He saw a need in the market and he went after it.

Rich kids who didn't want to study or go to class but still wanted the grades to keep mom and dad writing the checks, needed Dan. This need, coupled with large classes, enabled him, for a fee, to take the class for you.

The fees ran from three hundred bucks for an easy class, to six hundred for organic chemisty, which was notoriously difficult. Of course it wasn't all that easy to pull off. Sometimes, it took disguises. Other times, especially in the smaller classes, it took doctored student Id's. Dan wasn't into making fake Id's, he was only into taking classes for you. You had to supply the Id card with the fee. Dan supplied the picture and the brains.

In addition to his own course load, he would take anywhere from three to six extra classes a semester for others. For most classes he just took the tests. Rarely, if ever, would he need to go to class. He demanded and received bonuses for receiving A's. He also gave refunds for any C's.

He never needed to give a refund.

Between his classes, his 'business' classes as he told his parents about his money making venture and playing lacrosse, I hardly ever saw him.

When I did, it was usually to go out drinking. And boy could he drink. Earlier, I mentioned that like people attract like people, well with Barley this was ridiculously true. His friends from home were just like my friends from home. His dad was a larger than life character just like the Mole. And his father's friends could make up at least three novels, or at least three volumes of psychiatric journals.

Is it any wonder we are friends to this day?

Dan's second job, as I said, came to him accidentily. Let's just say it was a joint venture with me.

As I said, like most college kids, Dan liked to drink. He would go out with his lacrosse buddies after they cleaned the football stadium every weekend. Hard to believe that one sport had to clean up for another, but such is the power of college football.

Anyway, the stadium was a considerable distance from our dorm. The guys would get a keg to drink while they cleaned. They would hit the keg all day. The coaches turned a blind eye. It was the least they could do, since the lacrosse players were financing their own sport by cleaning the football stadium.

The players would make a day of it.

When they were done, both the cleaning and the keg, the players would have to walk about two miles back to campus.

This pissed Dan off.

"It's bad enough that we have to clean up afta the football playas," he'd say in his thick long island accent. "But then they expect us to walk back? Fuck that! It's BULLSHIT!" he'd complain.

One night after a cleanup it started to rain. Barley was hammered. He was also furious. He was holding court with the other players under the bleachers. Comparing the history of lacrosse to the history of football.

As I mentioned he is the smartest guy I know. When he was fired up and on a roll he was like the incredible Mr. Whoppee on the old cartoon show Tennessee Tuxedo. You know the guy that explained everything to Tennessee and Chumley on his 'Fabulous Three D-BB' or his magic black board to those that don't remember the show.

He would rail on with his accent, "Lacrosse is really the American spoat, not Footbuall. Footbuall traces it's roots to European footbuall or socca as its cualled. It is a derivation of rugby," he rambled. "Lacrosse on the otha hand, derives from the American Indians. It was played in this country longk before the Europeans even settled here."

"What's your point Barley? A point is a good thing to have in a story," one of the players egged him on.

"My point is, that the fucking football players should be cleaning our stadium for their keep. Not the other way around. The college should at least get us a bus to get us back to campus."

He took a big drink from his red plastic cup and looked out toward the field house.

That's when his business opportunity came to him. Well the business opportunity came later. What came to Dan on that rainy day was tranportation. Specifically, one of the football players' brand new bikes.

Since it was raining, the football players were all holed up in the field house watching film and getting treatments from the game the day before. As a result, their bikes were lined up in front of the stadium. They weren't locked. Who would dare take a football players' bike? They were the big men on campus. The top of the collegiate food chain.

To Dan, he saw his ride home. He quietly excused himself from his lecture by telling his teammates he had to go to the bathroom. Then he walked over to the bike rack to case the joint, as it were. Sure enough, the bikes were both new and top notch. For all we knew the college bought them for the players.

After looking around to see if anyone was watching, he realized the rain provided the perfect opportunity. He took the nicest one and began his ride back to the dorm.

The next day I woke to see a brand new tenspeed in our dorm room. Dan looked as surprised to see it as me.

"Where the hell did this come from?" I asked.

I looked over at Dan, who looked like he was struggling with the same question. In hind sight he was probably getting his story straight.

"I found it," he finally offered.

As a liar he sucked.

"Alright, I fuckin took it from those prick football players," he crumbled, even though I hadn't said so much as a word.

"Well get rid of it before the RA sees it," I said as I turned over to go back to sleep.

"What am I going to do with it?" Dan asked.

I could tell **his** problem was now **our** problem.

"Leave me alone and let me sleep," I said.

I couldn't sleep though. My mind kept kicking around how to get rid of the bike. After a while it came to me.

I lived only about twenty minutes from campus. Dan lived over two hours away. I had a network of shady friends and petty criminals. Dan did too. It's just that Dan's were farther away. I could tap into these 'friends' to sell the bikes. What was I thinking, it was only one bike. Okay, I admit, It came to me that it didn't have to be one bike. It could be many bikes. Shit, I even had an uncle who had a chop shop. Why did it have to be only bikes?

My mind raced.

Dan was reading my mind. "Look I screwed up. I took a bike. I won't do it again," he lied. "If you get rid of it, we can split the money," he added.

"Sixty forty," I demanded.

"Done," Dan said, closing the deal.

Dan was always generous.

Dan's second business was born. He never walked home from a drunk load again. Instead he rode in style on any bike he could find. Often he would wake to find a junker in the dorm room that he didn't even remember taking.

"What are you doing Steve, adding to our inventory?" he'd ask.

"Hell no, asshole, I told you, I don't steal, I only fence. You brought this gem in last night. Don't you remember? Do you forget eating my pizza too, fat boy?" I added.

He obviously remembered neither.

"How am I supposed to get rid of that clunker, take it in for scrap?" I busted his balls.

"Ok, you can keep anything you get on this one. No split expected," he practically begged.

"Just this time. Next time pick a better ride. My customers are very discerning," I joked.

So the second business thrived. Thankfully, he only ever delivered one car to my uncle with the chop shop. I don't think Dan stole it though. At least I hope he didn't. Remind me to ask him some time. Maybe the next reunion.

I also made money in college legally. But, like Dan, I had an angle too. My angle was based on the fact that I hated math.

In order to graduate from college you had to take math. No matter what the major, you had to take it. Most majors required more than one math class. Even English majors had to take one. This fact scared the shit out of me.

As early as my senior year in high school I had kicked this fact around. I rolled into college with confidence about almost all things, except math.

I was able to put off taking the required basic calculus class-freshman math my freshman year by waiting until the last minute to enroll. By the time I registered, the class was filled. The faculty advisor had assured me that I could take it my sophomore year.

That's what she thought.

After my freshman year, Dan had realized my math phobia. He offered me a one time offer to take Calculus 115 for me for free. It was a generous offer.

I couldn't take him up on it though. As strange as it sounds coming from a bike fence, it just wasn't honest. I may have been a lotta things but I was going to get my own education. It just couldn't include math.

When my freshman year was almost wrapped up, it came to me. I was leaving the meeting with my faculty adviser. Because I was undeclared, that is, I had not yet chosen my major, I received the help of a fulltime academic advisor—a professional guidance counselor. Not some professor seeing their allotted fifty kids as part of their tenure package. No, these were fulltime advisors for all the kids who couldn't figure out what they wanted to be.

As I left the office I saw the sign.

"Wanted: Three students to train as student academic advisors. Paid position."

I scanned the job description. As part of the college's efforts to diversify, they were creating three paid positions for students to advise other students in choosing majors and selecting classes. You received your own office, a paid salary and you could make your own class selections. This was too good to be true. If I could grab one of these slots, I would be the first sophomore guy to get a look at the incoming freshman girls. I would get my own office, get paid, and if I was reading the ad correctly, pick my own classes.

My dream was out there and I could taste it.

No math.

I went back in and filled out an application. I would need to interview. Fortunately for me, my counselor was on the interview team. I would have to work fifteen to twenty five hours a week and fulltime in the summer or at least the month of August. Last but certainly not least I would need to maintain a three point average. No sweat, since I now wouldn't have math to pull down my cumulative average.

Where do I sign up?

When my interview rolled around at the end of the freshman year, I started to get cold feet. My friends thought I was nuts. I remember Dan telling me I had no chance. "Diversity Steve. They are looking for diversity. This school wants blacks and women. It is not a man's world any more. At least not a white man's world anymore," he said, not half joking.

At first I thought he was right. The day of the interview, the waiting room was filled with all kinds. Shit, it looked like the United Nations or at least the United Colors of Benetton. I didn't stand a chance. But after my interview, I realized Dan was right.

They were looking for diversity.

I would be their token white trash kid done good. Maybe that's too harsh, but the truth was they were into diversity. Racial and economic. I just fit the latter.

I got the job.

By the time my bird watching trip was on the horizon, I was the most popular student counselor on campus. The real deal. Everyone wanted a session with the plain speaker.

Screwed up with too many electives? I knew the quickest and easiest way to get back on track. Want to change majors? I would show you what would count in the transfer and what wouldn't. Professors? I always was brutally honest. My class mates appreciated it. I could name my own hours, the number of hours and most importantly make my own curriculum.

Yes, by the time of the trip, I was well on the way to graduating in four years, with a three point two grade point average, money in my pocket, my resume reflecting this impressive, if bogus position, and the best part —NO MATH!

When you can't make it in the system become part of the system. Or as the oldtimers say, 'If you can't beat 'em join 'em.

That last two weeks before the trip I remember, was also when I decided never to speak in class again. Looking back, I'm sure I didn't keep the pledge to remain silent, but after what happened in Human Sexuality class that last week it's a wonder I ever spoke in class again.

Dan and I were in different majors. He was Biology and I was Fundeclared. Sooner or later I would have to choose, but for the time being undeclared was a nice place to be. Since we had different course requirements we rarely had a class together. So, when we both had the need for an easy elective to boost our grade point averages, we chose human sexuality.

It met one night a week for three hours from seven to ten. The first two were lecture. Over two hundred undergrads watching videos of Swedish test subjects masturbating with electrodes on their head to measure brain activity. I kid you not. I received college credit for this.

Is it any wonder China now owns the U.S.?

The last hour was a lab. It was really a discussion group. The young ladies and men of the class were expected to engage in open and frank discussions about sex.

Since the class took place at night, Dan and I would hit happy hour before class. The week before finals was the next to last class. For some reason we got really drunk before class. Since we came in late we couldn't find a seat together. We split up. I remember hearing Dan somewhere close, giggling during the movie portion of the lecture.

After the lecture we broke up into our discussion group. There were about thirty students to a lab. Since it was so close to the end of the semester the mood of the class was very loose and relaxed.

The professor, Dorothy Torchia was a large breasted ex gym teacher who had the tendency to well up with emotion when talking about the 'beauty and wonder of the gift of sex.'

The whole semester all I got out of her, between bouts of joyous crying, was to 'Always wash up before and after lovemaking and always clip my fingernails before doing the deed.'

Tonight, hoping to capitalize on the relaxed mood of the class, she suggested we split the boys from the girls and engage in an open, no holds barred question and answer session. She even made this sound sexual "an open, no holes barred sex talk" I imitated her voice to Dan in my best stage whisper.

She must have thought so too, because as soon as she said it she launched into a tearful digression about how she and her husband still enjoyed the pleasures of the flesh even after twenty five years of marriage.

Dan laughed and whispered "thanks for the visual, Dorothy."

She then gave the obligatory 'always wash up, before and after sex talk'.

Then the questions began.

At first everyone was shy and guarded. We all just sat there looking at each other and grinning.

The silence didn't last long. You see, we weren't the only ones that had been drinking, so it was no surprise when some drunk football player asked a specific girl how many times a week did she "jerk off or whatever girls call it".

The teacher Ms. Torchia quickly intervened.

"Mr. Campbell, it is called masturbation and there are to be no personal questions. Any question you ask, just remember to keep it general," she gently scolded and brought the group back on point.

No one else said a word.

A couple of ass kissers asked innocuous questions they thought would impress the professor, but all in all it was pretty lame.

This cautious give and take went on for some time. In many ways it mirrored verbally what goes on physically in a first date.

A lot of posturing.

Just when I thought the study group's verbal date wouldn't get past the heavy petting stage, a cute girl I recognized as a cheerleader, blurted out "Why won't boys kiss you after you give them oral sex?"

The whole class burst out laughing.

She immediately blushed, realizing what her question said about her.

Everyone pounced.

The instructor quickly came to the rescue. "Good question Kirsten," she said to the now red faced girl. To the class she said "Ms. Talbot was asking the question solely from a hypothetical perspective."

The class quieted down somewhat, but the football player continued to laugh and make rude comments to his friends around him.

Now it was the professor's turn to pounce.

"Mr. Campbell, a legitimate question has been asked, I am requesting that you answer it for the men."

Mr. Campbell fidgeted in his seat from the unwanted attention. "Its just gross. Kissing someone with cum breath has got to be nasty would be my guess." He smiled at his cleverness. He didn't say it was nasty, only that it **must** be nasty.

The men all mumbled in agreement.

I saw my chance to score some points with the ladies in general and Ms. Talbot in particular.

I put on my best sensitive new age guy act and calmly said to the girls "I don't speak for Mr. Campbell of course but I speak for myself when I say that if I'm with someone and we care enough about each other to make love, then I would be so in the moment that I would kiss you after that," I paused, and looked directly at the cheerleader "Ms. Talbot", I finished.

The girls cheered and the guys started hootin and hollerin and calling me a fag and a kiss up.

The teacher finally quieted everyone down and asked everyone to move on. I looked at the girls side, I could tell I scored points. Shit, I might even get laid out of this class discussion.

My reign as the class Casanova didn't last very long though.

Since the boys had answered a girl question, the boys got to ask the girls one. Someone yelled out crudely to no one in particular, "What does come taste like?" without missing a beat, my newly acquired scope cheerleader, Ms. Talbot answered, "Why don't you ask Mr. Molineux."

The whole class exploded in laughter. I was set up perfectly by my girl! Oh, the highs and lows of romance. The professor, even though she was laughing herself, quieted everyone down. Before she could regain control of the discussion, another girl in the back snapped her gum and, obviously without thinking said, "It tastes salty."

When everyone turned to look at the self-proclaimed cocksucker, she corrected "So I heard. So I heard."

Everyone laughed again. The girl herself even joined in.

Ms. Torchia calmly retook control of the discussion by saying, "What we have been discussing, when a man kisses a women after he ejaculates in her mouth is called 'snowballing' or at least that is it's slang name. Some people find it enjoyable."

I looked over at Dan and he whispered, "Let's go back to the bar Snowball."

To this day, to a select few college buddies I am 'Snowball'. I guess someday I will have to invent a more reasonable story about the nickname in case my kids ask.

Remember, you can't like your nickname and you can't give yourself the name.

Chapter 13

On the Importance of Music on a Road Trip

I heard a friend of mine describe Bruce Springsteen's music as providing, "the soundtrack of his life." At the time this sentiment almost made me puke. Not because I thought it was an over the top cliché about a possibly overrated musician. No, it was because you should have more than Springsteen on your life's soundtrack.

Much more.

I have always been interested in music. It may border on an obsession. I still routinely send and receive mix Cds with my friends. Music is listened to and discussed, dug and dissected. My I-Pod is almost always in my pocket.

I still go to concerts, even though concerts, at least the kind I grew up on, are becoming more and more like relics, ancient rituals in danger of dying out like dinosaurs or old Indian dialects.

When you are paying a hundred dollars to see a graying or balding old man phone in a song written thirty years ago, maybe it is time to move on.

Christ, a couple of years ago I went to see Elton John. I was treated to a heavy old bald guy with his hair spray painted on, wearing a purple jumpsuit that made him look like a rancid sausage, or Barney in control top pantyhose! The old ladies next to me literally banged their walkers on the ground demanding an encore. Damn, I think I even heard the crinkling of their Depends as they boogied in their chairs.

But you know the truth? When he started to perform, he could still, as Pete Townshend wrote, 'Sing a razor line every time." Despite this, even Townshend must feel silly singing, "Hope I die before I get old," at sixty something.

Yea, and he is laughing all the way to the bank.

Keep on rocking people. It sure beats today's canned choreographed lip sinc'ers.

Despite the graying of rock, I still have a passion for music.

It is with this passion that I dove into the mix tapes for the trip. I remember debating with my college buddies what would work and what would not, given the ages of my father and the other Birders. I knew my father and his friends came of age in that 'between time.' The early sixties before the British invasion. They had lived through all the changes that came between the time of bubblegum do—wop and the time up to my college years; late eighties and early nineties.

The trick, my friend James told me, was to get them hooked, then gradually expand their minds. Depite the ominous sound of it, like I was going to feed them some acid or something, all he really meant was that I needed to feed them their usual diet of Stones, Beatles, Beach Boys and Steppenwolf. Then, when they were not expecting it, expand into REM, The Cult, The Replacements and Nirvana. Alright, maybe they wouldn't handle Nirvana, but Pearl Jam was attainable wasn't it?

Besides, I had a secret weapon. The mother of all road music, as Saddam himself might have said had he chosen to be a disc jockey instead of a dictator. Truly the all time number one road trip band—Creedence Clearwater Revival.

It is a scientific fact that if you can't get two people to see eye to eye, put them in a car and let Creedence rip. I even heard tell of an old redneck, dead and in the casket, who's foot started to tappin when the grieving widow played *Traveling Band* at the dead guy's request.

Don't believe me? Look it up.

There is a reason why the Coen Brothers' Big Lebowski loves them. Mole and his friends did too.

Creedence would be my base. I would intersperse this with some others.

Any Allman Brothers or at least *Blue Sky* and *Rambling Man. Good Vibrations* by Brian Wilson, The Stones, pre-*Some Girls*. Anything by the Beatles. Anything by Dylan, except maybe his holy roller shit. What was the best Dylan album was always good for a debate with the Mole and his friends. I couldn't wait to bring it up. Of course it would be

Blood on the Tracks, although I could see arguments made for *Desire* and *Blonde on Blonde*.

All manner of Motown would be welcomed, especially Marvin Gaye and the Four Tops. That crazy genius Sly Stone. Gamble and Huff—The Sound of Philly. George McCrea, *Rock your Baby*, for the funk.

Anything by the Kinks. Traffic in traffic would be great. Blind Faith. Steely Dan's *Kid Charlemagne* and *Reeling in the Years*, if for no other reason than the rippin guitar solos sound great at high speed. The Who, *Who's Next* and *Quadrophenia*. Bob Marley—at least *Three Little Birds and Redemption Song* for built in optimism. The Chambers Brothers-*Time Has Come Today. Magic Carpet Ride*, by Steppenwolf. Van Morrison. Plenty of Van. *Into the Mystic* sounds like a religious hymn. Early Aerosmith—back when they still did drugs, *Toys, Rocks* and *Get Your Wings*. Peter Gabriel, either with Genesis or solo. Definitely not Genesis without Gabriel. Early Yes, like *Fragile*. Some U2 but let's not go overboard. Hit them with AC/DC *Back in Black* once in a while. Little Feat, Elvis Costello, The BoDeans, Jackson Brown, The Pretenders. Strummer and his boys The Clash.

Keep it coming!

Coltrane and Monk for Mole.

Some Tony Bennett and The Chairman of the Board for Josh, in moderation.

I would intersperse this with REM's *Reckoning* and *Murmur*, Pearl Jam, some World Party and a little of the Violent Femmes. Of course, that twisted degenerate Warren Zevon and his under rated guitarist Waddy Wachtel. Paul Simon's whole catalog.

The Band. There is a reason they were Dylan's back-up.

I would add a little Bruce. Along with *Greetings,* who couldn't dig *The Wild and the Innocent* or *Darkness*?

Neil Young would glue it all together.

Perhaps I was obsessing, but like I said, music has always meant a lot to me. On a road trip, besides your traveling companions, it is **the** most important thing. And if you got bad traveling companions it can make up for them.

Almost.

I made a lot of mix tapes in the weeks leading up to the trip. All painstakingly mixed and labeled. One for every mood, and time of day. They would come in handy.

For my trip with Mole and his buddies, I would have good traveling companions and great music.

Chapter 14

How Josh lived in the sixties
and why he walked with a cane

He looked like Robert Goulet. Yea, that Robert Goulet. The sixties, *Camelot*, you know who I'm talking about. Josh Keenan had the whole look, right down to the smoking jacket. Like some blue collar version of Austin Powers or someone you would spot in a hot tub with Liza Minnelli and Sammy Davis Jr.—not in the rat pack days either, I'm talking last week.

The amazing thing was, he didn't have to look like this, he chose to. He had what Jimmy Buffet would call a pencil thin mustache. He had so many nervous tics he looked like a batting coach signaling with Tourettes syndrome. He wore his hair slicked back in a fifties style DA.

The duck's ass.

All well and good except this was 1990.

He didn't give a shit. He was Josh Keenan and if you didn't like him, well go fuck yourself. That was Josh. Yea, he didn't give a shit, and he didn't take any shit either.

He was friends with Mole since the seventh grade. They had become friends after meeting in wood shop at the old Harris Junior High School. It was not your typical junior high friendship. Then again Josh wasn't your typical friend, ever.

He was always hyperactive and he liked explosions. He was a pyromaniac in a time before we labeled kids.

Today, he would be poked and prodded, analyzed and evaluated. The experts would probably label him with attention deficit disorder, or ADHD, or operational defiant disorder, or bi-polar disorder. His chart might note that his preoccupation with cleanliness or his "hand washing kick", as he called it, might have the makings of obsessive compulsive disorder.

Today, he would be given a psychological risk assessment, and an offense specific arson evaluation by some mothball smelling, boozing child psychologist at the request of some meddling middle aged school principal.

They would find many things.

They would do nothing.

He would have definitely been on Ritalin or at least Adderall.

But like I said, he was a kid back in a time before we became obsessed with medical labels. Back then he was just a kid who was hyper and liked explosions.

Josh Keenan.

Mole told me when he first met Josh in seventh grade he thought he was a prick. Even back then Josh looked like Robert Goulet, or maybe a young version of Art Carney in the *Honeymooners*.

He was that creepy kid who pulled girls bra straps, peeked in the girls locker room, teased all the slow kids and put firecrackers in frogs' mouths. He would throw snow balls at cop cars just to get them to chase him. He wasn't that smart, but as he said, "I ain't wearing a hockey helmet and I ain't ridin in no short bus".

Mole stayed away from Josh at first. Josh claimed that he didn't even know who Mole was until Mole got suspended for not pledging allegiance to the flag.

Josh said, after that, not only did he know who Mole was but he hated him. Further, he pledged to "Get that unpatriotic commie bastard".

It is from these flawed beginnings that Mole and Josh became friends.

Under Mole's high school year book picture it reads "Rebel Without a Cause." Just like his favorite actor James Dean. Hell, he even named me after him—Stephen Dean Molineux.

In the seventh grade, the rebel without a cause got suspended because he refused to pledge allegiance to the flag. Years later, he told me he didn't have anything against the flag or the country it represented. It was just that he wasn't going to be forced to do something that was nothing more than a mindless rote exercise that didn't mean anything, or at least didn't mean anything to a bunch of thirteen year olds at eight in the morning.

He had been laughed at and ridiculed by students and teachers alike. Some, like Josh, even hated him for it.

Years later, when the Supreme Court overturned laws compelling you to participate in the pledge, Mole told me he didn't gloat. However, he did tell me, that it was one of his best days ever, especially when the same principal who suspended him called to apologize.

Not Josh. He wanted Mole to apologize. He hated Mole for not pledging.

Because of this, he plotted vengeance.

He would eventually get his revenge, although he had no idea it would lead to a lasting friendship between the two very different personalities.

Both boys were in the same shop class. Mr. Michener was their teacher. Ben Michener. Since he always had huge sweat stains under his arm pits, Josh had given him the nick name B. O. Benny. Body Odor Benny. All the years B.O. taught he had no idea he was called B.O. Benny. If he did, it certainly didn't lead him to change his antiperspirant.

B.O. Benny's other claim to fame was that he was the only shop teacher at Collingdale school with all his appendages. That's right. Out of the three shop teachers in the district, he was the only one with all his body parts.

There was Lee Longhorn. Leapin Lee Longhorn, the West Texas wonder. He was a former college quarterback who was the metal shop teacher. He couldn't throw worth a shit anymore because he lost a finger in a sheet metal cutter.

Then there was Mr. Lilly.

Mr. Lilly taught mechanical arts and drafting. Unlike Longhorn, he had all his fingers. Instead, he was missing half his leg from a motorcycle accident.

At the start of every school year, his big trick consisted of pretending to get angry at the class and during the tirade he would stab a compass into the trouser leg of his prosthesis. This chestnut never failed to send a least one kid to the nurse for an upset stomach.

Josh liked them all, and despite the name, B.O. was Josh's favorite. He really liked B.O. Josh would joke that B.O. Benny was the only 'complete' shop teacher at the school.

In fact, the feeling was mutual. Josh was the teacher's pet. He was that kid that was just born for shop class. He was great with his hands.

Because of this, B.O. Benny let Josh act like a teacher's assistant. He even gave Josh keys to the shop so he could work on his projects whenever he wanted. Josh was always hanging around the shop helping B.O. with the projects and cleaning up the classroom. It made his classmates sick. They would tease Josh, and accuse him of all sorts of nastiness.

"Keenan, did you help B.O. buff out his flag pole last night?" Or "Josh, did B.O. give you the wood last night?"

It went on and on.

Josh could care less.

"You tools are just jealous that I am the best shop student. B.O. is merely recognizing greatness," he boasted.

They would shut up because they knew it was true.

Mole on the other hand, was the worst shop student. While he always did well in English and to a lesser extent Science, he sucked at shop.

During his less than stellar shop career he had not produced even one project that could ever begin to be used for it's designed purpose. They laid, dusty and unused, in his basement, gathering mildew with the abandoned board games and a castaway electric football game from some long ago Christmas.

His towel racks wouldn't rack. His napkin holders wouldn't hold. His bird houses wouldn't house.

In short, he was the worst shop student in B.O.'s class. He never did get a chance to make something that would work, something that would last. Josh saw to that.

When Josh got his revenge, it was almost the end of the school year. B.O.Benny had given Mole one last chance to pass his class. He allowed Mole to pick his own final wood project. If Mole could get an 'A' on the project, B.O. would pass him.

Mole picked out a simple two hinge jewelry box. He would use maple wood and he would line the box with felt. Not only would the felt add a layer of elegance to the box, it would also hide any mistakes Mole was bound to make. It was a basic no-frills shop project. Not too complicated and guaranteed to get Mole a passing grade.

Mole was cautiously optimistic. Well, at least until Josh Keenan volunteered to help Mole with the project. Mole told Mr. Michener that he really didn't need any assistance, he could do just fine by himself.

B.O. Benny thought Josh's idea was great. His best student helping his worst.

In front of the class, he thanked Josh for his generosity.

So, Mole had a partner.

At first, Mole found Josh overbearing. Whatever Mole did, Josh would do over. If Mole made a mistake, he wasn't allowed to fix it, Josh made him do it over. He hated Josh's perfectionism.

Mole really could care less about shop. All Josh cared about was Shop. It was a match made in hell.

This went on for a couple of weeks.

During this time Mole developed a crush on a pretty field hockey player named Linda Marabella. Even though he only had one class with her he was always finding excuses to be close to her.

Today we call it Stalking.

During shop class one day, she came in to ask Mr. Michener if he would sand down her hockey stick because it had chipped during a game. Mole noticed her immediately. Josh immediately noticed Mole noticing her.

"She's a looker that one, hey Molly?" Josh teased.

Mole hated being called Molly.

"Too bad, she doesn't even know you exist Molly," he taunted. "I bet, if you got your shit together and started to work with me on this jewelry box, then gave it to Ms. Marabella, well sir, then you would be the bee's knees."

He whistled and said, "Who wouldn't want a custom made personalized jewelery box?" He pulled out his own project, a multidrawered heavily lacquered deluxe jewelry box. It looked like he had bought it from a store.

It made Mole's box look like a cheap cardboard cigar box.

Mole got excited.

"Ok. I will take this project serious. Thanks for the help Josh."

Josh had him roped in. "Mole, if you give me the key to your shop locker, I can work on this in my spare time. I can do some extra detail work, and if you want, I can carve her name into the box with a router. It is up to you," Josh added.

Mole was smitten. Not only to Linda Marabella, but also to Josh and his generosity.

He handed over the key.

True to his word, Josh worked on that box with Mole at every opportunity. Since Josh had the key he was able to work on the box after class too. He even got B.O. Benny to chip in by doing some mother of pearl inlay. The box was going to be awesome!

Mole began to get excited about his project. As the box became more elaborate he started to get more confident—in his shop skills, and his pick up skills.

He found himself fearlessly starting conversations with Ms. Marabella. He told his friends it was just a matter of time before he would be going out with her. He hinted to her about the wonderful surprise he was working on for her.

All the while Josh helped. His assistance was a godsend for Mole. He was genuinely growing fond of his odd new friend. Now, when the two were done their work, it was Josh that tucked the box safely back in Mole's shop locker, always making sure to lock it with Mole's key before he closed up the class.

The day finally came when the box was done. In fact, mostly all the projects were finished and ready to be presented for review and B.O.Benny's final inspection. By now Linda Marabella knew Mole had made her a jewelry box. The whole school knew.

Not only would Mole get an "A" and therefore a passing grade in shop, but he would also get the girl. As Ethel Merman sang in Gypsy, 'Every things coming up roses.'

Class was still in session. Although most projects were finished, the shop was still a beehive of activity. Some kids were finishing up. Some were doing extra credit projects. Still others were doing volunteer bird houses for the local 4-H club.

Mole went to the locker and removed the finished jewelry box. It seemed to positively radiate. It was Mole's Opus.

The whole class turned to gaze at the remarkable work. It looked professional. He couldn't wait to give it to Linda.

He owed it all to to Josh. He knew he needed to thank Josh. Not in private but in front of his class mates.

But where was Josh?

Mole looked around, Josh was no where in sight. That was odd, since Josh rarely missed out on shop. Surely, he wouldn't miss this; the final unveiling of the project he had contributed so much toward.

Oh well, Mole thought, his loss.

He presented the box to his teacher.

B.O. Benny turned to look at Mole's work.

"Looks pretty tight Mr. Molineux," he said as he began to inspect it. Before he could finish the review, another student called. He needed Benny's help on the band saw.

What happened next is still subject to much debate. Many barroom conversations have centered on who did what and when. Time and time again, over the course of countless teacher lounge lunches, the issue of who was behind the tragic shop class bombing has been discussed and dissected.

Theories abound.

Some say Josh Keenan entered the room and placed the explosives in the box, then slipped out undetected. Some say he placed them in earlier and then used a timer to detonate them when he wasn't around.

Still others blamed the Mole. They claim the rebel without a cause was getting even for his suspension after refusing to pledge allegiance. Still others claim it was a rival suitor of Linda Marabella, who was pissed about the Mole's advances and the gift he planned to give Linda.

What is not in dispute is the following.

B.O. Benny began to assist the student on the saw. Everyone turned to look at him saw the board. As he cut, a loud explosion ripped through the class. Wood chips flew in all directions. The sound was deafening. Most people instinctively ducked. Those that didn't, either covered their ears or their eyes.

B.O. Benny. Poor B.O. Benny. He was so frightened and shocked by the sudden explosion that he sliced his finger off in the band saw. Witnesses recall, that he didn't even make a sound. Instead, he uttered under his breath "Shit" then calmly turned the saw off, put his now severed digit in his mouth and ran out of the shop.

The class sat dumb founded. Most just sat, in shock. Some wore looks of horror.

One wore a strange mischievous grin.

When the smoke cleared, the only damage to the room and the students within, was to Mole's jewelry box. All that remained were splinters and a few pieces of felt.

Of course an investigation was undertaken. Inquiries made. Interviews conducted.

Eventually, reports were filed and safety changes made.

No more were students given access to the shop after school hours. Locker keys were held only by the instructors. Projects could no longer be group projects.

Perhaps it was because of the changes, perhaps not, but there were no more explosions at Harris Junior high school.

No one ever was caught.

The crime remains unsolved to this day.

As I said, Josh and my father became good friends and remained so.

Linda Marabella never really liked Mole, what with him being a rebel and a beatnik and all. She went back to her old boyfriend, or as Mole and Josh called him the-Main Suspect.

B.O. Benny?

Mr. Ben Michener collected worker's comp for two months then quietly returned to teaching. He no longer could claim to be the only shop teacher with all his appendages, but hey, at least now all the shop teachers were alike.

Josh Keenan was just a hyper guy who likes expolsions.

He grew up still liking explosions. He was always driving to the Carolinas' to buy M-80s, cherry bombs, and roman candles. Even as an adult he would get all worked up at Fourth of July, making sure to get an up front spot to spread his blanket for the annual Collingdale Fourth of July fireworks display. Afterwards, he would always host the Josh Keenan 'After Shock Party' at Seconds Flat.

The A fter shock party usually consisted of Josh setting off a shitload of explosives. This included all manner of fireworks as well as assorted home made explosives. One year he even set off a home made pipe bomb. He would also shoot a variety of guns into the air. As part of his yearly grand finale he would detonate four quarter sticks of dynamite at the same time. The twist was that he would usually attach them to some inanimate object. One year, it was a watermelon. Another year a scarecrow. One time he brought down the house by exploding a blow up doll he had tied to the top of Beans' shed.

The year before the birding trip he conducted what would be his last After shock celebration. The show was going off as usual. Josh pretty much had all of his usual explosives and then some, placed on the top of the shed in the back of Seconds Flat.

The drunken crowd was going crazy. They had already experienced a show to rival the town's display. Now they wanted more.

Josh always delivered.

That night, Josh was sober. He never got drunk until after the show. He claimed, rightly so, that was why he still had all his fingers.

When he was finished setting up the finale, he got down from the roof of the shed. He trailed behind him a long fuse he had rigged up to act as a master. When the crowd was absolutely at their frenzied peak he lit the fuse.

The fuse sparked to life and started on its burning path across the yard and up the side of the shed to the roof top and the various explosives waiting to be blown up that evening.

When the fuse reached the top it disappeared onto the roof and out of sight of the revelers.

Everyone grew silent in anticipation.

Nothing happened.

Seconds went by, then minutes. The partygoers began to bitch. Some started to boo.

In an attempt to quiet the crowd, Beans told everyone to watch. With an elaborate flourish, he did a little curtsy and then a drunken pirouette during which he almost lost his balance. He quickly regained his footing only to then lay down on his back on the lawn. Lifting his legs behind his head, he fumbled with a lighter. When the Bic finally flamed to life, he calmly placed it to his ass and lit an enormous fart. The combination of sound and fury, while not rivaling Josh's show, was never the less pretty funny.

The crowd, temporarily distracted, laughed along.

The laughter increased when Bean's revealed that during the stunt he had shit himself.

"Damn it, these are my patriot pants!" he joked about the white painter's pants specked with red and blue paint. "There ain't no brown in the Stars and Stripes," he yelled.

He slowly walked bowlegged to the back door of Seconds flat, and quickly retired into the house. You could hear him drunkenly laughing and complaining as he fumbled in the bathroom with the shower.

Mole quickly launched into a impromptu history of fireworks. He began by explaining that the Chinese had invented the rocket. Then, he somehow digressed into the Dupont family and how they supplied gunpowder to the government during wartime.

The crowd wanted none of it. They screamed for Josh to do something.

During Beans' side show and Mole's rant, Josh had pulled out a stepladder and was on his way to the shed roof. As he climbed to the top of the shed to check on his explosives, something happened that has been known to occur when dealing in fireworks; namely, they went off.

The explosion was deafening. It took the party by surprise. After all, it had been over five minutes since the fuse was lit.

The crowd let out a collective "OOH!" Then as the secondary shower of sparks and smoke acended into the sky, the obligatory "AAH!" arose from the crowd.

It was beautiful. Almost as good as a professional show.

Josh had done it again. The crowd roared it's approval. Glasses were raised, toasts made.

But, where was Josh?

"Where is the maestro of this maelstrom? Where is this famous Chairman of the Bombing?" Mole yelled above the crowd.

Josh was nowhere to be found.

"He was on the ladder," Beans' mother mentioned. "Yes! Right before the explosion," someone added. "He is the one who lit it, didn't you see?"

"No, it went off on it's own. It was never out. Josh never got off the ladder," the crowd added.

Someone had gone behind the shed.

"Here he is. Somebody give me a hand." It was George Conchon, Josh's buddy from work.

A couple of people ran to George's call and disappeared behind the shed.

A few minutes later, they carried Josh out. He was conscious but in obvious pain. They gingerly put him down in a chaise lounge. He grimaced from the movement.

"What happened? Did the explosion hurt you?" His friend George asked as he examined his hands and face.

"He's got all his fingers, and he's not blind," George beamed.

"No fucking shit," Josh responded, yanking his hand away from Conchon. "Who are you, C. Everett Koop M.D.?" he sarcastically added. "I fell off the ladder and hurt my back. The explosion caught me by surprise and I fell. The explosion didn't hurt me—I'm a professional," he puffed out his chest to back up his boast.

He immediately cringed in pain.

The crowd grew bored with Josh. The show was over. Like motorists who slow down to look at a wreck, the crowd went back to driving, or in this case, drinking.

"Shit, my wife is going to kill me," Josh began. "I've got to work tomorrow." Someone handed him a shot. He drank it and handed the glass back for another. "Work! What am I going to do about work?" Josh moaned. "Someone needs to take he to the hospital."

It was his coworker George Conchon who took the floor.

"Josh, you can't go to the hospital, at least not yet. You have got to suck it up. Go home, go to bed. Tomorrow, me and Tony from the machine shop will pick you up. We need to at least get you into work. You can take a shitload of Advil, and maybe a muscle relaxer or too. Any one got any drugs?" George announced to the party. Immediately a crowd gathered.

"Someone got drugs?" Cokehead Ziggy asked.

"Get the fuck out of here. We are **looking** for drugs, Muscle relaxers, pain pills, shit like that," George said as he pushed Ziggy back.

"Oh sorry dude. I thought you said **you had** drugs," Ziggy mumbled, then drifted back to the party.

"I've got Percocet, Dilaudid, Placidil you name it." It was Gonzalez. He always had everything.

"After I hook him up he will be feeling NO pain," Gonzalez boasted.

"No drugs," Mole calmly stated. "George is right. Somehow Josh has to get into work. Then once he's there he can pretend to get hurt. At least this way, he can collect comp."

Mole nodded in appreciation to Conchon.

"Good thinking George," he added. "Boeing personnel will automatically drug test him. If he has controlled substances in his system they will terminate him. At the very least, they will know he had a previously existing condition. NO DRUGS," Mole finished.

They helped Josh to his feet. Someone handed him a fistful of pills.

Suitcase intervened to prevent Josh from taking them.

"It's okay, Suitcase, it's only Advil," they said as they pushed the Advil to Josh.

Josh took them all without a chaser.

The group helped Josh to the car.

George took him home.

Somewhere, the old shop teacher B.O. Benny felt a tinge of feeling where his digit used to be. He absently rubbed the stump of his missing index finger and the feeling passed.

Karma?

The next day, with the help of his friend George, and a ton of Advil, Josh was able to pull it off. It went exactly like George said it would.

He got to work at the Boeing plant early the next day. There weren't too many people to witness the hung over metal worker as he stiffly made his way to the line. He went through the motions of setting up his work area for about a hour. When no one was looking, he feigned falling over a section of the 737 plane wing near his work station. He screamed in real pain. His coworker, Mr. Conchon scrambled over from his spot on the line to help his injured friend. Together they made their way to the infirmary in D shop.

The Boeing doctors were skeptical, but with co-worker George Conchon verifying Josh's version of the accident, there wasn't a lot Boeing could do.

Josh had a herniated disc.

For his trouble, he got a cane, and eighty percent of his yearly salary for life, or at least until he got better.

Josh had no intentions of ever getting better.

The cane he customized by adding a compartment that held a small test tube of whiskey. The handle also pulled apart to reveal a dagger.

Josh would pull out the dagger at the drop of a hat, especially when someone questioned his story about his back.

"Damn those airplane parts on the shop floor," he would say to anyone who asked about his injury. If George Conchon was around, he would give him a conspiratorial wink.

He planned on never working again in his life. At least that's what his lawyer kept saying.

Never mind what his Doctor had to say.

Besides, Josh thought, in a slip and fall case, a lawyer's opinion was more important then a doctor's any day.

By the time the trip rolled around, Josh really didn't need the pain pills or the cane. Shit, he certainly didn't deserve the worker's compensation. He had been working under the table for the last six months, either with Mole kicking carpet, or tending bar at the Half-Way Tavern in town.

Never mind what he needed. He was keeping all three. The percocets, the comp and, when people were watching—the cane.

Remember, in the world Mole and his friends inhabited, it was okay to screw the man. Josh screwed the man and never thought twice. In fact, asked about it years later, he would sincerely relate that he got hurt in an work accident at Boeing. Like O.J. Simpson, he actually convinced himself that his story was true.

And by the way, he would also tell you he never blew up Mole's jewelry box. That's the story and Josh Keenan is sticking with it.

Chapter 15

How school ended and summer started

I love the beginning of summer. As soon as the chill of the spring nights is permanently gone it feels to me, like prisoners must feel when they are paroled. I can feel my mood suddenly improve. It's like you wake up one day in late May or early June and suddenly anything is possible. If you could bottle the feeling it would probably cure cancer or at least, clinical depression.

Instant optimism.

Any one who grew up or lives in an area where you experience four truly distinct seasons knows the feeling.

Maybe it goes back to my school days, when the knowledge that summer vacation was fast approaching and your responsibilities, at least your classroom ones, were in your rearview mirror. Maybe it is seeing girls in there summer clothes as Springsteen would say. Perhaps it is some funky genetic holdover from our caveman times; summer being the season when plants and animals are most abundant, and man was sure to be able to eat.

Whatever it is, I most definitely was in it's grip in the weeks before the trip.

My roommate Dan had paid me back and then some. He had overloaded on taking other people's finals and as a result he had cashed in big time. He had even received a couple of bonuses from the rich kids for ace'ing their classes.

He gave me four hundred bucks and a bag of blow.

I didn't want Beans to know about the coke but the money was welcome. I made a mental note to get rid of the bag before the trip. Who was I kidding, his gift wouldn't even last out the school year. This was college after all.

His generosity, combined with the money I saved from the academic adviser position, left me, as Beans would say 'fat and flush.' I was in good shape for the trip.

It was only a week away. I had the money and the time. What I didn't have was a friend. Despite pleading with Triangle Head to come along, he balked.

His family was very active in the church and his brother, a junior reverend or something, had commandeered his baby brother into attending Bible camp with him in some upstate Pennsylvania camp for holy rollers and other assorted Bible thumpers.

Triangle's summer was going to consist of going to church, reading the Bible, and getting the Lord.

Mine would to consist of drinking, gambling, womanizing and Bird watching.

When I told Mole during a rare phone call, the irony did not escape him. He had a good laugh since he was certainly no fan of organized religion. He boasted that Triangle would get closer to God by living life to the fullest on our adventure, than by reading 'bad history' as he called the Bible.

"Organized religion has done more to block man's path to his maker than any other thing in the history of man," He began. "On our trip, we will visit with God in his most beautiful church; the great outdoors-viewing all God's creatures in nature."

He was on a roll.

I looked at the line of guys looking to use the dorm phone and I cut him off.

"Dad, let's continue this discussion on the trip. Long story short, Triangle Head is out. It is me, all by my lonesome. It doesn't matter, Triangle would have worn out his welcome after a day or so anyway.

Gotta go. Tell Mom to call me tomorrow."

I hung up and walked back to my dorm room as the line of students eyed me with contempt for hogging the dorm's only phone.

That night I went to bed early. I had one more final, and I wanted to be well rested. None of this all nighter crap, that was for amateurs and freshman. No one learns any thing at four A.M. or so I thought.

Tonight, Mole sounded okay. This trip just might be a good time, I thought as I drifted off to sleep, the light of Dan's desk lamp the only light in the dorm room.

The next day my final came and went. In college, when you go to class and do your reading, most classes are pretty easy. So are the finals. My finals were in the can. Now, there was only some academic advisor work to do and then I was homeward bound.

My mother called me the next night to see how I was doing. In actuality, we both knew, her call was to reassure me that she was all right.

In fact, she sounded damn near happy.

She told me that Mole had worked every day since I was last home. She said that he was on the wagon at least until the trip. He was drinking only beer. No booze and no drugs.

Over the years, since this was as clean as he got, we both called these times his 'on the wagon periods'. Apparently, Larose was experiencing one such, almost dry spell.

She explained that he was also on a fitness kick. Each night after work he would go out on his ten speed. He would also go running sometimes to break it up. He was augmenting these workouts by eating raw eggs and wheat germ along with every sort of vegetable from his garden.

He had apparently regained interest in the garden.

If the news about Mole wasn't enough, Larose told me she had gotten a big promotion at her job. She was a payroll clerk at the Philadelphia shipyard, but had recently been promoted to the head position. She was still a clerk but her pay grade had been bumped up.

I was happy for her. Too many times the government promotes the little guy in title only. I was tired of hearing my mother tell me she was promoted to assistant manager or head clerk or administrative assistant, or whatever other titles the government could think of for the workers in the defense procurement division of the naval yard. It too often meant nothing to her take home pay.

Some times I think the government has a whole division of workers locked away in the bowels of a mountain somewhere, their sole job to invent meaningless titles to bestow on the countless minions who toil for Uncle Sam.

This was different. This was a title **and** a pay raise.

No wonder she was as close to happy as she could be.

We were both realists though. We had gone through so many of these manic episodes with Mole in the past, that we both were careful to keep the Mole's recent sunny days from blinding us.

My mother mentioned it first.

"You know what this means, he is going to be full of piss and vinegar on your trip. You better not beat him up again. Are you sure you want to go?" she began to ramble.

"Maybe he will surprise us this time," I lied.

She allowed herself to play along.

"He is doing great. He even helped Maddie with her homework, and it was with math no less. Maybe you guys will have fun," she added.

We both had had enough of the mutual bullshit fest.

"Who are we kidding? He won't even last til the trip," I said, pissing on the parade.

"One day at a time," she said. "One day at a time."

It sounded like a prayer coming from the other end of the phone line.

Too bad most prayers are never answered.

Chapter 16

How do you get off the ride?

When you marry, the preacher, or for most of the weddings in my family, the justice of the peace, asks you—Do you take this person to be your lawful wedded husband or wife as the case may be?

Without exception, people answer "I do."

It is a shame that no one fully comprehends the words that go along with this vow. 'For richer or poorer in sickness and in health.' These words accompany the vow. They were not put there for filler.

They were put there to warn you.

But on a person's wedding day, no one thinks of—poorer, they only think of—richer. No one ponders—in sickness, they think only of—in health.

On the happy day, no one wants to spend time getting their mind around the possibility that some day their spouse may fail as a breadwinner, or worse, that their loved one who they have just agreed to spend the rest of their life with, may someday become an alcoholic or a drug addict or perhaps even suffer from mental illness.

Perhaps the one delivering the vows should be charged with the duty to inform the happy couple on the joyous occasion of these very real possibilities.

Perhaps, young couples, before the nuptials, should be shown the inside of a divorce court, or given a tour of a drug and alcohol rehabilitation center or maybe even given a peek into a mental institution.

Is this somewhat drastic? A little dramatic? Yes and yes. But from what I went through, maybe these precautions merit some additional discussion. Perhaps these suggestions might change the course of many a potentially dysfunctional family. Perhaps not.

In any event, they would do more to enlighten couples than say, being tutored about marriage by a priest who takes a vow of celibacy and will never marry.

My parents didn't even get this.

The Catholic Church, in their infinite wisdom, does not counsel those that get pregnant out of wedlock. As such, my mother was screwed in more ways than one. Not that it would have made any difference.

My old man hated the church, and would have never subjected himself to the Catholic Church's counsel. Besides, what priest could have predicted what a life with the Mole would be like?

Let's just say, when my parents married, my mom was embarking on a ride with a lot of blind corners.

How do you get off a ride that hasn't turned out to be what you expected? How do you get the ticket taker to stop and let you off of the roller coaster that has gotten out of control or in some cases has turned terrifying and horrible? Especially when you know that to do so, may cause you to leave others behind, whether it is children, or sometimes the spouse themselves, such being the power of love.

These thoughts must have been carried around by my mother her whole life. Why she didn't act on them sooner?

Only she knows.

I guess when your nineteen and pregnant you don't pay much attention to what a justice of the peace is telling you. You are so nervous about the day and the future that you don't listen, or at least you don't comprehend. Instead, you concentrate on what you can control, and you practice quietly under your breath. You just don't want to mess up the part where you say "I DO".

I said earlier, my mother stayed in there and I think I'm better off for it. In reality, I will never know.

By the time my sister and I could talk Larose into throwing in the towel, the fight had been long over. Hell, the ring had already been torn down. The fighters well past their prime, relegated to bar stools not ring stools. Each fighter, clinging to their own version of history, as remembered by one punch drunk father and one mother content to see through the cliché of rose colored glasses and disregard the bad memories, or worse, act like they never happened.

As my school year came to an end and the trip was close at hand, Larose was still 'all in' to use the poker term. Unfortunately, her chances of getting a winning hand had long ago passed. In fact, she must have known that she would never break even. More likely, she knew at that point, that she would one day go bust.

As summer approached, my mother steadfastly continued to play the game.

And so did I.

The trip was coming up. Since there would be a lot of drinking, I chose to see the glass as half filled.

What is a life without hope?

Chapter 17

How we laid out the route
and settled on our wheels

School ended sometime near the end of May. It may have even been a couple days into June. I can't remember. I remember that it was very warm and I was very ready for the break. My mother picked me up. I was relieved to see her, if only because she drove the Dodge Dent and not the Ting thing.

The whole campus would torture me if they saw the Mole pull up in his carpet truck.

As it was, the only thing my dorm mates saw that day was that we had a beatup car. They could infer that my family didn't have a lot of money or that we were the type that didn't splurge on our ride.

If Mole showed up in the Ting Mobile, any number of inferences could be made. Most of which would be true. Of course the same ones that applied to my mother's car would apply to Mole's.

I could handle that.

But there would be so many others that I didn't care to have the other students making.

For instance; Steve's dad was a old hippy and he was a crazy writer or at least his Father had an odd way of showing his writing, what with it being displayed on the side of his truck.

Or, Steve's dad was a drunk. Okay, maybe they couldn't infer that from the truck's appearance, but the psychedelic painting would draw their attention to the Mole, and Mole would then draw attention to himself.

You see the problem? You understand why I was glad to see my mother?

When I was a kid I remember thinking it was cool. You know, being different can be cool. Being an alcoholic is not cool. Mole tried to hide one behind the other. Most people try to hide alcoholism behind a veil of normalcy. Not my father. He let his freak flag fly and he was a crazy drunk to boot. Not a good combo for a teenager to experience.

Did I mention I was glad to see my mother?

Larose was glad to see me as well.

I could tell that things were okay. For once she was just happy to see me.

No other reason.

No unfolding drama at home. No pending family saga for me to diffuse.

Just glad to see me. Her college kid was coming home for the summer.

We made small talk on the short ride home.

As we neared the house she began to recite the ground rules. It was like she went on automatic pilot.

"When we get home remember don't provoke him," she began. "Don't make a lot of noise if you know he's sleeping. Don't talk about money and whatever you do don't mention his drinking." She finished.

She looked at me like someone who forgot an item on their grocery list.

"I thought you said things were good?" I asked.

"They are. You know, I just worry Stevie." She sighed.

"Don't worry, I've learned to deal with all the versions of the Mole. I'm actually looking forward to going away with all those crazy bastards," I added.

"Stevie. The language!" she said half-heartily. She continued, "I'm glad Suitcase is going. He will keep them out of trouble."

"What about me? I will keep an eye on dad to," I promised.

"I know you will but I need someone to watch you both. NO FIGHTING! You remember what happened last time," she said as she turned the car off.

We went in the house.

It felt good to be home. I looked forward to seeing my sister and my friends from the neighborhood and yes, I was looking forward to seeing the Mole.

When I saw him sitting on the floor in front of the TV, I was genuinely glad.

My mother wasn't kidding, he looked great. Even with only two weeks of his health kick under his belt you could notice a difference. He must have been ten pounds lighter, and his belly was obviously slimmer.

He got up from his seat on the floor and quickly gave me a hug.

This was back before television remote controls or at least remote controls in our house.

In our house if you wanted to switch channels you needed to sit close to the T.V. Before I left for college **I** was the remote. Mole would tell me to change the channel and I would get up and do it. With his short attention span I would get quite a workout some nights.

Now, as he looked me over, I wondered whether my sister had now inherited the same job.

"Well how did you do in that English class? Did the teacher like the paper I wrote for you?" he began.

My mother's ears pricked up at this comment. He looked over at her then backpedaled, "I mean the one I helped you write," he corrected, lamely.

I always let him write at least one paper a semester, in a variety of subjects. At first, I let him write a paper because I was swamped with school work. Then, with his appetite whetted he began to insist. Insist is actually not strong enough a word. He would torture me.

Finally, I gave in and committed one paper a semester to him. He picked the subject, I picked the paper. I had full editing powers, although I rarely exercised them. Consistently, I was guaranteed an 'A' or at least a 'B' if the teacher suspected I didn't write it myself. Most of the time the papers were so good the teachers always suspected.

It would frustrate the Mole to no end for him to get a 'B', I mean for **me** to get a 'B'. He could not fathom that a teacher would lower a grade merely because they suspected it was not authored by the student. I begged to differ, having seen students failed or in some cases expelled for cheating.

I felt lucky.

In a philosophy class, he had written beautifully on reestablishing ties to Cuba. The teacher talked in class about Mole's line that 'instead of raising the **altitude** of our spy planes, we should raise our **attitude** about our closest island neighbor.'

The paper had netted me an 'A' even though the professor had to know I didn't write it.

Mole was a human thesaurus. Me? I thought a thesaurus was a skeleton in a dinosaur museum.

This semester was no different. I fumbled around in my backpack for the graded paper. I handed it to Mole. It was a English paper. Mole loved English. If I had let him, he would have written every one of them for me. As it stood, he got one. I can't remember if it was on Vonnegaut or Brautigan, but I remember it was a 'B+'.

He became furious.

"How dare this sum bitch grad student give me . . . ah . . . give **you** a 'B+'? That paper was good stuff" he protested.

"No biggie Dad, I still got an 'A' in the class," I explained, taking the paper back and putting it in the book bag.

"It's all bullshit anyway Stevie. They shouldn't even give out grades. It detracts from the learning process," he said. "The only person who should be graded, is the teacher—by the students. That would improve the quality of your education at least." He finished, then turned back to the T.V.

"Check out this asshole on the idiot box," he started right back up again. "You really thinking about law school? Lawyers are ruining this country. Watch this," he said jabbing his finger at the television. "I've heard it all now!" he railed. "I saw this story earlier today."

He turned up the volume.

On the news was a local Kensington guy who was suing the Philadelphia Eagles. It seemed that before a playoff game he had been hired with a group of other diehard fans to shovel the snow from the stadium. He was paid fifty dollars and given a ticket to the playoff game. Unfortunately, the idiot did not wear gloves. Since it was below freezing and he didn't bother to stop, he got frostbite and lost three fingers. He and his lawyer were practically screaming into the camera about the injustice of it all. The lawyer, who was dressed in a shiny suit (readers note: **never** use a lawyer in a shiny suit) was talking about the Eagles' organization's negligence in not providing the guy a pair of gloves.

"They were responsible for supplying the tool of the trade. They supplied the shovel, but they did not supply all the tools my poor suffering client needed-namely GLOVES! A PAIR OF TWO DOLLAR GLOVES! The Eagles' organization should be ashamed."

With that, he brandished a pair of work gloves that he waved at the camera in that awkward way, like someone who doesn't know what to do with his hands in front of a T.V. camera. He reminded me of a used car salesman or those cheap cable commercials with aluminum siding guys acting as their own pitchmen.

Mole immediately lunged at the set and turned down the volume.

"How can you watch that and really think of law school?" he asked.

"That is what is wrong with this country. We are a nation of victims. Every person is so sensitive, we are hamstringing ourselves with political correctness and feelings of entitlement!" he argued.

If Mole's arguments were projectiles launched from a weapon, it is obvious they would come from a shotgun. Loud, rapid and scattered. And, unless they were fired at close range, not likely to bring you down.

"Do you think our ancestors complained about shit like this? What happened to the America that pulled itself up by it's own bootstraps, made it's own fortunes, took care of itself, and didn't so much as cry a peep?

Now we get every son of a bitch looking to grab their fifteen minutes and a quick buck by whining about bullshit to some asshole with a microphone, and there is always some asshole with a microphone!" he fumed.

"This puss gut **volunteered** to shovel after he found out it would get him in the game. He didn't bring gloves to an Eagles' game in sixteen degree weather, and then he wants to sue the team after he gets frostbite. What? . . . Did the owner Leonard Tose put a gun to his head? Too much! Shit, I need a drink" he finished, and immediately realized what he said.

He backpedaled.

"Christ, shit like this could drive a man to drink," he sheepishly said looking over at Larose.

She frowned but didn't say anything.

"Mole I couldn't agree with you more. I never said I was going to law school, only that I was thinking about it" I responded.

"On the other hand what's the matter with sticking it to the man and getting paid in the process?" I asked, following what I thought was Mole's logic.

"There is enough injustice out there committed by the 'Man' that needs to be righted, without assholes waiving bogus claims and giving the little guy a bad name. It fucks up everyone's credibility," he said, warming to the debate.

I realized I was being sucked in.

I wanted nothing of the sort. Shit, I had just walked in.

I changed the subject.

"Why don't you show me the garden and those 'tomatoes' in the middle?" I said, glancing over to my mother.

She gave me a knowing look, rolled her eyes and retreated to the kitchen.

Saved by the weed, I thought, as Mole smiled and gave me another hug.

"To the garden," he said.

The garden looked better than any time I could recall from the not too distant past. Someone had done a nice job weeding and generally cleaning up. They had even placed a slate path through the the whole plot. It made it easy to get to all the plants without muddying up your feet.

Mole began to show me all sorts of produce.

"Look at this big Beefsteak," he bragged.

"How about these squash?" he crowed.

I really couldn't get too excited over a tomato or a zucchini. Although I must say, Mole had a ton of them growing and they all looked impressive.

We made our way to the pot plants. There were certainly plenty, but it was obvious Mole's forte was with legal crops, not marijuana. Apparently, he had not bothered to remove all the male plants. This must have occurred during his last extended drinking jag, when the garden was neglected. As a result, the plants were not 'budded up' as much as if the females had been completely cleared of males. Oh, there was a crop, just not a bumper crop like the rest of the backyard bounty.

Mole read my disapointment.

"Don't worry I hooked up with Roads. He have plenty of smoke for the trip," he said as he plucked some weeds from between the weed plants.

"By the way, Roads invited us to stop in if we are in Cape May. We may have to stop there after A.C. Maybe check out the World Series of Birding. Maybe just to hang out."

He grunted as he bent down to pick one of the what seemed like hundreds of zucchinis that had just started to grow from the bright orange flowers that dotted the yard. They would most likely dot my Mom's salad that evening as well.

"Speaking of the trip, what mode of transportation shall we use on this sojourn? The Ting Mobile? You know it will accommodate all of the Birders and then some," Mole said, turning back toward the house with a couple zuchini and an early tomato.

I thought of the dayglo painted truck and the attention it would draw to a car full of drunks and marijuana.

As I thought of a way to let Mole down easy, I remembered the linkage and the way it jammed.

I threw away all thoughts of diplomacy.

"Screw the Ting Mole. It is summer time and the livin is easy," I sang jokingly like some hammy gay version of Paul Robeson.

Mole laughed.

"Next you will be singing Swing Low Sweet Chariot, or better yet Camptown Races. What vehicle do you suggest?" He joked.

"Let's take Suitcase's convertible," I offered.

"Lucille? Do you think the old girl has got it in her?" He shook his head answering his own question.

Lucille was Suitcase's 1969 Chevy Impala convertible. It was named 'Lucille' after the girl in a scene from *Cool Hand Luke*. You know the one; where a scantily clad sexy blonde spends a hot southern afternoon washing her car in a very provocative manner. In plain English, she dick teases the hell out of the inmates who watch her from the other side of the road during work on the chain gang.

The movie is a classic, and so was Suitcase's car. By the way, I think Suitcase identified himself in the George Kennedy character. If not, he certainly identified with the scene.

Who doesn't?

We went back in the house. Larose had started dinner

Mole continued, "A road trip with Lucille, with the top down in early summer would be a lot more appealing than a carpet truck, Stevie. Remind me to ask John."

He handed the veggies to Larose.

The rest of the evening was great. My mother was a great cook when she had the time. My sister was home and we all shared dinner around the kitchen table. It was a regular, normal evening.

During my childhood and teen years we had many normal days. Days when you ate as a family. Days when you watched movies or went to sporting events as a family. Days when you went shopping or just went out for a drive with your parents.

Unfortunately, it never lasted. It was always punctuated by some craziness on Mole's part. Always some cringe worthy event to make the brief period of normalcy disappear like your sister's coin collection when your old man needed cigarettes or cheap vodka.

How long would this last? I thought, as I helped my mother clean up the table.

It was just a matter of time.

That night I slept soundly in my old bedroom.

Today I'm fortunate to live in a house with a closet the size of my old room. Americans want the big house, the big yard, a big car. Today we always feel we need more room, more space.

Bigger is better.

Thinking back to that old room, with its space for only a single bed and a chest of drawers, my parents' room not three feet away, and my sister down the hall in a tiny room a mere six feet from mine, it was plenty.

Bigger is not better.

That morning, the sun flashed through the blades of the fan like some beacon from a distant light house. I dreamed I was on a beach with the Birders.

I awoke, my face not six inches from the window and the tiny fan on the pane, it's blades crusty with the WD40 oil and the dust it had gathered. The working man's air conditioner. More noise really, than relief from the heat. It never the less gave me a sense that I was fending off the hot weather, or at least keeping it at bay.

To this day, I cannot sleep unless I've got the constant whirling buzz of a fan in my room. Even in the winter it runs. The sound it provides is more important to me than the breeze.

Old habits.

With the sun came the summer heat. No need for alarm clocks in my parents' house. The June heat dictated the schedule.

It woke you at dawn, and kept you up late, at least until fatigue and boredom were able to tag team it and pin it to the ground. When it was finally beaten, you might be able to steal six or seven hours of fitful, restless, sweaty sleep. When I was a little kid though, heat was not something I recall recognizing. The trusty fan was more than enough.

Heat, like bills, cholesterol and seatbelts is something you only think about as an adult.

It was June and I was twenty years old in my little claustrophobic room in Glenolden, Pennsylvania and I definitely felt the heat.

Mole was already up, I could hear him downstairs. He had the stereo on low and he was making breakfast. He was singing George Harrison's *My Sweet Lord*. He sounded pretty good. Then again, George Harrison makes everyone sound pretty good.

I went down to eat.

"What's up?" I asked, still waking up.

The old man was making chipped beef—shit on a shingle. He had some scrapple going too.

Over the years, eating all those Mole breakfasts, my veins must look like sticks of butter. Who cares. Good food will kill you. So does everything else, including living.

I sat down at the table.

"Today is Bean's birthday," Mole said, pouring himself a cup of coffee.

I passed him the milk that was on the table.

"I like it black like my women," he joked, sitting down next to me.

"Suitcase figured a couple of day trips are in order before we shove off. Practice runs. You know, work out the kinks, loosen up the livers and acclimate the eyes. All designed to hone our birding skills."

He lit a cigarette and leaned back. He lazily looked at the cigarette end then licked his finger. Carefully, he dabbed his wet finger on a small section near the end of the butt. Satisfied it was burning evenly, he returned to his discussion.

"We will road trip for the day and celebrate Mr. Walsh's forty third," he paused, "or is it his forty fourth year on this planet?" he finished, and sat back in his chair. Absently, he scratched his stomach and sat, enjoying his breakfast of champions; a cigarette and coffee.

As I ate, my mom and sister came in.

My mom got some tea and sat down with us. She lit a Kool and reached over to pull the ashtray to the middle of the table. Immediately, my sister complained to both of them about the need for two cigarettes at the same time in our little kitchen.

For her complaint she was quickly banished to the living room. She happily obliged, having complained merely to get sent there.

She quickly left the table. Now, she could now watch her Saturday morning cartoons and enjoy her Count Chocula cereal in peace.

I sat quietly as my mother and father silently circled each other as we sat around the breakfast table.

It always amazes me to see the politics of relationships. The endless posturing. The marital dance. Who leads, who follows. The feints, the charges and then the retreats. Give ground to gain ground. The constant marital bartering and trading. The hageling and the deal making. The saving up of tender, and the cashing in and purchase of favors. What Seinfeld refers to as "getting and having the hand."

The really talented couples could engage in this crazy phenominum without ever even needing to speak a word.

Watching my parents that morning was like witnessing a classic boxing match. The 'sweet science' of Frazier and Ali (being from Philly it is always announced Frazier first). Mole versus Larose. Or maybe, that day, fighters weren't the right analogy, maybe they were dancers; Rogers and Astaire or Gene Kelly and Debbie Reynolds. No, maybe they were more like Gleason and Audrey Meadows from the Honeymooners, with a drinking problem thrown in.

Larose knew something was up. It was the first Saturday in three weeks Mole wasn't working. Also, since he wasn't drinking he was getting up early, but today he was up at six. This was way too early, even for a relatively sober Mole.

Something was up, she knew.

What was up, was not going to reveal itself too quickly. Not a second, as Orson Welles would say from Mole's favorite wine commercials "before it's time."

The two sat across the table smoking and sipping their morning pick me ups, speaking the silent, long verse poetry of a damaged marriage. Dueting, without speaking, the free form jazz of a dysfunctional relationship. All the while the only sound in the house; the tinny speaker of the living room television blaring *The Smurfs*.

"I'm going over to see the O'Hanlons," I said breaking the deafening silence.

"Tell Mrs. O'Hanlon that I will return her casserole dish later today," my mother said, welcoming the break. She put her cigarette out and started to clean up Mole's mess.

"What did you do, use every pot and pan in the cabinet?" She complained, grabbing the plate in front of Mole.

He had put his cigarette out on his plate.

"It's not an ashtray for Christ sake!" she made a face like someone had farted, and practically threw the dish into the sink.

I stand corrected.

This was a chess match between two masters. Spassky and Fischer.

Larose was Spassky. The old guard Grand master. Stubborn and set in her ways. She had opened with a variation of the Sicilian Bitch.

Mole was Fischer. Remember, Fischer was crazy. Fischer could also not be beat, plus he lived by his own rules. Did I mention he was nuts?

This could take some time.

I left the match.

"I'm going to take a shower," I said getting up from the table.

"Shower is broke. Take a bath," Mole commanded.

"Ok I will."

I glanced over at my Mother and my eyes told her to back off.

I went upstairs to take a bath.

Nothing like taking a bath in a regular size tub when you are twenty.

At my house, I had taken a bath every day for as long as I could remember. No one had a choice. I never took a shower except at school or the gym from the time I was eight until I left for college.

Our shower stall leaked and my family could never afford to have it repaired. Oh, there was always money for cigarettes, booze and pizza deliveries, just not shower repairs.

Today, I refuse to ever sit down to bath again, but back then I had no choice.

I took a bath.

When I got down from the bathroom, I could hear Mole telling my mom that he didn't have work, and that he would not be driving. He sounded like some teenage kid asking for permission to use the car.

I laughed to myself.

Who were they kidding?

Why did they go through this charade each and every time he went on a bender?

No matter what was said or done in this regular Molineux marital ritual, he would end up doing what he wanted.

Going out with his drinking buddies.

I finished up in the bathroom and headed to my friend's house.

The O'Hanlons lived directly behind us. They were a big Irish Catholic family. When I say big, I'm not talking the extra kid or two that represents a big family today, today's yuppie sign of affluence They were not even one of those Brady Bunch blended families you also see in this age of disposable razors, disposable cameras, disposable diapers and disposible marriages.

They were the real deal.

The O'Hanlons had nine kids. Eleven, if you count my sister and I.

You should, since we practically lived there.

Nine kids, all a year apart except for the baby Janie. She was a 'surprise gift from God' as Mr. and Mrs. O'Hanlon described her.

I was friends with all of them, and I hung out with the ones closest to me in age. I even dated Bridget, the sister that graduated high school with me. She was the only one to go to public school.

Three of them were in college at the same time. Daniel in St. Josephs, Bridget in Lycoming, and Seamus in LaSalle.

Between the money the parents' spent on Catholic high school and Catholic college tuitions, the O'Hanlons should have had a wing in the Vatican named after them. Instead, all they got was a mention in the church's bulletin and the 'privilege' of assisting in the weekly passing of the collection plate at Saint Gabriel's Church.

They knew my parents, and despite my Father's antics they liked them both.

Since they were older and since they did not approve of Mole's behavior, they were always trying to parent me and to a lesser extent the Mole too. This was done in many ways, some subtle, some about as subtle as an insurance agent's convention.

From the casual comment, to the actual parent sit down, the O'Hanlon's were not above both, not just with me but also with the Mole.

Despite this forwardness, my father did not seem to mind. He seemed to take Mr. O'Hanlon's lectures the same way I did, like an embarrassed school boy.

To my family, the O'Hanlons were good friends and great neighbors.

I cut through Mole's garden into the O'Hanlon's yard, past the old apple tree that, during my childhood, had provided a never ending supply of ammunition for bombing cars or for the occasional apple fight. I walked up the back steps and let myself in the porch door.

No lock, no knock.

Mr. O'Hanlon sat at the kitchen table reading the Boeing magazine he had brought home from his job as a plant helicopter quality control inspector. He smiled and put down the magazine. He eyed me up like he was thinking of hiring me, or letting me marry his daughter.

That day, Mr. O'Hanlon started by messing with my head, literally.

"Stephen, my boy, Daniel is not back from food shopping yet. Why don't you stick around. When he gets back we are heading over to Richie's Barber Shop for a buzz cut. It seems that you haven't seen the inside of a barbershop in quite some time. Parents are still letting you wear it long, I see. What do you say? My treat," he finished and took a bite of toast that was left on his breakfast plate.

Just then, his youngest daughter Janie came in.

"Leave him alone Dad, he has his own parents," she playfully scolded. "His hair looks just fine the way it is. If you had your way the whole world would look like Gomer Pyle," she said taking some milk from the refrigerator. "Next, you will be recruiting him for five o'clock mass."

She sat and poured a glass.

"Great idea little lady," Mr. O'Hanlon said passing her a paper towel to wipe up a little milk she spilled.

"No use crying over it," I joked.

No one laughed.

"Why would I cry over it son?" Mr. O'Hanlon said giving me a brief confused look. Then it dawned on him. He smiled again.

"You have your parents wit," he said, playfully punching my arm. "Why don't you come to mass with us tonight," he added.

"No can do Mr. O, I'm going out with my Dad and his buddies," I said, hoping my friend's father would not press for details.

He pressed.

"Not those same characters who were out shooting the bow and arrows a few weeks back now is it? Pork and Beans or some crazy nickname I heard them called."

He looked at me with a combination of pity and disgust.

I knew it well, I had seen it many times before, from many people.

It is a look that is both easy to put on and lazy to wear.

Mr. O'Hanlon was a nice man, but I hated that look.

"Their nicknames are Suitcase and Beans. John Sampson and Bernard Walsh. They are my father's oldest friends and its Beans' birthday today," I said defensively.

"Does your mother know?"

Before I could answer, he said smugly, "There will be drinking, no doubt?'

His daughter came to my rescue again.

"Steve, doesn't your mom have our casseroule dish? I want to make macaroni and cheese tonight. What do you say we go get it? Dad, say good by to Stevie."

Mr. O'Hanlon must have realized he was coming on too strong, he blushed slightly and said, "I will tell Dan you stopped over. Think about the church invite though."

He went back to his magazine.

Janie drained the rest of her milk and led me to the back door.

Saved by the belle.

When I got back to the house Mole was looking for me. Whatever he had said to Larose must have worked, because she did not look angry as she folded clothes and listened to her music on Country 92.

I handed the dish to Janie and told her to tell her brother and sister I was home. She yelled in to my sister for her to come over later, then she left.

"Dan wasn't home I take it?" Mole asked.

I shook my head.

"Well are you ready?" He grabbed the Ting Thing's car keys and headed for the driveway. "We will see you some time tonight, hon," he said kissing Larose and my sister good by.

I gave my Mother a hug and told her not to worry. She just shook her head and said something about growing up, then went back to the laundry.

We went out to the Ting Mobile. He must have seen my face because he immediately began to defend the choice of the truck.

"I know it's a pain in the ass with the linkage problem. But mom needs the car today," he began. "It is just until we get to Seconds Flat. Then we will switch to Lucille."

We pulled out of the driveway and headed to Seconds Flat.

"Let me guess, Mr. O'Hanlon tried to Shanghai you into a date with a Father, Son and Holy Ghost at the local St. Gabriel's drive in?" He said as he gently eased the Ting into third gear.

The gears grinded but did not jam.

"You are correct, oh great one" I said imitating Ed McMahon. "He means well, I guess," I added, thankful that the Ting Thing's gears had not frozen.

Mole began, "Some of the worst things ever done by man have been done in the name of religion by men who meant well. Mr. O'Hanlon is a nice guy but he should lighten up. At least he should stop recruiting for Notre Dame so to speak.

There are hundreds, perhaps thousands of religions in this world. Why do almost all of them believe they are not only right about God but that they are the **only** way to God?" He paused and looked over at me, a little too long for my liking. We were driving afterall. I noticed his face was turning red and a vein pulsed in his forehead.

He continued.

"As though the inventor of both phlegm and the orgasm would ever grant us the enlightenment to understanding it all." He took his hand off the wheel and swept it in front of him as he drove. "That our maker, if he or she exists, would tell us 'thou shall not kill' then give us burgers at a drive thru McDonalds. It is ludicrous.

Do you remember that debate I had with those Jehovah Witnesses that knocked at our door that time?" he asked.

I nodded. There was no getting a word in any way.

"Well, it really wasn't much of a debate after I offered them the Scotch. Chivas Regal too, not the cheap stuff. If you are going to fall off the wagon, better to be wearing Gucci shoes than work boots," he winked.

"Where was I? Yea, I asked them, did they honestly believe that every Jew, Muslim, Hindu or Buddist, was going to hell because they were not Christian? Well you know their answer, you were there.

They said yes. They had the audacity to believe they had the only map to God! I think that's when I showed them the door," he chuckled.

I thought about reminding him that they ran for the door after the mention of blood transfusions, but I let it pass.

"Stevie, isn't it more likely that there are many paths to God. That all religions, if they are based on the Golden Rule, might just get you there? Wherever 'there' might be. I believe there are many roads to God and they are all paved with one thing: kindness. Love thy neighbor. Tread lightly on this good earth. Its as simple as your kindergarden teacher taught you; share and play well with others," he finished, and doing his best Sean Connery said, "so endeth the lesson."

"Now fetch me the jug o' punch in the back in my toolbox. I've been on the wagon too long. Also, we need to stop and get Beans a card and a gag gift." He smiled conspiratorily and pointed to the back of the truck.

We drove on in silence. The drive punctuated only by the sounds of the grinding linkage and the bottle top being screwed on and off by Mole as he sipped the Gallo wine.

Later, as we pulled into the five and ten store parking lot he looked over and said "If you get a chance, you should try and go to church with the O'Hanlons next week if we are around."

He smiled and took a long draw on the wine then added, "Alcohol and the Lord, both good in moderation, but too much of either will make you a bore."

"What are you getting Beans?" I asked as he parked.

"Correction, what **you** are getting him," he replied.

"Ok, what am I getting him?" I played along.

"I don't care what card you get, but I want some Aqua-Velva for Beans," Mole said, handing me a ten spot.

"Here is some laughing lettuce, it should be enough."

I took his word and the money.

When I came out he was in the passenger seat.

He had spared me the first fight.

I would be the designated driver today. I silently thanked him, and settled in to driving the Ting and its temperamental gear shift.

"So what's with the cheap cologne?" I asked. "Beans doesn't look like a Velva man he looks more like a High Karate or even a Canoe guy." I joked.

"He's neither. Actually he's an Old Spice man. I **said,** it is a gag gift," Mole laughed.

In my best Brogue I said, "Manly yes, but I like it too!"

"That's Irish Spring not Old Spice but nice try" Mole said, smiling and shaking his head slowly.

He sat back and closed his eyes. Obviously, he was enjoying the wine, but he was also enjoying me.

Amazingly, I was enjoying him as well.

Now, I couldn't wait to see his friends too. A wave of good feelings enveloped me. I wanted to bottle it and store it away, keep it for the times when he was mean or nasty, or worse.

I tried to keep it going, so I joked, "What are you the expert on pop culture now Alex Trebek?"

He sat up and started looking out the side window to the right lane. He signaled for me to switch lanes, then said, "The old man knows a thing or too about a lot of things but not too much on any one thing.

Here, pull in to Coppen's Beer Distributor. Beans and Josh don't like the wine."

To make the right turn in to the now rapidly approaching store, I down shifted as I changed lanes. Of course, the linkage jammed.

"Shit!" I yelled.

"And shove you in it!" Mole finished. "Don't worry, I have the hammer in the tool box." He said as though it was the most natural thing in the driving world.

We glided in to Coppen's Kegs and Cases.

In Pennsylvania, you can not get a case of beer anywhere other than a licensed beer distributor. Oh, you can get marked up six-packs at bars, take outs and some restaurants, but you are limited to two at a time. If you want more than that you must leave and come back.

It is a joke. Some leftover law from the end of prohibition.

The state also controls liquor sales as well. You can only buy liquor at selected 'State Stores'. The state of Pennsylvania is one of the biggest buyers of booze on the planet. It is also one of the most expensive places to buy it.

Whenever Government is involved you know it is going to be expensive, complicated and more than likely, extremely inconvenient.

I remember one night, when I was a kid during a beer run from a party, Mole made about ten trips back and forth, from the trunk to the bar. He must have spent a hundred dollars on beer that would have cost only thirty dollars in a distributor.

With Mole's buddies, a beer distributor was the cheapest and easiest way to go.

Coppen's parking lot was not paved. It was an old gravel lot. As we glided into our parking spot, with the wheels crunching over the stones, I was reminded of an old seashore restaurant, or maybe a bait and tackle shop lot. It just had that beach feeling to it.

I asked "Mole when do you think we will start the official Bird watching trip?"

"Consider yourself on it. We might stop back to get some binoculars and perhaps some bathing trunks, but we are now officially Bird watching.

I'll run in, you fix the linkage. Too bad you are only twenty or I would switch jobs with you," he said, handing me the hammer he had gotten from the back of the truck.

I reluctantly took the hammer.

"I'm twenty one, remember father of the year?"

I threw him a look and climbed under the truck. The gravel stuck to the back of my shirt from sweat. So much for a clean shirt, I thought as I shimmied up to the linkage and gave it a couple whacks.

With my legs sticking out from the underside of the truck, I laughed at the thought that any drunk walking through the lot was sure to think that Mole had run over some one in his haste to re-up his beer supply.

He came out of the store just as I was finishing. He carried two cases of Miller High Life, a carton of Kools and and one each of Marlboros for Suitcase and Josh and Camel no-filters for Beans.

The show had begun. Smokes and beer were a sure sign.

He dusted my back off.

"If we are on the trip, I'm going to need to get a lot more than binoculars and a bathing suit," I protested.

Mole looked over and boomed "Thoreau said, 'Simplify, simplify, simplify.' I never understood why he didn't just say it once."

He laughed and got back in the Ting.

"You don't need anything son, simplify."

He opened a beer.

"If you insist, you can pack proper when we get through with the day trips."

He turned on the stereo. *Skating Away on the Thin Ice of a New Day*. Jethro Tull.

Turn it up!

We pulled back onto the pike, I noticed the general rundown look of the area and remembered Triangle's comment. When the song ended, I turned down the radio. "Triangle joked that this area is so run down it was one stop shopping for the black man. I thought it was kinda funny."

Cautiously, I looked over for Mole's response.

He bit his lip and quickly balled his fist. He immediately must have had second thoughts because he unclenched his hand and began to rub it with his other hand. "You are lucky your driving, wise ass. Don't dare let me hear you talk like that again," he said menacingly.

"No, you are lucky I'm driving, cause if you hit me again I'm fightin back. I'm not takin your shit any more Mole," I finished, and glared right back at him. With my anger up, I briefly thought of pulling over and beating the shit out of him.

I let it pass.

"Look Stevie, you know better. Some of my best friends are African American, do you think they would appreciate that kinda talk? Please, be careful with language.

Most of the time language is like a butter knife, safe and easy to use for many different situations, but when it comes to race, it can be a razor, and a razor leaves nasty scars."

We both sat silent while our anger ebbed.

When the anger had cleared he continued, "Now I apologize for raising my hand to you. Please don't lose your temper with me. The last time you did, I had to wear those big black wraparound sunglasses to cover my shiner. Christ, I looked like Richard Petty at a domestic abuse shelter," he smiled at his own description.

"No dad, you had to wear them because you got shit faced and took a swing at me after I told you to leave mom alone," I said, my anger rising again.

"All right, maybe I was contributory negligent in your infliction of chin music, but you have to admit the description of my appearance after the pummeling is certainly dead on."

"Chin music? A pummeling? . . . I hit you once! You were so drunk you don't even remember it," I protested.

"Whatever. I looked like Jerry Quarry after a Frazier beating," Mole insisted.

"No, you looked more like Charles Nelson Reilly hiding a black eye, what with those stupid giant sunglasses covering your face. Weren't they your mother's? Anyway, they were definitely women's glasses," I said.

I could feel the anger leaving me like some unwelcome spirit.

We laughed.

He tried a few more descriptions of his condition, none were really worth mentioning. This was odd because he was at that stage of a load where those that are funny become hilarious. You know, louder but really funny.

A little alcohol can really get the sense of humor humming. Of course, this is not to be confused with the time when those that are hilarious then become obnoxious.

It's a fine line. One desirable, one to be avoided.

If only I could consistently find that line.

With the air cleared, Mole changed the subject.

"Speaking of black guys," Mole said, switching gears about as easily as the Ting Mobile. "Our first stop on this trip, after Seconds Flat of course, is to see my old friend Roger Keysey up at Swarthmore College. You remember him don't you? He's the professor who got me that big commercial carpet job with the college. I installed all the carpet in the dormitories at the school. Big money. I had Seamus O'Hanlon, Josh, and your Uncle Tony workin on that job with me. You might have tagged around too.

Roger called, and wants to return some books I lent him. I tried to tell him that books cannot be owned, that they belong to everyone," Mole paused and looked over at me.

"In a global library Stevie, no book can be property. The only thing a book might be is overdue to the next reader. Books are knowledge, and knowledge is meant for sharing." Satisfied his point was made he took a sip of his drink and put his feet up on the dash.

"None the less, despite my opinion, he still wants to give them back." He paused and took another drink. "Seeing Roger will also give us a chance to visit the library and pick up some birding books. Plus, I'd like to find Mailer's new one," he continued, now fumbling with his wallet. He pulled out a old tattered college ID that showed him as an employee of the school. He had blacked out where I assumed it had once said 'temporary.'

It looked pretty good. As far as college Id's went, Dan Barley would be proud. "Roger got me this identification. It allows me to use the facilities whenever I want," he said.

I pulled the truck into Bean's driveway and grabbed the gift. Mole grabbed a case of beer and the smokes.

Chapter 18

How the Birders wished Beans a happy birthday and Beans had the freshest breath in town

Beans was glad to see us. Not so much for the trip but for the smokes. It was amazing how many cigarettes these guys could smoke. At least a pack and a half a day, more when they were drinking. And they drank everyday.

Do the math.

Beans' cigarettes were Camel no filters. They were disgusting. Each one was only about two and a half inches long, but they packed a wallop. Only tobacco and rice paper, nothing to filter the smoke.

"Filters are for pussies," Beans would yell whenever some one tried to give him a regular cigarette.

I remember smoking one once and I got so light headed I almost passed out. It was worse than chewing tobacco. I might even have thrown up.

Beans loved them.

He had started smoking them in the service. He was an MP in the Marines. Like a lot of servicemen, he started smoking as a way to get a break from the physical fitness training during basic training on Parris Island.

When the smokers heard the drill instructors bark, 'Smoke em if you got em!' they marched off for a ten minute break. The non-smokers had to continue their calisthenics. Beans quickly learned to 'get em.' Pretty soon he was 'smokin em' too.

While the other recruits continued doing push ups and side straddle hops as they watched the smokers, Beans relaxed with his new best friend, the Camel no filter.

Mole had started the same way.

Funny that the Marine Corps, which is already pretty adept at getting you killed quickly, would teach their recruits yet another method to die slowly.

"Well, well, well, if it isn't the mental defective unit, in formation," Beans drawled, imitating Jack Nicholson in Cuckoo's nest.

Mole you remembered my birthday," he gushed, eyeing the smokes. "Stevie you shouldn't have," he said lighting up what looked like the last one from the pack in his hand. He crumpled the pack and threw it in the direction of the trash can.

He missed.

He reached over, I thought, to grab the present which I had put in a cheap gift bag. Instead, he grabbed a beer out of the case Mole had put down next to me.

"Stevie, be a sport and get the other case out of the truck," Mole asked. "There is a little something for us in the toolbox too," he added.

Sure enough, there, under the carpet kicker in a empty staple box, was an ounce of what looked like some pretty stinky weed. I took enough for a couple of jays, grabbed the beer and made my way back into the house.

Beans had opened the gift. He was holding the cologne and laughing. Slowly, he ran his hands over the bottle like Ray Charles being introduced to a new lady. With a smile on his face, he looked over at Mole

"Dare me?" he asked.

Mole laughed and said out of the side of his mouth Bogie style, "For old time sake, play it again Beans."

Beans opened up the Aqua Velva and took a drink. I damn near gagged on my beer just watching him.

"What the hell are you doing? You will die from that. What are you crazy?" I said in disbelief.

"It didn't kill me before, although it did make me a little sick. Then again I drank a whole bottle last time," he laughed, then smacked his lips. He went for an another swig, thought twice, and took a sip of beer instead.

"No need to brush my teeth today that's for sure," he said. He took a draw on the Camel. "Guess I should be careful the cigarette doesn't ignite me breath. That would be another type of dragon breath I could do without."

Mole sat down across from Beans.

"Tell Stevie about the time you drank it on the ship," he said.

"Oh it was nothing," Beans said, in a way that let you know it was going to be something. He sat down on an old wicker chair that I did not recall seeing the last time I was at the flat. He took another long drag on his cigarette, allowing the smoke to lazily exit his nose and mouth. He obviously was in no hurry.

Like many good story tellers he would let the story come on its own.

Anticipation makes all stories better.

The smoke from his cigarette wafted up to his eye. This caused him to close one eye tightly, and squint with the other. As he sat there preparing his thoughts, he was the picture of Popeye the Sailor, about to tell us a sea—faring yarn.

He began.

"For a time, I was stationed on a Navy ship. They would come in for repairs or for leave. They put some MP's on every Navy vessel that docked at that base in North Carolina," he paused and stared at the cologne.

Just when I thought he had lost his train of thought, he said, "I can't remember the name."

"Lejeune" Mole chimed in.

"No, it was after Lejeune. It doesn't matter. Anyway, They had taken the ship down the river and out to the bay to test the repairs. They ran the ship up and down the coast for a day or two, to work out the kinks.

It just so happened to be my birthday. I couldn't get any booze to celebrate. You know me, I was going ape shit. I was desperate.

On a dare, some sailors bet me I couldn't drink cologne.

They gave me a choice between a couple types. Since I used Old Spice I couldn't bear to try that, so I settled on The Aqua Velva."

He lifted the bottle back up and looked at it admiringly. He put it back down and lit another cigarette.

"I didn't even think twice. I chugged down the whole bottle. The sailors went nuts. They had me figured as a crazy marine and I guess they were right.

I won some money too.

I was pretty buzzed from the Velva, but now, because I was not bombed, I really wanted to drink. No cologne either. Real liquor, and some beer too. I wanted to get drunk!

I think I also fancied a little female companionship. It was awfully lonely on that hunk of steel. So anyway, I bet those sailors that not only could I get off the ship, but that I could get to town, walk into a bar, and have a proper drink for my birthday.

They bet me hundreds. After all, we were on a destroyer docked maybe a half a mile out in the bay."

He stopped to catch his breath and take a long drink of his beer. He then spit into his palm and nonchalantly put his cigarette out in his hand. Finished, he calmly rubbed the ashes into his pant leg.

"Mole, you tell the rest. You're the story teller," Beans began to balk.

Mole would have none of it.

"Finish it before Josh and Suitcase get here," Mole pleaded.

"Well it was startin to get dark but you could still see," he began once again.

"Dusk," I offered.

"Yea dusk. Any way, there was only a small crew, so no one paid much attention as we made our way up to the top deck. Besides, I was the military police officer on duty, so who could stop me?" he continued. "At first, I figured it was no big deal. You know, I can swim for days," he said.

Mole nodded in agreement.

It obviously was not a boast.

"But when I looked down I realized it would be like jumping off the Walt Whitman Bridge," he paused. "Okay, so maybe it wasn't that high. I mean I'm still here to tell the tale, after all."

"No fuckin way. You dove from the ship?" I asked incredulously.

"Hell no. I jumped," Beans said matter of fact.

Mole quickly added "A marine can jump from any height."

He got up to demonstrate placing one hand on his nose and cupping his balls with the other.

"Yea, yea, I know, quit playing with yourself Maureen and let Beans tell the story," I said and turned back to Beans.

"The jump wasn't that bad. It stung a little but no more than a bad belly flop. It was a calm sea so the swim was a piece of cake.

No one reported me until the nightly roll call. I don't think they realized the jump didn't kill me. I lost some of the money on the way in and I lost a lot more when I finally found a bar that would serve a waterlogged, drunk Marine.

They found me the next morning at some whore house. I was hung over and sick as a dog. I had lost or spent every dime of my winnings. I think I had a good time though. I must have.

I got a dose of the clap from that whorehouse. At least that got me out of the regular brig and into the prison infirmary.

I still can't believe they didn't court marshal me. Six months for going AWOL and six months for giving my sidearm to a sailor to hold. I got out in seven months.

Drank Aqua Velva in the joint too."

He took a drink of his beer then smacked his knees that peeked through his torn dungaree Bermuda cut offs.

"Any one need another?" he said reaching over and grabbing a fresh one.

"Got these shark tattoos when I got out," he said, as he pulled up his shirt to reveal two faded green sharks, one on each hairy breast. He flexed his chest and the sharks looked like they were swimming.

"Speaking of tattoos, how is the wee burn healing?" Mole asked leaning closer to view Beans' shoulder.

Beans rolled up his sleeve gingerly.

The wound had begun to heal nicely. It had scabbed up and it did not appear to be infected. Beans absently picked at the scab's edges. When he believed we had checked it out sufficiently, he rolled down the sleeve.

"That bitch scarred me for life," he shrugged.

"That she did lad, that she did," Mole added.

"Where are Suitcase and Josh? I want to get going," Beans said.

He got up and moved the nicotine stained blind to look out the window.

"Relax, we are not on a schedule," Mole answered.

Indeed. It was summertime and the living **was** easy. We were definitely not on a schedule.

It was still early when Suitcase and Josh arrived. I looked at the clock on Beans' kitchen wall and it said ten—ten. That had to be wrong. I leaned over and pulled Mole's arm up. His watch said the same thing. Mole had already been drinking for an hour. Beans no doubt about the same.

What is the old cliché? It must be five o'clock somewhere.

I grabbed my second Miller, and sat back to see what came next.

It didn't take long.

Josh and Suitcase came into the room singing some old doowop song at the top of their lungs.

"Blue Moon, Now I'm no longer alone, Without a dream in my heart, without a love of my own. Ba Ba Ba Ba Ba Ba Ba Ba Dang a Dang Dang Dang a Ding a Dong Ding Dong . . ."

They put there arms around each other, lowered there voices as far as they could and finished "BLUUUUE MOOOOOON!"

We all put down our beers and gave a round of applause. This turned into a standing ovation. Then, Mole, Beans and I did a mini 'wave'.

Josh and Suitcase joined hands and gave a synchronized bow like two stage actors.

"Bravo! Bravo!" Beans yelled, handing them each a beer.

Suitcase, seizing the moment, launched into Brando as Stanley Kowalski in *Streetcar Named Desire*.

"Stella! Stella! Where are these birding boozers to go on this fine summer day? Stella!"

Then he took off his wind breaker to reveal the white Fruit of the Loom tee shirt he was wearing and he was into *On The Waterfront*. "I cudda been somebody, I cudda been a contenda, It was you Chalie, it was you!"

"For once he does Brando. What no Steger?" Mole said, getting up to hug them both. "Well, where shall we go on Bean's forty third birthday?" he continued.

"My forty fourth. Remember I flunked third grade," Beans corrected.

"You were held back kid," Josh said, lining Beans up for punches.

"Forty four birthday punches. I don't know who is in more danger. Beans from my punishing right hooks, or me from a heart attack caused by too much exertion."

He began to wind up.

"Lets compromise. One punch, you old bastard," Josh said and gave Beans a playful tap on the shoulder.

"OW! Watch me fookin arm, damnit, she's still on the mend, for fuck sake. What did you do, forget your operation Doc Keenan?" Beans said and rubbed his shoulder as he sat down.

"Sorry old man, I did forget. Any word from that glorious bitch you call your ex?" Josh added.

Mole jumped in, "Easy, Josh, Bean's shoulder is not the only thing that is still tender. What do you say we step out to the yard to discuss the day's journey."

Mole got up, grabbed the now half finished case of beer and began a Monty Python's Ministry of Silly Walks, walk out of the room toward the back door. Suitcase followed, saying in his best Marty Feldman from *Young Frankenstein,* "Walk this way." He proceeded after Mole walking like a hunch back.

Josh and I just shrugged and followed.

As I explained earlier, the yard at Seconds Flat looked like a junk yard with bird feeders. There was plenty of crap, interspersed with bird feeders of all shapes and sizes. Hanging feeders and suet feeders. There were even a couple of humming bird feeders as well. They were set off by an assortment of old building materials left over from the Birders many side jobs. There was also the obligatory old tires, assorted aluminum products, mainly, siding and cans destined eventually for the recycling yard, and old and rusting car parts. An ancient Merc outboard that once pushed Beans' crab-boat *The Cannery Row,* now sat uselessly propped up in a beat up fifty-five gallon drum.

"Audubon's Auto Salvage" Mole described it once.

Despite all the junk, the yard attracted a wide variety of wild life. The secret, was the strip of woods behind the yard. This woods ran about three hundred yards long and about a hundred yards deep. On the other side was one of many graveyards that bordered Collingdale and Darby. This combination of meadow, woods and backyards with bird feeders was a song bird's wet dream, if song birds have wet dreams.

This morning, the birds were all over the yard.

"What the flock?" Mole whispered as he saw the flurry of activity at the many feeders situated all around the yard. "What did you do, fill them with Bird nip or some other such aviarian addiction?"

He slowly and quietly pulled up a lawn chair. The others followed his lead and sat down as well.

Beans was the last to come out. He carried two pairs of binoculars around his neck, a beer in one hand and his smokes in another. He looked out at the many birds using the feeders.

"Well, well, if it isn't my old feathered backyard buddies come to hang out with my old backyard buddies," he said smiling and handing a pair of binoculars to Mole.

"Look, a male and female cardinal," Suitcase whispered.

Sure enough, two birds, one a dull red and the other a flaming crimson with a large crest flew to the feeder closest to the hedges.

"I put sunflower seeds in that one, and a little suet next to it. The red birds love those sunflower seeds," Beans said, barely containing his excitement. "Last year, a pair nested in that hedgerow right next to the feeder," he continued.

"It is probably the same pair, they sometimes come back year after year," Suitcase chimed in.

"What do realtors say? Location, location, location. What bird family wouldn't buy in this neighborhood?

Bird supermarket within flying distance. Safe housing by way of a two bedroom hedgerow, and outdoor plumbing," Mole said pointing to the two birdbaths at the other end of the yard. A large group of starlings had landed there and were busy fussing and cackling in and around the base.

Looking at the cackling starlings, Josh joked, "There goes the neighborhood, always the darkies movin in."

The birders let out a collective groan, then decided to play along.

"In this particular situation if the cardinals decide to vacate, it would not be 'white flight' but 'red flight,'" Mole said to a louder groan.

Then, enunciating like a southern minister he said, "Segregation by migration, as the Reverend Jesse Jackson Bird might say."

"Shh, you will frighten our winged colleagues," Beans whispered.

Mole was not to be stopped.

"Ben Franklin said, 'Beer is proof that God loves us and wants us to be happy, and no doubt he was right."

Mole took a long drink from his bottle.

"But I bet you if Ben were here drinking and birding with us today, he would amend his statement by adding that yet another way God shows us he loves us is by giving us Cardinals. What other reason can there be? Other than perhaps to please God himself. Come to think of it, cardinals are a perfect example that God exists.

Evolution? Ok, but so much for the camouflage theory.

The cardinal always dresses to impress. Especially the male cardinal, he looks like he's always going to church on Easter or perpetually getting ready for the bird prom or something. In the animal world, he flaunts it baby! No blending in for this bird. It is as though Mr. Cardinal tells us Darwin don't got all the answers. That God still has plenty of tricks up his sleeve. He is, after all, the universal magician," Mole finished.

Realizing he was rambling, he continued, "Figure out where we are going today while I take a piss.

Stevie, tell them about stopping at Swarthmore, okay?" He got up and walked into the house.

The guys laughed. Josh looked at me and said "Your old man is crazy. You know that?"

Suitcase patted me on the back and added, "But he's probably right, and if not, he is at least entertaining."

We turned to look at the feeders again.

The birds had all flown away.

That was odd, since we really had not been that loud. Plus, our vantage point was partially shielded by rose bushes and an old stack of slates Beans once planned to use to build a walkway to the shed.

"That's weird. The birds all skedaddled. What do they see that we don't?" Suitcase asked as Mole came out with fresh beers.

"They see Brunswick, that fat lousy cat of mine. Look at him steppin across the lawn. Is he ugly or what? Look at his mug, he's got scars on him, man he reminds me of Sonny Liston or something," Beans said sarcastically.

"He is certainly as big as Liston that's for sure," Josh added.

"Brunswick?" I asked curiously.

"Yea, named after the shape of his big orange bowling ball head," Beans explained.

He was right, the cat looked like a bowling ball ex-boxer, or a street fightin pumpkin. He was a huge battle scarred orange tom. He had only one eye, so his head was in constant motion looking for unlucky birds or perhaps a new kitten to rape. He had an open cut over his eye and it was visible from across the yard.

"Well if it isn't Chief Running Sore" Josh said, calling the cat by his own nickname.

He called out to Brunswick.

The big cat just ignored him and continued his thuggish roaming of the yard.

Beans laughed, then pulled an old can from the recycle pile. Giving it a rattle toward the aloof feline bully, Brunswick instinctively turned his head toward the sound of food. He promptly turned and trotted toward his presumed breakfast.

"That reminds me, I have a batch of that homemade wine out on the car. For the life of me, I can't get anyone to give it a whirl. You know, after I got the mailman, Bernie sick last year with my first batch, no one will take the plunge," Josh said. "Bernie suffered an ass explosion as a result. I think there are still remnants of that event on the bathroom ceiling!" he said and laughed.

"Thanks for the visual, Josh That was too much information," I said disgustedly.

"What about Beans here? He just got done a shot of Aqua Velva. If he can take that, what is a little homemade wine to that stomach?" I suggested.

"You went back to the well Beansie? Damn, I can't believe I missed it. I still can't believe you drank that shit in your Marine days," Suitcase said, patting Beans on the back.

"We can't risk losing him to bad hooch, especially on his birthday. Besides, we have plenty to do today and we all need to bring our 'A' game," Josh added. "No, what I was thinking, is we put that nasty cat in Bean's laundry room with just his litter box, some kibble and a big bowl of the wine. No water. When he gets thirsty enough he will gun it down. Then, when we return from the day's festivities we will see exactly how safe and effective my vintage turned out," Josh suggested.

"That sounds a bit cruel, doesn't it Bruns?" Beans said lifting the big tabby up and rubbing his matted fur. The cat meowed what I swore sounded like 'Motherfucker', then playfully bit Bean's hand.

"A Guinea cat! It might work. It is not like we are killing the nasty bastard," Mole said, reaching out to Brunswick's enormous head. The cat hissed and scratched at Mole.

"Although if we are lucky that might just happen. This ugly mouser has ruined our bird watching one too many times" he added.

"The secret will be to leave him in there all day without water. Then when we get back, we put a bowl of Josh's homemade wine in the room. That way we can see the effects, before Brunswick can sleep it off," Suitcase said, settling it once and for all.

"Go put the bastard away and let's get going. We are burning daylight.

We will stop at Swarthmore then go on a little walk about. No itinerary, no schedule. Lets just see what this wonderful day brings us."

He slapped his knees and nearly bounced from his chair.

"To Lucille" he boomed.

After putting the cat away we grabbed the beer and some more weed and we were off. The sun was up and the top was down. Creedence blared from the stereo.

Chapter 19

Mole's field notes—On backyard birding

To those who think that Bird watching for Boozers or the AAS—Audubon Alcoholic Society as it is also called, is all exotic locales and rare species. If you think you could never possibly get to observe and drink in the many locations my friends and I have had the pleasure to bird watch, I suggest you get started on this pleasant endeavor in your own back yard. Many exotic and not so exotic but never the less interesting birds will pay you a visit if you know what your doing.

Like any good party planner, all the right birds, or the fun birds, or the 'in' birds will make an appearance if you know what attracts them.

Peanut butter for a variety of types of wrens, finches and warblers. Sunflower seeds and Thistle—this 'il get the striking red cardinals to make a visit. Commercial mix will get a large variety of song birds. If it is predatory birds you seek, a large ham bone or the left over turkey carcass from Sunday dinner can be left out.

Once you are set up, pour yourself some Chivas regal over ice. Watch the pour and behold the beauty; like pouring tea over diamonds. Now find a nice quiet spot to observe. Binoculars if you have them, at least take your reading glasses off if you don't.

The common Starling is the first to arrive. Large flocks mingle and gossip on the ground, rarely venturing to the feeder. They chatter endlessly.

"Do you believe ole Harriet got mauled by a tabby?"

"You don't say—and so young."

"What about Stanley and Iris—all their chicks flew the coop, now they're empty nesters"

On and on it goes.

Do you ever notice the starling walks—no pussy foot hopping for these guys. Like old, black shawl wearing Jewish ladies at the market. They spend hours kibitzing and walking throughout your yard.

They are not to be confused with the Purple Grackle. The Grackle always looks like the best dressed bird at the bath. They strut by in tuxedos, ready to fly off to the bird prom. Bird grooms walking down the aisle. Whereas the starling waddles like Groucho Marx, the Purple Grackle saunters like an avian Cary Grant, or a formally dressed Rhett Butler.

All mixing at the bird bath cocktail party.

In a flash the party goers, the gossipers and the old bird lady shoppers are gone. What has caused the party to break up?

A squirrel.

Okay, so not a bird, but what back yard feeder is immune from these bushy tailed feeder crashers?

Do you ever notice that squirrels are the most indecisive, wishy washy animals on the planet? They start across the road only to stop midway. Their legs doing a rodent's cha-cha. A furry tailed fandango.

"Did I forget my keys? No I have them."

Mr. Squirrel starts back

"Wait did I forget to turn off the iron?"

Turns around again.

"Let me get my wallet! No wallet is right here in my back pocket."

Crosses back—splat!

It is no wonder the leading cause of death for the squirrel is not cancer of the nuts as you might expect from this writer, but your basic road kill.

A fair size manila envelope could act as a mausoleum for a whole family.

If the squirrel could make up it's mind it would never end up being a pancake on our highways. As it is they are a welcome sights at my feeder, even if they scare away the birds. Just stay out of the road.

Chapter 20

How the Birders bided and birded their time away

Swarthmore College is only about a twenty minute ride from Seconds Flat, but it is a world away from the towns and boroughs that surround it. Geographically, it may be situated in the same county, but that is about all it has in common with the rest of its neighbors.

While most of the county are republican conservatives, whether oddly, union workers or white collar types, Swarthmore, on the other hand is perhaps more liberal than even the possible spawn of a Kennedy and Jane Fonda. It is a throwback to a time of patchouli and Dead concerts.

Oh, it has its share of button downs, my friend Kenny being one of them, but he was the minority for sure.

Mole loved the place.

He had been going there for years. In addition to using the library, he also ran on the track, and bird watched in the college's arboretum.

Over the years he had befriended a number or professors and other employees at the school.

He was very disappointed when I didn't even apply.

I would not have been accepted even if I had.

However, he was glad my friends Ken Schmits and Bruce Hires were there. Because of this, he knew I would spend my fair share of time at the campus.

He was right.

I would spend at least a weekend every month and even more time each summer when Ken and Bruce would act as caretakers for their fraternity.

I looked forward to checking in on my high school buddies now, since both lived year round in the frat.

At first glance the campus looked deserted. Classes had ended probably around the same time as Widener. Not many people were out. Then again, it was still early for a college campus. Especially one at the end of finals.

Mole and his buddies left to look for Roger. I left to track down my friends. We agreed to meet up in an hour or so at the frat house.

I talked them in to leaving the beer and the pot in the car. Although the school was pretty liberal, there was no need to draw additional attention to the four middle age drunks visiting the campus library.

We parted ways.

I spent the next two hours shooting both the shit and pool with Ken and Bruce. We caught up on everything. They had plenty to drink since, they explained, Swarthmore College funded all student parties.

That is my kind of school!

They told me that if they wanted to have a party, they merely wrote up a proposal, submitted it to the administration, then picked up the check.

Too much.

No wonder it cost big bucks to go there. Thankfully, both my friends had received scholarships.

Some time in the afternoon, Mole and the boys showed up. They left the car, since you could walk the whole campus in about ten minutes.

Beans now carried a small Igloo cooler and wore binoculars around his neck. Mole had a couple of books he had taken out from the library. Audoban's *Birds of North America*, and *Field Guide to the Birds of the Northeast*. He handed them to me. "When you get a chance you can read up," he said happily.

"Bruce, Schmitty, how are you lads? You both look well. Where might a man get a wee drink to quench a mighty thirst?" He clenched at his neck to back up his request.

Ken went to grab some beers.

Bruce and I went back to our pool game. Suitcase sat down to watch, while Josh examined the old fraternity pictures that adorned the walls.

"Mr. Mo did they tell you there is a nesting pair of eagles in the arboretum?" Bruce asked.

"Are you pulling my lariat, Hires? You know we are serious birders all," Mole said pulling up a chair close to Bruce.

"I have seen our national symbol a number of times, but I don't think the rest of my flock has ever set sight on the grand bird. Have you son?" he asked, getting back up to grab the rack.

"Only in the zoo," I answered.

"Suitcase, what about you?" Mole asked.

"Only on the back of a dollar bill, and the way I blow money that is too often a fleeting glance at best," Suitcase answered, then laughed.

Josh reentered the room. "Gentleman, you know I really don't give a flying fuck at a rolling donut about birding, but I would love to check out a bald eagle. I mean who wouldn't. Do you know where this nest is located?" he asked.

"They won't let us get too close, but there are a couple of good vantage points not too far off the main trail. It is not far away. Want to check it out?" Ken asked.

"Does a beer shit in the woods?" Suitcase asked. "Show us the way."

Ken was telling the truth.

It really was not that far away. Past some pines and planted Rhododendrons of the Swarthmore arboretum, we spotted them. The pair were situated in a very spare nest high up in a oak tree. Signs warned against going within seventy five yards.

We happily obliged.

The birds were taking turns gathering food for a small brood that looked to be three hatchlings.

I have to admit it was pretty exciting. I had gone with Mole on his 'birding trips' before. Most of the time I just thought it was an excuse for my father to drink and hang with his boys. But this was different.

This was breathtaking.

The day was beautiful; sunny and not too warm. I felt drunk with happiness and wonder. I was feeling the beer but that wasn't it.

I looked around at Mole and his buddies and they all had the same look on their faces. A look of both happiness and awe, wonderment and contentment. It was magical. Maybe it was the beer. No it wasn't, no matter how embarrassed I get remembering it.

It was something else entirely.

My friends told me later they felt it too.

We sat there for what seemed like an hour. In reality it was only twenty minutes. Finally, after the male had delivered a fish dinner from the nearby reservoir and then flew off to patrol around the nest, Josh said "That son of bitch has the right idea. I'm getting hungry. What do you say we go and grab ourselves a bite too. I need to call the old lady any way."

Whatever we had felt had flown away as well.

Mole reminded us to 'police up' our trash. Then we all hiked back to Lucille. We thanked my friends and got the car packed up.

I have to admit Mole had me hooked on the birding. I knew it was more than drinking and hanging with his friends.

He must have known too, because before we took off, he gave me a hug and said "Thanks for coming Stevie, that was grand, just grand."

Chapter 21

Mole's Field notes—On the the Bald eagle and other predatory species

The North American Bald Eagle is perhaps the most majestic species a bird enthusiast can ever hope to see.

Rightly so.

They are upwards of three feet long and have been known to have wing spans of up to seven feet. It is no wonder our founding fathers made it the symbol of our country. After all, looks are everything in the good ole US of A.

At the time, not everyone shared the same enthusiasm for this famous member of the hawk family. Benjamin Franklin felt a more appropriate choice for our national bird was the wild turkey.

Why?

Because he felt, correctly in my opinion, that despite the bald eagle's good looks, it is nothing more than a thief and a scavenger. A fake idol, more interested in stealing from other smaller birds than in getting an honest meal. A big bully, content to eat the meals of others or to feast on their leftovers, than to hunt for its own dinner.

He is also a loner and political exile.

It is therefore arguable that the bald eagle shares a lot of the same traits as many Americans.

Hell, the same can be said of most of humanity for that matter.

Perhaps the bald eagle is in need of a makeover.

Let's start with the bald part.

In this day and age of technology, where every middle age guy, for a few bucks, can undergo a hair transplant. Why can't the Bald Eagle obtain a head feather transplant, or at the very least a Clairol color job.

That's right, as part of the extreme makeover of America's bird, why not shave a few years off his look by getting rid of the 'bald' issue completely.

If America is truly interested in good looks, what better way to give the eagle a new start than to change his head to a new youthful full head of feathers look!

With the new full feather look, could also come a new reputation as a hard working, honest and trustworthy good neighbor. Isn't this more in line with the traits we as Americans would like to project.

It starts with our national symbol having a full head of jet black feathers.

The turkey would never stand a chance. It is not as handsome and not as majestic as the bald eagle. Certainly with the bald eagle no longer bald after his cut and blow dry head makeover, the turkey will forever languish, not on the back of our money but back on our thanksgiving table, where many believe it belongs.

With or without the extreme makeover of the bald eagle, the turkey never had a chance. Americans always go for looks over substance. And in the bird world they don't get any better looking than the bald eagle.

Whether the eagle is bald or sporting a full head of feathers as I suggest, or even a toupee as some have been known to embrace, seeing one in the wild is always exciting.

The bald eagle is very rare in the northeast. They are coming back slowly. Hopefully, my son's children will be able to see them in the same way we currently see robins.

Hey, we can all dream can't we?

In the meantime, there are other raptors that are more common and can be seen fairly easily all over the northeast.

Seeing these birds of prey is just as exciting as seeing the eagle. I suggest the next time you travel on any road that has a grass shoulder, you keep a hawk eye out for hawks.

In Pennsylvania, even close to Philadelphia where I live, you can see red tail hawks, cooper hawks, and some times sparrow hawks and even kestrels. These smaller hawks claim a section of the highway as their territory. They perch like toll takers or sentries looking for the rabbits and mice that make their home in the grassy areas next to the shoulder.

If you live near a river or other large body of water, you can also see ospreys or fish hawks as they are also called. These large birds of prey are just as large, and since they are mostly all white, just as impressive as their more famous cousins the bald eagle.

I like to drink Kentucky bourbon or maybe crown royal when looking for these regal creatures. The good stuff for the most impressive species of the bird world.

Enough on the birds of prey, I will take a break now, and pour myself a drink.

Wild Turkey any one?

Chapter 22

How Brunswick roared his approval of Josh's wine and the Birders planned their next trip

The trip home from the college should have taken no more than a half an hour. Instead, it took the rest of the day and then some.

My father and his friends wanted to stop at every bar they passed on the way back to Seconds Flat.

I remember they used to do this when I was a kid, but since DUI laws had gotten tougher, I thought they had given it up.

I was wrong.

When I was a kid on the weekends, Mole and his friends would pick a town on the map. Usually, within a couple of hours from our house. They would drive to the destination, stop in to the local watering hole and start drinking. Most of the time they would end up making friends with the locals and laughing and drinking the afternoon away. Rarely, if ever, did they get into any sort of scrape with the other patrons.

"It is about meeting people and having a good time. Our only goal is to laugh. Find the kindred spirit that likes the Marx Brothers or Mel Brooks, or Monty Python. Show me an old timer who remembers Ernie Kovacs and I will show you a friend. Have a good sense of humor and you can get along with anyone. Well mostly anyone," Suitcase would say, playfully punching Josh on the arm.

Because, almost without exception, whenever they didn't get along with someone on their regular barhops, it was always Josh in the middle of it.

Even with Josh's take no shit attitude, I can't remember them ever getting flagged or kicked out. I'm sure it happened just not when Mole took me along.

It must seem strange that my old man took me along on his drinking binges and I guess you would be right. Usually, it was the only way he could get out without Larose bitching. Oh, she would bitch when we got home, but at least he got out.

"Stevie, don't ever get married. But if your dumb enough not to heed my advice, remember, wives are going to bitch no matter what. Therefore, it does not matter when you come in or how you come in. If you are going to eat shit no matter what, make it worth your while," he would slur to me on our many white knuckled drives home, well before I was old enough to get my license.

What I do remember, besides the interesting drives home, was how unbelievably cool it was to go in a bar when I was kid. The sudden coolness coming in from the summer heat. The big change from the sunlight to what felt like pitch blackness. You had to stop, and allow your eyes to adjust like some subterranean animal, (a Mole?) before venturing inside. The bar smell; that combination of beer and smoke and fried foods. The way it would get on your clothes and in your hair. The way it felt like everything came to a halt when someone new entered.

It might not sound appealing as an adult, but as a child it was so foreign and different that that it was like traveling to another country.

The never ending cokes and seven-ups from the spray fountain. The bowl of maraschino cherries to put in the sodas. The lemons and limes and the olives all laid out neatly for the drinks. The hot fries and the peanuts. The chips and the pretzels. The ugly fat barmaids fawning all over the little kid, making me special burgers and hoagies from some never seen kitchen in the back.

The smiles on the drinkers, and their endless quarters given to you for the pinball machine or the juke box.

The juke boxes! Yes, the juke boxes, with their wild variety of music and songs. The opera music at the Gibbstown dive. Patsy Cline in the south philly punk bar, and Yes' *Tormato* and *Going for the One* in the Pocono truck stop. You never knew what gems you might find on those old record playing boxes. You just had to look.

The best however, was the playful banter of Mole and his friends mixing it up with the regulars. Their art of verbal sparring. The conversational give and take. The slow search for a similar sense of humor. The hit and misses of finding like people.

Stick and move.

Mole, Beans, Suitcase and to a lesser extent Josh, were always probing the ramparts of the bar patrons, testing their attitudes and prejudices and opinions. Most of all looking for a sense of humor.

Mole believed that where there was a sense of humor there was an intellect.

Many times the Birders would go too far, push the limits too much. They would then be compelled to pull back, regroup and reassess the situation.

Later, perhaps with a drink bought for the bar, or an easily thrown pool game against the locals, or even just an apology and a compliment, they would start back in. More jokes, more banter, more references; to books, to movies, to songs, riffs on every subject. Then, when an opening was revealed, when a potential convert was found, they would quickly breach the walls. They would gain access to these strangers in a bar and in a flash they would become friends.

Phone numbers and business cards would be exchanged. Promises to meet and to drink, pledged. Both the Birders and their new friends knew the barroom promises would not be kept. It was part of the ritual. It did not matter. What mattered, is, that at least for that afternoon, in that bar, Mole and his friends had shared drinks and laughs and a slice of their lives with others. They had arrived as strangers and they left as friends.

They had been accepted.

The bar, with its booze and food and smoke and conversation nurtured this phenomena.

There is a reason the Irish call them Public Houses.

To the Birders, every bar they went into they wanted to be **their** bar. They were always interested in meeting people, and befriending them.

Most of the time that's just what they did.

Beans' birthday was no exception.

With me as their designated driver, they were free to visit every bar, restaurant and taproom between Swarthmore and Collingdale. If you ever traveled the route, you would know that there are at least twenty.

We made at least ten.

It was a great day.

Since I was driving I took it easy. Even with only a few beers and a couple of one hitters of smoke during the day, I felt drunk and high. I realized I was having a great time. It was perhaps the first time I ever felt good and comfortable with Mole and his drinking. It was though he had lifted back a veil and let me peek in and see the whole picture. At least that is how I felt that day. In hind sight, it was more like looking through the same kaleidoscope I had always looked through, one that on many occasions had shown me ugliness, and embarrassment and sometimes even violence. That same kaleidoscope had now been twisted and spun, to reveal a beautiful, wonderful world filled with Mole and his friends, and with them their sense of humor and sense of wonder at the world.

It was a great day.

When we finally made it back to Seconds Flat we ordered a pizza and excitedly talked of our next trip. While we settled in, Beans put on the Phillies game. It must not of been real late, since it was an eight o'clock game.

No television, only radio.

Even if a game was on TV they would still listen to the radio. This drove me crazy. The Phillies on the radio, are the backdrop to most of my childhood summer memories. Harry Kalas and Richie Ashburn. Like two extra Birders, the Phillies announcers were two extra drinkers in the room, even if they only hung out in a little square radio on the coffee table.

"Gentleman, Beans bought this new color console the last time he got back from the oil wells. Why don't we watch the Phils in living color?" I pleaded.

Everyone was pretty drunk so I could tell they were not even paying attention to me.

I gave up.

Since they were not paying attention, I suggested to Mole that we head home.

He dismissed me with a wave of his hand.

"The game is still on," he slurred.

"You are not even listening to the game" I protested.

"How can I when you won't shut the hell up," he complained.

Josh gave him a look like he was out of line.

He quickly changed his tone.

"We can't leave yet. Not before we test out Josh's home made booze on that sum bitch cat, Brunswick," he said smiling back at Josh.

"Well he has been in that room all day without so much as a drop of water. He must be good and thirsty by now," Josh speculated.

"I don't know. That cat is a bully and a pain in the ass, but slipping him that shit seems a bit cruel," Beans said looking at me for help.

I guess, since I was the only somewhat sober one there, he looked to me to save his cat. What he didn't realize was that I was a dog person. I found myself blurting out, "PETA be damned, I mean they use monkeys for science don't they?"

Mole chimed in, "And Norman Mailer used Jack Abbott for culture didn't he?"

It was Suitcase that closed the deal.

"Cats don't bark, they don't scare off burglars or track down escaped convicts, they don't sniff out drugs and they sure as hell don't take orders. That nasty animal has been killing song birds for long enough. Let's dose the bastard, he can take it. If the shit, excuse me Josh, if the wine is ok, we can drink it our damn selves. Brunswick will show us the way," he finished.

Beans knew he was out voted.

Josh cautiously slipped a bowl of the inebriating juice into the panther's den, saying, "You're going to love this my little yellow open sored pussy cat."

The big tom immediately began lapping it up. Beans was peeking through a crack in the door.

"Brunswick's tongue looks like sand paper that has been sunbathing in the Sahara," he drunkenly explained.

We all laughed at his description.

Beans looked up from the crack to acknowledge our appreciation of his play by play.

It was certainly better than the Phillies game.

"Let us have a look at that crazy tabby," Josh said pushing himself up to the door.

Beans moved over to allow us all a peek in. He opened the door slightly to give us a better view.

At that moment the cat looked up from the bowl. He tilted his head like an old RCA advertisement with the dog listening to 'his master's voice'. Brunswick was definitely thinking this potion over. His taste buds were doing some serious contemplation. Then the big mouser sort of shrugged, as if to say 'What the hell, any port in the storm, I'm damn thirsty.'

He shook his head furiously then proceeded to polish off the rest of Josh's grape.

Then, he went bananas.

It is said that cyanide acts almost immediately, but this grappa seemed to be even quicker if possible. Brunswick had no sooner retrieved his tongue into his meow hole, than he did three complete back flips like some crazed fat, hairy, middle aged feline Marylou Retton. He looked like an epileptic having a Grand Mal seizure while doing half gainers. At one point it seemed that he was actually standing on his tail. He then let out a howl like Linda Blair in the Exorcist, and came straight for us.

Beans hurried to shut the door.

"What the hell did you put into that shit Josh?" Beans yelled over the wailing cat.

"Never mind. We are sitting on some powerful spirits. We begin the human trials tomorrow," Josh said laughing and patting Beans on the back. "It can't be any worse than Aqua Velva."

I saw my opening.

"Mole if we are coming back tomorrow to try Josh's home brew, we better get going. I'm sure Mom is waiting up for us," I said, looking at Suitcase for some help. None was needed.

"Fellow birders, today was, and please excuse the pun, a flying success. We were able to see one of the truly inspiring birds of pray. We enjoyed each other's company, and we got to tie one on with Beans' ugly cat. Good night all," Mole said walking passed me out to the driveway.

By the time I said my good byes and talked to Mole's friends about our plans for the next day, Mole was asleep in the car.

As I drove home, I thought back on the day. Mole was right, it had been a grand day. I turned and patted my father's shoulder.

"It was a grand day Mole, a grand day."

He didn't stir, but he had a contented look on his face.

I drove home in silence. As I passed the same spots I had seen a million times before, it somehow felt different and new.

I looked in the rearview mirror and realized I wore the same contented look.

Chapter 23

How we visited Wink and his ponies, and Mole preached the gospel to some gobblers

The next day, Sunday morning, came quickly. Mole was already up and was doing his big, sloppy, breakfast thing. If he was hung over he didn't show it. My mother was up too, I heard her telling Mole that she was going to get ready to go out with her sisters shopping. My sister was going along for the ride. It appeared that Mole and I would be able to meet up with his friends again.

I took a bath, then came down. Larose and Maddie were already gone. I grabbed some eggs and a half of a grape fruit. Mole was already cleaning up.

"Well where to today? I said, as I poured myself some coffee.

"What are you drinking that for?" Mole asked.

"Christ, it's a cup of coffee," I answered.

The old man was a whack job. He would watch me smoke pot, even smoke it with me. Watch me drink beer, and obviously drink with me, and then suddenly get all health conscious and make a comment like this.

"Settle the fuck down. What's with the Sunday morning health sermon? This reminds me of the time in the seafood restaurant when you lectured me on the cholesterol in shrimp as you sat there drinking a stinger and smoking a cigarette. Does the word hypocrite mean anything to you?" I said.

I then took a slow and deliberate drink of my coffee.

"You are absolutely correct, son of mine. If you are my son. Your mother had a fondness for a young Portuguese fisherman about the same time as your Jose Conception, wise ass. Do as I say not as I do," he fired back.

"On second thought, we are all worm food anyway. So drink and smoke and pay no mind to a man that is busy committing a coward's suicide; slowly," he rambled on.

I realized the reason he did not look hung over was because he was still drunk. No wonder my mom had left so early.

Given his condition, I figured I should test the waters to see what kind of day was in store. After all, I could still make morning mass with the O'Hanlons.

"Well, what do you and the boys have in mind for today? When we left last night, they mentioned seeing the ponies. I assume that means the track?" I asked.

"Sorry to have mugged you first thing on a Sunday morning. That is certainly no way for me to act. Let me start over lad," he said.

To prove the point he got up and left the kitchen. He then walked back in and sat down.

"Good morning son. Did you sleep well? How is your coffee? Do you need more sugar?"

He pushed the sugar bowl over my way.

"Ok, I get the point. Thank you. Well what are your plans?"

"Rimbaud said 'Advance always.' I say, what other choice do we have?" he began. "The ponies Beans referred to are indeed thoroughbreds, but we are not going to see them on the job as it were. No, we are going to see the horses on their day off. Much in the same way that we are on vacation, well so are the cousins of Secretariat."

"Whatever that means," I said, as I reached for his orange juice.

"Easy son, That's no ordinary OJ, that stuff would put hair on Anita Bryant's tits, if those wrinkled milk bags are not already spouting a five o'clock shadow," he said, then laughed as I nearly choked on his barely orange glass of vodka.

We **are** off to the races, I thought.

He took back his drink.

"You remember Tommy O'Conner, that horse trainer Beans used to work with at Philadelphia Park?"

I nodded, remembering vaguely that Beans worked at the track years before.

"Well, he married into some horse money. He now runs his father in law's horse farm down in south Jersey, outside Vineland. He invited

Beans down to check out the spread. Apparently, he has upwards of a hundred and fifty acres and a bunch of horses.

He has produced some winners too. He said we could stay as long as we want. His old lady is away on business," he said, then drained his screwdriver.

"Let's clean up and get on the road, but before we get going, will you go out and get some produce from the garden? Beans asked for some tomatoes and stuff, so I am going to hook him up."

He handed me a Acme shopping bag.

I packed my stuff, then picked some veggies for Beans.

I put everything in the Ting Mobile.

Mole took the tomatoes, lettuce and zucchini I picked and packed it away.

"Remind me to take this with us," he said.

I drove.

We met the guys at Seconds Flat. This time there was no waiting. Josh and Suitcase were already packed and ready. They each had a bag, so I was glad I brought a couple changes of clothing. Of course they had Josh's homemade wine and it was apparent they had been hitting it already.

"Good morning sweethearts," Suitcase greeted us as we got out of the Ting Mobile. "We have been waiting for you candy asses," he said, as he put a cooler into the massive trunk of his beloved Lucille.

"Beans says Wink's place is about an hour from here. Somewhere past Vineland in the pine barrens. It is outside some town, something ville, I can't remember what he said.

Hey Beans, where is the farm again?" he called, as he went back in to the Flat with Mole and I trailing him.

The place was a wreck and it smelled like cat shit.

"What the hell reeks?" I asked, immediately backtracking outside to the front yard.

I heard Beans yell out from the back of the house "Thanks to Josh's experiment, Brunswick is a little hung over. He has graced us with Montezuma's revenge. That cat don't take no shit, but he obviously gives a shit" he yelled in.

"Nothing meaner than cat shit," Suitcase said laughing.

In the background I could hear Josh gagging and bitching. It was obvious that Beans had enlisted him to help with the cleanup.

I silently thanked my lucky stars we were late.

Mole ignored the situation.

"Since we are taking the Walt Whitman bridge today, I will bless this trip with a quote from Camden's favorite bard. 'Afoot and lighthearted I take to the open road, the world before me,'" Mole recited.

"Quit quoting that homo and get in here and help," Josh complained as he walked out with a t-shirt over his mouth.

"There is no evidence Whitman was gay. Perhaps you slander America's greatest poet because of his role as a male nurse during the Civil War," Mole added, defensively.

"I'm sure he was buffing muskets as part of his nursing duties. Anyway how can you have 'Leaves' of grass?, they are 'blades' of grass. Fuck Whitman and fuck poets. Help me clean up this cat shit," Josh bitched.

"Josh, Next you will be cursing Dylan Thomas," Mole said.

"Rage against the dying of the light, my ass. Help me clean up!" Josh continued.

"Your wine, your clean up," Suitcase said, handing Josh some rags he had pulled from his convertible.

"You bastard, Suitcase. No wine for you today," Josh teased back.

"Fuck poets? Stop the sacrilege Josh. It is the Sabbath after all," Mole joked.

Josh fired back, "I got a poem for you. There once was a man from Nantucket who's dick was so long he could suck it . . ."

Josh danced a little jig.

Beans came out. "Are you fucking dancing? Talk about a fucking fudge packing homo! I bet Whitman didn't dance like a Mary when he recited his verse. Enough! Now, I put that nasty shitting machine out for the day. The Flat needs to air out. Thankfully, mom is away. Brunswick can spend the day in the great outdoors."

He grabbed a bottle. "Let's get on the road," he said almost tripping as he put on his flip flop, balanced his beverage, and got in the car all at the same time.

"There is a beverage here," he said as Josh tried to shove him.

He reminded me of the *Big Lebowski*.

He didn't spill a drop.

We were off.

Again, it was a beautiful summer day. Suitcase had the top down. Even though there were five adult men in the car there was still plenty of room. If you have ever been in a 1968 convertible Impala, you know it is a tuna boat.

They are huge!

Say what you want about Detroit and the big three now dying car companies, but in their heyday they could make some steel sleds.

Twentieth century chariots.

They weighed tons and guzzled gas like Sherman tanks. Detroit's last gasp of American automobile dominance.

Lucille was just such example, a car created and built before gas prices and mileage concerns started to control the designs.

With the top down and the music blaring, you felt like you were in a moving stadium.

The dashboard felt like it was a mile away. It was made, like the rest of the car, with nothing but steel. The car was indestructible.

In an accident it would surely crush anything that came in it's path. But as an occupant without a seat belt, you would no doubt crush your scull on that steel dash, oh so far away.

Since I was not asked to drive, I took a back seat. Let my old man deal with that dash board.

I handed Mole some Creedence and we were off.

"Although we associate Jon Fogerty and company with the Bayou and swamp music, Creedence Clearwater Revival are in fact from San Francisco," Mole began to explain over 'Fortunate Son'.

"Enough of the background facts there Mr. Whoopee, lets listen to the music," Josh said. "Turn it up Suitcase," he leaned up and offered Mole a drink of his wine.

"Creedence beats my bullshit anytime," Mole said and took a big drink from the flask.

We drove on, content to listen to Creedence and take in the Sunday morning sights. When we got to the Walt Whitman Bridge, Suitcase turned down the music.

"Somebody give me a fiver," he said, as he pulled the car up to the toll.

"The toll is only a buck," I said handing him a dollar.

"I said a fiver. Any one who sits here for eight hours a day sucking exhaust fumes deserves a little tip," He insisted.

Without turning around, he stabbed his hand back again.

Josh handed him a five. "You are a fucking pushover John," he said, calling him by his real name.

"It is Suitcase to you, Robert Goulet. And I will pay your cheap ass back when we get to Tommy's."

He gave the money to the toll taker, then waved off the change. The man smiled and shook his head.

"Thanks," was all he said.

We drove off towards Wink's place.

Driving through South Jersey, it is hard to believe it is the most heavily populated state per square mile in the whole country. After going through Camden, it quickly becomes scrub pines and deserted two lane highways.

Today of course, like the rest of the country, there has been a ton of construction. Housing developments and strip malls. Back then though, it was called the Pine Barrens for a reason. It was indeed barren with nothing but small gnarled scrub pines for miles and miles.

Some areas had been ravaged by fire. The ground burnt and barren. The remaining pines blackened and twisted. They were interspersed with areas that were green for as far as you could see.

These scrub pines were interrupted only by isolated communities that still apparently eeked out a living from the cranberry and blueberry culture. Rusting pickups and dilapidated autos seemed to be a popular crop.

We passed a small town whose outstanding piece of architecture was a feed store church. That is to say, it had once been a church. It's owners had never bothered to tear down the steeple. Now the only services it held were for farm animals.

Next we passed a huge deserted orchard. The fruit trees long dead, their grey trunks and gnarled empty branches stretched out in rows like old parched parishioners praying for water.

Surveying the orchard graveyard Mole observed, "Look lads, an arbor with arthritis."

We drove on. The music blaring and the beer cans popping.

With the deserted and open road, Suitcase picked it up. At one point I looked over his shoulder and the speedometer said eighty five. If we got stopped for speeding, there would no doubt be trouble. Open containers and joints in the ashtray do not lead to a happy ending after a car stop.

Mole must have read my mind.

"Slow down old boy, there isn't any hurry . . . there is a bad moon on the rise," Mole sang, to the words of the Creedence song that was playing.

"I didn't even realize I was going that fast. It is the music and the open road," Suitcase apologized.

Not to mention the booze, I thought, but bit my tongue. Instead I asked "Who is this Tommy O'Connor? Mole mentioned him this morning but I really don't remember him."

I pointed to the cooler at Josh's knees, "Grab me a beer Josh please?"

Josh handed me the beer.

"Tommy O'Connor, you remember, Wink? He has that one funky eye. Squints all the time so he's called Wink," Josh said.

I nodded.

It was Beans' turn next.

"I used to work with the prick at the race tracks in Jersey. When they closed, we both got picked up by Philadelphia Park. I get stuck mucking out the stalls, he gets to fuck the boss's daughter. Go figure. I shovel the shit, he steps in it."

"What the hell do we have here?" Mole said, as a large flock of turkeys came into view as we came around the bend in the road.

"Pull over, I need to piss anyway," Mole said.

Suitcase pulled the old Impala over.

"This is strange, I thought it was nothing but blueberries and cranberry farms in this a here parts," Suitcase drawled. "Turkeys ain't something I reckoned on seeing," he continued with a exaggerated country twang.

We all got out.

Aside from the pen full of turkeys there was no other signs of life.

"That farm house back a mile or so must have been the owner," Josh said.

He started to case out the pen for his next meal.

The turkeys, being big followers and thinking Josh was there to feed them, began to congregate by the fence.

"Easy there partner, these friendly feathered friends at least have until Thanksgiving before they meet their maker," Beans said.

Mole finished pissing and chimed in, "Or that amount of time before they are made into meat."

Everyone groaned at Mole's bad play on words.

Just as I was getting back in the car, I let out a loud sneeze.

Now it is well known that turkeys are the bird equivalent of Lemmings. They have a group nervousness caused and inculcated over the years, no doubt, from being slaughtered in mass at certain times each year. Our Thanksgiving is the Turkey's holocaust after all.

At the sound of my sneeze, all the turkeys responded with a rousing standing ovation of gobbles. This tickled Mole to no end. Sensing a very live audience, he jumped at the chance for a speech. He climbed onto the trunk of Lucille.

"My fellow Americans," he boomed out over the sprawling pen. Letting his voice drop like Martin Luther King he continued, "I yearn for the day that we are judged not by the color of our meat, white or dark, but for the content of our character!"

The turkeys went wild, with a mass round of gobbled kudos as they scrambled away from Josh and toward their new leader. Seeing this, Mole scrambled to the podium of the picket fence. Now separated only by chicken wire, he spoke to his captive audience.

"The time has come for a new generation of turkeys," once again the flock let out a unified response, "born in captivity, tempered with grain, yet raised to be stuffed," he paused for affect, but the turkeys were impatient, they gobbled their encouragement at the end of the noise, "Let the word go forth, from this day on, that the feast is over!"

A thanksgiving touchdown was scored. A thousand turkeys in unison gobbled their approval. Mole continued, obviously enjoying himself, "But I say to Mr. Swanson and to Butterball and their ilk," the birds let out a low rumble of acknowledging gobbles as if they understood the words, "that they can stick to mashed potatoes and gravy, we have families to raise!"

Beans nervously looked down the road toward the farmhouse, certain that the owners would be coming soon.

No one came.

Suitcase slapped Mole on the back.

"That was amazing. You are like Gandhi of the gobblers."

He looked over at me, I just shook my head and drank my beer.

"A regular preacher to the poultry," I lamely added.

The turkeys lined up around Mole. I half expected them to reach out for his autograph.

"He's like a turkey dictator," Josh joked. "Keep talking while I get us some for dinner," he continued.

"And I say to all Americans—you can take your cranberry sauce and shove it!" Mole shouted.

The feathered congregation went wild. Mole was a turkey rock star. He was Castro and Bono and Foghorn Leghorn all wrapped up in one.

By now the turkeys were so worked up, they we delirious.

"I guess no one ever delivered a speech to them before Mole," Beans said, having abandoned all worries of being caught. He and Suitcase stood next to Mole on the fence like two drunk secret service agents guarding their poultry president.

"So let all of us gathered, send a word out to the turkey packers everywhere, those of you who have seen your parents slaughtered in the Christmas and Thanksgiving day massacres, let them know, that I am not afraid . . . for I have been to the mountain top and I have seen the promised land!"

All hell broke loose.

At the very same moment that Mole finished his turkey sermon, Josh dove over the fence in a mad grab for dinner. It was an emotional peanut scramble. The whole flock let forth a thunderous roar of gobbles. They flapped their wings and swarmed over each other in a mad effort to escape Josh.

Mole was shocked.

"What are you doing Brother? These are my people," he said only half joking.

Josh cursed him from the pile.

It was like a poultry version of Jonestown without the Kool aid.

"You son of a bitch. Why did you stop talking? I could have caught a shit load of those stupid birds," Josh complained, picking himself up off the ground. He had one bird by the neck and he was covered in turkey shit and feathers.

With the whole pen in a panic, he calmly snapped the gobbler's neck.

"Let's get out of here before the cops come," Suitcase yelled.

I was already in the car when the rest jumped in. Josh was the last to reach Lucille and he banged on the car with the still squirming bird until it stopped moving. Only then did he throw it in the trunk.

We sped off laughing.

After we were safely away, Mole turned to Josh and said, "After that performance Keenan I'm thinking of becoming a strict vegetarian."

He took a long drink of his wine and settled back in his seat. Then he laughed and said "Josh I should snap **your** neck."

We laughed and broke Josh's balls about his appearance.

After a lull in the action, Suitcase called Josh 'chicken shit'. Josh gobbled and said "Never mind all the ball bustin fellas, we are having turkey tonight."

//

We reached the stables well before noon. Wink was there to greet us. He seemed excited to see Beans.

Before I was out of the car I realized why.

"Beans did your friends bring the weed? I haven't been able to get diddly squat since the winter," he asked excitedly.

Mole patted Wink on the back, "Don't you worry there, Wink old boy, we have the giggle weed and we look forward to sharing some with you."

Wink's mood improved immediately.

"Let me show you gentlemen to your lodgings. Once you are settled, I will give you a tour of the stables and the surrounding acreage."

He grabbed Mole's bag and led us in to the main house.

The place was a sprawling old Victorian. It looked like it had been added onto a number of times throughout it's history. It had a wide open wraparound porch with rocking chairs and a sliding wooden bench.

Although the house was old, it was kept up nicely.

Fresh paint and stainglass windows were just two of the details I noticed when I entered the foyer. There were a number of people in the place, mainly Hispanics. A maid, a cook and a couple of groundskeepers or perhaps stable hands, from the look of things.

They spoke in hushed Spanish and smiled and said 'ola' as we went to our rooms. There was no sign of Wink's wife.

Mole and I were given a large room that overlooked the back yard. From the big back window you could see the stables, the paddock, and the surrounding pastures. As far as you could see, there were fields, broken up only by the white pickets that separated the parcels. At the far end, were what looked like overgrown meadows. After that was a large wooded area. It was difficult to tell if there were trails leading from the fields to the woods. Only a closer look, or perhaps binoculars would reveal it.

"Did you get a load of this spread Mole?" I asked turning back from the window. "Yea its something else. Wait until you see the horses. Wink had over twenty last time. Beans thinks he has even more now," Mole said shaking his head.

He took some pot out of a big bag and placed it into two smaller bags.

"For the dude?" I asked.

"Yea, I don't want the prick bothering me all week. I figured if I give him his own bag then I can avoid being tortured by him, at least until he smokes this batch, or lies and tells me he smoked it."

"Why don't you like this guy?" I asked.

Mole looked out the window then back to me.

"He's not so bad, he just seems to forget that he was a stable hand just like Beans. He thinks his manure doesn't stink that's all," Mole said, then changed the subject. "We should go out for a hike. Check out the grounds, then do some birding. Maybe finish the day with some canuding."

He put his arm around me.

"If you are ever going to marry, make sure you marry up!" he laughed.

"This is some crib huh?" he continued.

"Lets see how the boys are making out."

We walked out of the room and down the hall.

"What the hell is canuding?" I asked, not knowing if I really wanted an answer.

"Ask Beans or Suitcase later when we are on the hike. I don't think Josh ever had the pleasure," Mole said as the others met us in the hall.

"Where did Wink get to? I would like to get something to eat," Suitcase said.

Josh added, "Yea, don't forget I got that bird in the trunk. I would like to get one of those hatchet head spicks to pluck it and gut it. Maybe we can eat it for dinner."

He rubbed his hands together like some crazed cartoon mad scientist.

"Easy Josh, first you murder one of my flock, then you insult the very wait staff that are charged with our care and comfort," Mole said, looking around at the rest of us for our help or at least our reaction.

Suitcase joined in.

"Yea, who peed in your wheaties lad? What you need is a toke of the kind bud, or perhaps a healthy dose of some aged whiskey. I am sure that a home to thoroughbreds has it's fair share of Kentucky Bourbon. Come, we will ask our kindly Mexican helpers where we might slake our thirst," he finished and winked at Mole.

Mole gave him a look that said well done.

We all went down stairs. Wink was waiting for us. Mole took the opportunity to introduce me, "Tom, this is my son, Steve. He is a sophmore at Widener. He is interested in the horses and is a novice birder. As such, we have brought him along to further his education in both disciplines."

Tom O'Conner sized me up as he shook my hand.

"Stay away from the ponies and the female birds and you will be all right."

He let out a huge laugh that boomed throughout the house. Then he led us through the kitchen and out the back door.

"Let me show you around the place," he said walking towards the barn.

"Wink, I got a turkey in the trunk, any chance your cook can tend to it?" Josh asked.

"Tend to it? You make it sound like it is wounded and needs medical care," Wink joked. "I assure you Marta is already plucking that bad boy. It should be ready to eat this evening. By the way, I will be sure to ask my neighbor Henderson if he is missing any Toms," Wink added sarcastically.

Josh, not content to let this comment go, responded, "Yea and while you're at it remind him next time to keep his birds penned up, so they are not running loose in the road and almost causing us to wreck."

He smiled and winked to me. When Wink turned his head he mouthed, "Fuck him if he can't take a joke."

We entered the barn.

There were at least ten stalls on each side of the massive barn. Each stall had a door that was about six foot high. The first thing I noticed were the heads of the horses. Almost without exception, they peered over the stall doors. These animals were huge. It seemed like a rogue Budweiser Clydesdale had paid a past visit to these stalls and his amorous adventures had left these thoroughbred mutants in his wake.

"Oh my God! These suckers are gigantic," I yelled.

The horses let loose, rising up and kicking the stall doors, their winnying and snorting rattled the whole barn.

I was petrified.

"Relax son, these are stallions. They are always riled up. Interested like most studs in fightin and fuckin."

Wink laughed again.

"Not to mention eating and shitting," Beans added.

"You would know more about that than I would Beans," Wink said, dismissively.

I could see Beans bristle but he didn't say anything.

"Guess I'm just not used to seeing racehorses this close, Mr. O'Conner," I said. "They are magnificent creatures, that's for sure," Wink answered. Then he smiled and said, "Come on out side and I'll show you my wife's latest love affair."

We went out side.

We began walking to the far end of the barn, past the pastures I saw from the window and closer to the woods. There on the edge of the field was a small pond. Next to it, hidden by a grove of trees was a small enclosure. I expected to find a beautiful mare or at least another stallion, instead there were two black pigs.

"Well, Northern Dancer and Sunday Silence they are not!" Mole joked.

"The wife just loves these porkers. They are Vietnamese Pot Bellied pigs. All these horses, and the old lady says she needs a pet. I say get a fuckin dog. Instead she comes home with two tiny pigs. Moves them right in the main house! Tells me they are going to be house trained. Pigs. Can you believe it?

That was a year ago. Now these monsters are over two hundred pounds and still growing. My wife is attached to them worse than if they were dogs. She adores them. I have to admit I'm sort of fond of them too. They are cute, don't you think?" he said, He began talking to his wife's pets in some sort of baby talk. The animals came over and clamored for their master's attention. Wink leaned in and scratched them both behind their ears.

"Shit, they are just like dogs," Josh said, reaching in to pet them like Wink. The larger male immediately squealed like Josh had stabbed him and proceeded to bite Josh's hand.

"Mother fucker bit me!" Josh screamed, pulling his hand back and grabbing it with his other hand. Immediately, blood began to spurt through his fingers.

"I'm bleeding like a stuffed pig!" he yelled.

We laughed.

Mole handed Josh a hanky he had in his pocket.

Wink glanced at the wound then went back to petting his pigs.

"I'm sorry about the mishap, but you should not have stuck your hand in there while I was petting them. They are very possessive, not to mention territorial," he added smugly.

Suitcase, angered at the lack of concern from Wink said, "You left out, tasty and delicious. Especially with a little mayo, some lettuce and tomato and some wheat toast."

Everyone but Wink laughed.

I looked over at Josh and I could tell he was furious, not with the pigs but with Wink.

Mole, sensing the awkwardness, said "Enough of these nasty beasts. We came down to drink and to bird. Wink, do you mind if we take in the rest of the grounds?"

Wink responded, "Of course not. I need to meet with the stable hands about a sick mare. After that I've got some calls to make. What do you say we meet back up in a couple of hours for some drinks and a late lunch?"

He began to walk back to the barn.

"I'm going back to the house to clean my hand up," Josh angrily said.

We all followed.

His hand had only been nicked. It should have been no big deal. Instead, as soon as Wink left, Josh said, "Beans I can't stand that bastard. Why did we come here again?"

"Easy Josh, Wink's alright. Besides, like Mole said, we are here to bird watch and party a little. So just chill."

I couldn't tell if Beans' words had any effect on Josh, but if history was any indicator they were in one ear and out the other.

We went in and grabbed some clothes from our rooms.

After I had changed into some swim trunks, we grabbed a backpack full of beer and some binoculars and headed out for a hike.

Josh's hand was bandaged and he was still angry.

"That lousy mother fucker," Josh complained. "He's taking sides with swine over yours truly," he continued. "I have just one word for that prick; Bacon. That's right 'The Other White Meat' is going down," he added.

"Josh! Enough with that shit, they are his wife's pets for Christ sake," Beans protested.

Josh shut up, but I could sense the wheels spinning.

We walked to the end of the pasture. There were two paths leading out to the woods. Mole and I took a path that led left through a meadow and to the woods in the distance. Josh, Suitcase and Beans went right, on a path that went directly into the forest.

According to Wink, the two paths met about two or three miles down at a old deserted quarry. We said we would meet up at the quarry for a swim. Each group would check out the area for the best birding.

Beans claimed the last time he was there he had seen a vulture convention as he called it. I didn't care what we saw, I was just glad to be out on a beautiful day.

This was the first time I had been alone with my father for an extended period of time in as long as I could remember. He must have planned it too, because no one said anything when we split up.

As soon as we hit the trail, he lit a joint. He inhaled deeply and then handed me the jay. I took a toke and handed it back.

We walked on for a good bit in silence.

Then, about fifteen minutes in, he pulled out a bottle of vodka.

"You want some?" he asked.

"Why would I want that rot gut?" I asked digustedly.

"What's your problem?" he asked. Then not waiting for an answer, he added "I'm on vacation."

I fired back. "That's just it, you are always on vacation. Or, you are stressed from work. Or Mom is giving you a hard time. Or you are worried about the bills. It never ends. Why can't you just get high and drink a few beers? Why the vodka? Shit, its ninety degrees out!" I said incredulously.

He looked at me, then at the bottle. He started to put it back, then changed his mind and took a long swig. It reminded me of the Chief in Kesey's *Cuckoo's Nest* describing his father's drinking, 'When he put his lips to the bottle he didn't suck from the bottle, the bottle sucked from him.'

After the guzzle, he barely grimaced. He just shrugged his shoulders.

We continued our hike.

After a bit he said "I guess I just drink so much because I like it. It is a fun way to escape, to fly away. Plain and simple, I have too much fun with the sauce. Its like a dance with a partner I can't seem to shake, or in truth, I don't want to shake. I can't help it, I'm in love."

He paused for a moment, then laughed, and continued "Sometimes I lead, sometimes the booze leads, but I always like to dance." He smiled then looked down at the path.

He stopped briefly and poked at something in the dirt with a walking stick he had picked up somewhere along the trail. Whatever he saw, it didn't reveal itself to me.

"It seems more like you are always wrestling with the bottle and the booze is taking you down and pinning your sorry ass on a consistent basis," I said.

Mole looked up at me.

"Son, there is hope for you after all. You should be a writer not a lawyer" he said approvingly. "It reminds me of the time you told me, if someone shits on you, turn it into fertilizer, and grow from it," he laughed.

"Yea, I'm a regular Steinbeck," I said sarcastically.

"You are missing my point. The booze is screwing you up."

Mole waved his hand dismissively, "I am screwed up. The booze has nothing to do with it."

"And denial is only a river in Egypt to you Mole," I said, and shook my head.

Mole laughed, "Fuck it, I will be worm food shortly. We all will lad."

He took another drink of the vodka.

"There is nothing sad about the demise of a species, me included," he boasted.

I shut up and walked ahead of him on the trail.

We walked on past the fields and into the woods. After an uncomfortable silence, broken only by the sounds of the forest, Mole began to lecture.

"The pine barrens of New Jersey are one of the most unique ecosystems in the world. They are the home to over four hundred ninety species of animals. This includes fifty-nine types of reptiles and amphibians, thirty-nine types of mammals, ninety-one types of fish and two hundred ninety-nine types of birds. This does not take into consideration the migratory birds that pass through each year as they travel from their summer digs to their winter homes.

Birds been doing it well before senior citizens started their winter migration to Florida. Where do you think the term 'snow birds' came from?"

"This is great, I get to go on safari with an alcoholic Alex Trebek," I joked. "Screw the statistics there Thoreau, and tell me something interesting," I taunted.

"Like what? You cocky bastard," Mole fired back.

"Like, what's the deal on the Jersey devil?" I blurted out, then realized, I really wanted to know. "Come on know it all, what's the skinny? Or are you too busy with Audobon, Whitman and Emerson to engage in a discussion on some New Jersey myth?"

"If it keeps you from giving me shit about my drinking, I will educate you in Greek mythology, urban legends, or JFK assasination conspiracy theories, until the cows come home, whatever you want," he boasted.

"Speaking of which, the phrase 'until the cows come home' originated in Scotland in the early eighteen hundreds to signify a long time. Since cows are notoriously slow and languid creatures, it certainly would take them a long time to get home," Mole rambled.

"Look, you long winded tool, I asked about the Jersey Devil. If I have stumped you, just let me know and I will inquire about another topic. Don't sit there and give me your digression bullshit in an effort to stall," I said and laughed.

"I am not stalling, it is just that in the pursuit of knowledge, one is apt to take frequent detours and explore little factual side streets while traveling the main information highway," he continued.

"Mole, you should have been the lawyer, because you are so full of shit. Now, do you or don't you know the deal with the Jersey devil?" I asked, finally cornering him.

He said nothing and continued to walk.

Just when I thought I had stumped him, he began, "It's funny you mention the Jersey devil. For some it is not a myth, it is real. The Jersey devil is supposedly a large beast that looks like a gargoyle and has large bat wings, hoofed feet and red piercing eyes that can paralyze a person.

This area was named 'Pouessing' by the original inhabitants, the Lenni Lenape Indians. This meant dragon.

The Swedes, who settled here after the Indians, called it 'Drake Kill' or Dragon's channel. So, you could see where the legend could have started." Mole said.

Just then, we heard a sound like an animal running through the woods.

Mole looked at me and raised his eyebrows.

We kept walking.

"The earliest reference to the present day Jersey Devil legend is Mother Leeds. She was an actual women who lived here in the early seventeen hundreds. She was rumored to have been a witch. She had twelve children and claimed if she had another it would be the devil himself. When she had a thirteenth child, it was claimed that it developed hooves, wings, a long forked tail and a bird face and it flew off. It was said that it came back to carry off children and livestock."

I must have appeared very skeptical, because Mole added, "There was a real Leeds women. In her will, she named twelve kids so there was some historical basis for the story. There have been periodic sightings of the beast over the years but no specimen has ever been captured," he finished.

"How do you think this shit gets started? Bigfoot, Yetti, The Jersey devil, the list goes on and on," I asked.

"I don't have a theory on Bigfoot or the Abominable Snowman, but the Jersey Devil, that's easy. It is real. It's a bird.

The rare Sandhill Crane calls the pine barrens home. They have a wing span of up to seven feet. They are all white with piercing red eyes. To the early settlers, seeing one at night, they must have been scared shitless. The Jersey devil is a sand hill crane," Mole finished.

Satisfied, he lit a cigarette.

"Well, what about the part about the devil carrying off livestock and all that shit?" I asked, now fully interested in Mole's talk.

"That's easy too. Again, I turn to our feathered friends for a reasonable explanation. It has been documented that on rare occasions eagles and hawks have preyed on lambs and newborn calves. They have been able to swoop down and carry off their quarry. Some one probably witnessed this take place, and a legend began.

It could have been at night or before people had access to good eyeglasses. It is also possible that they might have mistaken the screams of the captured animal to be the Jersey Devil's. It follows then, that perhaps the animal's hooves were mistaken for the devil's as well.

Who knows?

What is neat to me, is how over time, the story builds and is added to and refined, until it is taken for fact. All as a result of an erroneous perceptions over time.

If you tell a story well enough, it will be true even if it didn't happen, I think Kesey said that in *One Flew Over The Cuckoo's Nest*." Mole said, then laughed.

"Even a crazy story about a winged devil that steals children in the night, Ooooh! Ooooh!" Mole continued.

He raised his hands like Frankenstein and reached for my neck.

"Get the hell off of me you drama queen. Lets hurry up and get to the quarry I'm sweating and can't wait to dive in the lake," I said shrugging him off.

"And, it was Chief Bromden in *Cuckoo's Nest* who said, it is all true even if it didn't happen," I said, remembering the line from one of our favorite books.

"I think you are right son. But I was close, it was Kesey and it was *Cuckoo's Nest*. I turned you on to Kesey. Did you read *Sometimes a Great Notion?*" he said and picked up the pace.

"Yea, it was good, but I liked *Cuckoo's Nest* better," I said.

"Well you should also read *Fogerty and Company*, anything by Tom Robbins, Vonnegut, Mailer, and of course I know you have read Henry Miller," Mole continued.

We walked.

Despite talking about books, I was still thinking about Mole's Jersey Devil talk and the sound we heard in the woods, I admit, it creeped me out.

Just to be sure I looked back down the trail.

Nothing followed us that I could tell. Whatever was behind us was gone.

We heard the others before we saw them. They had reached the quarry first. I didn't hear any splashing, but they were very loud. Beans and Suitcase were singing, *The Band.* "Up on cripple creek, she sends me, if I sprang a leak, she mends me, I don't have to speak, she defends me, a drunkard's dream if I ever did see one . . .."

We came out from the woods to a little clearing overlooking the quarry.

Wink was right, the paths pretty much met up, although we were about fifty yards down from the other path.

As we made our way up the edge of the quarry to the Birders, we saw Josh cautiously climbing down the edge to the water.

Mole immediately took off running. As he did, he began to take off his clothes. First his shirt, which he left in a crumple where it fell. Then, without missing a step, he unbuckled his shorts. They quickly fell to his ankles. He nimbly stepped out of the shorts without slowing too much. He kicked off one sneaker then the other. At the sight of Mole running, Beans and Suitcase stopped singing and started to cheer Mole on as though he were one of Wink's horses.

"Here he comes, charging hard on the inside corner, direct from Wink's Jersey stables, it's the Molinator. It looks like he may have dropped a shoe, but it doesn't seem to have slowed him down," Suitcase yelled, picking up a stick to use as a phony microphone.

Beans joined in, "The Molinator has been known to run on all sort of banned substances. The shit this pony has been known to ingest makes Lasix look like baby aspirin!" he joked.

"He may not be from Kentucky horse country, but he has plenty of Kentucky whiskey in his veins," Suitcase announced.

Josh looked up from his perch on the edge of the quarry close to the water.

"Easy Mole I havn't checked it out yet. It might not be that deep, or it might have obstructions," he yelled up.

Mole didn't care, or he just wasn't listening.

"Here he comes down the stretch, he's wearing blinders," Beans improvised.

"No, he's not wearing blinders, in fact he's not wearing anything," Suitcase corrected.

"Don't tell me he's nude," Josh laughed. "What is the crazy bastard up to?" he added, stopping to look up for a view of the action.

Mole had hit a puddle before the edge. He kept running.

"As he approaches the wire, its sloppy going, thank god he's a mudder," Beans commented.

Mole hit the edge and he was over.

We ran to the edge and looked down. All we could see was a small white figure in a huge clear pool.

"Come on in the water is beautiful," Mole yelled up.

"You Goddamn nut! You could have broken your neck. I didn't even get a chance to check it out. What if it was too shallow? What if someone had driven a car in there or if there were rocks?" Josh babbled.

"God, would someone give that pussy a bikini top?" Beans yelled.

"Yea, get in the water before I come down there and make you give me some knob work, Josh honey," Suitcase added.

Mole called out "Come on Josh, stop worrying and jump in."

Josh carefully took off his clothes and folded them neatly on the rocks. Lastly, he took off his old Fruit of the Looms.

"Jaysus, Josh, your undies look like a used coffee filter," I yelled down as he placed them next to his pants like they were the golden fleece.

Everyone laughed.

Josh threw a rock up at me.

The floodgates were open.

"Hey Josh, I didn't know your ass was a smoker. Man they are some serious nicotine stains, what is your kiester up to, a couple packs a day?" Beans joined in.

Mole yelled up from the water, "Looks like they are some nasty skid marks or perhaps just a couple of strips of ass bacon."

He splashed Josh.

"Screw you guys," Josh said and dove in.

"It is fucking gorgeous. I might even change my mind about Wink with this place." He dove under and disappeared.

"At least wash those drawers out," Suitcase said trying to keep the ribbing going.

Beans was next.

"I dove off a ship that was ten times higher," Beans lied. "Can't get shown up by Mole," he said, then dove head first to the water thirty feet below.

Suitcase looked at me. "Well son are you going in?" he said, as he took off his shirt. Before he could finish I jumped in.

Unlike Mole, I left my shorts on.

Josh was right, the water was gorgeous. We swam around for a bit while Suitcase sat on the ledge, his legs dangling down, his pant legs rolled up.

No matter how hot it got Suitcase always wore long pants. Usually Painter's sometimes jeans. No shorts, ever.

Since he wasn't swimming, he roamed the bank of the quarry where it leveled out and there was a shoreline.

He disappeared for what seemed to be a long time, although I seemed to be the only one to notice.

After a bit, he appeared around a bend, paddling a canoe.

"I knew Wink had some boats down here," he yelled as he approached.

He docked the canoe, and climbed back up the ledge.

Mole and Beans climbed in the canoe and began to paddle off. With the exception of Bean's crocheted Beer can hat and their paddles they were naked.

"Canuding I suppose!" I yelled.

Suitcase laughed and handed me a beer.

Mole and Beans apparently couldn't hear us, but they waved anyway and paddled out of sight.

"Did your mom ever tell you about the time those two got swept over the Schuylkill river dam in a thunder storm?" Suitcase asked me.

Josh gave him a quick look like 'shut up' but Suitcase paid no notice.

"No, I can't say she did, although I have a recurring memory of watching some one go over the falls on television," I said, vaguely uncomfortable. I leaned back and let the sun soak into my face. I took a sip of my Beer.

Suitcase continued. "Funny, this story played out live on Action News, maybe you didn't imagine it."

Josh quickly added, "Yea, you couldn't have been more than six or seven, too early for you to remember this."

He looked over at Suitcase with resignation.

"Well you might as well tell him, although its better with those two assholes filling in the details."

Josh sat back and cracked a beer.

"Your dad and Beans were on a load some years ago. Your dad had just bought a canoe. He no sooner had bought it, then he painted it up to match the Ting Mobile. To Christen the paint job, they decided to take it out on the Schuylkill. Your old man loves that section in Philly where all the college crew teams practice," he paused and looked over at Josh, "What's it called Josh?"

"Da! . . . Boathouse Row there Lenny," Josh teased.

Suitcase threw an empty beer can at him and continued, "Boathouse Row. They planned on showing off for the college girls before the Dad Vail Regatta. They had the canoe registered, they had life preservers, they had a air horn, they had everything. It was the only time they were legal in their lives. Man, they didn't even bring a cooler, because they didn't want to get arrested by the river patrol."

"Are you telling me they didn't drink?" I asked disbelievingly.

"Please! This is Beans and Mole we are talkin about," Josh said and tried to light a cigarette. Even though he had taken off his pants to swim, his lighter somehow managed to get wet.

Suitcase tossed him his own.

He lit it and sat back again. "Of course they drank. Since they did not bring a cooler, they drank a case of beer and a quart of vodka before setting sail," he finished.

He looked to Suitcase to pick back up with the story.

"Setting sail. Nice Josh. You make it sound like *Gilligan's Island* for Christ sake." He began to sing "A three hour tour, a three hour tour."

"I hate that fuckin show, stop singin and finish the story," Josh groaned.

"Anyway, they had all there bases covered. What they didn't plan on was a freak May storm. They should have known something was up when they didn't see anyone out for the regatta. The organizers of the race knew about the weather, they had called off the teams that morning. But drunk canoe'rs don't check the weather.

Your dad and Beans just figured the race was being held further down by the Boat houses. Since it was a hot day and this being your father and all, the boys were quickly completely nude paddling down the river," Suitcase paused to light his own smoke. "What's with your old man and nudity anyway? That man will drop trow at a moments notice," he continued.

We laughed at Suitcase's comment.

"What happened? I can't believe my parents never told me this story. I swear I remember it though. For some reason I remember a helicopter. Am I crazy?" I asked, picking at the edges of my pot and booze addled memory for the details of the story.

"Damn if you didn't see it on TV!" Josh laughed. "Finish it before those drunks get back and deny the truth," he added, tossing his cigarette butt over the edge.

Suitcase continued.

"All of a sudden a freak storm arose. At first, rain was no bother. In fact, the two of them started to belt out 'Singin in the Rain'.

Very soon after that they noticed the current pick up. They still weren't too concerned, Beans is a merchant marine you know.

Mole told me that he first started to get nervous when he saw tree trunks speeding by. By then it was too late. The current had picked up unbelievably. The debris and the current kept them from getting to shore. Plus, Mole claims, although Beans denies it, that Beans lost his paddle. Before they knew it they were in the middle of a flash flood."

Suitcase paused and took a sip of beer.

Just then Mole and Beans came in to view, still far out on the lake.

"Don't leave me hangin," I demanded.

Suitcase was a great storyteller. It's just that he told stories at different speeds. Sometimes he could weave a tale slower than a sports announcer who takes valium and then describes a Southern Senior's golf tournament.

This was one of these times.

"Well Stevie," Suitcase said pointing out to their canoe on the quarry lake, "There they are, so you know they lived. They knew it was pretty bad, but they still didn't panic. It wasn't until they saw the crowd that had gathered on the banks that they realized the danger. In addition to a ton of bystanders, there were river police, philly police and news reporters."

"I think even the TV anchor women Jessica Savich was there. How prophetic that turned out to be, poor girl, tough to save someone from a submerged car though." Josh volunteered.

"Nice fifty cent word Josh, what did Mole teach you that the last time he told the story?" Suitcase teased. "Her later drowning has nothing to do with this story. So please put a sock in it."

I interrupted, "Stop breakin balls. So, I didn't imagine this. I **did** see it on the News. **Now** I remember. My mother at first was laughing, then she was angry, then she was crying uncontrollably. The phone just kept ringing and ringing. At some point, she got my neighbor Otis Zook to take the calls," I said, now remembering yet another fucked up memory of my old man. "Each call must have been someone asking if she was watching the news. The Horror. The horror!" I said, quoting Brando in *Apocalypse Now.*

I choked out a laugh.

Suitcase went on.

"Well, it was too fast to get them by boat. Besides, the Coast Guard boats could only make it up to the dam, not above it. Beans told me he thought of swimming for it, but he did not want to desert your Dad.

I think, he was too drunk to swim. In any event, they both stayed with the canoe. It was over in a few minutes. The current washed the two naked drunks over the Fairmont park dam quicker than shit through a goose.

The canoe broke in two.

The police rescue plucked them both up with a Coast Guard rescue boat."

"There **was** a helicopter, But they used it only to keep them in sight, not to pick them up. Although, remind me next time to say they got saved by the helicopter, it will definitely make the story better."

He finished, and tossed his beer can. It clinked off the others that formed a small pile next to the cooler.

He got up to go to pee.

Josh shook his head and patted me on the back. "Larose had us pick them up at the police station. It was on all the stations. Two naked drunks go over the Schuylkill river dam. Classic! They got risking a catastrophe and drunk and disorderly. They got off easy."

"Your poor Mother. She's got her ticket punched for heaven. Shit, so do you Stevie. So do you."

Josh laughed, but it was a sad laugh.

Sometimes you get pity when you least expect it.

You could tell this story was fucked up even by Josh's standards.

"What an asshole. No wonder they didn't tell me. How fuckin embarrassing is that?" I said with anger and disgust.

"No Stevie, they didn't tell you because that little stunt almost got them killed," Josh said, then got up and yelled out to Mole and Beans as they paddled back.

"Hey, your ears must be burning, we were just talking about you. By the way, it looks like you brought along a friend," he said and pointed to the sky.

Sure enough, a lone turkey buzzard swooped lazily over the lake and the nude paddlers.

"See I told you there were vultures out here. Where there is one there are bound to be more," Beans yelled back.

Mole joined in, "How about a couple of cold ones for Lewis and Clark?" he said, as they beached the canoe and climbed up.

We gathered up Mole's clothes and picked up the beer cans.

We headed back.

The lone vulture circled slowly in the distance.

Chapter 24

Mole's Field Notes—On Vultures

The East Coast vulture festival is held in Gettysburg, Pennsylvania. While the backyard birders sometimes make the trip, we haven't been up there in a while.

Our first trip started not because of the birding, but because Suitcase and Josh are big Civil war buffs. They were looking for a reason to visit the site of the worst battle ever fought in North America. It was from this interest that we discovered another fact about Gettysburg; it is one of the largest summering resort areas in the Eastern U.S. for vultures.

It has been like that since July 1863,when Robert E Lee's confederate troops headed north from Virginia up through south central Pennsylvania to take the fight to the North. Foremost in Lee's mind was taking control of the North's railroads. Foremost in his troops minds were shoes. The boots they had were either shot to shit or AWOL. Lee's buddy J.E.B. Stuart had all the cavalry down around Washington.

Lee's soldiers had to hoof it. They couldn't even hitchhike, for even though Henry Ford's parents were pretty horny in 1862, he wasn't born until 1863. Newborns can't design mass production automobiles.

The rebels were left to the ankle express.

What ever was on the mind of the confederates, neither General Lee nor his troops had any intention of going to a vulture convention. They certainly had no intentions of being a main course for a vulture smorgasbord.

As it turned out, they were to be only one carving station at the banquet. The union army was the other. Even though Gen. Lee's army served up 20,000 men, prepared in a killed, wounded, or missing buffet, the union course offered up 23,000 men.

The vultures didn't care. Vultures don't read menus. Vultures live on carrion. They eat dead animals. Don't knock it. When is the last time you ate a live one? Vultures are the winged crabs of the sky.

Outside Gettysburg on July 1st, 1863, Gen. James 'Old Pete' Longstreet met and attacked the union army. Eight thousand confederate troops were killed in one battle alone. Within six days, 43,000 soldiers were either dead or dying. Bodies covered the hillsides. The townspeople worked frantically to bury as many as they could.

It was another losing battle.

The creeks looked like Borsht. Thousand of dead horses, there bellies swollen and popped. Millions of flies were whistling Dixie. If the wind was blowing, right after this carnage, it carried the stench to distant locations.

Vultures flew in from all over. They came in from North and South.

Vultures can spot a dead or dying rabbit from over a mile away, but even if they used binoculars it can't explain how they flew from Canada and Louisiana. There eyesight is excellent, but not that good.

It had to be word of beak.

Black vultures and turkey buzzards soared high in the sky, never moving their wings, riding on thermals. The scavengers soared so high up, to the dying soldiers laying and moaning, looking up to the heavens, they must have looked like specs of pepper spilled on a blue table cloth.

The huge grubbing buzzards came to Gettysburg in such numbers that they probably had to wait in holding patterns up near the stratosphere for their turn at the morbid meal. This was the greatest Valhalla ever, a banquet to tell their grand birds about, and they must have, for as I have said, to this day, Gettysburg is one of the largest gathering places for vultures in the eastern U.S.

Although graceful as kites, gliding high up, vultures are ungainly and ugly on the ground. They would circle until they would spot an unattended body or a horse that only hosted a few diners. Down they would swoop, faster than a bob-sled entering hell, and with their long crooked, un-feathered necks and obscene bald heads, they would tear off the flesh and swallow it like a ravished ectomorph.

They didn't have to fight for food, there were bodies for every birdie.

The whole Civil War was a boon to scavenger bird bellies, but Gettysburg was something else. Turkey Buzzards perched, stomachs full, on fence posts, rested and digesting.

Toothpick time.

Hundreds posted in trees, peering down on their companions pecking indiscriminately at Yank and Reb.

These birds were shittin in high cotton. Huge mounds of their guano covered the stripped bones like monuments. Burial crews worked in the heat and stench on the two hills whose names sound like ski resorts today; 'Big Round Top and 'Little Round Top'. Two hills where the battles were particularly gruesome. They had to kick the brazen buzzards off the bodies to bury them.

The bloodiest battle in the Civil War was over.

But the word must have passed through the generations of vulture's genetical grapevine, for they keep coming back in flocks. Like some morbid Mardi Gras Mecca.

Enough is enough about Vultures. Although they provide a valuable ecological garbage collecting service, it doesn't mean birders have to like them. Worms and maggots do the same kind of work, but at least they are discreet about it and work under cover. They don't go flying about in the skies, reminding us of our mortality, as if a funeral home rented one of those little Piper planes that pull advertising banners over resort beaches. Their's would say 'Die at Joe's'. Buzzards come to think of it, even dress like morticians. With a blackish grey plumage, and their wrinkled nude necks they look like Bertrand Russell's viewing.

Where was I? I seemed to have gone on a bit long about the vulture. Excuse me while I freshen my drink.

Chapter 25

On the benefits of word games, a pig in a blanket, Beans in the trunk and zucchini saved the day

That night, we dined on the bird napped turkey. Perhaps, because I had seen it dispatched so nonchalantly or maybe because I saw how dirty the birds live, I couldn't really enjoy it. Surprising too, considering I had the stoner munchies. If the Domino pizza guy was in the neighborhood things might have been different. As it was, freshly killed Tom would have to suffice.

It was pretty dark by the time we finished dinner. Wink told us some of his wife's girlfriends were coming over. In hindsight, I realize this was for my benefit. In reality, he had some professionals lined up for a visit.

Whores.

I didn't think Mole was into pros, not because of any moral dilemma or any sense of loyalty to Larose, no, his was a purely economic reason; he could not afford prostitutes.

Wink on the other hand, not only had money to burn, he also lacked any internal compass to point him on the righteous path. Not only did he think nothing of "paying for pussy" as he drunkenly referred to it later that night, he also had no qualms about living dangerously, by bringing the girls into his own home while his wife was away.

Looking back on it, with money not an issue because of Wink's generosity, my father and the other Birders probably felt, 'when in Rome'.

They anxiously awaited their "short, horizontal dates" as Suitcase called them.

We all sat out on the front porch, drinking, smoking and taking in the evening sounds.

"It's still hotter than hell," I said, more for a conversation starter than for any real commentary about the weather.

"Son, clichés are nothing more than the brain being lazy with language," Mole said, taking the bait. "Although I guess they do allow a little verbal shorthand for the masses."

"Easy Mole, the boy is just makin conversation. And anyway I disagree. Clichés are not only a verbal shorthand they also allow us to instantly understand a feeling or a point of view, they facilitate communication," Wink debated.

"Fuck all that, it is hot as hell!" Beans boomed. "What the hell would you have said to describe the fact that I'm sweating my dick off?" he challenged.

"You better hope your dick don't fall off before our short horizontal dates get here," Josh said. Then clinked glasses with Suitcase, "What would our resident wordsmith say to describe the evening then?"

He looked over at Mole.

Mole took a long sip of his scotch. He slowly put it down.

"While I don't like to be pressured, I would say off the top of my head that it's hotter than a middle aged female pizza oven going through the change of life on the Gaza strip."

Every one laughed. Wink took his hat off and nodded to Mole. Beans whistled. Josh just shook his head and Suitcase pretended to bow down before him. I got up and pissed off the side of the porch.

"Wonderful commentary on my description son," Mole said, then turned to listen. The laughter had stirred things up. The farm and the surrounding woods and fields had come alive with sound.

'Wanh wanh wanh' came the sound of a frog. It might have been down by the pond but it sounded like it was on one of the porch's Adirondack chairs having a whiskey with us.

The next sound we picked up was a fox somewhere off to our left. It's howls and squeeks made it sound like it was either being tortured or raped. Assorted insects each called out in the darkness.

Suitcase began to sing out "The hills are alive with the sound of music!"

"Shut up and listen. Nature is on the prowl. All around us, the biggest singles bar of them all—the forest, is having ladies night. We aren't the only species looking for love," Wink joked.

"Screw me—screw me—screw me," Wink said imitating the frog.

Then it was Beans' turn.

"I'm horny, I'm horny. I'm horny," he called out, like some night insect.

"Hoowwllss about some doggy style?, Howl, howl about it!" Suitcase howled, sounding every bit as tortured as the fox.

We laughed.

"Pussy—Pussy—Pussy. I want Pussy! Pussy—Pussy—Pussy!" Mole chimed in, sounding pretty convincing as a love struck cricket or summer cicada.

"Big cock, come and get my big cock. Big cock, big cock," Josh bellowed, although we had no clue what animal he was imitating.

We all shut up and looked at him.

He shrugged his shoulders and said "Hey I really do have a big cock, wanna see?"

Just then, three girls materialized at the foot of the porch.

"Jesus H Christ! Are you guys desperate or what? Outside on the porch beggin for a piece of tail? What do you think, you can scream out vulgarities and it will turn us on?" said a cute peroxide blonde as she stepped up on the porch.

We were all taken aback by the suddenness of their arrival.

Wink quickly recovered.

"Ladies, welcome, we have been expecting you."

To us, he said "See boys, Mother nature is on to something. The creatures of the night have taught us well. Ask and ye shall receive."

Everyone blushed at being caught in such silliness. In an effort to compensate for their embarrassment, the birders leaped at the opportunity to give the girls their seats.

"What on earth were you doing?" said a dumpy little red head. Mole kissed her hand like some cheesy knight in a sword and sandal flick. "Madam may I take your coat?" he asked, even though she wasn't wearing one.

"No, but you could get me a fucking beer!" she answered, and rolled her eyes at Wink.

Wink stood up.

"We were just admiring the night sounds and remarking on the night creatures pick up lines is all," he explained as he popped a beer and handed it to the girl.

"Glass?" he asked.

"No glass, but five hundred dollars for the first hour or so would be nice," she answered stiffly.

"Girls, we will take care of business in a bit, I promise. First let's relax, get to know each other. While I am already well acquainted with Sophie," he said as he hugged the blonde, he continued, "I would like to get to know you and your friend here."

He took the hand of the third girl, a rail thin dirty blonde with obvious fake tits.

"Candy," she said blandly.

"A Christian god given name no doubt?" Josh said, coming over to greet the girls.

"Let us retire to my study to get acquainted," Wink added, putting his arms around the two other girls and leading them in the house. He looked over at me and since his one eye lid was always shut, he lifted it up at me.

A reverse wink! I thought. I laughed and followed them in.

Mole goosed my ass as we left the porch and entered the house. I smacked his hand and said "Careful, I'll tell Larose."

He frowned.

Once the girls were settled, their attitudes got noticeably better. After drinking a bit, they really loosened up. They thought it was 'adorable' that I hung out with my father. I felt like telling them, I was only looking out for him at my mother's request, but it might be a buzz kill.

I let it pass.

The Birders, no doubt invigorated by the healthy lust vibes of the girls, played a game of sex-Scrabble. It was regulation Scrabble, with the handicapping clause that every word, be it vulgarly pornographic, or biologically obscure had to do with reproduction or sex in general. I had seen them play variations of Scrabble like this, e.g. car scrabble, movie scrabble, geographic scrabble etc. over the years whenever they got together.

On the second word, an argument broke out. Wink had tried to use the word 'Yoni', which is the Arabic word for pussy. Not only did he get a double word score but the 'Y' could claim squatters rights to a triple letter score.

"Not allowed! Overruled! Foreign words are not kosher! Illegal!" protested a pretty sloshed Suitcase.

"Well, what the fuck is kosher?" objected an angry Wink. "Kosher is Yiddish, it's Hebrew." Wink was worked up.

The girls fidgeted.

"Yeah but I didn't use 'kosher' in the game."

Suitcase dropped the anchor on the debate.

Four words later, I used the word 'hormone.' This too caused a little disagreement. The Birders finally accepted it as having to do with reproduction. But when Mole, stroking the redhead's shoulder and casually firing up a Groucho Marxian sized joint put his twelve point 'W' in front of hormone, making it 'Whoremone', all hell broke loose.

"There is no such word, you goofy pot head," Beans complained. The rest jokingly bitched along too.

"Ah, so it's a new one. You got to give a little slack in this game. We're not playing by the Marquis of Doonsbury rules here. You want our language should become stagnant? Whoremone, it's a good word, sounds good. Consider it a defined genetical slut."

As Mole pleaded his case, I looked over at the girls he was in effect slandering. The girls didn't seem to care, in fact they looked bored.

Josh and the skinny girl were flirting in the corner.

"Bullshit . . . OK, OK you people got constipated imaginations, go out and overdose on poet's ex-lax," Mole rambled. "How about this," he said as he placed the letters slowly and carefully, taking a toke in between.

He spelled out 'twat'.

"Now is that Kosher enough?" he said satisfied.

The game was deteriorating as fast as the attention spans of the whores. The sex scrabble only seemed to increase in raunchiness. The slang term 'quim' was argued briefly, mainly because Wink had palmed a 'Q' as if they were playing some literate poker in some western saloon. Just when I thought it could get no worse, Suitcase tried to get away with 'Volvo'.

"Volvo is a Swedish car not a cunt," Wink corrected. "It's 'Vulva' you mean. You got an 'A' or what?

"Vulva is the entrance to the vagina. It includes the labia majora, the labia minora, the clitoris, all the external genital organs of the female," Mole drunkenly lectured.

"Give it a rest there Doctor Ruth, enough of this game," Beans said, and drunkenly flipped the game. Little wood squares spilled all over the floor.

The game was over.

While the debate was raging, Josh had walked out with his whore.

Wink and Suitcase realizing that Josh had paired up with 'Little Miss Bolt—on', as Beans had called her after squeezing her fake breasts, made for the remaining two.

Beans, after his brief tirade, had kicked back on the couch and was about passed out.

Mole and I tidied up a bit, then went back to the porch.

For all of the festivities I was pretty sober. Guess I still couldn't really let my hair down around the old man. We sat and listened to the sounds. In addition to the mating calls of the forest we now had to endure the mating sounds of Wink's house and the snoring of Beans.

After a while Josh's whore walked up on the porch.

"What happened to Josh? You kill him with your lovemaking?" Mole joked.

"Your friend finished up pretty quick. He led me back from the woods and said he was going to take a walk and collect his thoughts," she said, putting a blanket on the porch chair.

Mole tried to hand her a beer.

"No thanks honey, how about a smoke instead."

Mole lit her a cigarette and handed it to her.

"Either of you guys looking for a walk in the woods?" she said trying to sound sexy. Instead she only sounded tired.

"No thanks sweetheart" Mole answered. "My son and I were just catching up. Probably going to hit the hay in a minute." He smiled at his use of the cliché, then looked at me. "We are at a horse farm for Christ's sake, its okay to use that one," he laughed.

To the girl he said, "Go in and go to bed, I don't think your friends will be around until morning."

He opened the door and let her in.

He returned to the porch.

"What do you think Josh is up to?" I asked.

"He probably passed out in the barn or one of the out houses," Mole said. "Let's take a walk around," he suggested.

We started out toward the stable. Remembering earlier how riled up the horses had been when we went through, I took Mole by the arm and made a wide berth around the barn.

"Shhh!" I said. "Remember how rowdy the horses were today. They are pretty quiet now. Josh is definitely not in there."

We walked back behind the stable. It was quiet. The sound of the insects had suddenly ceased. I looked at Mole. He was too drunk to notice.

All of a sudden we heard a loud squeal of a pig, and then a sound like a feed bag hitting the ground. We ran to the sound.

There, outside the pig pen was Josh, dragging something.

"Shit, you scared the hell out of me." Josh said, obviously startled.

Behind him lay a pig. It did not move.

"I thought you were that prick Wink, or one of his lackeys," he hissed.

"Josh what the hell are you up to?" Mole slurred.

"I fixed that sorry ass porker that bit my hand today. Help me get rid of it before that asshole finds out," he pleaded.

"What did you do?" I asked, looking back at the house to see if any one heard.

The lights were out, except a lone spot that shone on the stable.

"I clubbed the fucker with a tire iron from Suitcase's car that's what," Josh laughed.

"Be quiet, if he hears us we are screwed," I whispered.

"That pompous asshole is either asleep or got his ears covered by a dirty whore's thighs," Mole said, grabbing the pig's front leg and starting to drag the dead animal. Josh dragged the other.

"Where should we hide it?" I whispered.

"Hide it? We are going to eat it. You know how much meat is on this beast?" Josh said.

"I know a butcher back in Collingdale that will do the deed for a slice of the pie or in this case the pig," Mole snickered. "Can you drive Stevie? Its only eleven. We could be back by twelve, sleep at Seconds Flat, drop Wilbur here off at Stan's in the morning, and be back here before they even wake up," Mole said and switched hands on the pig.

"I'm okay to drive but what will we say when they ask why we left? Not to mention how will we explain the missing pig?" I asked, realizing the plan had a lot of loose ends.

"Easy, I left the pen door open. The other one for some reason won't leave," Josh explained.

"No shit, he's petrified. His bunk mate was brutally murdered before his very eyes." Mole laughed and smacked Josh's back. "You are one crazy fucker, Josh," he finished.

"We can grab Bean's crab boat, *The Cannery Row* and tow it back. That way we can say we went home to get the boat for when we head to the shore," Josh added.

"Despite the old cliché, the beast is barely bleeding, so there won't be any trail. Just to be safe we will wrap this dead porker in a blanket so we don't fuck up Suitcase's trunk," Mole said, now sobering up as he realized the extent of the situation.

"Biggest pig in a blanket I've ever seen," I joked. "Lets get going, I don't want to be driving when the bars close."

I turned for the car.

"Where do you think your going? This thing is heavy. Help drag it," Mole jokingly pleaded.

"Sorry gentleman, the driver is not a pig pall bearer. I will meet you at the swine hearse."

I headed off to the car.

It took them at least fifteen minutes to get the porker in the trunk. Josh was right, The thing hardly bled at all. In fact, with the exception of a bump on it's head it looked like it was enjoying a nice quiet sleep. The blanket only added to this appearance.

"You sure that fucker is dead?" I asked as I poked the huge animal.

"I'm sure. I swung that tire iron as hard as I could and hit him smack dab on the head," Josh assured me. "That reminds me, I will be right back, I forgot the tire iron," he said as he ran off.

We got going around eleven thirty. The ride through Jersey was uneventful. I was more sober than I thought. I guess the event straightened me up. We barely saw any drivers until we got near Camden. Then, it seemed, traffic picked up.

Mole was asleep in the passenger side. Josh put his cigarette out then settled back behind me.

As we got over the bridge, I felt a shift in the back. I looked in the rearview mirror thinking Josh had shifted from one side of the car to the other. Although he was now asleep, he had not moved. I refocused on my driving. I certainly did not want to get a drunk driving charge.

When we got onto Hook road in Darby, about three miles from the Flat, I heard a loud scream. I looked back to see what was wrong with Josh. His eyes met mine. We both instantly knew.

"That monster is back from the dead!" Josh yelled.

Mole sat bolt upright. "What the hell is that?" He asked.

"Quiet!" Josh commanded. "It can't be, I fucking clobbered that boar," he insisted.

We listened.

"Nothing . . . see. We are imagining things. It was just the spare tire that moved when you made that turn," Josh said, although you could tell he didn't believe himself.

Then the squeals began again in earnest. This time they were accompanied by the sound of a caged animal.

"That pig is alive Josh!" I screamed. "What the hell, am I supposed to do? Should I pull over and let it out?"

"When we get home, I will carefully open the trunk and personally dispatch that porker my damn self. I should have known you would fuck up the sow's assassination," Mole complained. "That future ham is certainly complaining about it's hotel accommodations."

During the commotion I had taken my eyes of the road. At some point I must have drifted into the other lane.

I didn't even see the cop until he was right behind me.

His lights flashed.

"Fuck. I am screwed. Bring on the DUI!" I said immediately pulling over. The pig seemed to have quieted down. "Thanks guys." I said with disgust. "Not to mention we are all going to be charged with theft of a farm animal. If there is such a charge," I added, taking my license out in anticipation of the nightmare.

"Keep your cool. No one is screwed yet. Let me do the talking," Mole calmly stated.

"Yea Sherlock, how am I going to explain the deranged pot bellied porker in the trunk?"

Before Mole could answer, the officer tapped on the window. You were swerving a lot back there. You been drinking son?" the cop began.

Son? He was almost as young as me. A part timer, I'm screwed I thought.

I handed him my license. Mole handed him the registration and insurance information from the glove box.

He walked back to his squad car.

"I don't know this kid, do you Josh?" Mole asked turning back to look at the car.

"No Mole I don't. My guy in this town is Jack Kokal. Hopefully he's on duty." Josh said. He began to tap his foot nervously.

The officer was in his car checking my information over the radio. I briefly thought of running. Only with Mole could this shit happen, I thought.

Another squad car pulled up. It was a Collingdale cop! Apparently due to the time of night the neighboring town's officers backed each other up on calls.

It was Pete Murphy. He was the son of one of Suitcase's buddies. He might be able to put out the fire with the potential drunk driving, but we still had the stolen pig in the trunk. If they open the trunk, not only would they be opening a can of pigs, but I remembered, Mole left a bag of weed under the spare.

As Murphy exited his car, the first officer got out to walk back to me. Before he could talk, Murphy spoke.

"Hey isn't this John Sampson's old Impala? That you Mole?" he began, squinting in the darkness to make out the occupants.

The young cop spoke up. "I pulled them over for swerving and I suspect drunk driving," he said excitedly.

"Easy there Reynolds. You are Officer Reynolds, Bob's boy right? Murphy said.

"Yes sir, and if you will help me out I was just about to conduct some field sobriety tests," he answered reaching for the door handle. Thankfully, the pig had taken a break from bitching or maybe it had finally checked out for real.

I stepped out of the car.

Josh and Mole tried to step in. "Officers, I can explain. Both me and Josh here have been drinking quite a bit. We were with John Sampson at a friend's house in Jersey. We needed to leave and get home in a hurry, we had . . . ahh . . ." he paused . . . "an emergency" he said.

"We had to get home. I couldn't be messing around all night, I've got work in the morning," Josh added.

"My son Stevie here offered to drive us home. He doesn't drink, do you Stevie?"

I looked over at Mole, than the cop. "That's right officers, these guys reek of booze. That's what you probably smell," I offered.

"Well why the hell are you swerving all over the road?" The young officer demanded. He could feel his DUI bust fading fast and he wasn't about to let it go.

"These guys were sleeping, so I lit a smoke to keep me busy. The ash dropped in my lap. I'm sorry, but I was paying more attention to not burning my ass than to the road." Then for good measure I added, "It won't happen again officers, I promise."

"There Reynolds, you satisfied? I know these fellas, they may like to drain a few once in a while, but they ain't that bad. What do you say we let them go with a warning?"

Murphy looked over at Mole and winked.

"I don't know. I'm thinking I might need to give the driver a breath test just to cover my ass. You know how Mothers against Drunk Drivers are," Reynolds protested.

"All of you out of the car."

We all got out, and walked to the shoulder.

"Is this necessary? I just said I know them. My family are good friends with the car owner. By the way, where is Suitcase any way?" Officer Murphy asked.

He looked at Josh then the young cop and he shrugged.

Before we could answer, the car began to rock. Lucille looked like it had to take a pee.

I looked at Mole, then over at Josh. The cops took a step back.

"What the hell . . . . What are you guys up too?" Reynolds demanded, looking a little frightened.

From the trunk came a series of grunts, shrieks and guttural wailing. The porker was obviously not liking his pig pen.

"Yea, what the fuck are you guys up to? I just went to bat for you and now you got some weird shit going on in this trunk," Officer Murphy said and reached for his pistol.

Thank God the inebriated jumper cables in Mole's brain came to the rescue.

"I can explain," Mole stammered.

He looked over at Josh.

"Yea, Mole can explain," Josh lamely offered.

Mole gave him a dirty look then continued, "You know that emergency I mentioned earlier? Well what happened was, me and Josh here got to drinking Tequila with Suitcase and Beans."

Murphy jumped in, "How long has that crazy fucker been home? I know where this story is going and it doesn't have a happy ending. Everyone knows you don't give tequila to that loony jarhead! Beans, what a piece of work!"

"Yes, well that crazy Jarhead just about tore up our friend Wink's home. When he started fighting us, we over powered him and put him in the trunk. I know it sounds cruel, but he got so screwed up in Vietnam with the Corps and he is a mess when he drinks. Throwing him in the trunk is the only way.

We drove home as fast as we could," Mole said convincingly, or at least it sounded good to me.

Officer Reynolds wasn't buying it.

"I don't give a crap how drunk he is. He acting disorderly, not to mention he's publicly drunk. Open this trunk. Let's see what a night in the slammer does for this drunk animal."

Josh stepped forward. "You really don't want to do that. Trust me. We can handle him. Once we get him to his house he will calm down. I promise."

He looked over at Officer Murphy and raised his eyebrows.

Murphy thought for a minute then said, "I know that bastard is a son of a bitch when he's on the tequila that's for sure. I certainly don't want to mess with him." Murphy shone his flashlight toward the trunk. "Officer Reynolds, why don't you go check out the interior of the car for any contraband, I want to speak to these gentleman about their problem with their friend Beans."

Reynolds looked back at Murphy, hesitated, thought to say something, then hurried off for the car search. As soon as he left, Murphy asked "You guys don't have anything for him to find do you? Tell me, cause I just needed to get rid of him for a minute. Fuckin rookies!"

During this time the trunk had settled down some what. Now, with the young cop searching the interior, it started back up. It was worse than before. It sounded like we had bound and gagged Linda Blair and were taking her to her exorcism.

"He really sounds like a fucking caged animal," Murphy laughed and shook his head. "You guys need to get him home as soon as possible. If he gives you any shit at Seconds Flat let me know, I'm on an eleven to seven shift."

We were getting out of this. I couldn't believe it.

Beans in the trunk. For once a reputation as a nasty drunk was actually a good thing!

"Not so fast."

It was Reynolds.

He approached us with a large shopping bag. Strangely it was folded at the top. I didn't remember seeing it in the car, but it looked familiar.

My heart went in my throat. Mole's weed, I thought.

"And what do we have here?" Reynolds gloated. "It smells like maybe these boys have some marijuana."

I looked over at Mole, he was calm. Was that a smile on his face?

Our luck had run out. Larose would be furious with me.

Murphy looked at us and shook his head.

Reynolds opened the bag.

"What the hell? Lettuce, tomatoes and fucking zucchini! Shit!" he said, and threw the bag down in disgust.

Officer Murphy let out a sigh, and reached for the bag.

It was the produce we picked from our garden. We had left it in the car all day.

"Well I guess you could say it's home grown Reynolds!" Murphy teased.

"My wife loves garden tomatoes and grilled zucchini. Boys, do you mind if I take some home to my better half?"

"Take them officer. My pleasure. Plenty more where that came from," Mole babbled. "Now if there is nothing further we need to get this pig—Beans home."

"A pig! That's great. Beans the nasty ass tequila drunk does sound like a pig!" Murphy laughed.

"Yea, get out of here before I arrest all of you. Take your drunk buddy back to Collingdale and don't come back," Reynolds said trying to sound tough.

I didn't need to be told twice. I hurried back into the driver's seat. Josh and Mole followed me.

As I drove off, I looked back in the rearview mirror. The cops were dividing up the produce.

When we were safely away, Mole suggested we go back the next day and offer them some bacon with their lettuce and tomatoes.

We all laughed nervously.

We hit Seconds Flat late. It was dark. Bean's mom was not home.

It took me a while to wind down from all the excitement, but when I did I slept soundly.

When I woke the next day, both Josh, Mole and the pig were gone.

I didn't ask and they didn't tell, but we did have pork chops all summer.

Chapter 26

On Cannery Row, borrowed corn and riding a horse

We made it back to Wink's place before noon. No one said a thing. Mole had called before we left and laid the bullshit on heavy. He explained the boat, mentioned Josh's wife, and explained that I couldn't sleep and had offered to drive. I thought the last part was a bit much, but he claimed that no one suspected a thing. If they did they didn't accuse us.

Then again Wink hadn't mentioned the missing pet.

The girls were gone and the workers were back. The place was buzzing. Actually Wink wasn't even around. Despite all the activity, Beans and Suitcase lounged on the porch drinking Bloody Marys and eating a late brunch of egg sandwiches, grapefruit and coffee.

"Thanks for getting the boat, that's a great idea. The fire company boys want to meet us this week to do some crabbing out of Margate. *The Cannery Row* will save us from renting. Plus, it's got all the gear already on board," Beans said. "What made you think to go home and get it? I don't remember mentioning the Darby Fire Company's crab trip," he added.

"No biggie. Stevie couldn't sleep and Josh needed to check in with his wife. You didn't mention the fire company, but you did mention crabbing. All's well that ends well," Mole lied. "By the way where is Wink?"

"He needed to head to the track. He won't be back until tonight," Suitcase answered. "He said to hang out for as long as we want. His wife won't be back until the weekend."

"It must be nice to have your old lady go away and leave you alone once in a while," Josh said enviously.

"What are you complaining about. You go away and leave her alone all the time. It's the same difference," Suitcase corrected.

"Double negative. 'Same difference,' it's a double negative," Mole corrected. Suitcase didn't say anything.

"And it's not the same," Mole continued, adding his two cents. "When we go away we give the wives something to bitch about. When they go away, they got nothing to rag about," he concluded.

Josh fired back "I wish. My better half . . ." he started.

We immediately cracked up.

He hesitated then started over, "I mean, my ball and chain, bitches about the house and why it's so dirty. She bitches why I didn't cut the grass, why the litter box is full, the dishes not done, fish not fed. On and on she will drone. I don't get a moments peace. I have no sanctuary anywhere," he sighed and took a drag on his cigarette. "She does her best ragging while I'm shaving, she sits right down on the toilet in front of me while she takes a shit—with hemorrhoids no less!

Trust me, it's a nightmare whether I go or whether she goes," he finished, and took a large guzzle from a pitcher of screwdrivers that were on the porch table.

"Ain't love grand? You taking this all in Steve?" Mole asked me.

"Thanks for the visual Josh," I said. "With you guys, it is a wonder anyone would have you at all," I said truthfully.

I could never understand anyone wanting to be hitched for life to my old man or any of his friends for that matter.

"Don't worry Josh, your wife can't keep track of you in Jersey cause her police scanner covers Delaware County only," Beans teased.

Josh groaned and took another chug of the orange vodka. It looked tasty, so I poured myself a tall one. After last night, I vowed to get tuned up today and not to drive unless it was absolutely necessary. It was a good time to start on the load.

"She doesn't have the scanner on **for me**. She's just a nosy bitch is all," he explained weakly.

We weren't buying it.

There was a reason she was nicknamed 'Xtra Betty.'

She was the first with all the news and all the gossip in the town. Josh was too. The scanner gave her the jump on all police and fire calls. Thankfully Beans was right—we were out of her range.

"Don't worry about 'Xtra' I gave her the business this morning, she was right as rain when I left her," Josh boasted. "Two in one night," he said referring to the whore. "She said I could take the whole week if I want, and that's just what I plan to do," he added.

We knew that was bullshit. He slept on the couch like everyone else.

"Well the crab trip is not until tomorrow. That leaves today to do whatever we want. What are you fellas thinking?" Suitcase asked.

As we sat, a large friendly cat came out of the house. It began to purr and rub it's head and body on our legs. Then it began to paw at the wooden table base. Strangely it left no scratches.

Beans went to pet it.

"Look, Wink declawed the poor thing. Now, instead of scratching the furniture the poor bastard just polishes it!" Beans said, as he picked up the housecat.

That reminds me, we should follow this cat's lead and polish up the house, then go about getting ourselves some pussy that wants to polish *my* woodwork," he continued.

"Didn't you get your fill last night Beans?" Mole asked.

"Oh, that's right, you passed out after the game. Josh and Suitcase were the ones who scored," he said, answering his own question.

"Sorry Beans, but that looks like the only pussy you are getting, at least until Wink gets back," Suitcase teased.

Ignoring the small talk, I asked Beans and Suitcase about Wink.

"Enough about housekeeping cats, polishing the furniture, and enough about getting Beans a piece of trim, what did Wink say about the pet pig?" I asked.

Mole and Josh gave me a look.

"Why should he ask us about the pig Stevie?" Beans asked, looking over at Josh and Mole.

He knew immediately.

"What the fuck did you do? Josh you no good son of a bitch!"

He began to step to Josh.

"You bastard. How many times I tell you to keep that temper of yours in check?"

Mole got between them.

"Easy there Mr. Walsh, not to worry, we left no trace of Josh's little outburst. Here, take a drink and a toke of the giggle and relax. He went to refill Beans' drink.

"Look, if you are the least bit forgiving, we might even cut you in on some pork steaks," Mole tried to joke.

Beans was having none of it.

"Josh, you always have to look a gift horse in the mouth. Why do you have to screw up a good thing? Wink is showing some real hospitality, letting us stay here. When he finds out you killed his wife's favorite pet he will kick us out quicker than shit through a goose." Beans finished and took a long drink of his Bloody.

"Beans, you used more clichés there than my old Italian mother in law. Christ you were even able to use two separate animal chestnuts in one sentence, I guess that's in keeping with our barnyard surroundings, no doubt," Mole joked.

We all laughed.

It apparently had the desired effect, because Beans smiled and lit a smoke.

Josh seeing Beans smile added, "Relax Beans. What does the man who's been caught cheating say? 'Deny, deny, deny!' We don't know nothing. That's our story." He patted Beans on the back, "Who can say? Maybe the helpers left the gate open," he shrugged. Satisfied with his story he sat back and took a drink.

As we sat on that porch, I felt we Birders had good load coming on. Sometimes it's best to just go with the good time. I decided to ride the alcohol wave.

Sure enough, we spent the next couple of hours drinking, smoking and hanging out. Mole, Josh and I retold the pig story for Suitcase and Beans. It was only one day later and the story was already better than what I remembered.

In fact, I realized, that was the beauty of the Bird Watchers, they were all born story tellers. Raconteurs at heart. Always looking for one more bedtime story.

Even everyday boring life took on a mythical feel when it was put in the tumblers of the four drunk friends, polished up to a luster and spit back out.

I found myself drinking and laughing with my four friends that day.

Before I knew it, it was late in the afternoon. The workers were already packing up to leave. Apparently, when Wink wasn't home, the concept of a full day's work took on a new meaning.

The sun, that had blazed hot all day, began to look like it might be starting to relax and kick back as well. With the bulk of its work done, it began its slow decent toward slumber. If it were a suburban homeowner the Sun would have put the mower away, grabbed a beer, hit the couch and would be looking over the TV guide for the evening shows.

In the distance the whitetailed deer had come out from their wooded hiding places and were beginning to enjoy the tender grass at the far end of the meadows.

You could feel the day switch out of the passing lane.

The birders seemed to take the change in their own way.

Beans, who had passed out early the night before began to get rammy. He demanded we go out to a bar so he could "get what he missed out on last night." He paced the porch and would not sit down.

Josh seemed to want to kick back and do nothing. He contented himself with smoking and taking in the surroundings. Content to admire the shadows that fell over the farm and the fields surrounding it.

Suitcase, he was hungry. He played the food game. To him, the ritual of the discussion of food was every bit as important as eating itself. He would spend hours kicking around the merits of various restaurants and different entrees and specials. He would sometimes start the talk of what's for dinner even while he was eating lunch.

That day he talked cheesesteaks.

"I like Geno's better than Pats. Don't get me wrong, they are both good but Geno's is better. I think it's the roll." He leaned back and scratched his belly. "In Jersey the only place I know that makes anything to rival the Philly Steak is maybe the White House in Atlantic City, but even that pales in comparison."

Josh cut him off.

"Shut up! Your making me hungry. I'm content to just hang out, maybe make a turkey sandwich later. Where are we going to get a cheesesteak out here in Bumblefuck Jersey anyway?"

"Screw it, I will drive," Suitcase announced. "There has got to be some place that sells a decent sandwich around here somewhere."

I guess he was listening earlier when I told them that I would not be driving after what happened the previous night.

"I don't care if I have to drive back to Philly for Pete's sake," he pleaded.

"To hell with Pete and his fucking cheesesteak, I'm not leaving this porch," Mole announced. He promptly kicked back in a recliner and shut his eyes. "Ah yes, my little chickadees, I'm taking a Spanish pause, boys," he drawled, doing his best W. C. Fields.

"I'll go."

It was Beans, and it was no surprise, since he had been itching to go out for some time. "I need smokes and we could use some more beer while we are at it," he slurred. "Suitcase, the only thing I ask is, if we see a club, we go in for one drink."

Looking over to me, he held up four fingers. He winked, "Stevie you can navigate."

It was settled. The three of us would go.

Suitcase was his usual steady self. If he was drunk it didn't show.

He backed out of the drive and we barreled down the road. We left the farm in the rearview.

"Where are we going?" I yelled over one of my mix tapes; *Jagger—Memo For Turner.*

"Does it really matter Son?" Suitcase answered, then tossed me a smile in the side view mirror. It appeared that food, beer and smokes were not the most important items on the agenda.

We drove off through rural south Jersey.

After about fifteen minutes out, the terrain changed. What had been scrub pines and forest now became flat farmland. There were acres of corn fields and other crops—mainly they looked like soybeans and tomatoes. The fields were punctuated by small farmhouses and the occasional industrial building. There weren't too many people, it being too early for the migrant pickers. They wouldn't arrive for another couple of weeks.

"There has got to be a place around here somewhere," Suitcase yelled above the music.

A place. I began to think Suitcase was wrong. There wasn't going to be a place any where around here.

"These farmers got to eat and drink somewhere," Suitcase reasoned. "Shit, we may have to drive back to Camden after all," he complained.

"Why don't we pull over and check out a map? I know men don't ask for directions but there ain't no shame in checking with Rand McNally now, is there?" I asked. "I needed to piss anyway."

"Drain the main vein, sounds good to me," Beans seconded.

Suitcase pulled Lucille over. He stayed in the car and retrieved an old dry—rotted map from the glove box. It was folded up like it was done by a child and it looked like it served as a coaster for many a coffee mug.

"This will do the trick," he said.

While he checked the map, Beans and I got out to pee.

"Check this out Stephen my boy. Corn as far as the eye could see. Feels like we are in Iowa, not the most densely populated state in the union."

Beans swept his hand across the corn. "All this corn, Mr. Farmer won't miss a bushel or two."

He began to pick ears off the stalks and toss them back towards the car's trunk.

"What the hell you up too there Beans? What are we going to do with a bunch of green corn?" I asked, looking up and down the road to see if anyone was watching. Of course, there was no one.

I began to pick some too.

"Open the trunk there Mr. Sampson we have some very important colonels to transport," Beans said, banging on the back of the car.

Suitcase laughed and got out to open the trunk. When he did, the smell almost overwhelmed us.

"Whew! Now I know where the purloined pig got to," Suitcase said, placing the sleave of his shirt over his mouth. "Quick load up, and let's get out of here. Remind me to scrub out the trunk when I get a chance."

We took about a bushel or so, but Beans wouldn't quit. He kept on picking and tossing the ears into the trunk. When Suitcase closed the trunk, Beans tossed a dozen more ears into the back seat.

"Enough! You crazy bastard, let's go before a Statie passes by and arrests us for stalking," Suitcase barked.

We groaned at his bad joke.

Beans swatted him over the head with an ear.

We hit the road again.

"Did you figure out where we are?" I asked when we were safely underway.

"I know where we are. I just can't figure out where there is a place to eat." Suitcase explained. "There should be a little town up here called Millsville or something, they got to have a burger joint at least."

Sure enough, after about another ten miles we entered a town. Ten seconds later we were through it. Just when we were going to turn around and ask for directions we spotted a place. I call it a place, because it defied description. It was not a gas station although it had an old fashioned gas pump out front. It wasn't a feed store but it did advertise chicken feed in the window. It wasn't quite a bar even though there was an old neon beer sign hanging in the window as well. It wasn't a hotel but it did say 'rooms for let'. Lastly, it wasn't a Chinese restaurant, it couldn't be, out here in the swamps of Jersey, to borrow Springsteen's phrase, but the sign said it clear as day, 'Fin—Foo' restaurant.

"Pull over. I know you wanted a cheesesteak Suitcase, but Chinese will have to do," I said.

Suitcase pulled in. "At least we can get some beer," he added cheerfully.

As we approached, Suitcase laughed and said in his best Chinese accent "Fin Foo, fine asian cuisine."

Beans was the first to notice.

"You asshole. The sign says *fine food*. The bulbs burned out on the 'E' and the 'D'.

Suitcase didn't miss a beat, "Fank you Mr. Beans—san. I no wike Chinese food in middle of nowhere, any way."

We went in.

The office was a bar. The bar had no name, unless the small orange Miller and Bud lights advertised the owner's names. It was a one story cement block building, long and wide. Two pool tables and a small stage, with a sign saying 'Live Country and Western music every Fri. and Sat. nights', off to the left was a general store of sorts. It was manned by an ancient man who stared at a small TV screen on the counter next to an equally ancient cash register. The place smelled like someone had been frying onions.

"A good sign," Suitcase mumbled.

Two guys were shooting a game of pool and there were a few people at the bar. There was a couple at one of the tables, their heads almost touching. He stared at the TV over the bar, while she gesticulated wildly with her hands. Whatever she was telling him he wasn't listening. There was even a waitress, she must have been fifteen. She wore flip flops, that echoed loudly off the cinder block walls as she tended to the couple of tables that were occupied.

The place could have just as well been in Alabama as South Jersey.

We must have reeked Yankee even though we were north of the Mason Dixon line, but the clientele took no notice.

A TV bulletin announced a possible tornado warning for the next day. Everyone stopped to listen, except some wrinkled garishly dressed old crow sitting at the bar. Looking at the television she said, "Who the fuck wants to hear this shit. I'm missing General Hospital."

The bartender gave her a murderous look, and she replied "Well, I mean, how you goin to watch for a goddamned tornado anyway?"

He came over and took our order.

"Don't mind that bitch. She gets flagged every day at four o'clock, and she owns the place."

We took a glance over at her again. She looked like Betty Davis in *Whatever Happened to Baby Jane,* with apologies to the memory of Betty Davis.

As we watched, she lit what looked like a Marlboro 'Eight hundred' smoke. The cigarette was at least two feet long. She took a drag like she was making love to it.

Suitcase ordered beers. Beans had a Southern Comfort on the rocks with beer back. We ordered some burgers and hoagies to go.

"I can't imagine they will be any good, but what the hell," Suitcase said to me as he ordered.

"More red—necks here than when I was stationed in North Carolina," Beans said.

Of course the whole bar heard him.

I almost got up and walked out on the spot, but nothing happened, except the pool shooters who said "Hey, you boys like to shoot a little pool? Just a fun game for drinks."

Beans put two quarters on the table and challenged them, then I really got worried. Suitcase called the one guy's huge stomach a 'Milwaukee tumor.' I cringed but the guy didn't seem to notice.

His partner wore a old cut off tee-shirt exposing skinny biceps. He had a bunch of tattoos on each arm. They were home made jobs. Jailhouse tattoos. Scribbled nick names in ink of girls and guys.

He saw me staring and said "My buddies did this to me. I ate two Quaaludes at a party and passed out. They used me for an auto-graph book."

I heard enough. I told Suitcase I would wait outside.

He understood and didn't fight me.

Behind the bar there were some empty cabins. I looked around but there really wasn't much to see. A run down peach orchard, a rusted car and two beat up boats on cinder blocks. An old rooster hurried out from under a boat. He ran past me toward one of the buildings.

I walked up the road about a hundred yards. There, where the orchard ended, was this little corral. In it stood this one small pathetic looking horse. He wasn't really a pony, but he was pretty small. The poor thing was a bad excuse for an equine. He looked depressed, like he had been quarantined. Mr. Ed in exile. He had his head drooped over the second rung of the fence, he was that short. He looked to be a reddish color although he was so dusty it was hard to tell.

After petting him for a bit, I ran back to the car and got some of the corn from the back seat. I fed him some and he gobbled it up like it was his last meal.

As I was doing this, I saw Beans and Suitcase leave the bar. They saw me as they got in Lucille.

"Stay there Steve we will pick you up," Suitcase yelled.

They pulled up next to the pen.

"Who the hell stuck this poor beast out here in no-horse land? He's in solitary!" Suitcase yelled. "A red pony all alone-y" he joked.

"I think he's part Appaloosa," Beans said.

They're bald spots, idiot," Suitcase answered.

"He looks like the shortest horse on the merry go round, the one the Grandfathers plop their grandkids on, the one that can't even go up and down," Beans joked.

"I've been feeding him the corn. I don't think his owner is taking very good care of him. He sounds like he has a cold," I said.

Beans got out to pet the animal.

"Or maybe he is just a smoker like us," he said stroking the horse's neck.

Beans thought for a moment then continued, "Hey, if they don't feed him, we should set him free."

It was obvious Suitcase didn't like the idea. He frowned and shook his head, but he didn't say anything. Beans gave him a look like a six year old asking for Gummy Bears and before you knew it, Beans had the Pony out and was walking him down the road. They were both staggering. Beans was drunk but the horse was just old.

When they came back Beans said, "Let's take him for a ride."

"You can't ride that old swayback, he'll collapse from the weight," Suitcase laughed.

"No, I mean let's **give him** a ride. In the car," Beans corrected.

"No way Jose, not in my Lucille," Suitcase protested. "He's probably the owner's daughter's pet. Refuses to put the oldtimer down. They still hang horse thieves in these parts don't you think?" Suitcase asked as he looked to me for help.

"Nah, I feel bad for this guy, who knows, tomorrow might be the glue factory for him. I say a little spin in a convertible would do him some good," I said, surprised that I agreed with Beans' madness.

"Suit yourselves, but I'm not driving. If the cops stop us I'm not taking the hit," Suitcase said giving in.

"Fine, I'll drive," Beans said, and in a flash he had the the keys and was leading the pony to the convertible.

The horse climbed in like he expected to be chauffeured his whole life. I half expected the animal to winny 'Home James.'

I climbed in the back, Suitcase shook his head at the craziness of the whole thing, then got in the front. The horse was standing with his two front legs staddled over the seat. Suitcase had the horse by it's bridle, but he was not going anywhere. In fact, he looked happy as hell.

Off we went.

The horse looked like some overgrown golden retriever with his head sticking over the top of the windshield, his mane blowing in the wind. He's biting at the wind and whinnying and snorting with happiness.

Beans was having a hard time steering but he's laughing his ass off.

"Look at this pony, he's having the time of his life!" he said and reached out to pet him.

"I'm not digging this," Suitcase complained. "What if we get pulled over?"

"Stop worrying, John. If we get pulled over, we just tell the cops that our horse trailer broke down, it's an emergency, and we are rushing the animal to the vet.

They will take one look at this car and think we are excentric horse breeders. Probably give us an escort or something," Beans said trying to make it sound plausible.

"Then what will we do?" Suitcase asked, thinking, I guess, that the crazy story just might work.

Beans answered "Hell if I know. Take him to the vet I guess."

He obviously had not thought it through.

Meanwhile, the horse couldn't believe his good fortune. Man-of-War and Secretariet were never treated so good. This nag wouldn't have been admitted to the equine peaceful acres, but for one day, he's a young colt again. In addition, to the wind in his mane, he had been taking in the sights and sounds of our little drive. He even snuck a look at some fillies we passed on another farm. They were jealous no doubt. He was so happy and relaxed that he even snacked on the corn we pilfered as well as a couple of green apples that Suitcase grabbed during a quick stop at an orchard.

About fifteen minutes out, the horse, maybe because of the sudden richness of his new diet or maybe the excitement of his first car ride, began to fart. I would imagine that most readers have never experienced the smell of an old, excited over fed pony but I can assure you it was not the proverbial 'bouquet of roses'.

Even with the open air, it was disgusting. The horse now got even happier and more relaxed, if that was possible. He farted some more. Since I was in the back, I took the brunt of it. My feelings of sympathy for this nag quickly wore off.

"Sweet Jesus, for a little horse that things farting like a Clydsedale!" I screamed. "Hey, I'm a little gassy myself," Beans defended.

"Beans, on your worse Bean eating, beer drinking day you have not smelled like this beast. If you think it's not that bad, you get back here and spend some time with the ass end!" I complained.

As I spoke, the thing shit itself. The stench was over powering. It barely missed me but splattered over the back seat and out the back to the trunk.

I laughed. "So much for Lucille's upholstery," I said to Suitcase.

"Do something!" Suitcase yelled. "That's rich Corinthian leather" he jokingly pleaded.

"Ricardo Montalban, what the hell do you want me to do?" I asked.

"Make that fucker stop" Suitcase railed. Then he started giggling. Then, it turned into outright uncontrollable laughter. Beans began to laugh out loud too. He had been trying to pay attention to the road, now, as he laughed he turned around to see how bad it was. He immediately swerved off into the shoulder. The horse careened over to my side of the car. No sooner than he gets on my side, he lets out another rectal blast. This time I wasn't so lucky. The corn/apple manure hits me in the lap.

"That's it!" I screamed. "You no good shitting machine. Fellas, I'm going to kill this son of a bitch."

"Put an ear in his ass, son," Beans laughed.

Hearing what Beans had suggested and not to be outdone, Suitcase added "Yea, toss him a Cobb salad!" and high fived Beans.

"I'm glad you assholes think this is funny," I said.

When they wouldn't stop, I flicked some shit up front.

"Arse shucks, Stevie, we are only kiddin," Suitcase stifled a laugh and wiped away the manure.

Beans laughed as well. "I told you, Stevie, corn hole that bastard," he said, not able to help himself.

"Suit yourselves," I yelled.

I grabbed an ear of the corn off the floor of the car and jammed it up the horse's ass. For some reason, instead of slowing down, Beans had put the gas to the floor. He had regained control of Lucille for a second.

It did not last.

The ancient animal did not appreciate my corn-cob suppository at any speed. He screamed out like he was a bitch inmate in an equestrian men's prison. It reminded me of *Animal House* when Belushi and Flounder shot Neidemeyer's horse.

Thank God there was no room for the horse to kick. Instead, the horse complained by chomping his teeth into Beans' side. Beans screamed, and the car careened off the country road and into a corn field. Beans grabbed his side with one hand and punched the horse with the other.

Fortunately, Suitcase had reached over and taken the wheel. He tried to keep the wheel straight as we barreled through the cornfield.

Now the horse shit mixed with the corndust. If either one of them could see they certainly weren't driving like it.

"I'm bleeding, I'm bleeding!" Beans screamed.

The car continued it's out of control race through the corn field. Shit and corn stalks and blood flew in every direction.

Finally, after what seemed like eternity, the car came to a stop at the edge of the field. For all the excitement the horse had caused, he was pretty calm. He sat contentedly as though this were an everyday occurrence. A farm house stood about fifty yards from our traveling catastrophe.

Two men rushed from the house and ran towards us. One carried a bat and the other a pitch fork. Briefly, I thought of running.

"What in the name of God do you think you are doing?" the first guy demanded.

To his partner he said, "Do you think we need the law, Tom?"

I had just finished with an animal caper involving the law, I certainly wasn't ready for another.

Since I was the most sober, again, I employed my best bullshitting skills.

"Sir, we are very sorry about the cornfield. We will certainly pay you for the damage. My friends and I were taking this poor creature to the vet, it has some sort of gastric disorder. We had to take the car because the trailer got a flat," I continued.

Suitcase and Beans looked over at me. They're eyes said go—man—go.

"We did not anticipate the poor thing getting scared in the car. It is such a nice old pet to our friend's kid. It unfortunately bit my friend Bernard here, causing him to lose control of the car. May we use your phone to call our friend for assistance, and perhaps you could give Bernard a bandage for his injury?" I finished.

Here comes the police, I thought.

The men looked at us, then looked at each other. I think they were so afraid that we were dangerous that they pretended to believe my story.

"Well son, that's quite a yarn. I would let you in my house but the misses doesn't take to highly to me cartin in horse shit."

I realized I must have looked a mess.

"Maybe your friend can make the call instead," he said, pointing to Suitcase.

"By the way, who is your friend? Is he from around here?" the other guy asked.

Suitcase said, "Tom O'Connor. Goes by the nickname . . ." Before he could finish the first guy said "Oh, Wink, why didn't you say so. What's he doing with a nag like this? A pet for his kid? More like a pet for his Mexican helper's kid. Why didn't you say so in the first place. Should have known you were friends with that crazy bastard. The Pennsylvania plates threw me off."

The other guy still looked skeptical. "Why didn't Wink take the thing in his own trailer?" he asked.

"Wink is at the track today. His helpers were with him. It was the only thing we could do," Suitcase said and took over. I was relieved to say the least. He continued, "Thank you. If you could show me where the phone is, I will call Tom and we will get ourselves out of your hair."

He looked over at Beans and I, and smiled. The owner of the place led him back toward the house.

"Beans, get the horse out of the car. I'm going to try and wash up," I said.

The other guy pointed to a garage behind the house.

"There is a hose over there next to the barn."

I cleaned myself up and brought some buckets back for the car. Fortunately for Lucille, most of the shit had blown out the back or had gone in my lap.

///

Later, after Wink had shown up with a small horse trailer, and we had paid the farmer three hundred bucks for the damage, we drove back to Wink's place.

We dropped the horse back at his pen.

If his owners noticed, nothing was said or done about it. The place was as deserted as when we first picked up the poor animal.

We left him, just as we found him—forlorn and alone.

At least he would have the memory.

We drove home like a bunch of school kids who had been caught soaping windows. Beans and Suitcase made funny faces behind Wink's back.

A farm hand from Wink's place followed in Suitcase's car.

Back at the house, Josh and my father pretended to be pissed at us. They clucked their tongues and shook their heads. They said loudly, so Wink would hear "We told you not to go, we told you, we said you were too drunk to drive, but you wouldn't listen."

When he was out of earshot they whispered, "You stole a fuckin horse? You took it for a joy ride! And you call me crazy?! Can't wait to hear this one."

Wink didn't say any thing else that night, he didn't have to, it was obvious.

We had to leave. He couldn't prove anything about the missing the pig so he didn't even mention it. But the horse? The horse was the final straw.

We had embarrassed him with his neighbors. We had cost him good money. No amount of weed was going to make up for this breach of trust.

We were gone in the morning.

"Screw that rich bastard."

"Yea fuck him if he can't take a joke"

"The quarry was neat though!"

The car reverberated with comments all morning. You would have thought it was Wink who had ruined the visit. The Birders drank a little, just beer. They nursed a couple of long necks, but the drinking lacked any spirit. There was no joie de vivre.

After a while they stopped talking about Tom O'Connor and his horse farm.

We had the *Cannery Row* hooked up on a trailer behind us, so Suitcase drove extra careful.

The boat was a aluminum skiff with a twenty five horse Mercury outboard. It was as old and beat up as Suitcase's car that towed it. Mole had named it because it was metal and most of the time the engine would die on them. It was a metal can that, most of the time, had to be rowed. As Beans had said, his boat would at least spare us the expense of renting.

Josh had the final word.

"It's getting so you can't steal and kill a pet pig or joyride with a pony without someone bitching. You just can't have any harmless fun anymore. Everyone is a tight ass. That Wink can kiss my Irish ass in Gimbel's window. Let's go crabbing."

Chapter 27

Moles Field Notes on Seagulls—Dolphins— Greenheads—and Blue crabs

Nothing better than drinking a hot Irish coffee on a grassy dune. The quiet magic of the morning surf pounding in. The light, waking ever so nicely and slowly.

Coastal dawns must smoke marijuana.

The gulls getting warmed up for their daily caucus. Like Atlantic City conventioneers lining up for free buffets, they tell raucous and bawdy jokes while they wait for breakfast.

There are millions, billions, trillions, what's the next big number? . . . of tons of food in the oceans, but to hear the gulls constantly crying, you'd think it was a famine. Food stamp sea-birds. Calcutta Gulls. Wait in line, soup kitchen flyers, queue up!

I ask you, have you ever seen a sea gull with it's ribs showing? Yet, if they're not fighting over a lousy piece of clam, then they are squawking over a few feet of sand on miles and miles of deserted beach.

Gulls are very human. If they are not always complaining, then they are complaining that their species is always complaining.

Life is grand. I mean it. It's grandly horrible, grandly beautiful, grandly sad, and grandly amusing, grandly petty, somebody quick! A suppository for adjectives. Air brakes requested . . . .

A fishing boat was going out to sea and with it, always a miracle to witness-a group of dolphins. Never a school of dolphins. They've already gone to school and got their Doctorates in Enjoy. Their masters in Play.

I turn my eye to a movement in the sand. A 'scuttling work of armament, crowned by the fore claws' gesture of menace and power' as the poet Mark Doty described the crab. The Blue Claw, working fiercely to return to the ocean, struggles to get off the beach, but it's no match for the power of the sea. Eventually the Atlantic completes the task and the crab disappears into the surf. I am once again, amazed and in awe of the world I live in, and whatever or whoever created it.

Oww!

A damn Green Head fly has bitten me. In it's greed to take my pound of flesh it has lingered too long.

Smack!

I hit it. The green head fly's bite is so bad, you don't just want to smack it, you want to erase all memory of it's existence from the planet. You better be sure you do. I have seen Green Head Flies smacked dead on with a swatter, arise like Lazarus and fly off to bite another day.

I crumble it in my fingers and laugh.

God has a twisted sense of humor. Reminding me, by the bite of a fly, that I must, as Whitman said, 'Be not curious about God. For I, who am curious about each, am not curious about God—I hear and behold God in every object, yet understand God not in the least.'

Time to get off the beach and continue my day.

Chapter 28

How the Birders met the Darby Firemen and spent the day crabbing and Mole shook hands with a Blueclaw

After the adventures in the car the past two days, I was pretty played out for anymore animal escapades, that's for sure. I also wanted to avoid driving, and luckily today, I had not been asked to take the wheel.

Suitcase was in the driver's seat and he pledged not to mess around. Everyone seemed to agree that we had been very lucky and that our good times could have caused us even bigger trouble.

We drove toward the shore, content to listen to music and take in the sights. Early Stones and the Pine barrens. Not bad. Jersey back bays and Dylan's Like a Rolling Stone. Sublime.

After a while the music, the road, the beer, and a few tokes of a joint, had everyone, except me, back in vacation mode.

Wink was all but forgotten.

The birders began to warm up to the day and to each other's company.

The crab trip was in Margate, a seaside town close to Atlantic City. It had a large bay and a lot of bait shops and boat rental outfits. It also had great crabbing.

The Darby Fire Company A, not to be confused with Darby Fire Company B, had been coming here for an annual crab trip for as long as I could remember. I say don't confuse the two, because other than fighting fires they had nothing in common.

Darby B was a "bunch of nozzle nut yahoos" to hear Josh tell it. Darby A on the other hand was a drinking club masquerading as a fire company. Beans' good friend Jake Hagan was the chief. My father said he was a "Glorious drunk capable of imbibing all manner of spirits for days on end."

The two companies hated each other and were frequently at odds over the issue of drinking in the firehouse. Darby B believed that liquor held no place around firefighters. Darby A of course felt differently. Because of these differences of opinion, Darby B was always trying to get borough council to cut off A's funding. Darby B said the 'A' stood for "alcoholics" and of course A said that Darby B stood for "bitches."

Hey, they were local Fireman who drank a lot, how creative could they be?

Recently, Captain Jake, as his men called him, had really gone too far. As a result borough council had placed the company on a sort of double secret probation.

There was a lot of overlap in fire company coverage, Darby being a small town. Since there were not a lot of fires, unless of course they were lit by the fire men themselves (that is another story), A and B companies would often cover the same fire calls. Most of the time the two rival companies would put their differences aside to fight the fire.

Usually they both did a great job.

Oh, there would be the regular practical joke, the water in the boot, the intentional kink in the hose line, but generally the companies acted professionally.

This run of professionalism came to an end when Captain Jake answered a two alarm call on a Friday night. Not just any Friday night, no, this one happened to be on Saint Patty's day.

It was eleven at night and Captain Jake was 'primed at the pump' in keeping with our fire company theme. The call came in for a blaze on fourth street by the old Mione soap factory. Although that was generally Company B's territory, the boys in A thought B could always use the help.

"Those bitches couldn't put out a girl scout's weenie roast for Christ's sake! Let's go and show them how it's done the 'A' way!" Hagan had roared.

Half of the members were already at the station, and strangely enough, of the half that were there, most were already dressed in their uniforms, complete with boots and helmets.

Perhaps this detail is odd, unless you happen to have spent any time at a volunteer fire company, then your question would be; why weren't the rest of the members there and dressed as well?

In any event, they were out the door and on their way to the fire in Darby B territory in seconds flat. Come to think of it, they passed the Seconds Flat.

Beans, who was staggering in that night, remarked later that he thought he was in England because the new pumper truck was driving on the wrong side of the road. Beans paid no mind and went about his own firefighting business; passing out in the living room and hosing down his couch as he slept.

He heard about it the next day.

Captain Jake didn't realize how tuned up he was. Although, publicly he attributed the erratic driving to his lack of experience handling the new two steering wheel pumper truck and a change in his meds, privately, he would tell Beans and his friends that he was so drunk—he had asked the rear driver to take over. This of course was impossible, the rear wheel driver controlled only the rear portion of the truck.

On the one and a half mile drive to the location, the firetruck got lost twice, went down a one way street—the wrong way, and side swiped six cars, including the mayor's new caddie.

When the Darby Fire Company A finally arrived at the scene an hour after departing and twenty minutes after the last flame had been extinguished, Captain Jake, who had been holding a monstrous piss the whole time he drove around looking for the fire, jumped out and began to empty his bladder on the nearest telephone pole, bellowing "Where's the show? The A listers are here!"

Captain 'Goose' Glover, the geeky leader of Darby B who's nickname came from his droning obnoxious honking voice, ran up to gloat about Hagan's crew missing the call completely. Captain Jake, not missing a beat, turned around and finished pissing all over his rival's leg and down his boot.

A brief but glorious brawl had ensued.

After it was broken up by police, the name calling continued for a bit, as did the crank calls between stations. The calls did not taper off until the A men passed out, or perhaps they merely ran out of insults.

The suspension had been swift and severe.

Captain Jake had been stripped of his leadership role, denied the ability to answer calls for a year and publicly reprimanded at the monthly commissioner's meeting. The A company was not suspended; as they were needed to fight fires. However, they were not allowed to answer calls on the B side of town.

Luckily, Captain Jake avoided both a drunk driving charge and any increase in his car insurance. Since the town did not want anymore bad publicity, the full details of incident were hushed up. In the commissioner's meeting's minutes, the Captain's actions were explained as "a change in his medication."

Captain Jake Hagan had been on the wagon ever since.

The crab trip would be the first time he was back on the sauce.

Beans and the rest of us wanted to be there to enjoy the show. The men were predicting a return to form for the Captain and his crew.

I was worried. Whenever there was some one to potentially steal the drinking limelight, Mole usually raised his game. This almost always resulted in a disaster.

I was hoping he wouldn't go overboard with the drinking.

Perhaps the events of the past few days would cause him to slow down and keep his drinking in check.

Who was I kidding.

These nervous thoughts crowded my brain as we approached the shore.

"Son, you look like I feel." It was Mole.

He had noticed that I was not saying much, and my head was down.

"Have a drink. That always shuts up the unbroken Brahma Bulls that keep slamming my cranium stalls in the rodeo that used to be my brain."

"You can't just tell me that a drink will help my head ache, can you, Mole?" I answered. "Besides, I'm fine, just worried," I added.

"Worried? You have no worries. Think of happy, or funny things. 'Life is what a man thinks all day', Thoreau thought all day," Mole said, laughing.

He was on a roll again.

"Everything we're taught is false; including that thought, says I," he rambled. "And of course don't forget, 'He who speaks doesn't know, and he who knows doesn't speak'—And someone **said** that! Don't pay any mind to me Stevie, my brain is a zen clogged drainage system, it's dropping like the big ball on the Time Square of my memories." he finished, and looked out at the salt marsh at the end of the expressway.

He was high as Cheech and Chong's kite, I thought, I was in for trouble.

He turned back at me now pretending to be mad.

"What the fuck is wrong with you . . . you maternal copulatin son of a bitch. Feeling sorry for your damn self, while kids in Ethiopia don't even know what Cheerios are, let alone eat them!" he finished and handed me a beer.

I cracked it and drained it. Can't beat em join em.

Josh also joined the conversation, probably to give me a break.

"Mole, you are one fucked up individual. Most of the time I have no idea what you are talking about. Leave the boy alone. Still waters run deep. He will talk when he feels like it."

He pointed to a paper on the floor. "Now hand me my paper so I can catch up on the news."

I reached down and took the tabloid off the floor.

"Not the damn National Enquirer, now, is it Josh?" Suitcase said glancing in the rearview.

The headline screamed 'Aliens Land-Reveal Exciting New Diet Plan!' Underneath, another read 'Minister Explodes on the Pulpit!"

"How can you read that shit?" I asked.

"It's entertainment. Like watching Pro Wrestling or Roller Derby, it's just a little mindless escape. Plus it is usually pretty damn funny," Josh answered.

"The whole world is a National Enquirer headline," Suitcase chimed in.

"John is right. The whole world is crazy. Irony is God's only consistency," Mole said. "Take the 'Greatest'—Muhammad Ali. He can't barely speak, and he can no longer stings like a bee, only shakes like a bee explaining to the hive where a flower is," Mole continued. "Now if that isn't some crazy shit?"

"You are ruthless Mole." Suitcase laughed.

"What about the guy over in Salem who's parachute didn't open but he landed safely in a mattress factory?" Beans said, joining in.

"Can't top the blind man walking into a manhole in front of the Institute of the Deaf." Suitcase topped him.

"No way," I said, not believing any of this bullshit.

But Suitcase wasn't finished. "And, the kicker? His seeing eye dog developed cataracts the day after!" He crossed his heart—hope to die.

Mole was next. "Abbee Backilla, Ethiopian barefooted Olympic marathon winner—three time; paralyzed from a car accident. A multi-millionaire in Florida goes and wins the lottery. The list goes on and on."

"No, it's true Stevie all of it. An astronaut killed in freak horse spill. A lady walking a baby carriage gets run over by a diaper truck. It's all there and all true—I read it," Josh added.

"Yea, you read it in the fucking National Enquirer! When are we going to get there?" I said. "I've had enough of this car ride."

"Just like when you were a kid; Are we there yet? Are we there yet?" Suitcase teased. "We will be there soon enough."

Suitcase was right.

We pulled in the Margate public marina around ten. There was no sign of the firefighters. We went into a diner for breakfast and to wait for Jake and his crew.

Beans stayed outside to check out the boat.

We ordered bacon and eggs to go with our coffee. Everyone ordered screwdrivers except me.

Mole seemed to be getting pretty gunned up. So were Josh and Suitcase. What are they going to be like when the Fireman get here? I thought.

Suitcase took a sip of his screwdriver then said, "Alrighty then, Mole perhaps a little fishing story is in order. Tell Stevie about the time we caught all the Blue fish from that jetty in Cape May."

"Speaking of Cape May, I know we were going to check home after the crabbing but as Birders, we should enter the World Series of Birding contest in the Cape May Bird refuge," Mole said.

"You have got to be shittin me! A World Series of Birding?" I said unbelievingly.

"Oh yea, biggest event in the birding world. If they had a category for drinkers we would be the reigning champs. Most of our birding brethren however, are as dry as Presbyterians. Hopefully we won't be disqualified like last year," Mole explained.

"I want to checkout Atlantic City, then I don't care what we do. That Birding series was an adventure last year, I'll check it out again," Suitcase said.

"We'll figure it out when Beans joins us. It's this weekend so we have some time. In the meantime, the blue fishing story with the Mole's unique spin, if you don't mind," he continued.

As Suitcase finished, Beans walked in.

"Boat looks good to go. Just need some gas and oil mix and some bait and we are ready for the crabs. Heard there are flounder running in the bay too. Better get some flounder rigs as well," he paused then looked around. "I'm hungry. Where is that waitress?"

"She just took our order, we got you some eggs and bacon. Mole was just going to tell us about the time we caught the bluefish off the beach. Josh you may have heard it before, but Mole never tells it the same way twice. Do you Mole?" Suitcase asked.

Mole began, "We were fishing off the jetty from the beach down Cape May years ago. You might remember Stevie, when we first started to go to the Hostel. Anyway, we were fishing from the surf. It was a beautiful day and we were enjoying it, but we weren't catching anything.

Then the weather began to turn. The sky's complexion changed quickly. It went from maybe light Cuban to dark Cuban with black Haitian on the horizon."

Mole's friends smiled at the description. So did I. My old man could bullshit with the best of them.

He allowed the waitress to refill his coffee. He nodded a silent thank you then continued, "The air was on edge like it had a hangover. We were just about to call it a day."

"I already had called it a day. Remember? I was laying on the beach watching the storm roll in," Beans corrected.

"You're right. You called it a day, but Suitcase and I wanted one more cast. While I went back to the beach for more bait, Suitcase made a last cast far past the breakers. As soon as the sinker hit, the ocean sucked it up. He had a strike, and whatever it was, it did not like the luncheon menu.

It's as if the big bluefish on the line had said 'Waiter! Waiter! I didn't order any Goddamn hook salad for lunch. I've heard of a fly in the soup but this is ridiculous. A hook in a piece of squid! I will sue. My brother in law is a lawyer—a shark. The best legal fish head in the sea. We'll take this all the way to Neptune's Supreme court.' But Suitcase wasn't listening he just reeled him in," Mole said and laughed.

Josh wasn't buying it.

"Now the fish is talking huh? You ought to take it easy on the weed today there Mole. Just the facts man, just the facts," Josh said imitating Dragnet. He took a drink of his screwdriver.

Mole paused and looked at Josh, for a second it seemed like his feelings were hurt, then he smiled and said, "You know, telling a story in the first person makes truth obligatory. But I like to bend it, stretch it, anyway I want it. I like to let the truth dance. The truth loves to dance. It went to Authur Murry's, the truth steps on everybody's toes."

"I've had enough of this bull, I am going to find the shitter," Josh said getting up to go to the restroom.

Mole continued, "Anyway, next I cast out with no bait, and bang! I hooked one. The storm must have started a feeding frenzy or something. We landed about ten fish in fifteen minutes. Beans acted like a first mate on the beach, unhooking them. Would have kept it up, except the storm got too bad. It started to blow in every different direction, like a tornado with schizophrenia.

We had to stop. We could barely see. Ended up with more fish than we could carry. Gave a bunch away to some folks on the boardwalk who had watched us from an arcade," Mole finished.

Our breakfast arrived with Josh close behind.

We were so hungry we barely talked while we ate. Their wasn't even a piece of dry toast when we finished.

After we were done and they had lit cigarettes, Beans said, "Maybe we will catch some today. Even if we only get one, Mole will make a great story out of it."

"Amen brother. Amen," Suitcase said, and paid the bill.

We went back out to the marina to wait for the firemen.

Like most firemen we heard them coming before we saw them. This time instead of sirens we heard horns honking, shouts, laughter and cans being tossed. Sure enough, barreling into the parking lot came four carloads of Darby Fire Company A members. By the look and sound of them they had been up all night and they were ready to go. The typical Delaware County weekend warrior. Shoobie yahoos looking to condense a summer vacation into two days in Margate.

The name 'shoobie' was the nickname the locals gave to tourists. It referred to the shoe boxes the weekenders used to carry their possessions, back in the day when trains were the preferred mode of weekend travel to the shore.

These firemen shoobies substituted cars and coolers for trains and shoeboxes. Looking at them as they barreled into the lot, I'm sure the locals wished for the days when the train travelers were all they had to deal with.

Greetings were made, boats rented and equipment bought and stowed.

Apparently, despite everyone's level of intoxication, there were a few real outdoorsmen who knew the best tide and the best locations to fish and crab.

For every 'real' crabber, there were three amateurs.

We divied up the boats accordingly. Josh, Suitcase, Mole and I went in the *Cannery Row*. Beans went with Captain Jake and three other firemen. Two I had never seen before, but the third one was nicknamed Ziggy. I think it was because he loved David Bowie, I'm not sure, although from his long mullet hair to his Led Zeppelin T-shirt, the name fit him perfectly.

All together there were four boats. Three rentals and The *Row*. The rentals had small outboards so no matter how hard they tried they couldn't keep up with us. At first it didn't matter much because we were in a no wake zone.

Everyone was laughing and partying. In addition to the coolers on each boat, there were bottles of liquor, mostly V.O. and tequila. My old man had his standard issue cheap vodka and a bottle of Gallo Vin Rose to go with the beers. Each boat had one cooler with home made hoagies and the token bag of chips.

I looked through the coolers on our boat and realized there were only four cans of soda, three cokes and a fresca.

It was going to be a long drunk day.

I hid the sodas in the bottom of the cooler so I would have something other than beer to drink.

We headed out to a place called the cove. It was a spot outside Margate closer to Ocean City. It had a beach and a place to tie off. In addition to crabbing and fishing there was an area for water skiing and swimming. If we got tired of crabbing we could head to the beach to swim or cast from the shore.

As we chugged along, it wasn't long before the smell of pot emanated from each boat. Thankfully their were no State police boats to be seen. Everyone continued to drink heavily.

True to form, Captain Jake had fallen hard off the wagon. Even though it was still early, the combination of the drink and the sun were already taking their toll. He sat red faced and grinning, a beer and cigar perched in each hand. You could hear his laugh above the engines as it echoed off the water on the way to the cove.

Mole on the other hand had grown quiet. At first, I took this as a good sign. I thought he might have been played out and spent from the previous day's festivities. I remembered Josh's line that still waters run deep, so I kept a eye on him.

Suitcase sensing my uneasiness, patted me on the leg and said "No worries lad, no worries."

After a short boat ride, we reached a sheltered spot away from the skiers and jet boats and we set anchor. We set out the traps and the hand lines. Some guys cast out fishing lines instead, opting hopefully to catch a few flat fish that breed in the back bays in early summer.

Although you caught most of the crabs with the traps, the handlines gave each man something to do to pass the time, besides drink and shoot the shit. Plus, it was fun to watch the guys drunkenly attempt to net the hungry crabs that tenaciously held on to the mullet or rancid chicken we used to bait the lines.

Even though most of our party were inexperienced crabbers and there was a lot of noise from the drunken laughter and small talk, we started to haul in some decent BlueClaws. In the first hour we had caught a couple of dozen keepers on our boat alone. I hooked a twenty two inch flounder to go with the crabs.

Mole may have been quiet but he was drinking heavily. In addition to the neverending beers, he frequently took a long pull from his vodka bottle and washed it down with the wine.

"Yo dad, the sun is pretty hot out here, maybe you should pace yourself, it's a long day," I said.

I looked over at Suitcase who was also taking a shot from the vodka.

Some help he was going to be.

"You are worse than your mother," he slurred. "Sweet Jaysus you can be such a women," he continued. "What do you care? I'm not driving."

He was right about that.

For some reason I was the operator of the *Cannery Row*. I say operator and not driver, because there was no steering wheel. Instead, there was a long handle that came off the motor. By pushing or pulling the handle, you steered the boat. Even a small movement on the handle would result in the boat turning very quickly.

Despite never operating a boat before I had gotten the hang of it on the way out. Once again, merely because I was the least drunk, I was relegated to the position of responsibility. It was getting old. I felt like a baby sitter for a bunch of alkies.

Which is exactly what I was.

To hell with that, I thought.

"Your right Mole drink up! Your son and first born once again has things under control. I am not your wife, therefore—no more advice. No more requests. No more demands. No more tips about the sun or the booze. Drink up!"

The last comment I yelled to all the boats anchored around me. A drunken cheer went up in agreement.

Everyone continued to drink like ten men. Although everyone had plenty of booze, no one, it seemed, had thought to bring any sun block. As the day wore on, the result was four boats full of intoxicated red lobsters most of whom were pretty high to boot. The trip was getting sloppy.

Soon the tide began to change. With it went the crabs and the flounder. We stopped catching anything. In addition to being drunk and fried by the sun, the Birders and the Firemen grew bored.

Mole attempted to educate the party about the Plovers and the Red Knots that darted up and down the shore line. He explained how the birds stopped here each year on their migration to feast on the eggs of the horseshoe crab. He told us how the bird's numbers had suffered because the horseshoe crab was becoming extinct.

Although the birders found this interesting, the firemen wanted nothing to do with a drunk bird lecture.

"Shut the fuck up," Ziggy yelled from Jake's boat anchored about ten feet from us.

"Yea, I got a bird for you—a ten inch white owl!" Captain Jake shouted. To illustrate the point, he whipped his dick out and waved it at our boat. "Members Only!" he taunted, "Throbbing Members!" he yelled for good measure.

"Ten inches,my ass! Your White owl looks more like a runt of a humming bird to me," Mole fired back, of course keeping with the bird analogies.

A war of words ensued.

The firemen started to yell insults at Mole and the rest of our boat.

"Yo Maureen! What does SemperFi stand for?" Ziggy yelled. "Always a faggot!" he answered himself.

Next it was Captain Jake. "Suitcase. Paint any trucks lately?" he shouted.

I could see Suitcase turning red.

"Easy there Jake, it's one thing to insult the Corps, even if Ziggy's insult was pretty lame, I mean, what do you expect from a second rate drunk and a third rate firefighter. But it's another thing altogether to insult my friend personally," Mole responded.

"Screw you and the boat you rode in on," a fireman yelled from another boat.

With that, Josh, who had been sitting quietly, now stood and calmly threw a piece of bloody sun baked mullet over to the other boat.

"Take that you pussy nozzle nuts!" he shouted.

The rancid bait fish hit Captain Jake on the side of his face.

"I guess you would call that being Starkist!" Josh yelled. He looked over at us, obviously proud of both his aim and his pun.

"You lousy bastard!" Jake screamed. He grabbed some smelly chicken necks from a bucket and slung them at us.

Josh ducked but the slop hit Suitcase in the belly.

Now the naval battle escalated.

Mole took a nasty hit from some fish guts. He peeled off his soiled shirt and his shorts and returned fire in his underwear. As soon as he threw, Ziggy winged a mullet at him. Mole caught the fish and fired it right back. It smacked off a fireman's back and skipped into the water. Josh, never one to fight fair, started hurling full cans of beer at the other boats. Cries of 'foul!' rang out from our opponents but it did not stop the bombardment.

I heard Beans yell that he was being hit by friendly fire. He took off his shirt and dove off Captain Jake's boat. He began furiously swimming to the *Cannery Row*. The fireman in the other boats began screaming that he was a traitor and a deserter. Ziggy actually began casting a lead sinker at him as he swam. With each miss he would reel in and cast again.

As I watched this drunken sushi food fight unfold, I could see people on the beach pointing and looking. It wouldn't be long before the police or the Coast Guard arrived.

"Fellas enough is enough!" I shouted, without result. I yelled louder.

"C'mon Mole knock it off—we are all going to get arrested. I don't want a drunk boating charge Goddamnit!"

He laughed in my face. "There is no such animal son," he said, as he threw my freshly caught flounder at the firemen.

"Not my fish you prick!" I shouted.

It smacked, wastefully off the side of Jake's boat and fell back into the bay.

Beans had now reached our boat. Mole reached down and grabbing Beans' outstretched hand took him on board.

Dripping wet, Beans immediately asked for a drink from the Vodka bottle. Mole yelled time out and handed Beans the bottle. Beans took a huge guzzle of the vodka, then handed it back to Mole. Mole took a drink too. All the while the fish kept flying.

To top it off, Sea Gulls had began to gather for the scraps that fell in the water. There must have been a hundred. They dive bombed the boats like crazy, cackling kamikaze flyers, while Josh swung at them with an oar and yelled for Alka seltzer to throw at them to make their stomachs explode.

I was furious.

"Always taking chances with my future, you prick!" I screamed, ducking a hunk of squid thrown at our boat. "I'll be the one who gets busted. Please stop," I pleaded.

Mole wasn't listening.

At least Suitcase heeded my request. He calmly sat back down and began to clean up the boat.

Soon the level of fire from the other boats began to slow as well, either because the firemen realized things were out of hand or because they had run out of ammo. The only two guys still at it were Captain Jake and the Mole. Both drunk, both being stubborn assholes.

In an effort to stop the fight, I started the boat and began slowly chugging away. I told everyone we needed a new spot, but they knew what I was doing.

Captain Jake would have none of it. He and Ziggy began to follow.

"Not so fast pussies, I'm right on your ass!" Ziggy shouted over the rumbling of the outboards.

The other boats were obviously out of bait and no one wanted to waste any more beer but Captain Jake and his mate Ziggy wanted the last say. As they maneuvered closer, I sped up. To keep up, they opened their smaller engine up all the way.

As they got closer they began hurling their freshly caught crabs at us. The first two landed in the boat and immediately began to scuttle around the aluminum bottom. This caused Josh and Suitcase to begin to dance around like cartoon fat ladies who had just seen a mouse. In their panic, they practically tipped the boat.

Finally, Beans calmly smashed the crabs with an oar.

"Relax gentleman. The stowaways have been taken care of," he said laughing.

I pressed on.

"Those son of a bitches," Mole said. "Get me over there."

He was standing in the front of the boat like some stoned Captain Ahab chasing his leviathan.

"Sit the fuck down now!" I demanded. "I've had enough."

"Fuck you. I don't take orders from some bratty puss gut college boy," he hissed. Immediately, by his tone, his friends knew this was different. *He* was different.

They may not have ever seen this act before, but I sure had.

Josh told him to stop. Suitcase said something to him too. It made no difference. He was drunk and nasty and he wasn't going to listen to any one.

"You heard me college boy, get me the fuck over there!" he demanded.

I wanted to get away from him before I killed him, but I was trapped on a sixteen foot piece of aluminum in the middle of the bay.

I was always trapped with the Mole.

Someone must have heard my plea.

At that moment, Captain Jake threw something big at our boat. It came flying toward us. I turned to avoid it. It was a huge crab. My drunk father, forgetting that this projectile had claws, instinctively reached out to catch it and throw it back.

This was no dead fish.

The crab clamped both claws down hard on Mole's hand. He let out a scream that was heard back on the dock. I know it was heard on the beach, since now everyone on the beach and a lot of boats in the area were watching. He began to dance about the front of the boat like an epileptic Joe Cocker doing an Irish Jig. Since he had both hands above him trying to pull off the crab, he twisted off balance at the same time that I turned the boat.

He fell awkwardly, hit hard off the side and splashed overboard.

I gunned the motor.

"Easy Steve, watch the prop!" Beans yelled. "Pull around and I'll get him."

"Fuck him!" I said turning away from him and heading back.

"You can't leave him Stevie," Suitcase said.

"Yea, go back around and we'll grab the asshole," Josh concurred.

"I've had enough of his shit. He can swim back or drown, I don't care!" I said adding my drama to the situation. I mean, there were three other boats, all within fifty yards of him. Who was I kidding? Any one of them could grab him in seconds.

It was the principle of the matter. I was sick and tired of his act. I was sick and tired of his pushing the limits. I was sick and tired of him always being drunk. I was sick of his mood swings. I was sick of him always being nasty. Most of all, I was sick and tired of always being embarrassed by him.

"If the shoe were on the other foot he would leave me," I said.

To end the conversation I opened the engine up, full throttle.

If they wanted to protest any more I couldn't hear them.

When we got to the dock, I could tell the guys were pissed at me. They didn't say much, but I knew. They busied themselves with unloading the gear and cleaning out the boat. Every once in a while they stole a glance out to the bay, where you could see the rest of the crabbers puttering back in the slower rental boats.

I steeled myself for his return. I purposefully tried to keep my anger up. It would help me if this thing got ugly.

I had the feeling it might. By the way I felt that wouldn't be hard.

To calm myself I went to the cooler and took out the bottle of Vodka. I certainly could use a drink. I unscrewed the cap. As I did, Suitcase looked over at me. He didn't say anything.

I closed the bottle and put it back.

Suitcase went back to unloading the boat.

About a half hour after we docked, the other boats rolled in. The men were all pretty spent. Between the sun and the booze, they looked like the half dead dozen or so Blue Crabs that managed to survive the sea battle.

The worn out fisherman unloaded the remaining catch proudly like they were world record swordfish or something.

Mole, wrapped in a blanket, sat brooding and drunk. He would not look at me or talk to me. He finally got up to retrieve his vodka bottle from Beans. After taking an exaggerated drink to torment me, he rummaged through the gear for some cut-offs and a clean shirt. He then walked past me and grunted on his way to the bar.

I felt my temper rise again.

It was all I could do not to knock him out.

He probably felt the same way about me.

Suitcase waved to me to come in the bar as well. I shook my head no and instead yelled to him that I was going to the beach and would meet back at the lot later.

He nodded, then disappeared into the tavern.

I grabbed a towel from my bag and walked to the beach.

Chapter 29

On being left behind

Later, after a quick swim in the ocean, I calmed down enough to actually begin to enjoy myself. It's amazing how a sunny day at the beach can get your head right. After about fifteen minutes, I completely forgot about dumping Mole.

It was late in the day and there was hardly anyone there. The whole beach was practically my own. I flopped down right in the sand. I let the feel and heat of the sand envelope me. I let my thoughts wander.

I must have dozed off. Who knows how long I slept.

It was Suitcase and Josh who woke me up. They looked more sunburnt and tired than drunk.

"So this is where you been," Josh said, handing me another towel.

I took it and wiped some of the sand off the side of my face. Suitcase handed me a soda.

"We got a couple of hotel rooms back by the bay. Let's go back and grab some showers and maybe something to eat," Suitcase said. "You should probably call your mom to check in too."

"Give me a minute to get it together. I was out like a light," I said as I walked down to the water to wash off the sand.

The cold water brought me back.

I dried off and we headed back.

As we walked, I could tell the guys wanted to talk about what happened on the boat. When they realized I didn't, they changed the subject. They talked about Atlantic City instead.

"We should take a break from the great outdoors and do a little gambling tomorrow," Suitcase said breaking the silence.

"Yea, I'm sick of the wilderness. I could use a vacation from this vacation," Josh joked.

"Sounds good to me. Now if I could only get a break from my father," I said.

"Maybe he feels the same way," Suitcase defended. He looked at me to see how I would handle it. When I didn't respond one way or another he continued, "You can sleep in my room tonight. Beans and your old man have their own room. In the morning we will get a fresh start. Everything will be right as rain," He added optimistically.

We walked on in silence. All of us tired from the sun and the booze and the Darby Firemen crabbing expedition.

////////////////

Suitcase was right. The next day I woke up feeling pretty good. I had touched base with my mother before I went to bed and she seemed to be okay. I made no mention of the incident on the boat. I just told her we had fun and Mole was sleeping.

I showered and went over to the diner next to the hotel. The firemen were long gone. Josh was with me. We drank coffee and waited for the others. The place was an old fashioned pancake house common on the Jersey shore.

Young college girls, waitresses for the summer, hurried about taking breakfast orders.

As we waited, we watched the boats roll out for the day.

"How you feeling today college boy?" Josh asked. "Have you been bird watching in this diner? If you haven't noticed these cute girls then you must be playing for the other team."

He playfully punched my arm and then tousled my hair.

He could be a goofy bastard.

As he spoke, the others walked in.

Mole looked a little hung over but no more than usual. He sat down next to Josh at the booth. Suitcase sat next to me. Beans grabbed a chair and pulled it up to the end of the booth.

Mole broke the ice and made a joke about having too much to drink so his son had to dump him in the drink or something like that. Everyone laughed. A little too much if you ask me. The joke was pretty lame, but everyone was a little nervous and still waking up, I guess.

I drank my coffee. Suitcase looked over at me. I knew what he wanted.

Fine.

"Mole I'm sorry I didn't pick you up after you fell in," I said, not looking at him.

I admit it was pretty half assed as far as apologies go.

In typical Mole fashion he feigned being the bigger man, at the same time letting me know he was pissed.

"Shit happens. While I admit that perhaps I had imbibed a tad more grog than I should of and for that I am sorry, I take issue with the categorization that I fell in. The negligent manner in which you turned the boat leads me to believe you wanted to dump me."

He paused, took a sip from his coffee, made a face, then added another spoonful of sugar. He sipped again. Satisfied, he returned to his discussion. "I was drunk, I admit, but if I were driving the boat and *you* fell in I would not have left you behind."

He reached for the menu.

"I say bygones are bygones," he finished.

His friends let out a sigh of relief and began to order breakfast.

Not this time I thought.

He wasn't getting off so easy. I was not going to let him play the victim for his buddies any more.

"You were beyond a little drunk," I began. "I asked you a couple times to chill and you wouldn't listen. All your friends realized things were out of hand. They all respected that I was responsible for the boat. They all listened.

You always have to be drunk, and then you got nasty with me to boot? I can take a drunk. What I can't take, is a mean drunk. You are lucky that all I did was ditch you," I railed.

"Easy son, I'm sorry. You made your point, but I wouldn't have left you out there." he offered by way of his own half-assed apology. He looked to his friends to weigh in like some Friday morning hung over jury.

Suitcase nodded in agreement, the others buried their heads in their morning papers or looked out at the bay.

"You are so full of shit. You wouldn't leave me?" I practically screamed.

The waitress looked over, thought to say something, then moved on to another table.

"Tell your buddies about the Bennie Briscoe/ Marvin Hagler fight when *you* left me. What was I, about ten?" I taunted.

"Mole, when you are working a scam, it's always nice to let *everyone* in on it before you do it," I said, now almost ranting.

Now everyone stopped what they were doing and looked at Mole.

"You don't need to remind me, that was a mistake. I've told you a million times before," he stammered.

"I was . . ." he hesitated. He began to turn red.

"What?" I demanded. "You were what? . . . drunk?"

"Don't do this," he pleaded. "It was stupid. I have apologized a million times before. Nothing happened, we laughed about it. Remember? You told your friends. It's part of your standup comedy act for Christ sake!" He looked around like he was trapped.

"You're right it is funny *now*, but don't act like you wouldn't leave me," I said.

Thankfully for him, the waitress arrived with our breakfast.

Mole looked like a death row inmate getting a call from the Governor. Too bad his friends were interested now.

"What did the drunk idiot do? Sell you to the gypsies?" Josh joked.

"I'll tell you what he did."

Mole got up and excused himself from the table. He grabbed his coffee and his smokes.

"Remember, my son is a bigger bullshitter than his old man."

He walked outside. I could see him sitting on a bench looking out at the bay.

"You know my old man is a big fight fan. Always loved boxing. He and Dan Erickson used to go all the time. Either the old Arena in North Philly or the Blue Horizon on Broad street. Especially during the golden era of Philly middleweights; remember Boogaloo Watts? Willie the Worm Monroe? Briscoe? Gypsy Joe Harris, Eugene Cyclone Hart?"

Josh interrupted "Gypsy Joe. Guy had one friggin eye and he was still great! Ahh, The Sweet Science . . ." his voiced trailed off.

Beans who had up to now been silent, chimed in.

"I remember Dan. He is a Marine too. I think he was a combat photographer in Nam. He told me during the Tet Offensive, he shot footage for one day and North Vietnamese soldiers for the next four days!

Never picked up a camera again. Said the M16 was the only film stock he trusted." He paused and took a drag of his cigarette, coughed, then continued "He was a boxer in the Corps. Twelve and one record. After the 'one' he hung them up. Yea, he loved boxing."

He looked at me, embarrassed that he had went on too long.

"Yea that's Ericson all right," I said picking the story back up. "Nice background Beans," I added.

To Josh I said, "Remind me to tell you about the Cyclone Hart fight too."

I continued.

"Well, every time they would go, I would beg them to take me. Most of the time they would tell me I was too young for the fights. Then, when they would say okay, my mother would put the kibosh on it. You know the deal. It was always a school night, or we had an early game or plans the next day. No matter what, I never got to go.

This went on for a year or so.

Finally, after I had bothered them for what felt like an eternity, they agreed to take me to Hagler versus Briscoe. Two of the best in Philly.

It was at the Spectrum so I guess my Mom figured it would be safer, you know, a little more upscale. Anyway, I was on another planet, I was so happy. Finally going to the FIGHTS! I was young. A little kid. I couldn't believe my luck. The fights. That night.

Like all little kids, all I wanted was to hold the tickets.

On the ride down Dan and Mole sat in the front of the old Volvo. I sat in the back.

Leaning up, in the middle I kept asking, pleading actually 'Can I hold the tickets? Can I?' I must of asked a thousand times.

I should have realized then something was up.

They'd say 'Shut up, and sit back, we will be there in a little bit'.

All the while, no tickets.

The only thing I got to hold was the Styrofoam cooler with the beers. My job consisted of handing them cold ones and taking care of the empties. But no tickets.

Then we arrived.

All around us were limos, fancy clothes, and celebrities.

Smokin Joe Frazier, Sylvester Stallone, Burt Young, Willie Pep the old lightweight. Jake Lamotta the Raging Bull. Even Floyd Patterson—looking like a million bucks. It was wild.

Still no tickets.

Then I notice that we are not going in. Instead we are walking around outside. Dan and Mole are drinking, smoking weed, of course I didn't realize it was pot until years later. But if he were in here he'd admit it."

Josh interrupted "Of course he was smoking, when doesn't he?"

The others nodded in agreement.

I continued. "I notice they are talking to various groups of shady characters who are huddled around every gate. Guys shouting 'need two, need two!'"

"Scalpers!" Beans announced.

"Shit yea scalpers. Boxing match scalpers—the nastiest kind!" I exaggerated, now fully into the theatre of the story.

"Gee, hard to believe the bastards didn't have any tickets! God forbid they tell me."

"I didn't want to dim your enthusiasm," Mole said reentering the diner. "I mean you were so excited to be going to your first boxing match, I didn't have the heart to tell you we might not get in."

"All these years later and that's the best spin you can put on it?" I fired back. "You were a drunk selfish prick and you could have got me killed!"

"What happened?" Suitcase asked.

"The pricks not only didn't tell me they didn't have tickets, they also didn't bother to tell me they planned on ripping off the scalpers.

Like I said, if you are planning a scam it's nice if you let your party, *all your party* in on it."

I stopped and took a drink of Beans' screw driver, then went on.

"Next thing I see is Mole talking to this big black guy. They are warily eyeing each other. Dan is looking all around like he is a getaway driver or the lookout man or something. Anyway, I hear Mole say 'You got the tickets?' And the guy goes 'You got the money?' They start this fucking grifter dance with Mole going 'Yea I got the money. You got the tickets?'

He pulls out the money and he waves it in the guy's face. He says 'Show me the tickets-how do I know they are good seats?'

The guy pulls them out and waves them at Mole. He says 'Yea they're good—hand me the money.'

Mole says 'Let me hold them. I want to see if they're good".

This goes on for a bit. They shuffle around. They both extend their hands slowly, Mole with a wad of bills, the scalper with the tickets, both staring at each other like a Sergio Leone close up.

Then, quicker than losing my virginity—Bang! Mole grabs the tickets and runs! Danny, knowing full well what was going down, bolts after him.

Me?

I'm just standing there. I have no clue.

The guy screams out, takes about three steps after them, then stops. Calmly, he turns around and look at yours truly."

With that, I shook my head and downed the screwdriver. The birders were waiting on my next word. Mole just sat there staring into his drink.

"Those mother fuckers took off and left me holding the bag!

The scalper can't go after them cause he has other tickets to sell plus time was runnin out. Not to mention now he has a hostage."

Josh who had been listening intently jumped in. "Mole you son of a bitch, is this true?"

Mole sheepishly answered. "I remember that we told Stevie what was up ahead of time. I told him to run when we did. I had to."

He looked to me to corroborate his memory, but I was silent.

He shifted direction.

"Or maybe it was purely a crime of opportunity, I can't remember." he paused, and looked off as though he was trying to remember, then said "Well then, finish the story Stevie. It worked out all right in the end, didn't it. You're here, aren't you?"

"Just because it worked out alright in the end, don't make it right," Beans pounced. He waved to the waitress for another round.

"Well what happened?" Suitcase demanded.

"The scalper can't believe he's been fleeced. He figured, two guys with their kid, it had to be legit. He's in shock too.

At first he grabs me by the neck, thinking I'm going to run. I immediately burst into tears. When he sees that I'm so upset and incapable of running, he lets me go. Then he starts to interrogate me. I am so scared, I can't tell him where our car is or anything. I don't think I could even talk.

He must have figured that Mole was just drunk and when he figures out he left his kid he would come back and straighten out the mess. So he starts to calm down. He even managed to laugh about it. I remember him saying 'White boy, you are a bad excuse for collateral.'

He sits me down on a step and he says 'I ain't gonna hurt you, but I can't say the same for your asshole father. When he comes back I'm gonna be on him like white on rice, that honky drunk!'

So we wait. And wait. And wait. The final call is made. No Mole. The undercard starts.

No Mole.

Finally, the scalper realizes Mole ain't coming back. He can't believe it. I can't believe it.

Now the collateral is a liability.

I can see he is thinking. He walks over and says 'Son, that son of a bitch ain't comin back. Damn if I'm gonna be responsible for you. I can't turn you over to the Po-leece cause they will ask too many questions. Here's what I'm gonna do . . . Those tickets they stole were in section 414. If you can get in to the fight you might catch up to them. If you do, tell them what goes around comes around. I'll catch up with them and when I do well . . . I won't be as nice as I was to you."

I paused from the story and took another sip of the drink. I felt a nice morning buzz coming on.

Josh grew impatient "Did you hook up with your dad?" he asked, casting a dirty look at Mole.

"Shit yea.

So I cry to the first ticket taker I see. I tell him I got separated from my pop when I went to the bathroom.

He lets me right in.

I walk to section 414 and sure enough there they are. Mutt and Jeff, drunk and happy. Acted like it was no big deal. I remember Mole going 'Hi son. I knew you would find us. Sit down, let me get you a soda and some cotton candy. Like it was an all—American father and son night!

Fucking surreal. Wasn't it Mole?" I looked over.

Mole looked up from his coffee, "I said I was sorry."

Suitcase asked "Well what did you do?"

"What the hell was I gonna do? I settled in to watch the fights. Didn't even say a fuckin word more about it."

The diner table got silent.

Finally Mole said, "See I told you it all worked out. Great fight too."

I laughed and shook my head.

"And Josh, remember I said remind me to tell you about Eugene Cyclone Hart?

Well Hart is fighting on the undercard. It is the fight I walked in on.

Poor bastard is getting beat good. I mean really pummeled.

The guy next to us starts screaming 'Hey Eugene pull down you pants and stick your dick in his eye!'

Now I'm amazed **and** confused. I mean, what kind of boxing tip is that?

I look over at my drunk dad and his boxing expert Dan for an explanation.

You know what those two scout leaders say? I will never forget.

Erickson started to calmly explain to my ten year mind that Cyclone Hart was known in fight circles to have 'pound for pound' the biggest cock of any Philly middleweight and if he was to stick his dick in his opponent's eye he would no doubt knock him out or at least blind him good.

Then if this whole adventure wasn't crazy enough. Cyclone wins. The audience is unhappy with the judge's decision. I remember his opponent got robbed. Anyway, the fans are pissed. They start raining bottles down on the ring. Glass is shattering all around us.

You would think that Mole would have at least *tried* to get me out of there.

No way!

The main event was still on deck.

He tells me to get under the seat. He and Dan slide down and put their heads under the seats. He puts me next to him. There I am, fresh off being left with a scalper and now I'm under the chair with two drunks, dodging beer bottles!

Classic. All true. All Mole." I looked over at my Dad. "So don't sit here and tell me you wouldn't leave me—you old drunk prick."

He laughed and looked around the table.

"Touché lad."

He paused and took a drag on his smoke.

"It happened. I ain't proud of it, I ain't ashamed of it. What is done is done. You know I love you and am sorry for any pain I have inflicted on you or will no doubt inflict on you in the future."

He began to pack up his cigarettes and his lighter. He called for the check.

"Now, if we are done with our mutual therapy sessions, I understand the Birders would like to take a break from the great outdoors and partake in some games of chance in Atlantic City. Are we going to wallow in yesterday's news or will we, as the poet Arthur Rimbaud said, 'Advance Always'? I have always found that we don't really have a choice in the matter."

"So you tell me Mole, so you tell me," I shook my head.

Fuckin Mole, it was hard to stay mad at him for very long.

I found myself laughing about the whole thing.

Before I knew it I blurted out, "To Atlantic City! Can I hold the tickets? Can I ? Can I?"

Mole and I laughed. Josh and Bean's just shook their heads.

Suitcase paid the check.

Chapter 30

On Dice, Rice, Little Beers and The Universal Power of Ole Yeller

Atlantic City used to be one of the vacation capitals of the world. From the glamour of the Miss America Contest to the diving horse of the Steel Pier, the Atlantic City of old had something for everyone. It was America's summer vacation destination.

By the seventies you couldn't pay people to go there. Like some other New Jersey Beaches; Asbury Park and Wildwood, Atlantic City had fallen on hard times.

Gone were the summer crowds. No more young couples walking hand in hand down the boardwalk. No more families sharing slices of Mack and Manco pizza or eating salty fresh cut French fries and washing them down with real lemonade as the Ferris wheel turned lazily round into the night.

Finally, in an effort to revitalize the town, the powers that be, as they have repeated across the country many times since Atlantic City's so called resurrection, figured when something goes to shit, waive a wand and say the two magic words-

Legalized Gambling.

In a flash, Resorts International was built. The first casino of what was to be a dozen flashy betting parlors that would save the town, and restore it to its former glory.

Unfortunately, in the years since this knee jerk political decision, instead of realizing the vision of an east coast Las Vegas, the transformation of Atlantic City has taken a less successful path.

Instead of high rollers, AC has attracted mostly rollers of an another kind—wheel chair rollers. The aged and the retired. The North Jersey and Philadelphia fixed incomers who can't afford to spend their golden years in Florida or Arizona, now get their jollies on day trips to the shore resort of their youth. Even though both the town and it's guests are a far cry from their glory days, they keep hoping that the next trip; the next round; the next pull on the one arm bandit (or push of a button nowadays) will deliver them.

The big one. The jackpot.

For most visitors it never happens. Most take that lonely bus ride home empty handed. Left to wonder how they will survive the month after pissing away their social security or their pension checks to lady luck.

Sadly, for most of Atlantic City it hasn't happened either. Half the town is fake glitz, the other half is real poverty.

Less Vegas at best.

Today, in order to get visitors, the casinos really do have to pay you. Desperate for patrons, the casinos offer anywhere from fifteen to twenty dollars in slot machine credits or meal vouchers along with a free bus ride.

My grandmother and her friends used to take these day trips and never even set foot in a casino other than to eat or cash their vouchers. Mole was known to do the same and spend the day in the Atlantic City Library. That is, until he decided to stop returning the multitude of borrowed books and became the most wanted book thief in the state.

At the time we visited, unless you could fly to Vegas, Atlantic City was the only show in town. It is because it was the only legalized gambling in the tri-state area that the Birders, mainly Suitcase and Josh, found themselves regularly betting with the bluehaired ladies and their hearing aid and cane escorts.

It was this Atlantic City that was being suggested as a break from our bird watching. Is it any wonder I hardly seemed enthused?

Sensing this, Suitcase assured me that the day would be a good time, and an even better story. He further hyped the trip by saying if he won big, he would surprise us with a 'happy ending.'

I reluctantly agreed.

It had to be better than the day before.

We pulled into Caesars in the early afternoon.

We settled on Caesars because Mole would not patronize Trump's casino. He bitched that he hated that "bad haired egomaniac."

When Suitcase tried to explain that he had comps at Trump Casino and that Trump didn't really own the casino anyway—it was in bankruptsy, Mole still wouldn't budge.

Caesars it would be.

We all split up when we entered from the boardwalk. Past glittering escalators and mirrored ceilings.

Beans took his usual spot at the slots. Not just any slots. For Beans it wasn't about the gambling, it was about the drinking. He would scout out the quarter machines and then position himself at one that was close to the waitress' station. That way, he could play without losing too much and all the while still get plenty of free drinks from the waitresses as they left their bar station. As soon as he got there, I watched him tip the first girl that came by with a ten spot. She took his order and I saw her giggle at something he said. She playfully smacked his arm then disappeared into the crowded casino floor. Beans wasn't stupid. His waitress would pass by on every drink run. Win, lose, or draw he would be hammered in a hour.

Beans, the craftiest drunk I have ever known.

Josh on the other hand got real cagey. Always a little hyper, he turned into a first time expectant father on meth as soon as he entered the place. He began rubbing his hands together like some cold weather quarterback executing a two minute drill. All the while craning his neck to view "the action" as he called it.

He walked away. Over his shoulder he mumbled for us to leave him alone, he would catch up with us later.

Suitcase and Mole just nodded.

"What's with Josh?" I asked.

"Nothing really. He is really superstitious. He gets weird in a casino. He will only play by himself and doesn't want anyone watching. Says it will jinx him." Mole answered. "Let him go. Different strokes for different folks. Let him walk to the beat of his own drum. We will catch up later."

"You and your dad come with me, I don't roll like Josh. I *need* an audience for luck. Let's play some craps. Josh will be around when he's busted. Don't you worry, but I'm feeling lucky." He turned to the face the tables.

"I FEEL LUCKY TODAY!" Suitcase bellowed.

Everyone turned to look. A few people cheered. One guy raised his drink as a toast. Some elderly folks whispered amongst themselves and hurriedly cashed out their machines to get away from the loud drunk guy.

Suitcase played off it.

"That's right, you osteoporosis mamas—out of old Suitcase's way. You are takin' up my oxygen! I'm a gambling man and I came to roll some bones not look at 'em!"

We made our way to a table. On the way Mole slipped me fifty bucks. "Here, have some fun, sorry about yesterday," he said.

"What about you?" I asked. "Don't you want to play?"

I tried to hand back the money.

"No. I'm not one for the games. I'd rather go out and watch the ocean. But I'll stay awhile, Suitcase is usually pretty entertaining. Watch."

He motioned for me to stand next to him by the craps table.

He was certainly right about Suitcase. Mole's old buddy might have been shy with women but he was pure extroverted entertainment on the craps table.

He jumped right in.

Like some carnival sideshow pitchman he began a playful banter with everyone around him. Starting first with the casino workers, everyone from the drink lady to the pit boss got dragged in.

He ribbed them about the dice, about the betting limits, about the drinks not being strong enough, he even commented about the Roman motif in the worker's uniforms. After that comment he looked over at us and said, "Bet you didn't think I even knew what the word 'motif' was, did you college boy?"

Mole cheered and clapped for his friend. "Look out! The Suitcase is packed," he joked.

The excitement he was generating was contagious. In addition to the enthusiasm he was also starting to get lucky. Nothing like a loud, fun, lucky guy in a casino.

Soon he had the dice **and** the crowd in the palm of his hand.

It was exciting.

Mole handed him some money.

Seeing this, I handed Mole back the fifty.

"You sure Stevie?" he asked.

"Give it to him, he's on a roll," I said. He shrugged and handed the bill to his friend.

"Let's get a drink," I said, flagging a waitress.

Mole smiled and said "Make it a double, I'm safe to drink since we are no where near a boat today."

I laughed and ordered. "Hey, I'm sorry about yesterday too."

"I needed a bath. Ancient history." Mole added.

It was two hours before Suitcase left the table. Mole and I drank the whole time.

I looked for Josh when I went to the bathroom but never saw him.

Beans had gotten flagged for not playing enough for the amount of free drinks he ordered. Apparently, some nosy security guard watched Beans pretend to put quarters in the slots every time a waitress walked by. As soon as he would order, he would stop pretending to play and would instead turn and watch his neighbor play. This was fine with the waitresses who liked his tips and his flirting. It was not okay with the old lady who claimed to the security guard that not only was the drunk guy next to her not playing, but the he had pinched her ass too.

The security guards had acted quickly.

"No extra charge for the grope. That ass hasn't been touched like that since The Civil War!" Beans had yelled on his way out.

With Suitcase fifteen hundred bucks up, and Beans on a boardwalk bench taking in the sights, it was time to leave.

We needed to find Josh.

We didn't need to look far.

He was in the casino lounge with a smile on his face and a little asian girl on his arm.

"Well, well well. If it's not the feuding boat captain and his drunk naked first mate. You boys made up proper now?" he teased.

He was flush. With booze and money it seemed.

Pointing to the girl he bellowed "Yu He here is my good luck charm."

He kissed her neck.

"I know I like to play by myself," he continued.

She giggled at his comment.

He laughed then corrected "I said play *by* myself not *with* myself, you fresh little girl."

He gave her another wet sloppy kiss.

"I had lost for an hour straight. She came and stood by my side and I won two grand. Gave my partner here five hundred."

He pulled her close and kissed her again.

"She works at an Asian bathouse around the corner.

What say? My treat!"

"Just the kind of happy ending I predicted!" Suitcase said.

We scooped up Beans and followed the prostitute out of the casino and down the boardwalk.

She led us off the boards and to her place of employment a couple blocks off the main drag. It was a big rambling two story brick building that stretched almost half a block. It originally looked to have been separate buildings, but over the years they had been connected by a series of additions and renovations. The different building ages and styles gave it a ramshackle look that made it stick out from amongst the glass and steel of the casinos down the street.

The first floor housed a family restaurant and the second floor had from the outside, what looked like office suites.

It was to these upstairs 'offices' that the girl led us.

We were buzzed in through a locked door by a Korean madam. We climbed a flight of stairs, and were buzzed through yet another door.

"Welcome! I know you," the old crone at the door lied in her broken English.

She looked over at Josh's girl and gave her a smile as if to say good fishing, or perhaps, job well done.

The girl excused herself and walked out.

"I be back," she said.

The old lady led us into a little waiting room with a number of hallways leading off. In each hallway there were three or four rooms with doors positioned on each side. A large television blared in the corner.

Magazines—*Sports Illustrated*, *People* and some Asian version of *Playboy* or something were fanned out on a couple of coffee tables positioned throughout the waiting room.

A man in a suit sat patiently read a magazine while he waited for his appointment.

The place looked like a medical clinic or a large dental practice, I thought as I entered. I smiled and looked over at Suitcase.

He must have read my mind because he laughed and said in his best Asian accent, "Hey Joe, you want the body exam, or you want the oral work?"

Then again, his comments applied equally to a washy-washy house too.

The waiting business man looked up, checked his watch and went back to his magazine.

He no sooner went back to reading when the mama-san came back and led him to a room down the hall.

He disappeared behind a closed door.

She returned with a tray of tiny cans of beer.

Beans jumped up from his chair and grabbed four.

"The little Chinese beers! I have been in whorehouses on three continents. You show me an Asian bath house and I will show you the little beers," he said and quickly guzzled one.

The old lady handed me one.

Budweiser. It was all of maybe six ounces.

I had seen pony bottles before but this was a miniature can. To this day, I have never seen another. Maybe Beans was right, maybe they are manufactured solely for the Asian prostitution rings.

Who knows?

She smiled and bowed then took the empty tray and walked out. You could hear her barking orders in some foreign tongue. Her machine gun bursts of Korean or whatever it was reminded me of the Russian Roulette Scene in *The Deer Hunter*. I made a mental note to rent the flick when I got home.

My mind raced.

What had I got myself into?

We waited like high school football players before a big game.

Instead of a coach's pep talk I got Josh.

"Now remember Stevie, when they come out, don't waste too much time pickin. The longer you take, the less chance you have of snagging a Thai, like mine. If you don't pick quick, you will get stuck with a panface," he said as he paced back and forth.

He made a face, looked quickly around to make sure none of the girls heard, then went on, "I mean Koreans are cute but the Thai chicks are smoking," he continued like some perverted Vince Lombardi. I half expected him to say 'Screwing isn't everything it's the only thing'. Instead, he took a little beer and drained it.

Finally he sat.

After about ten minutes the Old wise women reappeared. She carried another tray of beers. This time she also led a group of young Asian girls behind her. They were all dressed in bras and panties or bikinis. They were all gorgeous. It looked like an Miss China bathing suit competition, or a 'wrap' party from some kung fu movie.

Josh was right. Before I could even figure out what was what, the veteran bath house birders had sprung into action.

Josh was first. In addition to his girl YuHe he also took a smaller beauty standing shyly behind her.

Suitcase was almost as fast. He went right for a long haired girl with a thin face and almond eyes. Beans was going for her too

"Beat you to her Beans. You are getting long in the tooth. This young buck is taking over the herd," Suitcase joked as the girl led him off down the hall.

Beans didn't miss a beat. "Why run down the hill and fuck one when I can walk down and fuck em all," he joked back. "You are wasting energy that can be better spent elsewhere, Suitcase old boy."

He grabbed the next girl and sauntered away.

Mole and I still sat in the chair.

"I'm not much for professionals son," he said fidgeting in his chair.

"Don't worry dad, who did you used to imitate from that TV show—Hogan's Heroes? Sergeant Shultz?" I put on my best German accent. "I know nothing! I see nothing! I say nothing!"

He laughed and got up.

"What about you? I will if you will," he said walking over to the three remaining girls.

"Guess I would be letting down the team if I didn't give it my best college try," I said, also getting up and walking across the room.

The old lady gave me a toothless grin.

I studied the remaining girls. Josh's selection pep talk did have some truth.

The remaining girls were not as tall as the girls picked by Josh and Beans. They were beautiful but their faces were a little rounder and their bodies a bit more stout. Hardly the 'pan faces' Josh had exaggerated, but definitely very different from the Thai girls.

"Take your pick," Mole said smiling.

A pretty girl in a yellow bikini caught my eye. She smiled as I grabbed her hand. She led me to a room in the back.

The room was a nondescript square with a double bed, a closet and a small bathroom. It had a small refrigerator on the floor.

The girl retrieved two little beers from the fridge and handed me one. She looked at herself in the full length mirror that was against the one wall, and then motioned for me to get on the bed.

I nervously followed her direction.

I immediately had second thoughts.

She apparently spoke no English, however she did get out, "You want party?"

When I did not respond she said, "How bout massage?"

I did not want to 'party' but maybe only a massage would be okay.

A quick message to the reader: There is no such thing as 'only a massage' in an Asian bathhouse. The washy—washy is all sex, all the time, twenty four seven.

I figured this out quickly when she began to pull off my pants. She magically produced a hot towel that she tried to use to bath my junk.

I pulled my pants back up. "No, No. I just want massage." I squeaked out.

I noticed that I spoke broken and loud English as though that would make me easier to understand.

She laughed and said, "Bwow job?"

Now it was my turn to laugh. "No blow job. Just massage," I answered.

She smiled.

I had no idea whether she understood anything I was saying.

She pushed me onto the bed.

I rolled over to my stomach. For some reason, I was now resolved to only get a massage.

I motioned for her to rub my back.

She did.

What talented fingers!

I began to loosen up and enjoy her as she massaged my back and shoulders. Periodically she would work her way down my legs. When she did I would begin to get excited. I began to reconsider my decision to get just a massage.

As I wrestled with these thoughts, I opened my eyes and looked over to the far wall.

There, lying on the bed, was a slightly overweight ruddy white college boy with a receding hairline and a receding dick.

Really. The guy had a bad excuse for a cock. In fact it looked like a tuna can or a portabella mushroom or something.

The guy was getting ready for sex with a stranger that didn't even speak his own language.

For a second I was shocked, I mean I had private room!

A split second later I realized it was me—in the mirror.

Jesus. I looked ridiculous!

Cold feet? No, I had worse—Cold cock. I was cold cocked all right.

I jumped up from the bed and hurried into with my clothes.

The girl was in a panic.

"No, No, Joe stay. I love you long time. Me so horny."

She was breaking out all her broken English to get me to stay. Now I really felt like I was in *The Deer Hunter*.

"It's okay. I still pay. Me *no* horny," I brayed like an idiot. "Good massage, good girl," I babbled.

I broke away and went back to the waiting room.

No one else was there.

I sat down and grabbed the TV remote. I hoped she wouldn't follow.

I opened a beer I took from the tray on the table.

The old lady started yelling at the girl, then they both appeared.

"You not happy. I get other girl. We have wots," she said butchering lots.

"No, I happy. Girl good. I bad. I tired. No good. No boom boom."

As an after thought I pointed to my dick.

I felt like Tarzan describing his erectile dysfunction.

"You still pay," she said tiring quickly of trying to please me.

"I still pay. When Josh—san here," I said warming to my broken English.

Satisfied, she left the room.

I settled in to wait for the others.

I could hear the girl laughing and talking with the other girls who had not been picked by the birders or the other client.

I turned to the TV.

As I channel surfed, I began to get a little homesick. I tried to put it out of my head.

My mind wandered again.

What am I gay? I briefly thought. Passing on a beautiful young Asian prostitute? Especially one that is bought and paid for?

No, I'm just not in to pros, just like Mole, I thought.

"I just want to be held," I said out loud, then laughed.

I looked up.

The girl had returned to the room. With her were two others. They were just as cute. Since they were not working they were dressed in silk kimonos. They brought me more beers and sat down around me.

I turned back to the television. I had switched on an old film channel.

I recognized the movie right away. *Old Yeller*. One of my favorites.

You know the story. Classic Disney.

Young boy adopts a stray dog. His older brother doesn't like it. Eventually, after the dog saves them from various dangers, the brother warms up to the dog.

I started watching. The girls settled in around me.

"This movie is the best," I said to my new best friends. They smiled and bowed.

"Old Yeller—a great flick" I tried again.

"Oh yewer?" my girl said with a confused look on her face.

"No. Old Yeller," I slowly repeated. "He is a dog. The little boy's best friend," I explained.

They nodded in complete agreement.

Who was I kidding. They couldn't understand one word I was saying.

"You have no clue what I'm talking about do you. Jeez, you guys *eat* dogs don't you?" I said smiling and nodding back.

The girls smiled again. One repeated "No cwue, No cwue."

At least they were trying.

I went back to the movie.

The birders might be a while I thought.

I settled in with the little beer, the Asian girls and *Old Yeller.*

The movie was on for about twenty minutes. Despite some periodic noises from the rooms that distracted me, I began to get into the flick. It was *Old Yeller* after all; one of the best movies of my childhood.

Even though it was in English, I noticed the girls were watching as well. They seemed to be even more into it than I. All of them watched intently.

They cheered when the dog saved the boy from the attacking bear. They let out a collective groan when Yeller was blamed for stealing food. Occasionally, they would look over to me as though I might tell them what was going to happen next.

I didn't even bother to try.

"Watch it. It's Old Yeller—great movie," I said.

Besides, it was getting to the point when Old Yeller was about to die. You remember, when he saves the kid from the wolf, only to get rabies from it? You know, the older brother Travis has to shoot the dog to protect the family from rabies and to put the poor dog out of it's misery.

Well maybe it was my homesickness, maybe I was just tired, or maybe, just maybe, it was the enduring power of *Old Yeller.*

Before I knew what was happening, I found myself crying like a pussy. The tears just poured out. No matter what I tried, I couldn't stop sobbing.

I felt like some premenstrual bridesmaid at her best friend's wedding.

It was embarrassing. But, let's face it, if you have seen the movie you're probably welling up at the memory right now too.

I tried to hide my face from the girls.

First, I bail on sex, then I'm crying over a Disney flick?

I might as well turn on *Queer Eye For the Straight Guy*, I thought.

Thankfully, neither Mole nor the other birders had finished up yet. No one saw me.

It was just my sorry crying ass, and three Asian whores.

"I'm sorry but this movie always gets me," I tearfully tried to explain.

The girl I was with got up and gave me a hug. She stayed in the chair with me. I looked away from the screen. The other girls were still riveted to the set. They didn't even notice me. They sat, glued to the television.

I noticed that they were crying too. Now, my girl began to ball.

"Ohhh Ywer dead?" she asked, tears streaming down her face.

"Yes, Old Yeller died. The boy had to do it. It was the only way," I blubbered, falling back into her arms.

Now it was my turn to cheer up the whores.

"But watch, it is ok," I said pulling myself somewhat together and pointing to the TV. "He gets another puppy. It's okay."

I patted the girl on the shoulder. "Now, now. It's not so bad."

It was no use.

They all began to cry louder. "Ohh Yewer! Ohh Yewer!" they wailed. They began to carry on like my Italian great aunts at a stranger's funeral. I'm talking professional mourner shit. Flailing arms, faces buried in pillows. One girl even started to hit herself.

Damn, I thought it was only the middle eastern women who did that.

I had to stop them.

"Girls, it has a happy ending!" I yelled above the crying. "He gets another dog!"

It was no use. They were inconsolable.

Then the wise old women reappeared. "You want Happy ending?" she began having caught the tail end of my conversation.

She looked at the girls.

She didn't give me a grin this time. She was obviously not happy.

"What you do?" She shouted. "You hurt girls?"

"No it was Old Yeller, I swear!"

I pointed wildly at the television.

"Old Yeller!"

She looked at the TV. A commercial for Crazy Eddie's Appliances was on.

Now she looked at me like I was crazy.

"You get out. You bad man. Crazy man. Old Yeller leave!"

She started to push me toward the door.

"I'm not Old Yeller, I'm Steve. Old Yeller is a dog," I stammered. 'No, he is a movie! I swear. I didn't do anything."

The girls sat bawling. They didn't lift a finger to help.

No explanation.

No translation.

Before I knew it, she had kicked me to the curb.

I staggered down the steps and into the street.

Kicked out of a Washy-Washy.

All because of the power of *Old Yeller*.

Sad.

The birders caught up with me later in the restaurant down stairs. Needless to say they thought I had wigged out or something. Between the girls' hysterics and the Mama-san's anger, they thought I might have killed someone.

It was two hours and almost gallon of Jack Daniels later before I was finally able to adequately explain the circumstances that let to my bouncing.

I bet they still don't believe me.

We all had a good laugh though.

I swear, if I ever see the movie again, I will no doubt find myself uttering two butchered English words under my breath—'Ohh Yewer. Ohh Yewer.'

And I bet I will still cry like a pussy.

Murph
Smoking

Mobodog

Chapter 31

On a sandy slumber, a guaranteed cure for a hangover and a phat ride

We were smashed by the time we left the restaurant. If it was a family restaurant it wasn't after we were done. We were so drunk and loud, and we were laughing so hard about Old Yeller and the crying Asian Whores, it's a wonder we weren't kicked out.

We staggered to Suitcase's car.

That's the last thing I remember.

I woke up early to the sound of the ocean. We were on the beach. At least some of us were. I glanced around and saw Beans and Suitcase. No Mole and no Josh. We looked like we were escaped convicts from a drunk tank or hungover castaways washed ashore from some shipwrecked party boat. In hind sight we must have looked even worse than that. I mean, what's could be worse than passing out plastered on a beach?

My mouth felt like each tooth was wearing it's own dirty little sweat sock. My head screamed for help from the tiny miners that were excavating my brain.

It was that bad.

Fortunately for us, it was so early in the morning, the only people out were joggers and the occasional bicyclist.

We were alone with our hangovers.

As I began to focus, I realized it wouldn't be long before the crowds would show up for the all you can eat breakfast buffets at the boardwalk diners.

I tried to get it together.

I ran my fingers through my hair, and tucked in my shirt. I brushed off the sand and the salt as best as I could.

It didn't make much of a difference.

As we sat there gathering our wits, Josh and my father came walking down the boards. If they were hurtin from the night before they didn't show it. The only sign of their slumber was they walked with the stiffness of middle aged men who had spent the night passed out in a car.

"Good morning lads," Mole said greeting us. To Josh he added, "Would these boys be flotsam or jetsam?"

They carried four large Wawa coffees on a takeout coffee tray, along with a half a gallon of orange juice, some Danish, a bunch of bananas and a big bottle of V-8 juice.

"What the hell you got there?" Suitcase asked reaching for a coffee.

"Health foods?! Where is the grease? Give me a McMuffin or at least some bacon when I'm hung over," he complained.

"Don't forget the Advil, and some smokes," Josh added throwing a small bag to Suitcase.

Suitcase took the cigarettes like Sally Struthers grabbing a Care package.

Mole frowned.

"You don't need grease or any pain relievers. V-8, a banana and plenty of H-2O could probably cure cancer. For fook sake, it certainly can kick a couple of hangovers in the ass."

He looked over to Josh.

"Advil and cigarettes, now that is what I call a breakfast of champions" he shook his head then took a chug of V-8.

Josh surveyed Beans and Suitcase.

He reminded me of Donald Sutherland playing a phony general looking over the troops in the *Dirty Dozen*. He exaggeratedly scanned them from head to toe and jokingly pointed out Beans' missing flip flops and Suitcase's unkempt hair, which he referred to as "beach head". When he finished his review he let out a loud whistle and remarked, "Mole, I do think we made the wise decision to sleep in the car. It may have been a little cramped, but damn, look at these boys. The beach has gone and kicked their asses!" He finished and handed Beans a coffee.

I got up and grabbed the V-8 and a Banana. One thing is for sure, when someone with Mole's drinking experience tells you the cure for a hangover, you listen up.

You know what?

He was right. Just for insurance, I took an Advil too. I mean Josh was no slouch in the drinking department either. Might as well listen to them both.

I skipped the cigarettes.

We sat, drinking our coffee and curing our hangovers.

A lone tractor made it's way down the beach. The driver was lost in the music on his Walkman. Behind him, he dragged a large rake. He was grooming the sand for the day's beachgoers, ridding the beach of the trash and cigarette butts of the previous day. The beach looked like it was getting a shave and a haircut.

Mole seeing the tractor observed, "A new day. It looks like it is going to be a good one. We have plenty of dough and The World Series of Birding beckons. Look, the beach is getting cleaned up. We should follow it's lead and find a bathhouse or go rent a cheap hotel off the island so we can shower up before we head to Cape May."

No one moved. We sat sipping coffee and watched the beach wake up.

The ocean of course never slept.

Mole was the only one who was chipper. The rest of us were surly from the hangovers and our recent sleeping arrangements. We were not ready for such unbridled enthusiasm.

As he spoke, he began to clean up the trash from our Wawa break.

The seagulls began to gather around us looking for their breakfast. Where there is one there are bound to be a hundred. Their loud calls as they bickered for the scraps acted as our final wake up call. They also must have drawn attention to us.

We had been alone on the beach. Now, I felt a strange sensation that we were being watched.

I scanned the boardwalk. Sure enough, there above us sat a whole, big fat American family. Father, mother, two kids and an ancient grandmother. All of them with one common denominator; they were huge. I'm talking morbidly obese.

They must have gotten up early to take advantage of the breakfast buffet advertised at Uncle Bill's Pancake House situated on the boardwalk about twenty yards down from our night's sleeping quarters.

Each one sat gawking at us.

What was amazing about these fatties wasn't their weight; almost everyone in America is overweight. No, what was unique about this family was that they were completely comfortable with their obesity.

They were so resigned to their condition that each one rode a handicap scooter!

Together, they looked like an outlaw, sumo biker gang.

While I understand that bikers call their Harley Motorcycles hogs, these bikers **were** hogs.

It was ridiculous.

You could tell from their faces they were appalled to see grown men sleeping on the beach. They were more disgusted by us than we were of them. They were so close we could hear snippets of their conversations between the wave breaks. Short stacks and bottomless coffee mugs figured prominently in their discussion.

Beans must have followed my view because he was the next to notice.

Not good.

Remember, Beans laughed at cripples.

Who am I kidding. He laughed *and* pointed at the handicapped.

I acted quickly to head him off at the pass.

"Easy Beaner. Those folks are just out for a little family breakfast is all. No need to comment on their mode of transportation," I said delicately.

Beans laughed and shook his head. "A little breakfast my ass," he murmured under his breath. "That family ain't having nothing little."

He got up to relieve himself under the boardwalk. When the family realized Beans was pissing, they let out a groan. The fat husband, the leader of the fat pack yelled out, "Excuse me mister, but there are ladies present!"

Beans who had thus far contained himself, now yelled back, "Where? All I see are a couple of Sherman tanks with tits!"

To us he muttered, "Since when did the handicap scooter become the preferred mode of transportation for the obese?"

He turned to the family and yelled "The only handicap you have is you eat too much! Handicap scooters are for cripples and the elderly—not fat slobs."

"I beg your pardon sir," the man said in disbelief.

"Take a hike!" Mole said joining in. "No, really—take a hike. You might just lose a few. Since when did our country's citizens start to look like Bulgarians?"

Now the faucet was turned on full blast. All the Birders started.

Suitcase turned and yelled, "Quick get the pod of beached whales back in the ocean before they get baked by the sun."

Josh's contribution was "Hey, when you stand in the corner by yourself do they tell you to break it up?"

Mole came back with "Do you wear 'wide load' designer jeans?"

I should have been embarrassed, instead I found myself blurting out, "Cut your toenails and you can drop ten pounds!"

Beans continued to pile on. "Hey buddy when you're old lady backs up does she go 'beep—beep—beep?'"

Suitcase followed up with "Instead of bellybutton lint I bet you have a whole ball of yarn in that cavern of a naval."

Josh, trying to top it added, "Looks like you got two asses—a front and a back! A Frass. Get it? A front ass!"

The man was mortified.

The poor family looked around for help, but it was too early for the beach patrol. They were alone.

The father, realizing he was dealing with madmen turned his portly posse around and headed towards the restaurant. The sound of their scooters echoed off the boardwalk.

Over his shoulder he feebly yelled back.

"That's discrimination. I will have you know—I have a thyroid condition!"

"Yea, your thighs look like they are on roids alright! That is quite a condition!" Beans said, not letting it go.

Hearing this, the rest of his family sped up and continued to look back as though we would give chase. They kept up until they pulled off for the Pancake house.

As they got out of earshot, our hung over wrath next turned to Beans.

"You got nerve Walsh," Josh said. "You are not exactly a thin man you know. How dare you tease a nice fat family on their way to feed their fat faces." He laughed, then continued. "Check out your own belly. You haven't seen your dick since Nixon was President."

"An interesting choice," Mole interrupted. "Nixon's nick name was 'Tricky Dick'.

It is only fitting that you are describing Beans' penis, certainly a tricky dick if there ever was one."

"You might think of getting your own fat person scooter, you know Beans?" Suitcase added.

Beans laughed.

"Well can you two assholes tell me if my tricky dick is still present and accounted for under my Milwaukee Tumor. That chink chick did a number on my package that's for sure. Nothing like a long ride on the Orient Express to remind you of your manhood."

He stuck his pelvis out and pretended to try and look for his dick over his belly. He craned his neck in the exaggerated effort.

"Shit, I know it's down there somewhere. I feel a brush burn on my German Helmet. Boys, don't make me sprain my neck. Is it there or not?"

We laughed, but Beans was just warming up.

"I hate fat people even more than retards," Beans explained cruelly. "Retards don't have a choice. They are born that way. But fat people, I mean really fat people, they do have a choice. They **choose** to be fat. No ifs ands or big butts about it. No wonder our country is going to hell in a hand basket. If we can't take care of our own bodies, how can we take care of our world."

"So according to Beans' theory we are losing control of our bodies and therefore losing control of our world. It follows then that as the American people get larger, our influence as a world power will get smaller?" Mole said attempting to summarize.

Josh added "Well, if that is true than that handicap scooter family is turning our country into a Haiti or a Uruguay or some other irrelevant banana republic."

Everyone laughed at the thought.

Mole must have felt guilty about our cruel tirade. He shook his head and raised his hand to signal he wanted to speak.

"Speaking of the Scooter family, once again Beans' propensity for linguistic cruelty never ceases to amaze me. It is truly mean spirited and nasty, yet strangely contagious. We were like some kind of pecking party with the way we all piled on that poor family."

He continued. "Our portly voyeurs may have been a bit too nosy but they did not deserve the verbal mugging they endured from the likes of some hung over beach bums. What say we pony up a paltry portion of our winnings and hike down to the Pancake Emporium to pay there breakfast bill? An olive branch if you will."

"If you put French dressing on it they will eat it like a salad no doubt," Suitcase joked.

"Enough with the fat jokes. We need good Karma for the Bird Series. Give me a few bucks for their breakfast," Mole said.

He looked over and signaled for me to pass the hat.

I passed my baseball cap around.

The Birders all kicked in.

I gave Mole the money and watched him jog down the boardwalk toward the pancake house.

Beans yelled out, "We don't have enough money for their tab!"

Suitcase and Josh gave him a look that said, enough already.

He must have got the message because he then yelled out, "Tell them I'm sorry."

To Mole he yelled, "We will meet you at the car."

He looked over at us. "There, you happy?"

We walked back to the car.

Mole caught up with us in the parking lot.

"So, were the two ton family happy with our peace offering?" Suitcase asked as we piled back into the car.

As he spoke, I couldn't help but notice old Lucille smelled like booze and bad breath, like the odor of a cheap fleabag hotel after a big night. I guess that's what the old Impala was the night before.

"Boys, I chose to remain anonymous. The gesture is more important for our peace of mind than for any recognition we would receive from the Large family. I paid the waitress in advance and skedaddled back here. The wrong is righted," Mole finished. He began to make himself a screwdriver.

We pulled out and headed for the Garden State Parkway and the last stop on the line; Cape May New Jersey and The World Series of Birding.

Chapter 32

Of a concrete shipwreck and diamonds in the sand. A needle in the Road and how the boozers almost took the World Series of Birding

Cape May is at the southern most tip of the Garden State. Originally it was a small fishing village. Over the years it has grown into a large seaside town, but unlike its northern cousin Atlantic City, it never lost its quaintness nor its property values.

The town's year round residents are an eclectic bunch. Sweater wearing granola types, bed and breakfast owners who gave up the rat race, middle aged college professors, and bifocaled old gay couples. Mixed in with these diverse groups were old school fisherman and their families who still managed to scrape out a living from their clam and scallop boats.

Together, this mixed bag all shared the town. Many of them often drank beers and gossiped at the local tappies that dotted the main strip.

With names like The Nor'easter or the Ugly Mug the bars conjured up another time. A time of perhaps Melville or *Two Years Before the Mast.*

The place seemed to balance the old and the new. The conventional and the quirky. Like other 'end of the line' places in the U.S.—Cape Cod, Key West, and San Francisco, Cape May collected the odd, the individualist, the free spirits and the gay. Cape May had them all.

It was from this varied group of people that the World series of Birding was hatched as it were. Over the years it has grown into a big,

big tourist attraction. Birders from all over the east coast flock to the site (sorry again for the bad pun but the descriptions seem to flyout as I write.)

Enough already!

Suffice it to say, the World Series of Birding has become a big deal.

Mole and his friends had been coming to Cape May long before the Series had even been in place. They came because it was the least crowded Jersey beach. They came because it was cheap. Now they added the Birding Series to the list of reasons why Cape May was their favorite Jersey beach.

Most of all they came because of the Hostel.

The Hostel was just that. A group of no frills cabins centered around a shower house and a communal kitchen. It was low budget, took cash and was downright Ray Charles like in turning a blind eye to drinking and recreational drug use. The place not only turned a blind eye to drugs but its present owner, like Mr. Charles also appreciated his drugs

In other words the perfect sanctuary for the Birders.

It was owned by an old Delaware County family.

The Laughlins.

Mr. Laughlin had been a Westinghouse worker with Beans' father and Josh's uncle. Mr. Laughlin had been severely injured when an outside contractor accidentally dropped a steel plate on him as he walked to lunch at the plant.

He suffered massive injuries, including shattered ribs and a collapsed lung. His injuries landed him in intensive care for a month. He was in a doctor induced coma for two more. To top it all off he had a trach tube for four months.

Despite the seriousness of the injuries he somehow survived.

He had purchased the Hostel and the ten acres that surrounded the place with the settlement proceeds from his personal injury case. He retired from Westinghouse to run the place.

It didn't last.

Although the place was beautiful and the job of running it pretty easy, the constant wet salt air did a number on his damaged lungs.

He didn't last three years.

Josh related this background as we drove down the parkway.

"The amazing thing is he was a chain smoker," Josh said as he smoked his tenth cigarette of the day. "Laughlin smoked two packs a day since he was in the service. Even when he had the accident they would sneak him a pack in intensive care and he would smoke the damn things through his trach tube!" he said placing his own smoke at his throat and making an exaggerated sucking sound for effect.

"We get the picture," I said and playfully punched his arm.

He continued. "God is pretty sick. I mean the guy smokes two packs a day and has his lungs collapsed by a steel plate and he gets sick and dies from the salt air?"

"True story." he finished.

Now it was Beans' turn. "I agree that he died a few years after he bought the place, but it wasn't the salt air, it was most definitely the smoking and the accident that did him in. Cape May sea air is the best thing in the world for your health."

He tilted his head up and took in a deep breath.

He immediately began to cough.

"Inconclusive on both versions of the story," Mole said and laughed. "Is the cough because of the salt air or because Beans has been smoking like a coal mine fire since he was thirteen? The debate rages."

He turned back around and messed with the stereo. While he looked for music, Suitcase, who was driving, began to belt out *On The Way To Cape May*.

We all groaned and called for Mole to put something on the radio.

"Dad, if Josh and Beans' friend Laughlin is dead why are we going to this place anyway?" I asked, curious as to the connection.

Mole put in a home made Beach Boys mix. *Pet Sounds* with *Good Vibrations* and some early surf songs. *Sloop John B* started in.

"Cause Laughlin's son Chuckie runs the place now," Mole said then turned up the music. "The Road goes on forever," he muttered.

We drove through the toll at Wildwood.

After the music ended, Josh leaned up and said to Mole, "Do you really think the Road goes on forever? I mean, shit, the guy parties like Elvis. He might as well wear a white jump suit and scream, 'Cilla where are my Amphetamines?' Damn, the last time I was at the Hostel he snorted an eight ball and gobbled percs like they were candy. He was up for three days straight!"

Mole laughed. "He reminds me of Hunter S. Thompson if Hunter couldn't write. But look, if you went through what he did in Vietnam you would probably hit it hard too."

Suitcase just shook his head.

Beans, however, leaned up and said, "Your shittin me. He was doing drugs? Where was I? You know how I feel about that. Its bad enough with the wacky tobaccie, but hard drugs? He better not pull that crap on me. I won't stand for it, even if it is his place."

He took a deep drag of his Camel and a big gulp of beer.

"Who is the Road?" I asked, my curiosity getting the best of me.

"Roads," Mole corrected. "Or Graves if you are a veteran or he is in a good mood. He goes by a couple of handles."

Josh added, "Jack Laughlin's oldest kid. Chuckie Laughlin. Four kids and he was the only boy. Crazy fuck. I think your Dad's friend Dan Erickson served with him in Nam. He was a recon squad leader who was supposedly on a ton of missions. A real bad ass. He did two tours."

Mole nodded.

Josh went on. "On his second tour his squad got ambushed. Shot to shit. Him and one other guy survived, the rest were killed."

I interrupted. "Yea I saw this story. It was a flick, *The Deer Hunter*. Or was it *Platoon*?" I joked.

"You know I am a veteran . . . a veteran of Vietnam—movies. I have seen everything from *Boys in Company C* to *Coming Home* and *Apocalypse Now*. I served at the front lines of movie theatres all over the place. I haven't been in the shit but I have watched the shit! Many, many tours of duty. I wouldn't be surprised if I had Post traumatic stress disorder from watching Vietnam flicks."

"Enough funny guy, let Josh finish. You asked, now let him answer." Mole looked over at Josh to continue.

Josh smiled and continued, "For the record you ain't no veteran. The only war you may have ever served in was the Cola War—When Coke went head to head with Pepsi."

He laughed.

"Where was I? Right. Chuckie Laughlin. Well, after his squad was wiped out, the powers that be realized that Sergeant Laughlin should probably be rotated back away from the shit. He was, shall we say, a little battle fatigued."

Beans interrupted. "Get this. The brass sent him to the rear with the gear alright.

They gave him a nice calm, no stress job . . . Made him a body bagger."

"After seeing his men shot up, his reward? . . . Processing the bodies of all the others killed in action."

He spit out the side of the car. It immediately blew back.

"Gave him a promotion and a title; Master Sergeant. Director of the Soldier's Grave Reclamation and Identification Program," he finished and wiped spit off his face.

It was Mole's turn to run with the story.

"Leave it to the Army to come up with a title like that. All the other soldiers started to just call him 'Graves'. Well, as you could imagine he did not particularly like the title or the nickname. Plus, he was not nearly over the post traumatic stress disorder he suffered from his previous tour and the ambush.

So on leave in Saigon, one night after a two day load, he began to have his whole body tattooed as a map of Vietnam. The next day, instead of coming to his senses and realizing that he should leave well enough alone, you know, maybe not getting the tattoo finished, he embarked on filling in the map.

After a week's worth of sessions that cost a couple of paychecks, he had a pretty good road map of Nam, complete with all the providences and most of the major highways."

"Roads was born. He has been Roads ever since, although some of his Army buddies still call him Graves too."

Finished, Mole turned back to the music.

"What should I call him?" I asked.

"I would stick with Roads. Or maybe a simple greeting of Hi, Way!" Suitcase said, then giggled.

"You been hittin the weed behind my back?" Mole asked Suitcase as he handed him another beer.

Suitcase ignored the comment but paid attention to the beer.

He looked at me through the rearview mirror and said, "Anyway he is a good guy. Let's just say he is pretty liberal in his attitude concerning drug use. Not to mention he doesn't usually charge us for the stay, ever since your Dad did him a favor and carpeted his mother's house in Cape May Point."

We pulled off the Garden State Parkway at the Cape May Point exit.

It was a beautiful day. If we were going to waste it nursing hangovers it might as well be at the shore.

"Whadda ya think, should we head over to the Hostel, or should we check out the bird refuge and get our registration in?" Josh asked as we crossed the bridge into the Cape.

I was still hurtin from the night before, I certainly wasn't up for any major exertion. "Why don't we head down to the cement ship and look for Cape May Diamonds like when I was a kid?" I suggested.

For some reason I always get sentimental in Cape May.

"You remember that?" Mole asked.

"Shit yea. You and Suitcase took me there when I was little. I thought it was great, searching the beach for the polished stones and colored rocks. Only now do I realize it was a way to occupy me while you both slept off your hangovers on the beach," I answered and reached for my first beer of the day.

Both my dad and Suitcase feigned ignorance.

"No way, we never did anything of the sort. We love it there. It is beautiful." Suitcase protested. "What about the old World War Two lookout tower? That's even cooler than the cement ship. Do you remember that Stevie?" he continued.

Josh interrupted. "Hey Mole, you're the professor. What is the deal with the cement ship. It has been sunk there at Cape May Point for as long as I can remember. You know anything about it?"

"Suitcase you might as well head over that way. The registration for the Series is at the Cape May Wildlife refuge nearby. We can kill two birds with one stone. Although again, that might not be an appropriate cliché given the circumstances," Mole said. "You guys good with that?" he added.

"I don't care what we do but I could use a little nap. If we are going to be with Roads tonight I want to be at my top drinking form," Josh offered.

Suitcase turned Lucille toward the point. Taking control, he said "I will drop you guys off at the cement ship. Then I will head over and register us for the Series, pick up some booze and food for tonight, and check in with Roads. Hopefully I can dump the boat with him. I will swing back afterwards and grab you guys."

"Mole you didn't answer Josh's question. What is the deal with the sunken ship? Is it really cement? How did it get there?" I asked, now curious about something I remembered since I was little.

Suitcase maneuvered the old Impala into the Point's parking lot as Mole began to explain, "The cement ship is the wreck S.S. Atlantus. It sunk in 1926. It was one of a number of experimental ships built for use during World War One. It is indeed constructed of concrete. The other famous one being the Palto Alto on the west coast. Obviously, they proved to be impractical due to their tremendous weight. They were used as troop transports and to ferry supplies during the war. After the war the Atlantus was purchased by a business man to be part of a dock to anchor the Cape May side of the New Jersey to Delaware ferry. Before it could be put in place it came loose from its moorings during a storm and sunk off the Point. Due to its weight, it could not be salvaged. It has been there ever since. Although it has broken up pretty badly since I was a kid."

"A cement ship? What rocket scientist designed that? Jeez it's a wonder we won the war," I joked.

"Me and your dad used to dive off it when we were teenagers," Beans commented as he got out of the now parked car.

"Yea, but since someone drowned they won't let you near it," Josh added.

"Between the cement ship, the old World War Two watch tower and those quartz pebbles on the beach—the Cape May Diamonds, the place is a regular tourist attraction. You can hang out, get some lunch at the snack bar and maybe take a swim later," Beans said.

"Or take a snooze," Josh added.

"Get the cooler and the blanket in the trunk. I will be back later," Suitcase said.

We all got out and grabbed our gear.

Josh, my dad and I headed for the beach. Suitcase and Beans left to register us and run their errands.

We set up our stuff on the beach.

Josh settled in for his nap. That left Mole and I to ourselves. We found a nice spot away from Josh in an area that had some soft sand and not as many of the Cape May diamonds, which were nothing but little colored pebbles not yet pounded to sand by the waves.

It was a nice place. We sat right down on the sand.

We stared out at the sunken ship, that over the years, we had probably looked out at a hundred times. It looked the same. The beach looked the same. The whole place looked the same. It will probably always look the same.

But this time something was different. *We* were different. I felt it.

If Mole did too, he didn't say anything.

We let the beach take our thoughts.

The minutes passed. I heard a little girl yell out to her dad that she had found a real diamond.

I heard the father laugh.

I listened to the waves crash.

Mole sat looking out at the ship.

Finally, without turning to look at me he began to speak. "You know, I'm really glad you came along. I don't know how many more times we will be able to do this," he paused, hesitating I guess, so as not to sound too sappy. He fumbled with a pebble at his feet, looked at it then threw it in the water.

"I know my drinking bothers you and I know it has put us at odds some times, and for that I'm sorry. We have had our ups and downs on this trip too. It didn't take a dunk in the bay for me to know how you felt a couple days back. But I want you to know I love you very much and I don't want you to hate me for the drinking. If you do, that's your right but I hope you don't," he paused.

I went to say something. He lifted his hand to stop me.

"Listen. I know it upsets you, the drinkin and all, but its not your problem and its not your responsibility. You have nothing to be ashamed of. You are a great kid and my behavior is no reflection on you. Stop being embarrassed by my actions. It is me, not you, that has the problem.

Let's just make sure it stays that way."

Again I went to say something. Maybe a plea for him to get it together, maybe just to tell him I loved him, I don't remember.

Whatever it was I didn't get to say it, because before I could speak he said, "Anyway, I hope you see that my love affair with bird watching is not just about my love affair with booze. I really do love it. The bird watching that is. You already know how I feel about the drink. In a way they both let me . . ." he hesitated again.

I waited, but the words didn't come.

The moment passed. So did the thought.

After a minute or so he said, "Go get the Bird book out of my bag. We have some studying to do."

I thought for a second to ask him what he was going to say. Instead, I got up and went to get his bag.

Josh slept soundly on the blanket as I found the stolen Swarthmore library book buried in the bottom of Mole's backpack. *Birds Of North America*. I carefully lifted the book from the bag so as to not wake Josh.

Who was I kidding?

He was out. I could have dropped the book on his head and it wouldn't have made a difference.

I looked at the book, the Swarthmore College stamp emblazoned on the spine. I had completely forgotten that he had taken it. I smiled to myself and thought of his comment that books can't be owned. Of course they can't Mole, not when you are around to steal them.

I carried the book and a couple of beers back to our spot up the beach from Josh.

As I walked back, I noticed Mole looking at me. He had an ear to ear grin, like some buzz drunk Alfred E. Neuman.

"What? Is my fly down or something?" I asked, checking my bathing suit to see if my package was hanging out.

I handed him a beer.

"Son I am very proud of you. Despite your crazy temper, that I attribute to your Mother's side, you are a damn good son. I wish that you would become a filmmaker or a writer like you used to want to be. I don't know what you are afraid of. You can always be average. Don't let your upbringing limit you or hold you back. Don't let small town attitudes dictate your choices in life. You can always go back to law school if it doesn't work out. But if you must become a lawyer, as you have mentioned on occasion, I hope you are a trial lawyer, arguing in front of a jury. Because you are a born actor. That's why I named you after James Dean. You would be great. When you were little you always talked your way out of trouble. Either by being clever or by being funny. Either way I couldn't get mad at you."

He went to hug me. For once I didn't say anything.

No wise ass remark.

No, 'Get off me homo!'

No backing off or stiffening up.

I just let him.

Who am I kidding, I hugged him back. I hugged him like I was never going to see him again.

On my favorite childhood beach, with my father. For the first time; not as a child but as a man.

I hugged my father, and he hugged me.

My memory tells me it lasted as long as an important moment like that should last. My memory freezes it, suspends it or at least draws it out and slows it down.

It lasted forever.

But memories lie. Because at the time important moments happen you don't realize they are important. You don't have the foresight to take a mental snapshot. You don't record the moment. So in reality it probably lasted as long as an awkward hug between a drunk father and his angry son could last.

A second. Maybe a few precious moments? Who knows. What I do know is that was the closest I ever felt to the Mole. To my father.

He broke the silence.

"Now let's study some birds. We have a Series to win," he said finally.

He reached for the library book.

"Thanks Swarthmore College. Your book is going to carry us to victory!"

He sat back down in the sand and began to teach me.

We quizzed each other on every species. All the shore birds we were likely to encounter. The raptors and the wrens. The ducks and the doves. And we didn't stop there.

Mole knew them all.

He drummed all of them into my increasingly beer soaked head. We drained more than a few beers.

I was having a blast.

Before I knew it Beans and Suitcase were back.

Josh was still in a coma on the blanket.

"Well did you boys have some father and son special time?" Beans teased.

He began to pack up the cooler and the bags. He poured a beer on Josh.

"Drip drop in the bucket mother fuck it," Josh yelled. He obviously was not asleep anymore. "Don't waste the beer! I'm awake. Goddamnit."

He got up and wiped his beer soaked face on Beans' shirt.

Beans playfully slap boxed him.

Mole walked down to the water and dove in.

While he swam Suitcase pulled me aside. "How did it go?" He said seriously.

Playing dumb I answered, "How did what go?"

"Don't mess with me wiseass. You know what I what I'm talking about. You and your old man. Well?" He glanced down to the water to make sure Mole was out of earshot, "Did you get along?"

"We're cool."

"We're cool? Don't be a punk. Did you talk or what?" Suitcase pressed. "Don't shit me," he added like an exclamation point.

"I'm sorry Suitcase. I'm not trying to be difficult. We talked. Let's just say it was much better than the last time we were at the beach together. And his balls did not get sunburned. Thanks for asking."

"What's with the Bird book?" Josh interrupted looking at the hardback in my hand.

"Mole and I have been studying. He has it in mind to win the Series this year," I answered, relieved to be saved from Suitcase.

"Well the Series isn't until tomorrow, Tonight we take to the Roads!" Josh said.

Turning to the beach he yelled, "Let's go Mole, the Road beckons!"

Mole got out of the ocean and walked back up to the blanket.

"Nice dip in the drink is just the thing to get me going," he said as he toweled himself off. "Let's get over to the Hostel, I'm hungry," he continued.

We packed up the rest of our stuff and drove off.

In the rearview mirror I saw the Atlantic's tireless waves crashing onto the wreck of the concrete ship the S.S. Atlantus. Seagulls were perched on its bow, seemingly trapped, like sailors on a desert isle. It was no wonder the ship had broken up since Mole was a kid. The constant pounding of the drink was slowly wearing the old ship down.

Some day it will disappear, I thought.

We drove around a bend and it was gone.

/////////////////////////

The Hostel was about two miles up the road from the Point. We pulled in around dinner time. I remember, because the big communal kitchen was in full bloom. Like some hippy bees' nest the whole cinder block building bustled with people getting prepared to eat. College kids with their hot dogs and hamburgers. Young families with pots of spaghetti and sausage. Still others with nothing more than sliced Jersey tomatoes, corn on the cob and fresh peaches—the best summer meal of all. The smell of Crabs steaming in Old Bay seasoning. Cold beers and jugs of sangria all around.

In the middle of it all was a long haired tattooed man. He stood with a beer in one hand and a leather wine pouch dangling off his shoulder. He was directing the preparations like some culinary traffic cop. His muscle shirt and cutoff jeans stained with the signs of the pending meal.

He glanced over and waved to us.

"That would be Roads," Mole said when he caught me looking. "Let me introduce you." He led me over to the kitchen.

Friendly smiles and greetings came from some of the guests.

"So Mole, it has been a while!" Roads boomed. Everyone turned to look at us.

"Roads you old bastard you! How have you been? Neither you nor your place seems to change or age that much. That is a good thing," Mole began. The two men shook hands then half hugged.

"Who is the young lad with you? It must be young Mole no doubt," Roads said exaggeratedly looking me over.

"I'm Steve Molineux, Mole's son," I said and shook his hand.

His hand felt like a sandpaper vice. I tried hard to match his grip. It was no use. I felt like an animal in a bear trap. Just as my mind raced with the idea of gnawing off my own hand to escape the grip, he released me. He then gave me the same awkward half hug he gave my father.

He handed us each a beer.

"Mole's son. The Widener student. I have heard a lot. Anxious to hear some more," he said.

"I hope you guys are setting up in your usual cabin." He pointed toward a cabin about fifty yards away next to the showers. Just then Josh came out of the cabin. He waved to us.

"Perfect, the boys are already in. Bean and Suitcase were already here. I assume they got you from the beach?" Roads said.

Satisfied about the accommodations, he pulled off the flask. "Drink? young Mole."

I looked over at my dad.

Mole shrugged and said, "One from the Road."

I hesitated, then unscrewed the top.

I took a drink from the flask.

The contents burned my insides. My stomach felt like it had hosted a dinner party with the Ulcers and the Chili families.

"Mescal," Roads laughed. "Later you can eat the worm," he said taking the flask back and taking a slug himself. "I can't wait to get better acquainted with the son of Mole."

He patted me on the back and then whispered something to Mole.

I heard my Dad mumble, "hell yes."

Roads handed him something.

Roads then led us to a long picnic table in the screened dining area.

"Let's eat!" he yelled and beckoned the people to the table as though he were some tattooed benevolent Jim Jones or Charlie Manson. The various groups silently obeyed and began to bring the food to the table. After a brief pause, the pleasant chatter began again.

We sat and ate as though we were all one big happy family around a thanksgiving table.

That was another great thing about the Hostel. It was always a built in community. You don't see that very much anymore. Nowadays its rare enough to see a family reunion, let alone group dinners with strangers. When the Hostel was around all that came naturally.

After dinner, Roads started a bon fire. Coolers were brought out and the drinking started in earnest. Soon the smell of marijuana filled the air. Roads, who had been holding court telling stories like some crazed speeding Lenny Bruce, motioned with a head nod for me to go in the kitchen.

I put down my beer and went inside, expecting that he would put me on dish washing duty, or maybe ask me to bring out more ice for the cooler. Instead, he surprised me by offering me some coke.

I knew he was speeding. No one could naturally keep up the nonstop, hyped banter he was unleashing on his audience. No, it had to be chemically enhanced.

Even Robin Williams and Rodney Dangerfield used to jump start their shows with the devil's dandruff.

Most coke talk is just that—coke talk. Boring repetitious, inane, redundant.

Did I mention boring?

But not this guy. His stream of conscious rants were wildly entertaining, funny and varied. At one point he was able to weave William Burroughs, Gus Van Sant and Ken Kesey all together in a way that not only made sense but made me wonder why I hadn't seen the tie before.

Something about the Pacific Northwest being the locale for the movie *Drug Store Cowboy* and *Cuckoo's Nest*. Both stories were told by narrators through a haze of drugs. Now they were being described by Roads through a haze of drugs or something like that.

God I wish I had a tape recorder that night. No, on second thought, after what went down later, I'd just as soon forget the whole evening. But

I have to admit his conversation was definitely interesting, and the early part of the night was pretty fun.

I wanted in.

"I thought you would never ask," I said looking out the screen door to make sure Beans wasn't around. "I haven't done a line since last semester," I continued, handing him a CD case to cut out the lines on.

He pulled out a bag from his cut offs.

It must have been an at least an eight ball of solid rock.

"Colombian Shale. Peruvian Flake whatever you want to call it, it is good blow," he said. He began to gag just looking at it. "Jesus I'm going to have to shit just thinking about another line," he continued.

Ah, cocaine. To think, I used to pay good money for that feeling; gagging, and the urge to shit. Throw in the long winded redundant coke talk that rarely occurred with someone as interesting as Roads and you have described too many nights of my college years.

This night was no different.

Roads quickly cut out two rails. I snorted half, then rubbed the other half on my teeth. He quickly put out two more, even bigger than the first.

Just like that I was off to the races. I was flying.

We went back out to the party. Mole was pretty drunk, so he didn't notice anything. I can't believe he didn't, I mean I was banging. I could not shut up. I was pretty funny or at least I thought I was.

I was probably an asshole. Most times on coke you are an asshole.

I'm sure I was an asshole.

I can't remember where Josh had gotten to, or for that matter Suitcase's whereabouts. They might have snuck off to town or maybe they hooked up with a group of female teachers on a retreat staying a couple cabins away.

I do remember that Mole and Beans hung out at the bon fire. Like I said, they were pretty tuned up. We left them alone with their booze and their fire. We told them we were going to Roads' cabin to hang out with some girls that had shown up late. They didn't even notice us leave.

Roads' cabin was an interesting mishmash of things. An eclectic mix of books, movies, and music combined with the sloppiness of a bachelor with a drug problem. Picture Bill Murray's character's place in *Caddyshack* crossed with Bill Murray's character's place in *Stripes,* and his cabin in *Meatballs.* Add a little of the drug paraphernalia of Bill Murray in *Where the Buffalo Roam* and you pretty much have the place. While

I'm at it think Bill Murray's portrayal of Hunter S. Thompson in the same movie and you have summed up Roads and his place solely with Bill Murray movies.

"Beer is in the fridge," Roads said as he sorted through his extensive music. CDs, cassettes and vinyl records were strewn about like the place had been ransacked.

He chose a record and put it on.

When I returned from the kitchen with the beers, a girl sat on the couch. The record began to play.

"Stones most underrated LP," she said to no one in particular.

To Roads she said "Who is your friend Chuckie?" Calling him by his real name.

"This is Mole's kid. Stevie meet my friend Dawn. Dawn Mayer."

She gave me a smile and a nod. "Nice to meet you Stevie," she said drawing out the Stevie. I wondered if she was making fun of me.

"Nice to meet you Dawn," I said, now a little self conscious. "What Rolling Stones is this?" I asked trying quickly to recover.

"*Satanic Majesty's Request* rules!" Roads answered, now sweeping Dawn off the couch and dancing with her around the room. She did not appear too happy.

"Relax honey. There is plenty of time and plenty of shit," he said and winked at me. The song continued to play but she immediately changed her tune.

"Let's party then," she said and grabbed me to join the dance.

After the song, we sat down and did some more coke. I noticed them each take a pill. "What about me?" I asked, although I did not need a pill. I was already tuned up enough.

"Give him one Roads," she said and began laughing.

Roads reached in his other pocket and handed me one. "Just a little Perc," he said. "Enjoy the ride."

He and Dawn got up and went to the bedroom.

I sat listening to the album. I didn't know if it was the drugs or the booze but this did not sound like any Stones I had ever heard. It was really good.

I know there are those who would say it was the drugs, but after hearing it a thousand times since, I would disagree. Dawn was right; it is the Stones' most underrated album.

I don't know how long I sat there grooving to the record. But at some point Roads came back. Dawn was not with him.

"She crashed," he said. He began to fumble with the music again. "This calls for the Kinks.

"Lola—L-O-L-A!" I shouted. I realized how messed up I was.

"Son you need a Kinks education," he said and tossed a couple of CDs over to me. "*Sleepwalker* and *Village Green Preservation Society* are my two favorites. Ray Davies is the most underrated man in music. His brother Dave ain't no slouch on guitar either.

Full Moon on *Sleepwalker* is great. I feel like he wrote it about me. My hand starts shakin when night starts to fall and I have been known to mumble like a loon!"

He sang the last part as he placed another CD on his stereo.

For the next hour we listened to music. We talked about movies and books and Vietnam too, but it always came back to the music. We pounded beers and drank a couple of shots as well. I was pretty fired up but I was fascinated.

He was fascinating.

After we listened to a bunch of Ray Davies, the early Stones, some Nick Drake and some *Wish You Were Here* he lazily reached over and pawed for something under the stereo. At first I thought he was getting another CD. He finally pulled out a cedar cigar box.

I thought it might be his pot stash. "Let's get high," I slurred.

He looked at me with surprise. Then he realized I thought it was pot.

"This will get you high alright but it ain't weed. It's much much better," he nodded slowly.

"Roads' works," he said matter of factly. He lifted the needle and the rubber strap from the box.

"Does Dawn know?" I found myself asking.

"Why do you think she crashed? As we said in the Nam, she is in the land of Nod."

"Have you ever tasted?" he asked.

"Taste what?" I asked, now really feeling the Percocet, and the blow and the weed and the booze.

He laughed. "The White Dragon. Skag. Junk. Horse."

I must have worn a stoned puzzled look for he practically yelled.

"Heroin!"

Realizing how loud he was, he looked out the window and whispered.

"Do you want to try?"

I had always hated junkies. Hated the fact that humans had at least three natural orifices in which to ingest illegal substances, and yet people would create another by shooting a needle into themselves to get high.

At the same time, I was intrigued by the stories of the fantastic high. Fascinated by tales of those—artists, writers, actors, musicians and interesting people like Roads who dabbled in the White and lived to tell about it. Plus I had my knee operated on two years prior and the morphine they gave me in the hospital was pretty damn good. Some old timer hippie hospital orderly told me before I nodded out from the shot in the ass that heroin was even better.

I never forgot that.

If that wasn't enough, I wanted to come down off the coke so I could get to sleep. We did after all have the Series the next day.

I know it sounds stupid now to me as well, but looking back, that is the best that I can say to explain as to why I said yes.

What happened next I have never told anyone.

Roads worked quickly. He was an obvious pro. He tied off my arm with the rubber strap. I sat looking at the vein in my arm slowly getting larger. I tried to act casual while he cooked up the drug with a Bic lighter and a spoon.

I sipped my beer and waited.

Next he dipped the needle in a small tube of liquid.

"Bleach," he said when I gave him a look.

I sat back and closed my eyes. I held out my arm, looking to join Burroughs and Morrison and Coltrane and Lou Reed and all those other tortured geniuses that fascinated me. Looking to join Roads.

I heard a knock on the door.

Before Roads could react the door burst open.

"What the fuck are you doing? You no good junky!"

It was Beans and he was pissed. "I knew you were a no good piece of shit!" he yelled as he dove into Roads.

The two rolled onto the floor.

Beans began to beat Roads as Roads struggled to keep hold of his drugs.

"Beans stop! Roads didn't make me do anything. I was just going to try it, for Christ sake. I ain't no little kid. I can handle it!" I yelled, now trying to pull Beans off.

Still he beat him.

"You don't try heroin. You live it then you die from it! Plain and simple," he yelled, all the while continuing to pummel Roads.

Although Roads did not appear to be a slouch in the fighting department, due to his intoxication and the jump Beans got on him, he was no match.

"Stop! I'm sorry, I had no idea the kid was a virgin," Roads lied. "Easy Beans before you fracture my skull," he continued, now dropping the needle and covering up.

The damage done, although not the damage Neil Young was singing about.

"Get back to your room, Stevie!" Beans barked. He warily began to release Roads.

Roads did not continue the fight.

Seeing this, Beans began to tidy up the evidence of his attack. He righted a chair and picked up a spilled glass. He handed Roads a hanky for his bleeding nose.

"You heard me Steve get out of here."

I reached for my beer, thought twice, then ducked out. I did not look at either of them.

I walked back to my cabin.

I felt embarrassed. I felt angry. I felt sober.

Later, I felt glad.

I don't know what happened or what was said after I left. It was never spoken of again. To my knowledge neither Beans nor Roads ever mentioned it to anyone else. Beans didn't dime me out to my dad either.

They did tell Mole they had fought, although they never told him why. In fact Beans fell on the sword further by telling Mole he was drunk and had started the fight with Roads.

He never mentioned me. Oh, he talked to me about it, but he didn't talk to Mole about it. For that I am thankful.

Mole suspected the fight was because Beans hated drug users, but he never knew the real reason. He even gave Beans shit for disrespecting the Hostel's owner after all Roads' hospitality. He never really let Beans off the hook.

If I didn't already feel bad enough from the hangover the next day, I really felt bad seeing Beans take the blame.

I feel worse today.

Looking back, I am eternally grateful that Beans intervened. I don't know why he was up or why he was there, but I'm glad he was. Not that I blame Roads either. It was my own fault for getting in that predicament. Roads was just a mixed up Vietnam vet. He didn't make me do drugs. He didn't put me in that position. I put myself in that position. Thankfully Beans got me out of it.

Who would have ever thought that I would be saved from a heroin addict by an alcoholic.

Thank you Beans.

/////////////////////

The next morning was World Series of Birding day. Despite my partying I was up before the dawn. After the Roads incident, I had at least been smart enough to take an Advil and drink a ton of water. Even Mole's snoring and Roads' coke couldn't keep me up.

I slept well.

Appropriately enough, I awoke to the sounds of birds.

Before the dawn they sounded like a nocturnal nature's symphony warming up. I know what you are thinking, that birds whistling in the morning are not what you would like to hear if you were sleeping off a night of drinking.

For me, if you are awake and anxious to embrace the gift of a new day, especially a day with an adventure planned, than hearing God's feathered instruments outside your window is the most beautiful sound in the world. Sometimes the most beautiful music comes when we are not expecting it or even thinking about it. Like laying in bed and waking up early to the sounds of the morning. This was one of those times.

There is a reason Paul McCartney sang about Blackbirds singing in the dead of night. He found music in the same early morning symphony.

As I sat listening to the birds, I thought of that song. I wondered about the inspiration for the creation of art. It seemed to me that the birds were improvising; singing from the heart and not the mind.

Isn't that what makes the best art?

I thought of Marvin Gaye secretly taping Sonny Rollins' sax warm up for *What's Going On*. The art came from Rollins' heart not his head. Contained in his free form practice was the spark of genius. His non thinking improvisation was the art. Gaye knew that, and got what he needed from him without asking Rollins to think about creating. Rollins unexpected, non-thinking warm up was all Gaye needed for the start of his own masterpiece—*What's Going On*.

The birds know more music than man ever will, I thought.

Can the birds' improvised music be the start of my own magical day? If only we could all use nature's songs to launch our own greatness.

My thoughts wandered.

Maybe Mole and his bird watching were starting to influence how I thought. Was I my father's son? Seeing art in everything, including every man? Was I always destined to see things from odd angles, and through weird prisms?

At the time, in my little blue-collar part of the world, these traits seemed like quite an impediment. Certainly not the gift I see them as today.

Nah, maybe I was just still drunk, why else would birds chirping give me such crazy thoughts. I should go back to bed. Sleep it off. But if that were the case, then wasn't I my father's son for sure? My thoughts forever twisted by alcohol.

Enough.

I turned over and tried to go back to sleep.

Either way I am my father's son.

I no sooner closed my eyes then the door swung open.

"Rise and shine happy campers! Its medication time, its medication time."

It was Suitcase.

"Let's go. We have a Series to win."

He carried a pot of coffee and Mole's stolen library book—Birds of North America.

"What time is it you crazy bastard?" Josh complained. "Shut the door and close the blinds the birds can wait." He groaned, as he pulled a pillow over his head.

Suitcase calmly pulled the pillow away and farted on Josh's head.

"You son of a beatch!" Josh screamed in an exaggerated Italian accent. He bounded out of bed and swung the pillow at Suitcase.

"Easy man, there is a beverage here," Suitcase said, channeling his inner Lebowski. "You go to bed a mick and wake up a dago?" he continued, now putting the pot down on the nightstand.

"It must have been the spaghetti dinner last night," Mole chimed in.

"Did the spaghetti turn Josh into Luigi the organ grinder, or did it turn Suitcase into a methane factory?" I asked getting out of bed.

"Well well well. If it isn't Roads' new best friend," Suitcase said turning to greet me. I immediately stiffened up.

"Why would you say that?" I asked, now nervous that Beans had spilled the Beans.

"Just that you two seemed to hit it off. He is an interesting character that Roads. The illustrated man. Chuckie Laughlin . . ." Suitcase said, his voice trailing off as he concentrated on pouring the coffee.

Mole got down from his bunk and slapped me on the back.

"What time you guys wrap it up last night?" he asked and splashed cold water on his face from the sink next to the bed.

I took a chance that Beans had not said anything and that Roads was still passed out from the needle meant for my arm.

"Pretty early," I lied. "I knew we had a big day planned and besides Roads' girlfriend wanted him to come to bed."

I finished and pretended to look out the window. Anything not to look Mole in the eye.

"He still dating that junky Dawn? Nice piece of ass. Wasn't she Stevie?" Josh said as he stared down from his bunk. With his receding hairline and skinny white legs protruding from his stretched undies, he looked like some ugly baby bird perched in his nest.

"Now Josh, no need to be nasty. What did your parents teach you? If you don't have something nice . . ." Suitcase began. Before he could finish Josh cut him off.

"If I want to talk about the crack of Dawn at the crack of dawn then I will Godamnit! Now give me a hit of that coffee and toss me my smokes."

He sat up in bed.

Suitcase tossed him a pack. Mole handed him a lighter.

The door opened and Beans walked in. After the night he had, he looked like a cross between Albert Einstein and Don King if that cross breed had just received an electric shock. The bags under his eyes, always considerable, were packed for a long trip in the morning. They looked like Bela Lugosi recovering from a lobotomy. Now with the addition of the shiner and some scrapes on him, his look would make Kurt Vonnegut look baby-faced. But since he always looked rough in the morning the other Birders did not take much notice.

He looked at me then glanced away.

'Oh shit' I thought. Here it comes. I braced myself.

"Well are we going to see some birds today? Hopefully we can drinks a bit too. Just like Mr. Bojangles."

He laughed and did a little jig. He ended it by clicking his heels.

He did not mention the Roads incident at all. Or at least not yet.

"It is almost light out. You remember last time. We showed up at seven am., and we were almost the last ones out. We need to get going," Beans said grabbing the cooler and heading out to the car.

Mole noticed the shiner on Beans' eye.

"What happened to you Beansie?" he asked as he followed Beans out.

I heard Beans mutter something about a little scrap with Roads, then a dismissive, "I'll tell you about it later. We have birds to track."

We followed his lead and made our way to the car. Josh of course was the last out, bitching the whole time.

We started out for the bird sanctuary. Beans paid him no mind and continued with his caffeine fueled soliloquy.

"I love getting up early," he mused. "Even as a kid. Used to drive my old man bananas. He was a very practical man. He could fix anything. Neighbors would bring their lawnmowers, old sewing machines, watches, you name it. I think he was secretly glad that things broke down so much. Although, he never let on. 'Lousy engineering' that was his opinion about everything. He even thought God was a lousy engineer. If he'd see a comet or a shooting star it didn't occur to him that it was romantic, or stir a sense of awe. All he saw was an engineering flaw in the solar system. He thought crocodiles were a fairly good invention because they'd been around so long."

"I'm sure lizards have long warranties," Mole said, just when I thought no one was listening. He laughed and took a sip of coffee.

"Sorry to interrupt you Beansie."

Beans nodded then smiled and continued, "Anyway it would drive the old man nuts that I would get up early and not do anything. 'Boy could at least make his bed,' he'd say. So I'd make my bed in the dark, not to wake my brother, then take a cup of instant coffee and sit out on the back step and watch the field and the woods come to life. Wait for the birds to get theirs on."

"The birds get theirs on?" Josh interjected.

Mole leaned up and smacked Beans on the back. "Yes Josh, you heard the man. Birds get their's on! I know exactly what he means."

Suitcase nodded too.

"Get with the program Josh. We need the birds to get their's on a lot for us today," Suitcase said. "Hand me a beer," he added for good measure.

Mole continued. "For although Beans' voice does have a soothing treble to it, and it may cause you to treat Beans' morning lectures as pleasant background music . . ."

"Like listening to a baby snore," Suitcase offered.

"Beans does give good radio," I added, smiling myself at the Birder's morning dialogue. Mole handed Suitcase a beer then went on. "Josh if you would only listen more closely. Beans is always saying things that tickle the earwax. Of course Birds put their coffee on in the morning," Mole said, nodding at Beans in a way that said 'Let me solo a while,' he continued, "Brew it up in the branches, then sit around in the trees and swap bird lies, shoot the shit, rap, gossip. Trees in early morning are the diners of birddom. You figure, the worms aren't up yet, mosquitoes are just getting over their shift, its still too dark to see seeds, and most insects forget to set their alarm clocks half the time. So, what's to do? Have another cup and chat."

"Or chirp," Suitcase said playing along. Josh looked at him like he was nuts, then finding himself listening to the nonsense despite himself, asked, "What do the birds chat about there, morning storyteller?"

Mole continued, "Oh, the same things people do. How the job is going. Births, deaths, affairs, current aviary events. You know, 'So and so's aunt broke her wing . . . ' Mole began to jokingly flap his arms imitating some feathered gossip.

Seeing this, Beans began to flap his arms too. Laughing, he commented, "You don't say?"

Mole not to be out done chirped said, "Oh yes, nasty break it was, you didn't hear? Flew into a Buick Skylark she did. Week ago Sunday. Going much to fast, she was."

Beans now fully absorbed in his bird imitation, flapping and pecking his head like some spastic chicken asked "The Buick?"

Mole waited a beat then answered "No, the Oriole, bird brain!" Like he and Beans were an old Vaudeville act.

We all cracked up. Josh shook his head. All he could say was "We need to split these two assholes up today or we won't see any birds. We will be laughing too hard."

Suitcase turned down a road and headed toward Cape May point. The meeting place was outside the bird sanctuary. As we neared the registration lot we passed a little dirt road. Since it was mostly grown over I barely noticed. Beans nudged me and said, "There she is. Our ticket to the championship."

I didn't pay much attention. It was five thirty. Suitcase made another two turns and we were in the lot.

A crowd were already gathered. The sun had just opened a crack on the horizon, and it was yawning up. The mist was coming off the wide flat field that turned to marsh somewhere beyond the small tree line. Everyone was smiling and chatting. More than one group admired the sunrise. There was a sense of anticipation for the start of the bird watching competition.

I know it might sound strange to those who have never participated in the World Series, but even I, a first timer, felt it. Maybe it was the camaraderie, or maybe the competition. Maybe it was just being in the outdoors in the early morning with so many others who really appreciated nature. Whatever it was, it was worth the early wake up.

"Beautiful, isn't it Stevie?" Mole said and patted me on the back. "Times like this New Jersey seems like an apprentice Montana or something. Hard to believe we are only two hours away from Philly and couple from Washington."

"Less if we took the Ferry," Suitcase added as he handed me a notebook, a pen and a cold beer. "Me, Mole and Josh will head up state in Lucille and start out somewhere south of Trenton. Mole knows some spots.

Then we will make our way south toward Lake Absegami, in Bass River State Park. There are always a ton of birds there."

"Native and migratory. We always get lucky at Absegami," Mole added.

"You and Beans will stay in Cape May. Start out at the bird refuge then work your way over to the state beach, then back to the woods next to the Hostel. You guys should be able to spot all the shore birds plus the South Jersey species too."

"Might get some hawks and maybe an eagle on a early migration as well. You never know," Mole added.

I was amazed how much these guys were into it.

If their plans weren't enough, I now noticed Suitcase was looking at a map. He was carefully marking the locations up, placing different colored markers on each area.

"Taking this pretty serious aren't you Suitcase? Remember Josh said we are serious drinkers and casual birders. Not the other way around," I joked.

"Let me worry about Josh. That's why he is coming with me and Mole."

"Why is it me and Beans? Not that I mind," I asked and looked around for Beans. He was no where in sight.

Suitcase answered. "Beans didn't feel like a car ride today. He asked if he could stay local, and he suggested you stay with him. He knows there has to be groups of at least two."

Well Beans had not told my dad about my Roads incident but I was going to hear from him just the same. Fair enough. In fact, I thought I at least deserved a lecture or maybe even worse, even if it came from a guy who had his own substance abuse issues.

Hopefully he would drink heavily and forget all about it, I thought.

I was going to miss Mole and Suitcase's enthusiasm and their sense of humor though. I guess it wouldn't matter. I would hook back up with them at the awards ceremony that night.

As I thought about Suitcase's itinerary I glanced around at the other groups of birders. It was an interesting mix. Of course you had your share of the stereotypical National Public Radio types. Complete with the tan dockers or cargo pants along with the sun hat and binoculars. Greenpeace shirts and even an old Jackson Brown 'No Nukes' Tee were spotted in the crowd.

In addition, there were all sorts of school groups and boy scout troops. Glassboro State, Rutgers, and the University of Delaware were just three of the colleges in attendance.

Then there were the slightly off kilter independent birder groups. The Trenton Quacks. The Cape May Hawkeyes. Washington Twp. 'Who gives a Ducks.' The Runnemeade Road Runners. Never mind that there were no Road Runners within five hundred miles of New Jersey.

All of them had matching tee shirts and hats and were enthusiastically planning their day.

One group of particularly manly looking women were exiting their RV. They looked like the only other group that might actually be making a drinking party out of the Series.

Josh, seeing them remarked, "What, is there a bull dyke bar league softball tournament here as well?"

I laughed, but I stopped as soon as Mole gave me the shit eye. Of course the girls over heard this and the bad blood started immediately.

"Didn't know they let skinny little white trash drunks in the Series," a big girl said loudly so Josh would hear her. She looked like a cross dressing Ben Franklin in her knee socks and Black Doc Martins along with a grey pony tail and large forehead. She completed the look with John Lennon wireframe glasses.

Before Mole could intervene, Josh yelled back "Nice Adam's apple, you East German weightlifter. Why are you wasting time here? You don't even like birds, cocks I mean. You should be down eating at the Y!"

With that, she came at Josh.

Suitcase and my father got between them.

Josh began the 'hold me back routine'. You know, when you act tough but you really want your friends to hold you back. I guess he though it was too early to be messing with a pack of lesbian bird watchers. Maybe he realized he had met his match.

Mole quickly diffused the situation with some kind words and a six pack of beer. Finally the ladies backed off with nothing more than some dirty looks and a couple of them flipping Josh the bird.

Seeing this, Beans who had just got back from the registration desk shouted out "The first three birds spotted today. The middle fingers of some irate middle aged men. He exaggeratedly put on his glasses. "Oh, I'm sorry some middle aged ladies."

Josh laughed, obviously glad someone was with him.

"Thanks there, Beans. I was beginning to think Mole and Suitcase were on the rug munchers' side. I was about to get Mole a Martina Navratilova poster for his bedroom wall."

Suitcase handed Josh a beer. "Here. Keenan, always startin trouble. You should be glad Mole and I saved you. Nothing more savage than a flock of women in comfortable shoes. You need to chill. Enjoy the moment. Realize everyone here shares the same love of the outdoors and the winged creatures within it," he lectured.

He then continued with the rules. "Remember, everyone take binoculars and a pen and paper. It is not a proper sighting unless two people see it or hear it. Plus the species needs to be recorded along with the time, location and number of the specimens sighted. Here take a rule sheet."

He handed me a packet of papers that I shoved into my back pack.

I put a sleeve of beers into a backpack cooler and went over to Beans.

"What time will you guys be back and where should we meet?" I asked Mole and Suitcase.

Mole and Beans checked their watches like they were synchronizing some secret spy mission. Mole said "Some time around seven thirty. The thing shuts down at eight. There is an informal awards ceremony at eight thirty."

He looked at Beans, "The usual spot?"

Beans just nodded. "See you guys tonight."

To Suitcase, Beans added "Twenty bucks we spot more than you."

Josh walked over with a flask. He handed it to Beans. "No way. We will be covering half the state, in all kinds of terrain, with an extra guy. No way will you two spot more birds today. You are on foot and in only one location."

He took out his wallet. "I will take a piece of that bet. How about fifty with me Beans?"

"No sweat, and Stevie is in too," Beans said. "Don't worry Steve I will cover you. Although Suitcase ain't a bad birder and your dad is pretty good too, Josh is the kiss of death. The birds sense his lack of interest and avoid him like a feeder being staked out by my cat Brunswick."

"We are burning daylight. Let's get going. You got enough money Stevie? No way you guys will see more birds than us. But if you do that's great. Remember, we are on the same team," Mole said sounding like a verbal machine gun.

"See you tonight." Suitcase said as the three of them pulled out and left us in the lot. We watched them leave, then made our way out of the lot back towards the dirt road we saw on our way in.

We walked for a bit as Beans whistled the theme from *Bridge Over River Kwai*. The song was so infectious, I soon joined in. This led to Dueling TV Themes.

First Beans would whistle a song. I would guess the show. Then I would do one. I got him on a lot of cartoons. He got me on some sixties shows. I didn't know *The Outer Limits*.

"Before my time pop-pop," I joked. We both agreed that the Song from *Barney Miller* was the best jam song of all time when it came to television theme songs. We tried to whistle it but it was too hard. We switched to *Sanford and Son,* and then the *Andy Griffith Show.*

After about a half mile Beans began to explain his plan. "The place we are going to is the perfect spot. Me and your dad stumbled on it a couple of years ago when we first got involved in this crazy contest. It must have been an old cranberry farmer's shortcut or maybe a duck hunter's camp. I don't know. What I do know is that after spending the day there your dad and I came within six birds of winning the 'Big Day Big Stay' award. That's for the group who spots the most species in one location. It was the best we ever did and believe it or not we didn't even try. I swear. All we did was drink, eat, swim and snooze. All damn day. It was great."

He patted me playfully on the shoulder. "That's what I plan to do again today."

Just as I began to break a sweat, we turned off the asphalt and began to walk up the dirt path. I looked around but surprisingly didn't see another bird watcher. Come to think of it I didn't see anyone at all.

"Told you this is the spot. I can't believe all these so called serious bird watchers haven't found this place. Wait til you see." Beans grinned and wiped his face with his tee shirt. "I'm startin to pit out. I'm going to stink so bad the birds will think they have landed at a trash dump. Let's take a dip when we get there."

"Aren't we going to scare the birds?" I asked.

"The birds like a little noise. They are as curious as the next bird. A little splashing and laughing will draw em in. You'll see."

The path ended at the bay about three quarters of a mile from the main road. As we approached the water I could see what Beans was talking about. The place had something for every kind of bird. To the right of the bay was a pine forest. Next to it, back off behind us was a meadow that sloped gently off to a fresh water pond. There was also a salty marsh at the bay, a sandy beach and a scrub field that looked like it might have been an orchard or a blueberry farm at one time.

In the pond I could see all sorts of ducks and nesting water birds of all shapes and sizes. It looked like they were having a bird convention.

Beans pointed and crouched down. Quietly he whispered, "Our swim will have to wait. Seems the birds want to help ole Beans and his backyard boozing birders win the Series this year. Get out the bird book and the pad and paper. But be quiet."

I did as he asked.

"You know what all these types are?" I whispered.

"Most of em. What I can't identify we will find in the bird book."

He smiled and continued. "Now if you don't mind. I will do the callin and the drinkin. You be a nice lad and do the writin. Who knows? Might get to feeling like you are my personal secretary dictating my memoirs or something."

"I'll write for you Beans. I'll be the recording secretary for the Bird Watchers for Boozers Club," I said and laughed.

"Shhh! We are not a club. A club excludes people. We want our tent to shelter everyone. Isn't that what your dad would say?"

He paused and looked out over the pond.

"There. That is a wood duck. What the hell is it doing with those Mallards? Doesn't it know the Mallard is the horniest duck in the bird world? Mallards will screw anything. If that poor Wood duck doesn't get away soon it is liable to be ganged raped. Mallards are the biker gangs of the marsh—The Mallards! Sounds like a gang don't it? Should be written on the back of a leather coat or jean jacket or something. I've seen them try and get it on with muskrats for Christ sake."

He was quickly drawn to another sighting.

Look, there goes the Canadian goose. What a joke. Canadian. They are so lazy they never go back to Canada. Talk about an immigration problem. They are worse than Mexicans. Mexicans never leave either. But at least Mexican immigrants tend to our lawns while they are in our country. They work. The Canadian Goose just eats our lawns and shits up our parks and our ponds. I wish I had a gun. Guess that would go against the rules. Huh Stevie?" He shook his head and took sip of beer.

He then continued on with his bird watching monologue. I sat next to him feeling the sun warm my face and laughing quietly as I dutifully wrote down the species he called out as they came into view.

For the next five and a half hours I saw more birds than I have ever seen in one place at one time in my life. It was like Beans was the pied piper of birds.

At one point, after spotting a Red Headed Woodpecker, a Flicker, a Wood Cock, a Ring-tailed Pheasant, an Osprey, and three types of humming bird; The Ruby throated, The Rufous, and the Black Chinned, all within fifteen minutes, I half expected a blue bird to land on his shoulder and for Beans to launch into *Zippity Do Da'* like Uncle Remus.

Although he didn't sing, we did see four bluebirds land not five feet away from us as we sat drinking and bird watching that morning.

At around eleven thirty. I started to get hungry.

I looked at our list. We had seen seventy nine different types of birds.

Unbelievable.

Beans must have sensed my amazement at the number we had tallied. He laughed and said, "I told you this was the best spot. The secret is, it has four different environments converging at this location. Plus, it is a perfect place for migratory birds to take a break on their way south. It is like the South of the Border rest stop. It has something for every bird. Food, shelter, water and it is on a major migratory fly route of most Northern birds."

He continued. "I have pretty good eyes and I'm pretty patient but hey I'm no Roger Tory Peterson, the father of birding or even Pete Dunne the founder of this event. Hell, even they would admit that finding the right place is half the battle. What did Mole say in my backyard at Seconds Flat? When it comes to birds, it is Location, Location, Location." He smacked his thighs. "Now. Whaddaya say we get some lunch?"

He got up slowly, like some over forty bar league catcher nursing a rebuilt knee. "Damn I'm getting old Stevie. Don't know how long I can keep doing this."

He then let out a growl. "Son of a bitch. Beans you need to stop drowning in your own sorrows. You are alive and well. Stop your complaining," he said to himself as much as to me.

Surprised at the racket he was making, I remarked, "You are scaring the birds, Beans."

"Stevie it is a fact. You see most of the birds you are going to see in this Series between five am. and ten am. We won't see too many more until dinner. If we decide to hang that long. Let's go and get an early lunch at that bar I saw on the way into the Point."

He grabbed his empty beer cans and the sunflower seed pack he was working on and he began to make his way back up the dirt path. I followed behind with my backpack and my notebook.

What a great morning.

I had no idea what the others were doing but I was sure I would at least collect fifty bucks from Josh. Who knows, we might even win the 'Big Day Big Stay' award.

So far it had been about the birds. Now that we were taking a break I expected Beans would bring up the Roads situation from last night.

For an unpredictable guy Beans was pretty predictable.

I didn't have to wait long.

"Now that we have gotten most of our birding business out of the way I'd like to have a little one on one private chat about what I saw you doing last night," he began nonchalantly.

"What I was perhaps about to do, but didn't," I answered trying not to sound like a wise ass.

I must of sounded like a wise ass.

"Do you want me to do to you what I did to Roads?" he fired back, obviously wanting me to take my medicine. In this case a healthy dose of Beans' wisdom.

I launched in. "I was pretty banged up. It was a definite mistake . . . My defenses were down . . . . I was drunk . . . . I appreciate you coming in when you did. I promise it won't happen again . . ." I babbled.

"Son, thou does protest too much." Beans cut me off. "You bet it won't happen again. I won't tolerate drugs—hard drugs. Over my dead body. I catch you messin with that shit again I will personally kick your ass. Plus, I won't tell Mole, I will tell your mother." He looked over and nodded slowly.

He knew his shit, Beans did. He knew that I would be crushed if Larose found out.

"You have my word Beans. I won't do any hard drugs ever," I said solemnly.

"I believe you," he answered just as seriously.

"Why is it you are so against drugs anyway?" I asked. "I mean alcohol is a drug, so is weed. Shit, even nicotine is. I think it is just so much bullshit. We are hypocrites. All of us.

I say, it makes no sense, because the government subsidizes the liquor and tobacco industries. Booze and nicotine. The two biggest drugs known to man. Or at least the two that kill more people and ruin more lives than any other. They are legal. Yet we make the others illegal and lock people up for merely possessing them. Booze and smokes are glorified and all the rest are vilified."

I threw a stone off into the woods. Immediately, a flock of mourning doves kicked up.

"That makes eighty species," I said and laughed.

"This shit ain't funny. Fact is, booze and smokes are legal. We don't make the rules, we just follow them. It ain't for us to wonder about the whys and the hows. We are just regular Joes.

Besides, booze and smokes are a wave that you can ride pretty much your whole life. If you don't get nuts. No need to chase the big one or ride the wave everyday. If you play your cards right, both of them can give you a lot of enjoyment in this life. If you don't, then drinking and smoking only kill you slowly.

But that heroin. Or the crack, or that acid shit . . . well those drugs will bring a man down fast. There is a reason you don't see any recreational heroin users and there ain't no weekend crack smokers. Shit kills and kills fast."

He stopped and lit a cigarette.

"Hand me a beer," he said. "Where was I?"

"You were telling me about the evils of drugs, then you took a break to do **your own** drugs," I said, then handed him a beer.

He took the beer and nodded. He went to take a drag of his smoke. Then, realizing my comment he said, "Don't be a wise ass. What I am telling you is true."

He launched back in. "No one ever sucked a dick for a drink of whiskey. But it happens all the time on the streets of North Philadelphia. Women and men selling their bodies for a five dollar rock of crack."

Seeing my smile he added "So I am told, wise ass."

He continued. "Look. I'm not talking about marijuana. I think it should be illegal **not** to smoke pot. The whole world should be on the weed. Place probably be a whole lot more peaceful. Certainly sell a whole lot more Cheetos anyway. Only thing happening is people be laughing too much. No, I'm talking the hard drugs.

I have just seen too much hurt, too many times, too quickly when that shit is in the mix."

He sighed and took a seat on a felled tree.

I sat in front of him on the ground. "So what you are saying is that drugs that act slowly or are manageable are ok. But ones that act quickly and can be dangerous are off limits?" I asked.

"Man, you can be a difficult cocky son of a bitch, just like your dad. Both of you always questioning authority, debating issues, arguing for arguments sake. What I am saying is—don't do that shit. If you do you will deal with me," he said.

He got off the log and sat next to me. "You know you are like a son to me. Hell, you are a son to me. Same for Josh. Same for Suitcase. We love you. Always have, always will. We were there when you were born. Unfortunately, we won't always be there for you down the road. You need to learn from us even if you are smarter than us. You got a shot at being someone . . ."

"A contenda like Brando?! I wish Suitcase was here give us his imitation . . ." I joked.

"Shut up for once and listen!" he yelled and grabbed me by the back of the head. "You have a brain and a sense of humor. Everyone likes you. You got chances Mole never had. Don't fuck up a bright future on a lousy high. Your father . . . all of us would be devastated."

He let go of my head.

"I'm sorry. I won't have you joking about drugs. Now help me up.

Jeez, I feel like Henry Fonda in *On Golden Pond.* My knees are killing me. I have to pee. I'm crabby. Next thing you know I will be peeing my pants," he said trying to lighten the mood.

"Beans I hate to break it to you but you already pee yourself. Remember your couches at Seconds Flat?" I joked back, shaking my hands and warbling my voice like Katherine Hepburn, I said, "The only Golden Pond I ever see is in your trousers Henry."

I helped him up.

Beans started laughing. "That's a pretty good Kate Hepburn," he said.

Then before the moment got away, I looked him in the eye.

"I promise Beans. I promise all of you."

He smiled.

We walked up the path and headed to the bar.

He didn't mention drugs again. Later, he even took a couple of tokes of a jay before we ate.

"Good for the appetite," he said.

After lunch we walked back to the spot. We took the swim we didn't get a chance to take in the morning.

After a dip in the ocean we were able to swim in the freshwater pond. That way we didn't have that sticky saltwater residue on us.

I felt pretty good.

We crashed for a while.

When we woke it was dinner time. It was much cooler and it seemed less humid too. Bugs were not too bad. I stretched and yawned and in doing so woke Beans from his beer and lunch induced slumber.

As we sat, waking up and getting ourselves together, like clockwork, the birds started to show again. It was like the second shift had punched the time clock at the bird mill.

"Beans you are right again. The birds must have napped right along with us," I said marveling at Beans' predictions.

That late afternoon, Beans and I spotted nineteen more birds, and we heard three more too. Who would have thought there were Wild turkeys, Baltimore orioles and Pin Tailed ducks in Cape May.

As the sun began to descend, we spotted a night hawk and three owls; a barn owl a screech owl and a snowy owl that was passing through. We capped the day with a couple of Atlantic Brants and a small flock of Canvas Back Ducks.

The owls and the ducks were definitely the highlight of the day for me. Beans told me the humming birds were always his favorite.

"They are like little speed freaks," Beans joked.

As we were leaving to meet the guys back at the lot we spotted a lone black vulture. "I was wondering where those got to today. I always spot at least one. Either a black vulture or a turkey buzzard," Beans said and pointed to the sky. "Let's get out of here. Between the bugs and our new friend up there, I think I get the message. Time to leave. Besides I think it is safe to assume that Josh will owe us on the bet."

I put away the note book and picked up our trash.

It was a great day.

I had expected it to be boring but it was anything but.

Bird watching and boozing is a great time.

We made our way back up the path to the road and the rendezvous with the rest of the backyard boozers.

"For a first timer you are a natural. Now give me another beer," Beans said to me as we made our way back to the lot.

Did he mean a natural birdwatcher or a natural boozer?

I never thought to ask.

///////////////////

Later when Mole and the others got back, we went back to Hostel to clean up. Thankfully Roads was no where in sight. After we showered we returned to the Congress Hall for the awards banquet and cocktail party.

On the way Beans and Mole compared our day's lists to get rid of doubles and tally up our totals. Mole's group had seen or heard a little over a hundred and forty species. Unfortunately, there were a lot of the same ones Beans and I had seen. All tolled, I think we had a total of one hundred and fifty five different types of birds.

Of course Josh tried to break our balls about our total. No way could we have seen so many from just one spot. But Suitcase and Mole explained that in bird watching your word is your bond. Everyone is on the honor system and it never is a problem. Plus, Mole explained to Josh the beauty of Beans' bird watching spot.

"It is a bird watching gold mine," he said.

Either way, Mole's group had still seen more than us.

"What are you bitching about Keenan? You win," I said.

Beans paid up.

"We may not have seen as many but we probably drank more than you guys," I offered, now trying to rile Josh.

He just counted his money and smiled.

Surprisingly no one was drunk. For once it appeared the day's activity had been more important than tying one on.

"Let's get over to the party," Suitcase said as he slicked back the three strands of hair on each side of his head. Looking in the rearview mirror he realized he had a bad excuse for a comb over.

"You look like Mr. Softee," Josh teased.

"Just count your bird money jerk off," Suitcase responded.

He shrugged his shoulders and put on his painter's cap.

"Hair today gone tomorrow. Let's get there already," he joked.

We made our way to the Congress Hall in the center of town. The Congress Hall was an old wooden hotel that dated from the early eighteen hundreds. It was a beautiful old federalist building that had some how survived the various fires that had ripped through the town over the years. It was a rambling ramshackle of a hotel and convention center that for years had entertained the Birding World Series. It was made entirely of wood and with its painted green shutters and long square whitewashed pillars running the length of the hotel's porch, the place looked like it should be hosting the surrender of the confederacy not a bunch of bird watchers.

Since many of the birding groups were also history buffs and architecture fanatics, the oldest hotel in the town seemed like a perfect fit.

The Series cocktail party had never been held anywhere else.

We entered the lobby, where a sign read 'World Series of Birding Symposium'.

Josh looking at the sign said in his best English accent, "This way to the symposium."

I noticed the desk clerk and the bell-hop snickering to themselves.

"Here for the bird banquet?" The clerk sarcastically asked.

Mole noticed but didn't bite.

"Yes we are young lad and if you would be so kind as to point us in the direction we would be much obliged."

The bell hop rolled his eyes and pointed to the far hallway.

Amazing how one group of people will always make fun of another. If you are different, then you are ridiculed. We get mad at our kids for doing it on the playground, but who are we kidding? People never grow up. They never stop. It is always a playground.

Josh made a point of calling the workers 'bell boys' and tipped them each a buck. He intentionally dropped the money. The workers scurried to pick it up.

We stuck some nametags to our shirts and made our way to the reception.

As we entered, I immediately realized we had not dressed for the occasion.

Everyone turned to look at the 'Backyard Birding Boozers' as our nametags described us, as we sauntered in wearing our cutoffs and flip flops. Only Suitcase, who never wore shorts, wore long pants, and even those were paint splattered jeans.

"Mole, why didn't you tell me everyone would be dressed up?" I whispered, now beginning to gently ease myself back out the entrance.

"Relax old boy. While most of these partygoers have chosen to over dress for the occasion, choosing to ignore the fact that it is summer and we are at the beach, I suggest we split up for a while, get a few cocktails in us, and allow the rest of the birders to warm to the only group sane enough to shun formality and dress comfortably." He finished and immediately broke for the bar.

The rest of us did the same.

He was right. What did I care?

I didn't know anyone and probably wouldn't see them again either. Plus, I at least had on a golf shirt with a collar. The others had only tee shirts to match their shorts. I was the best dressed backyard birder.

But, you know, that wasn't it. The truth was, hanging with the Birders, I was beginning to see the world differently. I was starting to find my place. Or maybe I had already found my place but now was starting to get comfortable in it. Whatever it was, I really didn't care. I was having fun. I wasn't hurting anyone, and after seeing ninety odd birds in one spot not a mile from this hotel, I earned my right to be here.

Besides, What did Beans say about my father? We were not a club. Our tent was designed to hold any one looking for shelter.

Shouldn't everyone live by the same motto?

I had a couple of drinks and felt out the other guests. Now, no one seemed to pay any mind to our attire. I walked around the place, and looked for the others. I noticed there were a fair share of teetotalers, but all in all, most of the crowd seemed to like to bend elbows.

I came upon Mole and Suitcase sitting at a table. I commented to Mole about the make up of the birding symposium.

"The word symposium comes from the Greek word for 'drinking party'. And so if Plato could get plastered and Socrates a mite squiffed, I imagine then that even the well heeled bird watching aficionados can drain a few," he said then began to introduce me to the table.

I noticed that he and Suitcase were sitting with a whole group of strangers. The only familiar face was the Ben Franklin look a like lesbian from the morning. She appeared to be pleasantly buzzed and whatever issues she had with our group this morning had apparently disappeared.

With them was a couple of sport coat wearing middle aged guys and a couple of bookish thirty something women. Everyone seemed to be having a great time.

The Mole was in his glory. I don't know if he had done some speed with Roads or whether he was just fired up from the day and the booze but he seemed to have grabbed a shopping cart in his mind and had walked down his brain cell aisle looking for any interesting ideas on sale.

"Everyone has a drinking problem," he continued. Everyone at the table turned to listen. "I don't want to hear anymore cringing or hand wringing. Some people can't stand it. Prohibitionists want it made illegal. Some just can't get enough of it. I say it goes hand in hand with our beautiful sport. Yes, birding and boozing. Perfect together. It even has a ring to it."

He looked around. He repeated the phrase slowly allowing the girls at the table to join him.

"Birding and boozing," the table repeated.

Suitcase looked at me and smiled.

Mole's condition was infectious. The table's Neil Cassady like conversation went on like a bunch of chipmunks on Red Bull.

In retrospect, I guess I should have intervened right then. It was apparent that if I was waiting for the audience to boo him off, it was going to be a long night. Instead I decided to just let him go.

Let Mole be Mole.

And was he.

Instead of getting embarrassed or getting angry I was going to just observe. Soon I decided to switch to trying to record his stream of conscious ramblings. I pulled out the small notepad I used earlier to count our sightings. I started to discreetly take notes.

The thing of it was, most of the people that were in attendance were serious about ornithology. After all, they had paid to be here. They were respectable. They might enjoy their cocktails but they sure as hell were not stone cold alcoholics. Mole was a stone cold alcoholic, and there is nothing at all funny about that. But the rub was that, besides being a serious drinker, Mole also took his Bird-watching to heart.

Just when the people at the table were getting ready to walk away, Mole would grab them by their attention's shoulder. Like some nuisance distant cousin at a wake, he'd say something one didn't know about a favored aunt.

Chapter 33

Mole's Field Notes (as overheard at the World Series of Birding Symposium)

The speed of birds is amazing. What layman would know that a flock of Sand pipers was clocked at one hundred and ten miles per hour, by an airplane. Even the common Mallard can do sixty with no sweat. They eat fast too. No chewing their meals slowly, our birds. A young Robin, for example, may eat over fourteen feet of earth worms. And that is in one day! That would be his last meal in the nest. Of course that's fourteen foot of regurgitated worms. Not like it's one long piece of spaghetti. A diet like that your eggs would be colored blue too . . ."

The elderly couple that had joined the table earlier, thought about leaving, got up briefly, then sat back down to listen. Of course, the old bluehaired wife did not touch her pasta again either.

"Woodpeckers have it rough. It's no wonder some of them have developed red-heads. That's not decorative plummage, that's blood pressure. Imagine, coming home from work. 'What's the matter hon? Hard day in the tree?'

'Hard day at the tree is it? You bet your sweet feathered ass, lady. Peckity-peck-peck. And what do I get? Beetles, caterpillars, ants and moth larvae. You load sixteen tons of termites a day. I tell ya. You know that oak contract I hoped to land? Plowed under. Man-kind. Apartments. My beak hurts, I need a beer . . . . '

. . . The woodpeckers in California store acorns in the holes they drill in trees. Sort of putting the baby back in the womb as it were . . . The Ivory-billed woodpecker is assumed to be extinct. At least they haven't registered to vote, recently . . . . All woodpeckers have long sticky, barbed tongues. Which makes for limited, uncomfortable French kissing, but is great for extracting insects. They use their tail feathers for vertical bracing while eating, just like a back hoe . . . .

Woodpeckers have it rough, their beaks get dented and snub-nosed with age. Prostetics beaks are unavailable . . ."

Suitcase, like some stage manager or carnival host yelled out "Enough of the woodpecker. What else ya got? Tell them about the hummingbirds Beans and Stevie saw today."

The audience, that had now grown to about two tables worth of birders, clapped nervously. Who were these guys? Entertainment? They looked at each other and questioned.

Mole moved on.

"The Ruby throated humming bird has been studied by aeronautical engineers. Boeing would love to get their corporate mitts on this guy's act, no lie. But of all birds they are probably the most batty. Consider, they weigh less than one tenth of an ounce. And that's just normal. Some young girl hummingbirds striving to be models, have been known to starve themselves, developing anorexia and end up weighing less than a small flake of cigarette ash. Some reports claim that some hummingbirds go below sea-level so to speak, when it comes to weight. They are minus! They owe the scales.Now that's skinny.

They lay two small white eggs, which are about as small as a chipmunk's bowling ball. Their shells as thin as a butterfly's tissue paper. Their eggs weigh less than the thought that conceived them.

Yet this tiny bird eats fifty to sixty full meals a day. All sugar. They are crazed. They have been known to try to rape ostriches. Their diet consists of the nector of wild flowers. Now you get all the nectar, the sugar, the liquid sucrose carbohydrates fermenting around in such a wee body and its no wonder that their hearts beat six hundred seventy five times per minute.

Their wings can beat over seventy times per second. That's over four thousand two hundred times a minute. Now that's a lot of fucking flapping! They fly over sixty miles an hour.

The only solid food they eat is the occasional insect, and they only do this for the roughage when they are tired of having the shits all the time from all the sauce they put away.

They are hyperactive to put it mildly.

They are winged Sikorsky sops and they know it. They fly five hundred seventy miles from the tip of the Yucatan to Louisiana and back again, once a year. Drunk, the whole time. They're a disgrace.

I recall years ago, seeing three of them floundering around my Petunia bed, laughing like hell and telling old Hummingbird war stories. It made me sick. I tried to get the keys off them so they wouldn't fly, but they are elusive little bastards. You can't reason with them. It is that way with any migratory bird that has been hitting the sauce.

Yet they are beautiful birds. Indeed, when the sunlight hits them in a stand—still flight, just so, and it catches that lustrous red—throat patch, and the emerald green above . . . it is a wonderous thing to behold.

They can't sing, but they make a very small squeaky noise though. It sounds like a little rusty drawbridge opening on a toy Lionel Train . . ."

Suitcase and the women next to him, who I now noticed had her arm around him, began to cheer and clap. A couple at the table nodded slowly and commented that Mole's description "Although disjointed, really got to the heart of what its like to view the hummingbird. He is lyrical in his descriptions . . ."

Not to mention stoned drunk too, I thought.

To hell with it. I brought Mole another drink. Vodka on the rocks. He looked at me like it was a trick. I just smiled and raised my glass.

"You are in the zone Mole. In the zone," I mouthed to him.

We drank

Later, as the party guests got drunker, I overheard Suitcase say something along these lines: "I know that Storks are supposed to bring babies. Or if you are watching commercials on TV they bring Vlasic pickles, but for me they don't hold a perch to my favorite bird we spotted today.

The pelican.

For, you see, the pelican brings happiness. They deliver joy. How can you see one and not smile? They look like lazy, feathered Winston Churchills with wings. They seem like a bird you could drink with, or at least hang out and eat pizza. Of course with anchovies . . ."

The women, who was now his date, smiled and nodded drunkenly. The modulation of Suitcase's voice was like a verbal recliner. As she listened she tilted her ears all the way back.

The table overflowed with people.

Even Beans and Josh were overheard debating some other birders.

Josh boomed. "I tell you I saw two Delta Condors, the more common Yellow Cessna, and the Huey Chopper bird, or whirly bird for short."

Beans joined in the conversation.

"You heard him right. We saw two Delta Condors, a flock of single engine Yellow—bellied Cessnas and a rare Huey chopper bird."

Most of their listeners laughed along. One sober elderly man murmered something about "Disqualifying the boozers for claiming planes and helicopters in their totals." He shuffled off alone.

"The American Birding Association has no sense of humor if they disqualify us," Beans yelled after him. "They will rue the day."

Mole picked up the point. "The ABA has no vision at all. They just can't see that all planes are just new species of birds. That man created them, blinds them to the fact that man is just serving as God's tool in evolution. They're as myopic as the parasites that live on the hippo and the birds that feed on them, and they can't conceive of their hippo host being a living species. Cars are alive too. We are just so egotistically small-minded and dimwitted not to see the obvious."

He finished his drunken defense of his friend's boasts. The party goers laughed nervously.

I quickly changed the subject to the three types of owls we saw at the same spot. Mole began to spout some twisted nonsense about Owls, but one of the sport coats interrupted.

"Oh, so you are the group that spotted the three types of owls. You also saw three hummingbird species too. All in one spot? Right here in Cape May."

He pulled his card from his coat pocket.

I forgot his name but he was a professor at Cortland State College, and more importantly he was a judge of the competition.

He continued. "I guess the winners of the Big Day Big Stay Award would not be so inclined to show me their secret location?"

So we had won an award. Not the overall title we wanted but certainly not bad for a bunch of amateur birders and proffessional drinkers. Mole and Suitcase were so drunk they didn't even catch the man's comment. But Beans and I did. So did Josh.

"Hey Doctor. You are a doctor of birding or something aren't you? These assholes get any money for winning that award?" he asked skeptically.

"No, just some new binoculars and the satisfaction of knowing that they have contributed valuable information to South Jersey's birding and scientific community."

He smiled and shook my hand.

Beans had gone off to get another drink in celebration. He was on his way to blotto.

Josh looked at me with a barely contained smile and said. "Not bad college boy. But I will stick with my winnings. Thankyou."

We laughed and toasted our drinks.

Later when our names were announced, Beans advanced to the stage like a palsied kangeroo wearing flipflops. He had to use the tables as hand rails.

I helped him. For once I was not embarrassed, I was happy. Proud even.

Yes, Beans was drunk. Hell we all were. But we were having fun. Not to mention we had just seen more birds from one spot than all the science classes and ornitholical groups in the tristate area.

As we approached the lectern, seated at the front tables sat a huge overly made-up lady who looked like Jonathon Winters in drag. She sat with two women of competitive girth and cosmetics. Beans paused at their table. He took a long look at the largest of the three, took a sip of her drink, and whispered in her ear. Her laugh filled the auditorium. It's infectiousness broke the tension and we made it to the stage.

We were each given a new pair of Bushnell binoculars and a Plaque.

I looked out over the crowd of now tipsy birders. I waved the award at our table. Mole and Suitcase cheered. Josh whistled.

I pointed Beans to the microphone.

He removed it from the stand, and immediately began smacking it.

"Testing. Uno, dos, tres—testing!" he bellowed like some drunk Mexican Marlee Matlin.

The resulting blast was a brain exploding trumpet that no doubt caused San Andreas faults in the audience's skulls.

He adjusted it. "There that's better."

Beans let out a huge burp. The eructation hovered above the hall like a hawk. I let out a nervous laugh.

"What did someone step on a duck?" I said like Rodney Dangerfield in Caddyshack.

No one laughed.

In the suspense of the silence, couples glanced at each other. People lit cigarettes. Others took nervous sips of their drinks. Could it be this man was doing a Foster Brooks imitation of a drunk? Or was he going to fall flat on his face?

"Thank you. On behalf of the Backyard Birding Boozers, I say thank you birders all."

The crowd applauded to relieve the tension. Beans was not going to fall off the stage after all.

He continued.

"To a lot of people Bird watching and boozing seem to be an odd and unsuitable combination. Some may think they are harmless and unserious endeavors. Let me correct that notion once and for all. The hazards, dangers, and pitfalls of bird-watching and boozing are rampant It is the most competitive of all sports. By comparison Rugby and pro football look like scrap booking and crocheting. Bird watching can be brutal, friends. Make no mistake about it."

Beans smiled and tapped his empty glass over at Mole.

Mole got up and walked to the stage. He handed Beans a fresh drink.

"Doing great Beansie," he whispered.

Beans took a sip then continued, "And yet most of society, when they hear the phrase 'Bird-watcher' envision frail old ladies in tennis shoes, or some timid, milk toast librarian with a lisp and a field guide. They picture an Episcopalian minister, in tweeds and pipe, or perhaps a retired accountant with bi-focaled binoculars. To that I say Bull Land Fill!

To those that would have us in the same category with cribbage players, common stamp collectors, advisors on etiquette, and needlepoint fanciers, that lot. To those I say Au-bull shit-contraire. Hold it. Cease. Simply not so with our bunch.

We were, we are, as hard drinking, two fisted gang of rutters that ever put a smoking set of binoculars back in its holster.

Please say hi to my partners."

Beans pointed over to our table as he announced. "Suitcase Sampson our driver and shore bird expert. Josh Keenan our muscle, looks like Robert Goulet doesn't he? And lastly our founder and leader of the flock

Mole Molineux. We thank you for this Big Day Big Stay Award and hope that it is the first of many," Beans slurred.

The crowd clapped politely, although I now noticed some tables whispering and a few shaking heads and disgusted looks. I heard one man comment to his wife, "Look I spot the common Drunk White Trash bird. A whole table full."

At first I thought Beans was too drunk to notice the looks and the comments. Then I realized he didn't care. None of them cared. It is though my father and his friends realized all that mattered was doing their own thing. Have fun, get drunk, watch birds and laugh about doing it. Tent big enough for everyone.

Beans continued unfazed.

"Yes, and of course this award would have never happened without our newest bird watching boozer, Mole's son and my partner today Steve Molineux. Besides helping me spot so many birds he also provided a pleasant day's companionship and conversation. Thank you Stevie."

I waved shyly and tried to hide myself behind Beans.

Then I noticed it.

The looks and comments continued from some of the audience. It was the same look I had seen from the two workers earlier in the lobby. It was the same one as the waitresses back in the Margate diner. The looks from the audience reminded me of the stares of the fat family from the boardwalk. They were identical to the looks on the faces of people when they saw my dad and I driving in the Ting Thing. It was the same look Mr. O'Hanlon gave me in the kitchen, what seemed like such a long time ago; before the trip. It was a look I had seen my whole life.

I hated that look then, I hated it that night in Cape May and I hate it today.

The difference was, before I hated **Mole** for that look. I blamed **Mole** for that look. Now in front of that crowd, I realized Mole was right, it was his problem not mine and that look was everyone else's problem not mine.

Not everyone in the audience shared that look, but enough did that I wanted to leave. Not the symposium, not Cape May, but the planet.

Not because I was embarrassed, no, for the first time I wasn't embarrassed by Mole or his friends. I understood them.

I felt liberated!

I wanted to begin my life for the first time unfettered by Mole's drinking and more importantly, peoples attitudes about his drinking.

Why can't we let people live without judging? Why are we so interested in belonging? Why are we so quick to exclude those that are different? Why do people lift themselves up by pushing others down? These questions had been with me all along, but I had approached them all wrong.

Now this trip had shown me. Mole had shown me.

The rest of the night is a blur. I remember I had a great time. I laughed. I drank. I ate. I slept.

The next day I had the hangover to prove it.

It was time to go home.

////////////////////////////////

We drove out of Cape May the next morning. Between the hangovers and the sunburn we really didn't say much. No one ever says much at the end of a vacation. Especially after a low budget blue collar one. Everyone is lost in their own thoughts, dreading the return to reality. Most of the time the reality you are going back to isn't something to look forward to.

I slept for most of the way.

True to Beans' wishes we took the back roads.

I awoke as we crossed the Walt Whitman Bridge back into Pennsylvania and Philadelphia. Suitcase took the first exit off the bridge, to stay on the back roads. As we cruised past the Spectrum and the Veteran's Stadium home of our Flyers and Eagles, we approached the old Penrose Bridge. I craned my neck out the window for my favorite childhood landmark.

Sure enough, I spotted the Car Crusher.

The car crusher is the name my sister and I gave the auto demolition yard that sits at the foot of the Penrose Bridge. It is a fixture on the way through Philadelphia. It has been there for what seems like forever. As our name indicates it crushes cars for recycling.

The bridge is a beat up old four laner that used to be the main artery to carry Delaware County travelers to the New Jersey bridges and the shore. Since I 95 had gone up next to it, the old bridge didn't get much use. It was in need of repairs and upgrades. Instead all it got was a name change.

The bridge we crossed that day was now the George C. Platt Memorial bridge. Renamed after a little known Civil war general. The general's ancestors petitioned the state and after a while the change was made. It reminded me of my mother and her Government jobs. Always a different name but always the same old job.

Different name same old bridge.

Despite the bridge's name change the auto demolition yard still remained the same. The giant crane seemingly in constant use, picking up old and junked cars and carrying them to a conveyor belt to be crushed so small, my sister and I imagined them to be matchboxes, everyone of them, eventually to be made new again.

There it was as we passed on our way home from the shore. Same as it ever was, with apologies to the Talking Heads.

I was glad Suitcase picked the Platt or the Pen rose whatever you want to call it. The car crusher was always just the sign you needed to let you know you were close to home. It made you home sick in a nice comfortable way. As I said, it made me think of my mom.

I missed Larose. I even missed my little sister. I think Mole did too. It had been a week and although I did not see them much during the school year, this time seemed different. It seemed like it had been a long time.

I was anxious to see my mom, but I was also anxious to share with her my new understanding of my father and his friends.

After the Car crusher it would not be long now. Maybe we could be changed into something new and different too.

As we turned onto Hook Road for the final five miles, Suitcase was the first to speak. "You know Beans and I were thinking of extending this little vacation for another week or too."

I was taken completely by surprise. Apparently so was Mole.

"Don't look at me I've got carpet jobs," Mole said. "Where are you thinking about going?" he added.

"We have been invited to visit Beans' friends Junior and Skip in Florida. They said we could meet them in Ormond Beach and hitch a ride down to Key Largo on their Fishing boat," Suitcase said through a thick cloud of cigarette smoke.

Beans joined in. "I'm going. I am not due to work for a couple months. They would put us up free of charge and also would drop us back off at our car in Ormond Beach after the trip."

He patted me on the back.

"What do you say? Bird watching partner."

He looked at me then quickly looked over at Mole.

"He's his own man," Mole said. But his look said "No way."

"I don't have the money and I need to work to save for books in the fall," I answered as though I was responsible or something.

"Suit yourselves you pussies!"

It was Josh. He was drunk and he was going. "We will send you a postcard."

Let's drop them off and get right back out on the road."

"No way. I want to check on Seconds Flat and my mother. Not to mention Brunswick," Beans wearily said.

"Yea, and I want to do some laundry and get a good night's sleep. We can leave tomorrow," Suitcase added.

Josh was not happy but realized he was outvoted.

"Well, if the old lady catches me home I'm screwed. I will have to hide out at Seconds Flat if I plan on making it to the Orange State."

"That's the Sunshine State, Josh," I corrected.

"Just Joshing Stevie. Just Joshing. I am going to the Sunshine State then."

Lucille dropped us off at my parent's house. The car looked as tired and beat up as it's passengers. Suitcase was right, we could all use a good night's sleep and some clean laundry.

I went to shake Suitcase's hand and thank him for the trip and the use of the car.

"Handshakes?" he asked. "We don't need a handshake. A handshake is nothing more than a leftover relic of the cave man times. A survival mechanism. When Korg would look for rocks in the hands of other cave men he encountered. You don't have rocks in your hands, do you?" He let out a grunt and pretended to be a gorilla or a Neanderthal or something. "What we need is the good old fashioned hug."

He brushed aside my hand and gave me a big bear hug.

"Thanks for coming along. The trip would not have been the same without you. Try and be nice to the old man. He's not so bad."

He got back in the car.

Next up was Josh.

"I ain't huggin you like that homo Suitcase. I'll live with a handshake," he said grabbing my arm and pumping it like a politician.

"Anyway, be good college boy. Shame you can't make the second leg."

He got back in the car as well.

Beans was last. He had gone in to use the bathroom and to say hi to Larose. He hugged Mole and said something to him I couldn't hear. When he got to me, he just smiled and said, "I will take a handshake. I could use all the survival mechanisms I can get."

He turned and laughed at Suitcase.

Turning back to me he said, "Thanks there partner. Every time you watch those birds, you think of our day at our Cape May spot. Okay kid?"

They were off.

At the Molineux house, there was no tearful reunion to report, but I could tell my mother was glad to see us both. She must have sensed that it was a good trip.

She smiled and hugged us. She asked us if we had a good time. Her eyes asked me if everything was okay.

"I will tell you later," I whispered.

"It was fun and he was pretty good," I said when he went out later to get our bags from the porch.

For once I wasn't lying to her about the Mole.

Chapter 34

On Becoming an Assistant Manager of the Protein By-Product Removal Unit At The Local Meat Packing Plant

Time is an interesting concept. The clock tells us that time is a constant and never changes. Seconds tick by, then minutes, hours, days, and ultimately years; always passing at the same speed.

Life shows us otherwise.

Certainly time passes differently for different people. To a child, a school year may seem like an eternity. A summer vacation, a lifetime. Their life, if they even bother to think about it, will go on forever.

To an elderly person, a school year probably feels like a snap of the fingers or lone tick on the stopwatch. Time is short. The clock reminds them that it is indeed precious. Getting shorter and faster with every tick.

Time can also be different based on what is filling in that time. As the cliché goes 'Time flies when your having fun.' Certainly when things are enjoyable they seem to make time pass quicker. Who hasn't been at a party and looked at the clock only to remark, 'Where did the time go?'

Time also passes even when you are not having a good time. As my mother used to say "Who are we kidding, time flies when your having fun and time flies when you are not. Time just flies . . . Thankfully.'

In my case, for the remainder of that summer, I remember that it seemed like the upcoming school was not coming fast enough.

Now it seems, in hindsight, to have moved too quickly.

In any event, it was the first time I could remember ever thinking about the passing of time. Before that summer, I can't remember ever really kicking it around at all.

After that summer I can't remember ever really **not** thinking about it again.

Maybe it had something to do with my choices of employment for the remainder of that summer. Or maybe it was getting my hopes about my father dashed so quickly after our trip. Maybe it was what happened that fall after I went back to college.

Whatever it was, I have been conscious of the passing of time ever since.

//

Mole had lined up a few big carpet jobs before our birding trip. He had some new construction in Chester county. Big singles, in an up and coming housing development. He would carpet the new houses before settlement. No owners. No other workers.

This work was always there and he had until the end of summer to complete it. He did not need me for it, and there was no rush. The other contractors needed to finish first. Carpet is always the last job in new construction.

His other carpet job was subcontracting for his brother's carpet company. Residential work. Tear ups and carpeting of houses, like ours, in working class Delaware County. He needed me for these jobs. Not because I was a wiz at installing carpet. I most certainly was not. No. He needed me so that I could move furniture and deal with the homeowner.

My job was to keep the customer away from Mole. This allowed him to cover up and hide his drinking or to cover up and hide his hangovers. Either way he could not deal with the homeowner. With me there he didn't have to see them at all.

That was my job description plain and simple.

I called myself Mole's Customer Service Representative.

It was a good job title but not my best. My best was reserved for my other summer job.

For me, dealing with the customers was the easy part. Dealing with heavy rolls of carpet and moving furniture was not.

It was a pretty good deal.

I would prep the room by tearing up the old carpet and putting down new padding. He would install the new carpet, while I occupied the homeowner.

When he was done I would collect for the job. Most of the time it worked. Unfortunately for both of us there was never enough residential jobs especially in the summer. Because of this I had no choice but to take a second job. When Mole would work at his commercial new construction sites I would work at my old job from high school.

Fat remover.

This is not what you are thinking.

I was not some trainer at a health club. Nor was I some miracle diet salesman. Although both of these positions would have been welcomed.

I shoveled fat at Hygrade Meats in Philadelphia.

Technically, I cleaned out pipes in the basement of the factory. But, since the pipes were filled with fat and other rotted meat scraps, and the pipes, when sprayed with a high pressure hose, tended to dislodge their contents on the basement floor, I, for all intents and purposes was a person who shoveled fat. Since I liked titles, and shoveling fat was not, shall we say, too prestigious of a job, I had given myself the working title of Assistant Preventative Maintenance Engineer at Hygrade Meats.

It had a ring to it.

Besides, who wants to be a fat shoveler?

I would work this job on days when I was not working with Mole. Since it was summer and the carpet business is slow in the summer, I worked shoveling fat most of the week. The boss allowed me to come and go as I pleased.

It had to be the foulest most disgusting and possibly most dangerous job out there. I still can't believe it has not been chronicled on the World's Dirtiest Jobs.

As I said, I was a veteran at Hygrade having shoveled my share of the fat back in high school.

Back then, the job carried a couple of benefits. First, it allowed me to earn ten dollars an hour—no taxes. This in itself would have been reason enough to work at Hygrade. No one was making ten dollars an hour in high school at the time. But the money was just one reason.

No supervision was another.

Since the job was disgusting and took place in a dark, dank basement, the boss never bothered to come down. We worked at our own pace without anyone looking over our shoulders. This was a huge benefit, especially if you wanted to mess around, sleep on the job, drink or smoke pot.

We often did all four.

If all that wasn't enough to get you to sign on, my high school co-workers and I were all were all wrestlers. Most of the time we were expected to wrestle at weight classes far below our natural body weights. Because of this, we were constantly dieting. Most of the time that meant sweating off water weight before a match. Shoveling fat in a meat factory basement in close quarters with hot pipes was like spending a day in a sauna. Albeit, a disgustingly, smelly one.

With the addition of a rubber suit and the heat, after a hard day's work it was not uncommon for us to lose ten pounds.

When we were working at Hygrade we always made weight. It was the perfect combination for a high school wrestling kid.

It was not the perfect combination for a college kid.

When I came back that summer, I couldn't believe that I actually had not minded this nightmare job. Whereas in high school I liked the heat (all the better to sweat off the weight), I now found it stifling.

All of my high school buddies were long gone too.

Now I was left with strangers with whom I had nothing in common, nothing to talk about in this nightmare. They were stuck here because they could not find other work. Most were down on their luck. Most were not going anywhere.

Then there was the smell.

In high school there was a perverse pride we would get from having the plant's cafeteria cleared out before we were allowed to enter for lunch break. I thought it was funny how my mother would gag as she hosed me down in the yard before allowing me to go inside for the first of three showers before I could eat dinner. It was an even bigger hoot to see my sister eat with a look of disgust on her face if she was forced to sit next to me.

It was a joke that my clothes would not come clean no matter how many times they were washed, and had to be thrown out after one shift in the plant. Eventually I would burn them after the trash men complained one too many times.

It was no longer cute that the seagulls that congregated in the plant's parking lot, would go ape shit and dive bomb me as I walked to my car after work. They would be left to wonder why something that smelled as bad as me wasn't carrying their dinner.

The smell was worse than death. It is really indescribable.

I never want to smell it again

If all of this wasn't bad enough, there was the danger. Of course like any factory job there was the usual hazards. Industrial slicers and meat cutters in the plant. Forklifts and cranes in the lots. Enough danger that you had to wear a hard hat and always be on guard. Still, even with these regular factory problems the plant would suffer work injuries on a weekly basis.

Oh, to only have to deal with these mundane troubles.

In addition to the hazards all the plant workers faced, we had our own special ones unique to the 'cave dwellers' as we were called by the other plant workers.

The biggest and most prevalent problem was low hanging pipes. They were all over the basement. Some too low to go under, had to be climbed. Others too high to go over, you had to duck. Mostly all of them spouted steam or hot water or worse—fat. Not the gristle off your steak fat. I'm talking, been rotting in a pipe for months in hot temperatures fat.

Every day we would bang our heads on pipes. This would cause your hard hat to tumble to the ground where it would be swallowed up by the anywhere from six inches to two feet of rancid fat and meat scraps that were always at our feet. This left the unlucky person with a decision. Do they put the fat encrusted hat back on their head or do they go hatless and smash their skull a hundred times again in a typical day?

Newcomers usually went hatless. Veterans did not.

If the pipes weren't bad enough, there was also the rats and the roaches.

Fat is the leftover byproduct of meat. Pigs, cows, chickens, turkeys. You name it, it goes into a hotdog. I'm not talking sirloin or chicken breasts, or even pork chops. I'm talking tongue, and skin, and intestines and eyes and balls, and well, you get the picture.

There is a reason I don't eat hotdogs anymore.

Now just imagine, what does not make the cut from that illustrious group of meat scraps, that's what we found fermenting in the pipes at the plant on a daily basis.

The worst of the worst always brought out the vermin. Creatures that saw this disgusting filth as a banquet. There were so many nasty animals living in that basement that we were forced to constantly yell and bang on the pipes just to keep them away from where we were working.

Sometimes even this was not enough. Too often a rat or a opossum would just refuse to leave. It would just sit and stare back at us. It's shiny eyes glaring at us across the basement floor. Wondering when we would get out of the kitchen of their comfortable subterranean apartment.

I'm sure if you talked to the fat shoveling alumni today, and any of them were willing to admit to their old employment, some would say the hot pipes were the worst thing about the job. Still others would no doubt say the rats and the roaches were the biggest hazard. To me, by far the most dangerous thing about working at the 'Fat Factory' as my grandmother called it, were the electric wires.

The plant must have been built in the forties after the World War Two. You could not tell the age from the plant's exterior, nor could you from the plant's interior because it was obvious that it had gone through a lot of upgrades and additions through the years.

The way you could tell the plant's age was because, despite all the improvements over the years the plant's engineers had apparently forgotten the basement. Whatever improvements had been done to the top had not been done to the bottom. The cellar still had the original nineteen forties construction.

In addition to the faulty and failing pipes that led to my employment, there was also an antiquated electrical system. The electric could barely provide enough power for the few scattered bare light bulbs every twenty feet or so throughout the cellar.

My coworkers and I could deal with the bad lighting. What was almost impossible to deal with was the electrical wires that fell to the floor of the basement. The brackets that held them aloft had rusted out over the years, causing the wires to droop or lay on the ground. These live wires would electrify huge areas of fat, causing an unlucky shoveler who walked into that area to get electrocuted. Probably the only thing that saved us from being deep fried, was the fact that we wore high rubber boots. These acted to ground some of the current that ran through the fat, saving us from becoming French fries.

This problem was so prevalent that when we moved about the basement we would look like some platoon of soldiers on patrol. One guy would walk point. As he cautiously maneuvered up and down around the pipes he would gingerly feel for 'electric fat'. If he hit a patch he would yell out while the current snaked through him. Whoever was directly behind would hook him with a large stick and haul him out of harm's way.

Everyone dreaded 'walking point', and like soldiers in Vietnam, it was usually the new guys that got stuck with the job. Every shift, calls for the 'hook' to pull the unlucky guy out, were heard echoing though the basement.

As you could imagine, turnover was high in this job. Sometimes a guy would not even last the day.

Those that did stick it out could usually be seen wearing chest waders, more common on a trout stream then at a meat packing plant. This prevented you from losing a boot when the fat sucked the standard issue knee high boots right off your feet. Regulars also wore a knit hat under their hard hats. This served to keep the fat away from your hair, when your hard hat fell in the muck.

Last but not least, was facial protection. Anyone who did the job more than once wore protective glasses and a face mask. It didn't do much, but psychologically it meant a lot.

After spending so much time in the beautiful outdoors on the birding trip, I now found myself in blackness and filth indoors for eight hours a day. The only time I saw light was if I pulled the barreling and dumping duty at the fat tank.

Barreling and dumping consisted of filling fifty-five gallon drums with fat and then dumping them with the aid of a forklift into outside dumpsters. The fat would be shoveled from a giant tank the size of a backyard swimming pool. The tank was ten feet wide, eight feet long and maybe seven or eight feet deep. How deep I didn't want to know. My shovel never touched the bottom the whole time I worked there.

I wished Mole would get more carpet jobs for me. This job was even worse than I had remembered.

It was not to be.

Since we had gotten back, Mole seemed to bury himself even deeper in the booze. It was though he had tasted life on the outside of the cage and now he could not bear the thought of going back. Once he had taken wing there was no return.

He drank to excess almost every night now. He drank in the morning before work and even all day on the job too. First I found the vodka bottles in his truck. Then I would find them in our basement. Finally, I even found them in his tool box.

He had always taken pride in his work despite his drinking. Now, to see a vodka bottle in his tool box, meant that he had given up on his livelihood too.

Larose was angry and scared. "What happened to him on your trip?" she asked accusingly. "I thought you said he was good?"

"He was," I answered, as stumped and worried as my mother.

We settled back into life with an alcoholic. I called it trench warfare.

It is always the same. With an alcoholic you live your life in a hole, a trench really, because a trench is a hole you dig or is dug for you. A trench allows you to move but you never really go anywhere. This way and that, but never up, never out. Since you are always in the trench you get used to it. Even though you can't see that much around you, and it is usually overcast and wet, you still have each other and that is **something**. Why, sometimes when it is nice out, you can even see the sun.

Once in a while, when things go really well and it starts to dry out, you begin thinking about climbing out of the trench. You get all excited and begin making elaborate plans. Really they consist of either trying to put a ladder up to climb out or grabbing a rope that might get thrown down by someone trying to help. Either way, what happens is, once you start climbing, it starts raining again. You end up muddying yourself up as you futilely claw at the sides. If you are not careful or if you don't give up, you are liable to cave in the trench.

My mother and I gave up late that summer.

Suitcase and Josh came back from Florida in August. They said they had a blast. Beans stayed down to work on his landlord's fishing boat until he shipped out for the oilfields in the winter.

I called Mole's friends for help.

"What's up Stevie?" Suitcase asked with concern.

Suitcase came over when Mole was at work.

My mother didn't have much to say. Of course, now I realize that she knew-

Suitcase couldn't help.

I explained that Mole was partying even harder than before the trip. More important to me was that he did not seem to have a reason for the drinking anymore. He just drank, all the time, even on the job.

Suitcase listened patiently. He nodded at the right times. He clucked his tongue at the worst parts. He shook his head in disbelief.

During the time I took to brief him on Mole's situation he drank four beers, smoked a half a pack of smokes, and inquired twice about Mole's homegrown weed stash.

My mom was on to something.

He **was** no use.

He told us he would handle the situation and straighten it all out. He left with a promise to return.

That weekend Suitcase picked up my dad. Josh was with him.

"Don't worry Stevie I will talk to him," Suitcase promised as they drove off.

I could see a cooler in the back seat.

My mother and I looked at each other.

"Can't hurt. can it?"

Larose just shook her head and went back to the dishes.

They were gone for two days.

When they finally showed up on Sunday night, Josh had a shiner, Mole was limping and drunk, and Suitcase had a handful of disorderly conduct citations.

"Nice work fellas," my mother said disgustedly. She would not even look at Mole. He staggered up the gravel driveway with a bottle of vodka and a ripped tee shirt.

He slept until Monday night, missing work of course.

(Note to readers; Never use binge drinkers and alcoholics for an intervention.)

Two weeks before going back to school, the situation got worse. Mole lost the commercial new construction contract. He was drunk on the job again. The general contractor said something and Mole went off. He took a poke at the man, and that was it. Just like that he was unemployed.

My uncle would not give him any residential jobs without a guarantee that I would be there to handle the customers. I briefly thought about quitting school to help out but Mole would not hear of it.

"I break my back to give you the chances I never had. I will not allow you to drop out!" he would scream at himself as much as to me. "I made a living before you came on board and I will make a living after you."

As he got drunker and drunker his rambling monologues would increase in both volume and credibility.

"You see theesh arms?" he slurred one night. "They are not even the same shize any more from that goddamn tool box. Thing is fuckin heavy!" he yelled standing in front of Larose and I late at night. To prove his point he would take his shirt off and stand at attention. He would stand there swaying back and forth like an old Buster Keaton or Chaplin movie where the star's feet seem nailed to the floor. Just when you thought he had forgotten the point to his tirade he would snap his left arm out.

"She this one?" he would bellow. "Normal lenff. Not a thing wrong wif it."

Then with the left arm raised he would extend his right arm out, rotating his shoulder around so it was at least a half an arm's length longer. Never mind that he was now standing sideways. He had proved his point.

"I carried that damn, smoking heavy tool box for twenty-two years and look at my arm! It is a foot longer than my left," he would cry as though in pain.

The arm would drop, useless to his side, seemingly now paralyzed.

"I hate carpet installing and damn if my son is going to do it. **And** you are not going in the Marine Corps either," he rambled.

Satisfied his point was made, he would sit down Indian style on the living room floor and turn on the stereo full blast with some obscure jazz music.

Thankfully Larose had the sense to send my sister to bed.

She would look at me and we would laugh.

What else could we do?

It was like when he did his 'head' push ups during his show off workouts while he was drunk. Nothing would move but his head, and he would swear he did fifty of them.

His act was getting old.

The next day, when he sobered up a little he suggested I get him in at the Hygrade plant.

"Are you serious? You want to shovel fat? It's a nightmare dad. It is beneath you."

I bit my tongue as soon as I said it.

"I did not raise you to be judgmental. Any job where you break a sweat and work to earn your pay is good work. Besides I have bills to pay," he lectured.

"Alright I will ask Conway tomorrow."

Conway was the supervisor. He was an independent contractor. His company, J+C Industrial Cleaners, had the pipe cleaning contract for Hygrade. Because of this he could do pretty much whatever he wanted at Hygrade, including bringing in whoever he wanted whenever he wanted.

Mole was a shoo in.

"So your old man is out of work?" Conway asked over the phone. "Did you tell him it is dirty nasty work that is not for the old or faint of heart?"

I assured him that Mole was neither.

"Then bring him down tomorrow. We will give him a start at the fat tank. You can show him the ropes."

Mole and I spent the next two weeks working seven to three at Hygrade.

The other guys thought he was a bit odd with the way he would try and educate them as to various subjects throughout the day.

After about three days they nicknamed him Professor Mole. I told him it was only fitting since we **were** underground and he did know a lot of things. He seemed to take the name and the work in stride, never once complaining. It didn't hurt that he could drink on the job. Everyone did, even the boss upstairs, outside and in his trailer.

"Stevie, I have new found respect for you and your friends. How you did this job with a rubber suit on blows my mind," he joked.

"I still can't understand how you can do this for eight hours but I can't get you to put out the trash or rake the leaves." He laughed as he took off his rubber glove to wipe some fat that splashed in his eye.

It was the second week and we were pulling tank duty. We both stood on a rickety scaffolding over the tank. We took turns dipping our shovels in and scooping out the rancid fat, which we then placed into a fifty five gallon drum on the floor. Once the drum was full, the boss Conway would maneuver a forklift through a small door and dangle a chain drum harness in. We would then jump down to the basement floor and hook the drum up. Conway would lift the drum out with the fork lift and have it dumped by another worker stationed outside at a dumpster.

The work was back breaking and monotonous. Plus it got pretty hairy when the plank would get slick. If you were not careful you could slip and hurt yourself.

Still it was better than working in the bowels of the basement. Mole and I were glad to be on the tank.

Even though he was pretty drunk, he was okay. I mean he wasn't getting on my nerves like he usually did when he was banged up. He was a hard worker and the labor seemed to lift his spirits, as crazy as that seems, given the task.

He was shoveling and joking.

Besides making me laugh, he was cracking up Conway every time the forklift made an appearance.

Since Mole was the oldest worker, Conway bonded with him. They were about the same age. They were enjoying each other's company.

He was the hit of the fat shovelers.

What an accomplishment.

We were working at a good clip. Each of us alternating our scoops with the shovels. It was hot and the scaffolding was slick. We took turns singing Creedence tunes.

Just before we were about to break for lunch, it happened.

Mole fell in.

One minute he is plugging away like John Henry, the next thing he's submerged in the fat tank.

I screamed for help and fell to my knees on the scaffold. I dipped my hand in the muck like I was searching for the soap in a bubble bath. Before I could find him he surfaced.

"Ahhhh! I swallowed it!" he screamed as he tried to climb out. He quickly slid back off the slick metal wall of the tank and disappeared a second time.

My mind raced.

First I thought about an old lifeguard training film I had seen a long time ago at summer camp. I remembered it said if a distressed swimmer goes under three times he will drown. Mole had another dunk coming I thought.

The next thing that crossed my mind was Augustus Gloop from *Willy Wonka and the Chocolate Factory*. Remember, the glutton boy who fell in the chocolate river and got sucked up a tube? Thankfully there were no suction tubes for Mole, only tubes dumping fat in.

The thought of Mole as Augustus Gloop and the sight of him floundering in the fat, some how got me laughing.

By now Conway was there, as was Marty and Billy. Thankfully they weren't laughing. They placed two fifty five gallon drums next to the tank. Then, standing on the tanks they quickly dragged Mole out.

He tumbled to the ground, steam rising off his totally saturated body.

"You look like a mixer after making cake batter," someone yelled. "Don't want to lick it clean though, that's for sure."

"No, he looks like a newborn cow. Smells a whole lot worse too," Billy said throwing Mole a towel. Mole wiped his face, then gagged.

"Fuck all of you," Mole hissed.

"Take him up and get him out of those clothes. Hose him down, then go ask the shift manager if we can use the meat cutter's locker room so he can shower," Conway ordered, as though this happened every day.

"I got some fresh clothes outside in my car. Do me a favor Stevie and fetch them for your old man."

I was embarrassed that I had laughed, so I was glad to get out of there.

I climbed out and left him with the others.

When I returned Mole was gone. In the shower no doubt.

"He is done for the day, Stevie. Take him home. Get a good night's sleep. Tomorrow is a new day," Conway said. He looked at me and shook his head.

"I know it seems funny to you, but I assure you it is not. Happened to me years ago and pretty much wigged me out. Disgusting. Never want to go through it again," he finished. He waved to the others like he was rounding up cattle, and grunted "Back to work."

I thought of the shop foreman from *On the Waterfront*.

Even Longshoreman got it better than us, I thought as I gathered up our stuff to leave.

I met Mole at the car. He had on a pair of Conway's overalls and some work boots from my trunk. He was shivering despite the heat. He smiled and said "I felt like a piece of fried chicken."

He didn't laugh.

As I drove him home my mind raced for something to talk about. I remembered he had stashed a pint of vodka in the back. At a light, I reached back and grabbed it.

He took it without saying anything.

He drank in silence.

I remembered an incident that had taken place a day earlier at my on again/ off again girlfriend's house where I had gone to dinner with her family.

"Mole you would be proud of me," I began. "I know you like language and you always want me to become a writer or an actor, well I out did myself at Sally's a couple of nights ago."

"Yea what happened?" he answered trying to appear interested.

"You know her old man thinks I'm not good enough for her, right?" I paused to see if he was following me.

He finally looked over. "So?"

"So we are at the dinner table. Aunts, uncles, the whole family. The whole table is quiet. I'm a nervous wreck, trying to remember what fork to use you for my salad.

Her father says 'So young man, are you working this summer?'

Well I don't know what to say. The whole table is waiting on my answer.

I don't want to tell them I'm a fat shoveler for Christ sake. So I try and stall. I say Yea I'm working. Good money too.

A couple of them nod nicely, the mother smiles at me. I think I'm in the clear. But the old man won't let it rest. He says 'Well what are you doing exactly?'

You will love this. I don't miss a beat. I blurt out, I'm an assistant manager of the protein byproduct removal unit at a local meat packing plant.

I could tell the whole table is impressed. Jeez, even I'm impressed. Where did that come from? That is an awesome job title, if I do say so myself.

One uncle says 'That's a heck of a job. Must be very important. What exactly do you do?'

I go—I Shovel fat.

The whole table cracked up. Even the father starts laughing. He says 'You got a way with words Molineux. That's for sure. Where it will get you I haven't a clue.'

Her dad was still smiling when they served desert." I finished and let out a laugh.

"A good one huh?"

I looked over at Mole.

He was silent. Not even a smile.

Of course, now I realize I was an asshole. I did not even pause to think how that story must have made him feel. Telling him I was embarrassed to let them know what my job . . . what **our** job was, would be completely insensitive anytime, let alone after he had just fell in the fat tank.

I was getting out. Mole? He was just getting in.

I was moving up in a couple of weeks. Mole was moving down.

He had lost his carpet job.

He was reduced to shoveling fat.

He had just literally fallen in shit.

The realization that he was now reduced to an even more difficult dead end job with lower pay must have deflated him like someone stepping on a two day old helium balloon.

Today I am ashamed I told that story to him.

That day, I just piled on.

"What's with you?" I asked when he didn't say anything. "You look like that fucking Indian in that old pollution commercial. Are you crying? Please tell me that it's just irritation from the fat," I said oblivious to his pain.

"Just get me home," he said and took a swig of vodka.

I noticed some fat crusted behind his ear.

"You missed a spot."

He didn't move.

Chapter 35

On Going Back to School and Getting an Education

The next couple of weeks were rough. The tension in the house just continually seemed to amp up. Mole's drinking continued. All day at work he would sneak it. Then after a day at the fat factory he would drink himself blind.

I stayed out of his way. We all did.

My mother avoided him. I could tell she still loved my father but the booze was rapidly drowning any feelings she still had for him. They hardly spoke and when they did it was only to argue.

The usual suspects.

The working class trinity. Money, bills and the holy spirits. In our case the holy spirits were the vodka and wine bottles we were finding hidden all over the basement and the garage.

"I can't take this much longer. I don't know what I'm going to do when you go back to college," she said to me one night when he was out with Josh.

Suitcase was laying low after his failed intervention.

"Do you want me to take a semester off?" I asked.

Secretly I hoped she'd say no.

"No. Are you out of your mind? If you take off you will never go back," she said, and took a deep inhale of her Kool.

I thanked my lucky stars.

It was settled.

I was going back to Widener.

With college just a few days off, my awareness of Mole's escalating drinking problem receded away. It was though I was on a sinking ship and I had drawn the straw for the life boat.

I occupied my time readying myself to paddle off. I tried not to think of the others. If I did think of my mom and sister, I rationalized that the boat would right itself, the leak would stop, or another lifeboat would happen by. When those thoughts failed me, I lulled myself to sleep by dreaming I would paddle to safety then return and save the doomed vessel and its passengers.

I left the weekend before classes started.

Like usual, Mole sobered up long enough to give my mother and I small hope. He was there to wish me off and wish me luck. He was proud of me I could tell. The Mole I saw in the car after his fall at Hygrade Meats was no where to be found.

Still, I tried not to think what would happen now that I was out of the house.

On the other hand, Larose seemed to have changed since our trip. Maybe it was her job promotion, or maybe it was her realization that Mole wasn't going to change. Whatever it was she no longer took his shit.

With her new attitude, I felt better about their prospects with me back at school.

Then again, if she stood up to him like I did, she might end up like me—fighting him.

I selfishly put those thoughts away and went back to college.

School was a welcome distraction. For the next few weeks I didn't think about home or what was going on in it. I concentrated on the things all college kids do, classes, the opposite sex and partying.

Life was good.

At college I was just me. I was not the son of an alcoholic. I was not a first generation college kid from a working class family. I was Steve Molineux. I was a good student. I was an athlete. I was a student adviser. I was on the television crew of the campus station.

Who was I kidding.

I was the son of Steve Molineux.

I was on my way to receiving a college degree but I was receiving my real education from Mole and Larose and Mole's friends.

I spoke to Larose a few times during that semester. Her new attitude was causing her to bloom. She never sounded better. She was happy with work. She was happy with my sister's progress at school, and she was happy with her group of friends from the office.

She was not happy with Mole. She didn't talk about it but I could still tell from her tone.

She told me that on Friday nights after work she would take my sister to the Zooks and go to the base's Officer's Club with her work friends. She hinted subtly that some of the friends were men. When I didn't respond one way or another she moved on.

I think she was beginning to move on from the Mole as well.

I was happy for her. Instead of walking out, she was trying to find her place in a room crowded with the eight hundred pound gorilla that is alcoholism.

I hoped it would not squeeze the life out of her.

The semester wound it's way toward finals

I went back to my own worries. College worries.

In hind sight, really no worries at all.

///

As October rolled around, I settled into a routine. College is not really that difficult as long as you do your reading. Stay up on the reading and you stay up with your grades.

Every weeknight I was in the habit of going to the library to study. I found that getting myself out of the dorm, or now out of my apartment, was the best way to insure that I got my work done.

Now I admit there was also a lot of girls that hung out at the library so it wasn't all business. I would study from seven until nine or nine thirty then hit the library lounge to hang out.

Unfortunately, I was the guy that was every girl's friend but not their boyfriend. Still it was better than hanging out with the guys all the time.

Sometime in the fall, I forget when, I walked home from the library around eleven.

I had not talked to Larose or Mole in over a week. The last time I talked they were doing okay.

No news was good news.

When I returned to my apartment, Dan, my roommate was up drinking beer and eating pizza.

"Hey Steve. Your mom called. Said for you to call her when you got in. Said it didn't matter what time it was," he finished and went back to his pizza.

I panicked. Did Mole go off? Was she alright?

I hurried to the phone.

She picked up on the first ring.

"Beans is dead," she blurted out, then started crying.

"What?" I said. I felt like I was kicked in the balls.

"Your father got the call after dinner. Beans apparently drowned after falling overboard on his landlord's boat down in the Keys," she said sobbing.

"Where's Mole?" I asked now realizing the effect this could have on my parents.

She didn't answer for what seemed like an hour.

"You there mom? You alright?" I asked getting frantic.

"Yes," she finally answered. "Your sister just came in the room. I didn't want to talk in front of her," she said now more composed. "He left with Suitcase a couple of hours ago. He's not driving, but I'm worried. How could a swimmer like Beans drown? Didn't he swim from an aircraft carrier one time or something? It is the oddest thing . . . ." Her voice drifted off.

"I will be right home," I said now worried about the Mole.

"You will do nothing of the sort. You will worry me to death if you go out now. It is eleven thirty at night. Besides you don't have a car and you have class tomorrow. Get some sleep. I'm sure your father will be okay. You can come home this weekend. They won't have any service for a while. Not until they can get his body home. If they bring him home at all. Where will they get the money? . . ."

Again her voice drifted off.

By then I wasn't listening.

Beans was dead. If the initial news was a kick in the balls, then it settling in was now a one two combination to my head.

News of a sudden death kicks the shit out of you.

"I love you mom," I remember saying then putting the phone in the cradle.

Dan handed me a beer. "Late night phone calls are never good," he said.

"We got anything stronger?" I asked.

He smiled and said, "That bad huh?"

We drank until four.

He knew Beans a little, so he knew why I was so upset. He may only have known him a little but he knew a hundred guys like Beans. It was amazing how much his father's friends were like my father's friends. Plus he had lost his old man the year before at forty six, so he was still raw.

We swapped stories all night. I was glad I had him with me. Drinking with him took the sting out of the bad news.

To this day, it still does.

I slept in the next day. To hell with classes. My dad's best friend, **my** friend was dead.

How the hell could he drown? He was a distance swimmer.

I had seen him swim across the Springton Reservoir stone drunk, 'No problemo' as he would say. There was no way he could drown.

I needed to talk to Mole. Something wasn't right.

That weekend I hitched a ride to my house. No need to bother my mother. The funeral was Saturday afternoon. I had some time to get home.

I caught a ride quickly. A middle aged homosexual.

What's with middle aged white homos? Do they all moonlight as gypsy cab drivers?

Almost every time I hitchhiked in high school or college, and I hitchhiked a lot, I always got picked up by a homo. Don't get me wrong I've got nothing against homosexuality, but do these guys really think that I'm in the market for a good time just because I put out a digit? Keep in mind it is the thumb I'm talking about, not some other digit that might signal—green light.

I was a regular faggot magnet.

Anyway, I was in no mood.

The guy started with the usual homosexual hitchhiker pick up ice breaker.

"So you got a girlfriend?"

Then the awkward pause.

"Good looking guy like you probably has a lot of girlfriends."

(Note to reader: When hitchhiking, if you are asked about a girlfriend, just get out right then and there. Unless of course you are homosexual. If so, then stay. I'm sure a lot of relationships have started this way.)

He then reached over and put his hand on my knee.

As I said, I was in no mood, but I did not want to get out and hitch another ride.

"Look. I'm not gay and I'm not curious. You want to give me a ride great. You don't I will get out at the light. You tell me," I said looking straight ahead and speaking with a obvious tone of weariness at the whole thing.

"I'm sorry. I read you all wrong. Where you going?" the man asked.

I looked over at him. He was now redfaced.

"Glenolden," I answered. "Mind if I put on the radio?"

Not waiting for an answer, I turned up the volume. If he wanted to say anything else he couldn't.

He dropped me off at the Amtrak overpass in Glenolden. I'm sure he wasn't going that far but guilt sometimes is a wonderful thing. Just ask a Catholic.

I walked the four blocks to my folk's house. On the way I passed the Glenolden Pool. I thought of Mole and Beans sneaking a cooler of beers and all my friends in late night, years ago when I was a teen. I remembered Beans doing can openers off the high dive at two a.m. I remembered us all running when the cops came. Beans huffing and puffing and giggling like a child as we hid under the bridge next to the Arco refinery.

It hit me. Beans was dead. Forty five years old. A short ride. Too short.

I began to cry.

I pulled myself together by thinking of Lincoln's quote "Its not the years in your life, its the life in your years . . ."

Beans certainly had life in his years that's for sure.

I wanted to get my shit together before I saw my mother. I rinsed my face off with the O'Hanlon's hose as I cut through their yard on Elmwood Avenue. I crossed through the yards and went in the back door of my house.

My sister was watching television. She said hi then went back to *Scooby Doo*.

I went upstairs.

Larose was in the bathroom.

"Hi mom," I said through the door. "Where's Mole?"

"Oh. Hi Stevie. Your father went to the funeral home already. He wanted to help out Beans' mother. Josh and Suitcase picked him up. Be out in a bit. Do you need to take a bath, or are you ready to go?"

"I'm fine. I will be in my room."

I waited for her to get ready.

We left around noon. The sun was out but it was chilly. Definitely coat weather even though it was only October.

We pulled in to Griffiths' Funeral home. It was only a short ride from the house. What immediately struck me was the line of funeral procession cars. A parked hearse with a stretch limo behind it, rented for the family by the funeral home. Behind them were an long line of assorted cars. The procession looked like the starting lineup of a demolion derby. There were junkers of every make and model. Besides our Dodge Dent there were K-cars, an old Monte Carlo a couple of what looked like converted police cruisers, an AMC Matador, and I swear to God a Nova, and a Pinto. Remember, this is the late eighties maybe 1990. If there was a car called the the Santa Maria I would have thought a Pilgrim died.

We went in.

Mole came right up to us. He smelled like booze and cigarettes but he was drinking coffee.

He looked better than I expected.

"Thanks for coming, son," he began. "Do you believe this shit? Beaner, for Christ sake. Those shit bags better not show their faces," he said bitterly.

My mother went off to talk to some friends.

"What are you talking about?" I asked. Confused that my father would be so petty about who paid their respects.

"Those bastards from the Darby Inn, his landlords, the fucking drug smuggling pricks that killed him," he hissed.

People turned to look.

"What are you talking about Mole? Are you fucked up?" I asked alarmed at his anger.

"No I'm not fucked up. Anything but. But I assure you someone is going to get fucked up if Josh and I have our way."

He pulled me over to Suitcase.

"Tell him Suitcase. Tell him," he demanded.

Suitcase managed a smile. "Hi Stevie. Long time no see. You are a sight for sore eyes. Beans would be glad you could make it."

To Mole he said, "This is not the time nor the place. We will talk after."

Turning back to me, he said "Would you be a pall bearer? I'm sure Beans would have wanted you.

Me, Josh, your father and you will help out his two nephews ok?" he said in his softest undertaker voice.

STEPHEN MOLINEUX

"Of course," I said. "Let me tell my mom."

I walked off to find Larose.

The place was starting to fill up.

I noticed another trait of a working class funeral besides the cars in the procession.

The clothes.

Growing up in my neck of Delaware County, people didn't have nice clothes. Not only could they not afford them they really didn't need them. They needed work clothes and casual clothes. Weddings, funerals and court were the only times they got dressed up. Lately people didn't seem to even care what they looked like in court.

Since nice clothes were a luxury few could afford, any events that required dressing up always took on a comical feel to me.

Consider my own family's attire.

That day, Mole was dressed in jeans. Not any jeans, but brand new jeans, dark blue and stiff as cardboard. They were so uncomfortable that he was walking around the funeral home like John Wayne. Come to think of it maybe that's why the Duke always walked like that in his Westerns. Mole had on a corduroy sport jacket with big worn suede patches on the elbows. It reeked of mothballs and looked like it was from a 1960's Sears Catalog, which it was. To add to the look, the jacket had never been tailored. As a result the sleeves were so long, to the untrained eye Mole had no hands. The whole ensemble was finished off with ancient wingtips, sweat socks and a clip on square bottom knit tie, seen only on certain social studies teachers in the late seventies.

He was one of the best dressed at this funeral.

My mother was lucky. She worked in an office. As such she had decent work clothes. Not fashionable but decent. White blouse and black skirt.

Looked good. Larose always made it work on a limited budget.

My own outfit was no better. Like most of the attendees I had no overcoat. Unlike most, I chose to freeze instead of the alternative—Wearing a ski coat or cheap parka with the fake fur collar over your old or borrowed suit. In my neighborhood no one had a decent dress coat. Starter Jackets, old high school letter coats and army surplus. These were our Brooks Brothers.

Then there was the footwear. With the exception of Mole's wing tips which were ancient, no one owned a decent pair of dress shoes. I looked down at my own feet. I was wearing sneakers. Work boots, cowboy boots and even a few platform leftover disco shoes from the back of the closet made the rounds that day.

The whole room was filled with badly dressed people who knew that were badly dressed and felt uncomfortable by it.

Since everyone was dressed the same, those that dressed well were the ones who stuck out.

As I waited to go up to the casket, my informal count revealed only two or three tailored suits. Judge Narkin had one, the merchant marine union reps had the rest. Of course I did not count the funeral parlor workers. They all looked like spit shined Secret Service or the *Men in Black*.

Then I saw Beans. The informal blue collar clothing poll stopped. Dead.

Even though I was twenty, this was really the first time I saw a corpse. My great grandparents had died when I was young. If my mom took me to the funeral I didn't remember. My grandparents on Mole's side were cremated. My other grandparents were still kicking. I had a friend who had been killed in high school. He was hit by a train. Obviously it was a closed casket.

Beans was the first.

He was outfitted in a brand new suit. Probably bought by his mother or maybe even the the funeral home. It still had a tag on the sleeve. It had not been tailored. You could see where the sleeves were folded up and the pant legs pinned. He looked like a model from a wax museum. Nothing real about him at all.

I thought of a taxidermist's mounted deer head or a trophy fish. I thought of anything not to think of Beans in a casket.

His family and friends had taken to stuffing all sorts of mementos alongside his body in the coffin. He had his crocheted beer can hat, I remembered from the quarry. He had an Philadelphia Eagles shirt, a Flyers jersey and a Phillies cap. Someone had slipped him a bottle of Seagrams. Of course it was missing a few shots.

I watched as Mole and Suitcase placed a pair of binoculars, a feather and a Big Day Big Stay Certificate at his feet. My mother put some change in Beans' hand.

I looked at her quizzically.

"So he can pay the toll into heaven," she said matter of factly.

That's when I noticed it.

At first the body appeared normal. Aside from looking fake, Beans just looked like he was sleeping. As I looked closer I saw it.

A large bruise on his forehead. Following it upward, I saw a large gash in his scalp. It had been doctored up pretty good by the undertaker, but it was obvious. Before he died he had suffered a pretty nasty blow to the head.

"See it?" It was Mole. "See what I'm talking about?" he hissed. "Drowned my ass."

My mother grabbed his arm and gave him a stare.

He shut up. She led him away from the casket.

I stayed and looked a little longer.

"He loved you Stevie," Josh said, now coming up and putting his arm around me. "In Florida, after our trip, he told us the day he spent with you at the Series was the best day of his vacation and one of the best days of his life." Josh smiled. "Thanks for giving it to him." He finished then led me to a little room off to the side.

I sat on a leather couch and watched grown men stand around uncomfortable with their emotions.

Inside the room we sat and waited for the service to end. Someone had brought in a quarter keg. A large number of guys milled about drinking. Everyone had a flask. We sat pounding beers as a minister said some generic words about Bernard.

"Who the fuck is Bernard? His name is Beans, Padre," Josh said shaking his head. He was a little too loud.

Suitcase shushed him as he walked by and made his way back out to the casket. I listened to the sermon for a little while than I got up and went to the keg. I suddenly had the urge to get drunk. I felt all sort of emotions come over me.

Sadness, loneliness, futility. Most of all anger.

I sensed it in the others too.

The rest of the funeral passed uneventfully. Beans was laid to rest in a cemetery far from Seconds Flat. It was a shame he wasn't buried in Darby near his beloved bird feeders.

At least there is a woods next to his grave. You could spot a few birds from his final resting place I'm sure.

I tried to find the grave years later but I didn't have much luck. I found the cemetery but not the grave. Still, I don't need to go back. All I need to see is a hummingbird to be reminded of my dear crazy friend.

A living thing is always the best reminder of the dead.

//

That night Mole was strangely subdued. He was drunk of course but not gloriously so. He was sad but not falling apart. Most of all he just seemed tired and worn out.

Despite what Suitcase had said, they had not talked to me about the circumstances of Beans' death after the funeral. It didn't matter, it seemed to be the topic of conversation with everyone in attendance.

I heard the official version, the one told by the boat's owners. I had also heard the 'real' version, the one that had Mole so worked up.

What I gleaned from the snippets of conversation at the wake was that Beans was working as a mate on his landlord's boat. They had been fishing for dolphin. It was just the owners and some friends, not a hired trip. It was confusing as to who was on board at the time he went overboard, but according to the police report, Beans fell overboard about four miles out. He had been drinking heavily and he must have fallen overboard when the yacht accelerated, or perhaps made a sharp turn. In any event it was not noticed by the others on the boat for at least a half an hour. The cut on his head must have been caused by him banging it on the side during the accident.

The unofficial 'real' version was that the boat's owners were running drugs, mainly coke between the Keys and the Bahamas. Of course with Beans' attitude about drugs, when he found out he went nuts. He threatened to go to the police if it was not stopped. Instead, the owners had stopped Beans.

They had not shown at the funeral. Instead choosing to send the biggest flower arrangement, with a condolence note that said they had fishing charters they could not cancel. This just fueled the conspiracy theorists in attendance.

If it was true, no wonder Mole and his buddies were so pissed. Jeez, I was pissed.

Even my mom was pissed, although she told me not to leap to conclusions and to stay out of it.

Late that night, when I was in bed, I heard her talking to my father. She begged him not to get involved. She said nothing good would come from it. That what goes around comes around. She talked about Beans' lifestyle. She said while his death was obviously tragic, it was probably going to happen sooner or later.

Suprisingly Mole did not get mad. He did not argue or really even disagree with her. All he said was that he would let a sleeping dog lie. He said he wasn't sure Josh would though.

They went into the kitchen to smoke so I didn't hear anything else that night.

I returned to school the next day.

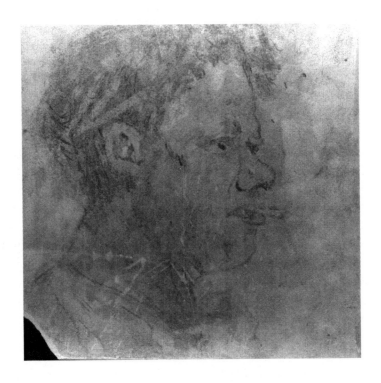

Chapter 36

On an eviction and pouring gas on the fire

The rest of that semester, I tried to put Beans' death out of my head. I concentrated on my studies and buried myself in my books. Looking back at my transcript, I had the best grades of my whole college career that semester. It is amazing how tragedy can refocus you and make you appreciate all the gifts you have.

I went home over winter break.

Mole seemed to be doing okay. He was working full time at Hygrade Meats, and he was back to doing small carpet jobs for his brother. He was drinking a lot, but aside from some crazy semi-nude late night banging on the piano, he wasn't too bad. The drinking I mean. The piano playing was terrible. He couldn't play. But that didn't stop him from 'going in concert', late into the night until he would pass out.

My mother and sister avoided him when he was smashed and tolerated him when he was merely buzzed. He was helping pay the bills.

My mother was still doing her own thing and my sister seemed to be alright too. She had friends and was doing good in school. She just never had those friends over the house, and it was a sure thing that my mother was the one helping her with the school work.

When I got home, my mother told me that two weeks after the funeral, after the police had ruled Beans' death an accident, his landlords had gone ahead and evicted Beans' mother from Seconds' Flat. She told me Josh and Suitcase had said this was the final straw. She made Mole promise to stay out of it. She was not sure he was listening.

I hooked up with the guys at the Halfway Tavern. Josh and Suitcase looked the same but something was different. It was different without

Beans. Everyone tried to pick up the slack or fill in the gaps, but that just made it even more noticeable.

They all seemed to be brought down a notch, their wings clipped, though they still kept their sense of humor.

Mole was now reduced to fat shoveling. Josh had obviously heard the title I gave the job, because he kept asking Mole to look at the 'protein byproducts' on every overweight girls' ass that passed our bar stools.

Suitcase had taken a job as an assistant janitor at a local high school. He said it was okay work, and he was glad to get benefits. He asked me to come up with a catchy job title for him too. He said he missed working for himself, but that those days were over.

Josh told a funny story about his latest short lived employment. Seemed his worker's comp allowed him to obtain partime employment. He was allowed to work up to twenty hours a week and earn a certain amount a year without jeopardizing his benefits. As a result, he had gone to work at Lowes Home Supply.

They had put him to work in Kitchens and Bathrooms.

From his perch on his bar stool, he looked around like he was telling a secret, then began. "It was great. I didn't have to lift anything because of my back. I had some lackey for that. All I had to do was wait on customers looking for new bathrooms or kitchens." He paused.

"You know who they are?" he asked lighting yet another smoke and gulping a 'little brown one' as he called a shot.

"M.A.B.'s—middle aged bitches!" he said as he slammed down the shot glass.

"I was getting more ass than a toilet seat at an all girls Catholic school."

The men around him listening interrupted.

"Bullshit!"

"Keenan the only ass you get is when you pay for it."

"Josh you worked in the 'Tool' department at Lowes. Who are you kidding?"

He ignored them and went on.

"Ever since Beans passed I seem to be drinking even more. Probably he's up there making me drink his share," he joked.

I looked over at Suitcase and my dad but they weren't laughing. They were drinking more than their share too. They didn't need any help.

"Because of that goddamn Beans I was going to the bar everyday at lunch. Usually just a few beers with my sandwich. One day though, I got to thinking about those bastards and what they done to Beans."

Suitcase interrupted. "Easy Josh. We don't got any proof of that. Besides they may have friends in here."

He finished and looked around.

No one paid any mind.

Josh continued. "Yea, that may be true but look what they did to Beans' old lady. Put her out on the street before he was even cold in the ground." He paused to take a drag of his cigarette. "Anyway I'm sitting there getting pretty worked up. Before I know it I'm into the whiskey. Bang, bang, bang. One after another.

I remember leaving but not much else. The next thing I know, I'm waking up in a display bathtub in the front of my department. An old lady standing over me asking my boss if I came with the fixtures!" he finished then started laughing loudly.

This quickly turned into a coughing spell that lasted a minute or so. Finally he took a drink of his beer and stopped coughing. He then spit into a hanky, looked at it and folded it back into his pocket.

"Thank god I still get the workman's comp, cause my supervisor kicked me to the curb."

"That reminds me. What the hell are we gonna do about those bastards that were responsible for what happened to Beans?"

It was Mole.

"You promised Larose you would not get involved," I reminded him.

"I will not get involved," Mole said and exaggeratedly raised his hand like a was being sworn in. He then winked at Josh.

"I promise to leave your dad out of it, Stevie," Josh said.

He to, raised his hand.

"What is this an induction ceremony for the Kiwanis club? You assholes. Let's drink to Beans," I said raising a glass.

"To Beans."

"To Beans and the memory of Seconds Flat," Josh answered.

This time it was Josh who winked at my father.

///

The next weekend, Mole told us he was going out with Josh and Suitcase. He did not say where. When I asked to go with him he told me he didn't know when he would get home, and claimed that I spent too much time hanging out with washed up old men. He told me to call Triangle head or hook up with the O'Hanlon boys.

I got the picture and begged off.

As he was leaving, I noticed him rummaging through the garage. I thought he was sneaking a bottle of vodka. Instead I saw him come out with a gas can. He didn't see me so I didn't say anything.

I certainly didn't tell Larose.

He was gone the rest of the day and well into that night. I was asleep when he came home so it must have been late.

The next day, my mother asked me to go to the grocery store for her. She knew I enjoyed food shopping. Especially with my Mom's shopping list. We may not have had a lot of money, but my mother never skimped when it came to buying food. Because of this when I food shopped I never felt poor. In fact I felt just the opposite. She would give me coupons of course, but she also gave me carte blanche. I could buy anything. She trusted me not to waste money and I earned her trust. I bought store brands when I could and didn't blow money on junk. In exchange for this, I bought food and lots of it.

Today, I love to cook and I do all the food shopping. Nothing makes me feel better than a full pantry and a great meal you prepared from it.

That day was no different.

When I left, Mole was still in bed. That was typical after a night out with the birders. What was not typical was the sight of his clothes on the basement steps.

That's odd. I remember thinking.

Usually he did that only if he was working at the 'fat factory.'

I didn't think he was. I was almost positive he was out with his buddies. Just to check I went to smell them.

Gas.

They didn't smell like that god forsaken Hygrades, they smelled like gas.

I left for the market.

After shopping, I went to load the groceries in the trunk. When I opened the Dent's trunk, there it was again—the odor of gas.

I loaded the groceries in the back seat instead.

When I got home my father was at the kitchen table drinking coffee and reading the local paper. Seeing me, he closed the paper and quickly threw it in the trash.

"Mind helping me with the groceries?" I asked as I put a couple of bags on the counter.

"Not at all lad. Not at all. Provisions for the pantry. Salt, mollasses, flour and lard. A job well done."

He didn't mention anything about the clothes or the trunk.

"Yo Mole. What's up with the gas smell on your clothes and in the car trunk?" I asked curious he hadn't mentioned anything about it.

He looked alarmed. "What are you talking about?" he asked.

I could hear the nervousness in his voice.

"The trunk reeks of gas and your clothes do too," I answered, now very curious.

"Oh that. I was helping Josh with some lawn cleanup and also winterizing the motor on Beans' old boat the *Cannery Row.* Spilled some gas on my clothes, not to mention I had the can in the trunk," he said. The nervousness in his voice was now gone.

"Do me a favor, leave the trunk lid open to air it out. Maybe wash it out later too, if it still smells," he continued. He got up and walked to the basement steps.

"I better get those clothes washed before your mother complains. Don't bother mentioning it to her okay?" he said and disappeared down the steps.

After the groceries were put away, I sat down to eat some breakfast. I poured myself the first of three bowls of Apple Jacks and got a glass of orange juice. Tiring quickly of reading the back of the cereal box, I wished that Kelloggs would start printing short stories on the back of their boxes, maybe a history of Johnny Appleseed, anything but the vitamin percentages. Knowing that would never happen, I rummaged through the trash looking for Mole's newspaper. I fished it out and brushed some coffee grounds off it.

"Good as new—news," I said triumphantly.

I sat down to eat.

That's when I read it.

There buried in the 'Delco Roundup' a column of short local news summaries was an article.

Two alarm Blaze Guts Darby Home
By Harry Cheqeum
Special to the Times

Darby Fire Company A working closely with Darby Fire Company B answered a two alarm call to 713 Clifton Ave last night, for the report of a house fire. The blaze was reported at approximately ten-thirty p.m. The fire was contained at around midnight. There were no reported injuries. The home appeared vacant.

Fire officials did report however that a cat was found in the rubble. It had apparently succumbed to smoke inhalation.

Chief Jack Hagan of Darby Fire Company A indicates that the cause of the fire is still under investigation. Asked for comment the chief gave the following statement. "My men responded quickly and professionally. Although back up in the form of Darby B were present, they acted purely as back up and were not involved in the actually battling of the blaze. It was A's quick response that prevented additional damage. We will actively investigate the cause of this fire, and report our findings at the appropriate time."

So, that's what Mole and Josh were up to last night. I thought. No doubt Suitcase was involved too.

Too bad about Brunswick. I'm sure the birders didn't know the old tom was still in the house.

Who knows, maybe Josh did. He never liked that cat anyway.

Good to see that there was still no love lost between the rival fire companies. Chief Hagan made sure everyone knew who was the boss, and who was the better fire company.

Thankfully there were no injuries. The fire was under investigation. Maybe Jack Hagan would label the fire faulty electrical, or the result of vagrants. The birders better hope he calls it accidental, I thought.

Does he know who really did it?

Did I?

"Stevie, you in there?"

It was my mother. She was now downstairs and in the living room.

"In here," I answered.

I threw the paper out a second time.

Later, when Larose went out I had a chance to talk to Mole.

After beating around the bush a bit he said, "Yea, we did it. Those bastards got off easy. Lucky we didn't burn the place with them in it. Does your mother know?"

He never could be cagey for long.

"No. I threw out the paper. I buried it in the bottom of the can," I said.

Mole shook his head. "She will find out soon enough. You will not tell her a thing. You hear me?"

"I'm going back to school soon. Right after the holidays. Remember I'm Sergeant Shultz. I know nothing," I said in my best German accent.

He smiled, then asked me to clean out the trunk before my mom got dropped off from shopping with her friend Heffie.

I did as I was told.

All week my mother would not to speak to him. He asked me a couple of times if I said anything. I told him the truth. I hadn't.

Larose had found out. Who knows who told her. Maybe she saw the news.

She knew Mole's friends did it. She must have known Mole was involved too. I mean she wasn't dumb. She knew what was up.

Between her anger at the burning of Seconds Flat, Mole's drinking and the upcoming Christmas holiday, the tension in the house was unbearable.

I would be glad to go back to school.

First I had to get through another Molineux Christmas.

My mother did her best to make sure my sister and I had everything we asked for every Christmas. How she did it on the money she brought in and the little she got from Mole I will never know.

That Christmas was no different.

Of course Mole always saved us a few bucks. He and Josh would always have their annual holiday Christmas tree heist. That year I went along.

Mole and his friends would meet a couple of weeks or so before Christmas. They would usually get a case of beer and cruise up and down the two main drags through our area of the county; MacDade Boulevard and Chester Pike. They would case the various tree stands for the easy pickings. Of course, in keeping with their rule to 'stick it to the man' Mole insisted on only the biggest tree lots or the ones run by a company. Each year the folks at Franks Inc. or Cannon's Corner or Home Depot found themselves a few trees short on their inventory.

This year would be no different. It always amazed me that the Birders would risk a felony burglary and jail time just to save twenty five bucks. I realize today that it wasn't the money. They did it for the fun of it. They did it to stick it to the man.

After about an hour of 'recon work' as Mole called it, we headed to the Toll House Tavern to drink and wait for the stand to close.

At about twelve a.m. we headed out. Josh had his pickup. An old Ford 150, with ladder racks and rust around the wheel wells. He proudly showed us the beer can holders he had bought from Pep Boys.

"Put your drinks right in there. Now we won't lose a single can to spillage," he proudly told us. We dutifully put our beers in the holders and piled in. We sat, packed in the cab, like migrant farm workers out to harvest a crop.

Josh maneuvered the junker out onto the pike and we drove towards Franks Nursery and that year's Christmas trees.

We pulled into the lot. A huge multi-store mall complex. It was well lit and patrolled by mall cops.

This was not going to be easy. In addition to the lights, the putt-putt miniature golf course looked like it was still open. Upon closer inspection, the only people we saw inside were workers getting ready to lock up.

We sat and waited for the cars to pull out. Mole sipped from a wine bottle as Suitcase and Josh drank beer. We debated movies.

"Nicholson's best was *Cuckoo's Nest*," I said tossing the first salvo. "In a supporting role he was almost as good as the astronaut in *Terms of Endearment.*"

"No way there, Gene Shalet. Jack's best was not *Cuckoo's Nest*. By the way Keysey's book was better," Mole said taking the bait. He seemed to have an edge to his voice, even though I didn't notice him drinking that much, I mean above his usual anyway.

He took a sip of his wine and continued, "His best was his early stuff *Five Easy Pieces* or that sailor in *The Last Detail* no doubt about it."

Suitcase pounced. "You are both full of shit, Siskel and Ebert, the best Nicholson flick is not either of the aforementioned, although they were fantastic movies. His best performance was not even supposed to be his in the first place. It was supposed to be Rip Torn's. Which, by the way would have been interesting to watch too, I'm sure."

He paused as the last Putt-Putt worker made his way to his car.

"I'm talking of course about the best road movie ever made, the reason I bought my first bike—*Easy Rider*. He was great as that crazy alcoholic lawyer. That my friends is Nicholson's best flick."

He looked around the lot, snuffed out his smoke and said "Let's move gentleman, These evergreens are gonna be ever gone."

We climbed out.

The trees at the nursery were kept in an makeshift fenced in area of Franks' parking lot. Suitcase had some bologna and some valium in case there was a guard dog. Thankfully, the stand did not have one. We walked to the back of the lot away from the street and as far from the mall's lights as possible. Mole found a spot in the fence that was missing a support pole. He quickly bent the fence down. While Suitcase watched for the security guards, Josh and I slipped over.

I was scared shitless.

The booze did nothing to calm me. Right then and there I decided this would be my last crime. I reached for the first tree I could find. Not quite a *Charley Brown* number but certainly the smallest one in the lot.

"Put that back!" Josh hissed. "I'm partial to Blue Spruce, not those Douglas Firs. They are a dime a dozen," he said as he began to casually look each tree over like some kind of forest ranger, or a cat burglaring Ansel Adams.

Seeing this, I sarcastically said, "Why don't we ask for a boy scout to assist us. I'm sure we could get one of the workers in here."

It was Suitcase's turn next.

"Would you two Marys hurry the hell up. Christmas will be over by the time you guys are done. Toss a few out for Christ Sake!"

I grabbed the next tree I saw and lifted it over the fence. Mole grabbed it and hurried off. Josh did the same with Suitcase. I then jumped back over and pulled down the fence for Josh and his last tree, a giant Blue Spruce.

"This baby is mine," he said proudly. The thing was so big it took us both to lift it. "Josh, you look like the Grinch who stole Christmas with that thing. Might have to donate it for the White house lawn," I joked.

"All I need is a sled and that little dog with the antlers tied on," Josh giggled.

We hurried back to the truck.

When we got to the truck I couldn't believe our bad luck. There, parked next to the pickup was the security guard's van.

"Shit, we are screwed," I said to Josh as I dropped the tree and prepared to run.

Josh said calmly "Hold it. I think we might of caught a break."

He continued to drag the tree toward the truck.

"What are you crazy? Let's get out of here. Mole and Suitcase won't rat us out," I pleaded.

I looked again. Suitcase and Mole were calmly talking to the security guard. He looked vaguely familiar. Were they actually laughing? Was the guard drinking a beer?

"Is that Jack Hagan Fire fighter extraordinaire?" Josh yelled.

A little too loud for all of us.

"Shut the hell up Keenan. You want to get me fired?" Hagan whispered back.

"A man needs to do what a man needs to do. Picking up a few extra bucks before the holiday. Working like a slave," he added, lifting his beer up and toasting Josh.

He had an ear to ear grin on his face.

"Hagan here has some good news for us as well as a fair business proposal," Suitcase said to Josh and I.

"Captain Jack, why don't you tell the boys what you just told us."

"Well lets see . . ." he began, taking his good old time.

Josh interrupted "What is it? Damn it."

"Patience Keenan you lousy ingrate. I have finished my investigation of the cause of the fire at 713 Clifton. Despite the presence of an accelerant, which will not be in my report, it appears that the fire was from some faulty wiring in the basement. Arson has been ruled out. It seems Second's Flat died of natural causes much like it's occupant Beans Walsh supposedly did as well."

He smiled conspiratorially and toasted everyone again. "To Beans," he said.

We all took a drink.

"Now after that bit of good news. On to the very reasonable business proposition, Mr. Hagan," Suitcase said trying to sound business like.

"Gentleman, I see that you are in the market for a few Christmas trees. Well I too would like to obtain a few nice ones for myself, and a couple of family members. Unfortunately, with all the hours I am putting in working here, not to mention the fire investigations etcetera, I have not been able to get out there to purchase them. Perhaps in the spirit of the season you might find the time to run a few trees by my house tonight. You know, as a holiday gesture. Just between us friends," he finished.

Josh and Suitcase were already walking back to the tree lot.

"Say no more Mr. Hagan. Consider it done. Now if you will excuse us we have deliveries to make," Mole said and shook Hagan's hand.

"Of course I have my rounds to make. Have to make sure no one makes off with any trees or breaks in the stores. My work is never done," Hagan said then drained his beer. He tossed the can and got into the van.

"I'm partial to Douglas Fir," he winked and drove off.

The Christmas tree heist was a resounding success. Still, that year, even with me along as new blood, there was something missing. It was though the Birders were just going through the motions. Even their drinking seemed to be labored. As they got drunker and drunker they seemed to get nasty. Whereas before when they drank they would get animated and funny, now they only seemed to get sullen.

"Gentlemen. Tis the season to be jolly, fa la la la la lalalala!" I said trying to rally them at a traffic light a couple of blocks from Hagan's house.

"Ba humbug," Josh said trying to play along.

Almost cutting him off Suitcase said, "Just shut up and drive Josh."

A flash of anger crossed Josh's face.

"Fuck you Ox," Josh said bitterly.

After that no one said a word.

We dropped off the trees at the fireman's house in Springfield. Even though the chief kept a house in Darby for residency reasons, his home was in Springfield.

The drive home was difficult. It was as though we were all blaming each other for the loss of Beans. Or maybe it was seeing everyone together doing an annual Birder's event without him was just too much. Or maybe it was just that we were alive and he was 'worm food' as Mole would say, that made the night so uncomfortable. Whatever it was we all wanted it to be over.

"Drop me off," I said when Josh took a turn back toward the Toll House.

"Me too," Suitcase said.

We looked over at Mole. He was asleep against the door.

Josh ran us home.

Suitcase woke Mole up.

He grumbled and fought at first, then realizing where he was, he staggered up the drive and disappeared through the side door.

"Good night guys. Be careful," Josh said and lit a cigarette. "Take care of your old man, I'm worried about him."

I said goodnight to them and took a Christmas tree out of the truck's bed. I have never felt more depressed around a holiday than I did that night dragging a stolen tree up the drive after seeing how the loss of Beans had so thoroughly destroyed my father and his friends.

I was glad school was coming up.

The holidays came and went. The only thing I remember about it was that was the year Mole's friend Dan Erickson and Suitcase got drunk at our house on Christmas eve. They partied until at least two in the morning. Larose was pissed because she couldn't get my sister to bed because of the noise.

If my sister wasn't in bed my mother could not put out the presents.

Danny's date that evening was a pot smoking, pill popping Jewish girl who taught high school English in Jersey. She looked like the old folk singer Pheobe Snow. She had a big mop of curly hair that Dan called a 'jew-fro' and she dressed in a funky pant suit with matching top. She laughed too loudly and at all the wrong times. Her big joke was since she was Jewish it didn't matter if she stayed up on Christmas eve. I remember Larose reminding her at least ten times that it did matter to us.

Mole and Danny gave her dirty looks.

Neither Larose nor the teacher got the hints.

Danny's girlfriend for some reason had a stack of her students' term papers with her. After drinking vodka gimlets and downing a seconal, she started to 'grade' them. She did so by arbitrarily writing a letter grade on the top of each paper. She ripped through the first bunch.

Mole saw it and took issue.

"Hey, you are not even reading them," he said.

"Who cares? The kids certainly don't. These kids are dumb. Trust me, my method is just as good." She laughed and gave a stack to Mole. "Here you try."

Mole spent the rest of the night drinking and grading papers. He took it very serious. He even read one aloud to the party. After doing so he awarded the paper an A.

"You really have a knack for this Mole, you should have been a teacher," Danny's date said.

The comment hit Mole like turning on his bedroom light after a big night out.

He did not say anything but he kept on grading. He kept on drinking too.

Everything seemed to be alright, at least by our house's crazy standards.

I went to bed.

The group continued to get pretty smashed. Everyone was pretty loud. Even my mother. I could hear her laughing and joking with Danny and Suitcase.

Later I heard them debating. Really it was only Danny and Mole. They disagreed over the quality of John Irving's writing. Danny was defending the author's work. He really liked *The Hundred and Fifty-eight Pound Marriage.*

Mole was dismissive.

The English teacher seemed to be the referee, or more likely the pot stirrer. She had fawned all over Mole before I went to bed.

To me, it sounded like they were fighting over Dan's girlfriend.

Their shouting match soon became a wrestling match. Upstairs in my bed I balled my fists up in anger. I looked out my window at the full moon and tried to lull myself to sleep.

It was no use.

I heard the crash of a lamp and Suitcase and Larose pleading for them to stop.

Enough.

I went down stairs to help my mother.

Danny had my father in some sort of wrestling move as they both sat shirtless on the living room floor. Danny had a big rug burn on his shoulder. Blood trickled from Mole's nose. They looked like two drunks in a homosexual Kama Sutra pose.

"Dad, it's Christmas Eve. What are you doing?" I pleaded.

"Go to bed college boy," he said bitterly.

"No, you should go to bed. You fucking drunk," I answered just as bitterly.

"Don't talk like that to your father," Dan said loosening his grip on Mole.

"I will talk anyway I want," I said, not so sure I wanted to challenge Mole's friend, the former boxer.

Fortunately, that wasn't necessary. Mole was going to make sure he was the only one I challenged.

He stood up and squared off in front of me. "I said go back to bed. This does not concern you."

His breath reeked of vodka and cigarettes.

I was so sick of his shit, I wanted to knock him out. Instead I pushed him out of the way, and tried to go back up the steps.

He was so drunk he fell to the ground. Thankfully he stayed down.

He protested, "See what he did to his own father? Did you? He struck me for no reason."

He continued to writhe on the floor like a professional wrestler. I half expected Vince McMahon and the whole WWF to come piling in my living room to back him up.

Instead Suitcase got between us.

"Enough!" he yelled to both of us.

"Stevie please go upstairs. You are just egging him on."

It was Larose. Was she siding with him? I couldn't believe it.

"Are you so beaten down that this shit is okay? It is Christmas eve for Christ sake! Why are you putting up with this shit? It is beyond dysfunctional," I cruelly said to her.

I backed my way up the stairs never once turning my back on Mole. He glared at me with a look that said this was not the end of it.

Once again Suitcase had intervened.

I went back to my room. I laid in bed and counted the days before school started. I tried to sleep.

The party quieted down but it didn't break up. I heard them arguing, then the next minute laughing. This went on late into the night.

I must have finally calmed down because I awoke the next morning to my sister in my room. She had gotten up early to see what Santa had brought.

By the look on her face she was not happy.

"There are people under the tree," she whispered.

"What did you say?" I asked, still not fully awake.

"There are people in the dining room. They are sleeping under the tree," she explained.

I followed her down the stairs through the living room and to the dining room. There, under the stolen blue spruce were Danny, his girlfriend and Suitcase, all passed out sharing a unzipped sleeping bag. They had pushed my mother's presents off to the side, so that it looked like Santa had delivered three drunks down the chimney to our house in Glenolden.

I looked over at my sister. She was scared and confused.

"Don't worry. Santa brought you presents," I said pointing her to the pile of gifts in the corner. It is only daddy's friends Danny and Suitcase."

Thankfully, once she saw the presents she was no longer concerned about Mole's friends under the tree. Ignoring the snoring mass she busied herself with sorting the gifts.

I went to find my father. I walked back to the living room. He was buried beneath an afghan under the coffee table.

Good. I thought. At least my mother got a bed last night.

I kicked at the blanket.

"What?" the blanket spoke.

"What's with the drunks under the tree? It scared the shit out of Maddie," I said, my anger boiling up again.

The blanket groaned.

After a minute Mole pulled down the blankets. He looked like the guy in the old 'Stoned Again' poster I used to have hanging in my room when I was sixteen. His eyes were bloodshot and he had dried blood around his nose, leftover from his scrum with Danny. He had bed head, and the beginnings of a beard.

He sat up. Looking around him as he got his bearings, he peered over at his friends sleeping under the tree. He rubbed his eyes as though he couldn't believe what he saw. He searched for his cigarettes.

Finding them, he smiled and said, "Look Stevie, Santa brought you just what you always asked for—a real live girl! Maybe you won't have to choke the chicken any more. Thank you Santa!" he said as he laughed and raised his hands to the sky. "Check your stocking, maybe there is a box of rubbers and some lube too."

I couldn't help but laugh. What an asshole I thought.

I shook my head and went back upstairs to wake my mother. She would be upset if she missed my sister opening her presents.

That Christmas morning my sister and I opened our gifts in front of my mother and father as well as my father's two hung over friends and a pill popping English teacher from New Jersey.

A Norman Rockwell painting we were not.

Chapter 37

How It's a Small World After All

I happily returned to school after the winter break. My home life was getting worse but my mother and I were content to ignore it. At least we did not talk about it to each other.

It was the same when I left. Just the usual 'Be good and study hard' along with the Raman noodles, the peanut butter and jelly and the folded twenty dollar bill.

I had no problem putting Mole out of my mind. I did so by filling my mind with distractions. Okay, only one distraction, an obsession really.

That semester I fell head over heels for my old girlfriend.

I know what you are thinking. How can you fall head over heels for your old girlfriend? Well the truth was, I was always head over heels, I just got a second chance that semester.

She had recently broken up with the whole football team to hear Dan Barley tell it.

We started to hang out. Some nights studying at the library, some nights in her dorm room. It didn't hurt that she did my biology homework for me.

She was smart and calculated.

It is really amazing the way some people are masters of their emotions while others are slaves. My girlfriend was always in control. Cool calm and collected. Dating me was always convenient. The easy thing to do. Same high school, same neighborhood, same friends. It made sense to keep me around.

Just not that close.

Me, on the other hand, treated dating her like it was life or death. I couldn't get enough. I had no control. I thought I was in love. Today, I realize I was infatuated.

Then, well I thought it was like Coke—The Real Thing.

Love, I mean real love, should make you feel like every door in the universe is opening to you. It should create a bigger world for you. When it happens you should start to feel that you are part of a greater thing.

Infatuation, makes your world close in, it closes and locks doors. It shuts you off from others. It makes things smaller.

That semester my world got pretty small.

Looking back, the whole thing is pretty embarrassing. Like looking at an old prom picture. You know the one—where you are wearing a lime green tux, a ruffled shirt with velvet bow tie and sporting a perm. Pretty painful to look at but you can't throw it away.

Sally is my prom picture.

Still I'm thankful for the distraction. It enabled me to get my focus away from my father's worsening alcoholism.

Things were going well. Sally and I were spending a lot of time together. We would take turns getting rides home on weekends. Her parents knew my situation so it was no big deal for me to spend weekends at her parents' house.

Her old man was a southern boy. He was self educated refinery executive who knew the value of hard work. He had been instrumental in getting my financial aid paperwork together when I enrolled at Widener. For some reason he liked me. Who knows, maybe he saw a little of himself in my hardscrabble life. Maybe I just made him laugh.

Every weekend I would come home with her. We would eat dinner at her house then go out with friends from high school. Most of the time we would get drunk, then stagger home to watch movies. Sally loved the Rocky movies and any Disney flick. Usually I would camp out with her in front of the TV. Most of the time she would get up to cuddle with her miniature dachshund on her living room couch. I would be relegated to the floor.

It would drive me nuts. Here I was drunk and horny, alone with my girlfriend, barely tolerating watching the *Little Mermaid* or *Snow White and the Seven Dwarves*, hoping to get laid, and I lose out to a seven pound hot dog?

I would sit there stewing, drinking a beer, while she would sit up on the couch spewing baby talk to that midget wiener.

I hated that dog and he knew it.

Some nights I would catch him out of the corner of my eye as she scratched his stomach. It was though he was saying 'Don't you wish she were scratching between your legs?'

I would look over and he would look away. The dog would not make eye contact with me.

This act went on for a few weeks. All the while I'm getting shut out. Oh, occasionally Sally and I would hook up. Usually when the older sister took the dog with her for the weekend.

When the dog was home though, I was not a priority.

My feelings about the dog were based solely on the fact he was a four legged cock block. If he didn't get in the way of our fooling around I wouldn't have had any issue with him at all.

Other than effective birth control, he was a nice pet.

For that reason I could not bring myself to be mean to the pooch.

Shit, how bad was I? Jealous of a dog.

Yet even though I couldn't be mean to him, I wished someone else could.

I got my wish late in the school year towards summer vacation. Sally and I had been seeing a lot of each other. I was becoming a weekend fixture at her house in Glenolden. Her parents had grown used to seeing me on the floor on Saturday and Sunday mornings. They would step over me on their way to the kitchen and a cup of coffee.

Most of the time I was so hung over I wouldn't even notice.

Since Beans died, I noticed I was drinking more. It wasn't just happening to the other Birders. I was doing everything to excess. You name it, I was trying it. Most of the time I didn't tell anyone. If someone took one, I took two. If someone drank two I had to have three.

One night I went out with some high school buddies. Sally stayed home for some reason. She gave me a key and told me to let myself in and sleep on the living room floor when I got home.

I was smashed. I did two valiums and washed them down with almost a fifth of vodka mixed with grapefruit juice. I was a chip off the old Mole alright.

When I finally staggered in to Sally's house it was late. I fumbled with the key, then wrestled with the screen door. I felt my way to the living room banging into everything on the way. I found my regular spot in front of the TV.

I passed out as soon as I hit the floor.

Sometime during the night I pissed myself. I'm not talking a little spillage.

I'm talking a gallon.

I awoke sometime before dawn. I looked around to determine where I was. My head hurt and my mouth was as dry and disgusting as a litter box. Odd, I was soaked. So was the carpet under me.

Funny, I did not recall taking a glass of water with me when I crashed. What did I spill?

I lifted up the blanket I had taken from the couch. Oh my God!

It smelled like a donkey stall.

It dawned on me, I pissed my pants.

I moved over to get out of the wet spot. I tried not to panic. I calmly got up and went to the downstairs bathroom. I took the hairdryer to my crotch. If any one was up to see me they would have thought I was giving new meaning to the term 'blow job.'

That's when I heard the father and mother stirring upstairs.

I panicked.

My crotch was dry but the carpet in the living room wasn't.

Before I could make it back to the living room I heard them.

"Jesus, what did a pipe break?" Sally's old man said as he went toward the door to retrieve the morning paper.

Then I heard the mother.

"Where is Stephen? Maybe he knows what happened."

As I walked back to the living room I saw him. The dog that is.

For once, he made eye contact. Our eyes met and his were saying a lot.

Who says dogs don't understand?

The moment he looked at me I could tell he wanted to take back all of those cock block evenings, all those flaunted belly rubs. He knew what I was going to do. He knew what I had to do. The dog practically gave me the idea, what with his knowing look over at me.

Too bad you can't talk little doggie, I thought.

I didn't hesitate.

"That goddamn dog pissed on the floor!" I said and pointed over at the little mutt. The dog started to nervously look around and his tail curled between his legs.

"He did what?" the father asked skeptically.

"He pissed all over the carpet. Even though I let him out when I came in," I said now bolstering my story with yet another lie.

The father, like some pet detective, started to analyze the size of the wet spot. As he did he would look over at the dog then look at me.

It dawned on me, maybe he was not buying a seven pound six inch high miniature dachshund being able to pee a three foot puddle.

As he sat pondering the spot, the mother leaped into action.

"You damn lousy mutt!" she screamed and began wailing on the confused animal.

"I am sick and tired of this shit. I walk you. I give you treats. I let you sleep in the bed and you thank me by emptying your bladder on my clean carpets."

She continued to swat the now terrified dog.

To add to the dog's problems he started to pee himself from fear. This only gave my story more validity.

This sent Sally's mom into a fresh tizzy. She held the dog in her outstretched arms like it was infected. She continued to smack it.

Her tirade ended only after the father took the dog from her.

Strangely, during this whole time Sally's father did not get upset at the dog at all. In fact he saved the animal from a further beating by taking the dog outside and putting him on a leash.

"Get a towel and help me clean this mess up," he said to me as he came back in.

I did as I was told.

No one mentioned the incident for the rest of the day. Sally could not believe it.

"The poor poopsie woopsie must have been sick," she said hugging the dog the next day.

I could have sworn the dog gave me the evil eye.

The carpets were cleaned and the incident soon forgotten by every **person** in the house.

Two weeks went by and I found myself again over Sally's on a weekend.

Her dad had been watching NASCAR and drinking beer. He offered me a few as I waited for Sally.

When his wife came down the stairs they went out.

I was alone in front of the television. The beer and the NASCAR got to me and I dozed off. I slept soundly on my back.

I awoke, after what seemed like only a few minutes, but now the six o'clock news was on the TV.

Sally was napping on the couch. The dog was on her lap.

The dog glanced at me then got up and scurried upstairs.

That's odd, I thought.

Then I noticed it. I can't remember if I saw it first or smelled it.

A dog turd.

On my chest!

That little prick had gotten his revenge. He had shit on me while I slept. He was so sneaky and so small I had not even awakened when he climbed up and used me as his own personal patch of grass.

No wonder he took off.

Of course Sally thought it was a hoot.

"Oh the little guy is jealous of you," she said as I sat there frozen with a pile of dog shit six inches from my face—on my chest!

"Why did my bumpkin do a do—do on Stevie?" she baby talked to the lousy four legged prick.

If only she knew, I thought.

I was beaten.

The dog won.

It was his house and she was his girl.

I should have known right then and there, I had no chance. If I couldn't even beat out a dog, there was no was I was going to beat out Sally's other suitors. The dog was the beginning of the end for us.

Later, when I was helping her dad unload groceries, he said "Serves you right. Blaming your pissing the floor on that poor dog. You might have fooled my wife but you didn't fool me."

He stopped to hold the door for me.

"You know, you better settle down. Chill on the partying a little. I don't mean to knock your dad, but you need to look in the mirror. You want to turn out like him?" He paused, thinking no doubt of the right thing to say, not wanting to offend me. He continued.

"My dad was a drunk. I very easily could have followed in his footsteps, but instead I used him as an example of what I did not want to become.

What do you want to become?" he asked.

I did not answer.

"What do you want people to think about you?"

I shrugged.

"That stupid little dog certainly passed judgment on you didn't he?"

As we emptied the last of the bags he said, "Don't give people a reason to shit on you. Clean up your act, because I expect a lot from you Molineux.

A lot."

Chapter 38

Schwinn some lose some

After that semester I needed a break from my girlfriend, but I still was not ready to return home and deal with Mole. I knew it was bad, because during that school year my mother had practically begged me not to come home. She said I would regret not getting the full college experience if I came home every weekend.

She was always a bad liar.

I didn't bother to tell her about going to Sally's house.

She was sketchy about Mole, saying only that he wasn't working at Hygrades that much and the carpet business was slow. She didn't mention his drinking at all.

That was a sure sign.

Given the state of my love life and hearing what Larose was not saying, I decided to live at the beach for the summer. I would then go back to school in August to work as an academic advisor with the incoming freshmen.

The plan allowed me to get away from my problems.

Or so I thought.

One thing Larose did tell me was Mole's truck the Ting Thing was broken down. The transmission was shot. Where I came from that meant your ride was done. No one had the money to replace a transmission.

Because of this I figured I was safe. From the Mole that is. Without his truck he couldn't crash my beach place. My mom wouldn't let him use the Dodge Dent, and Josh and Suitcase were not around to much. They were usually busy. Josh trying to patch things up with his wife and Suitcase caring for his nephews after his sister's divorce.

The Mole had no transportation and I was ninety miles away.

I obviously underestimated Mole's ability to sniff out a party.

I found a place in Sea Isle City on the Jersey shore. It was a two bedroom shack on the bay. The owners bought it for an investment. They were waiting for approval from the town to tear down the place to build new condos.

Like most shore communities the local politicians were taking their good old time with the permits. Since the approval would not come in until the next fall, the landlords rented us the place for next to nothing. Guess they figured we would keep an eye on it.

I found a job as a painter for a small outfit in Ocean City. My roommates were a childhood friend Eddie and my cousin James. Both were my age, both, like me summering at the shore for the first time.

It was early in the summer and the roommates had not yet found work. In truth they had not looked.

Each day I would go off to work in James' car. My roommates would spend the day looking for work. What they really did was sit around and get drunk and high. I would join them when I got home. I didn't mind, I knew it was temporary and they would both soon be working. At least they would have dinner waiting.

After a long day of standing on a forty foot ladder rolling stain on new construction, I pulled in to our house on the bay.

I was beat. I looked forward to a beer and dinner on the table.

That's when I saw it.

Mole's beat up Schwinn bike.

You have got to be kidding me. I thought. There was no way he could ride a bike ninety miles. He had to have suffered a heart attack or his liver burst or something.

I entered the place.

There, seated on a bean bag chair was Mole. He wore a pair of spandex bike shorts and an ear to ear grin. He was also bright red and breathing heavily.

"Stevie my boy. Thought I'd pay you a little visit."

With his flushed face and lycra shorts, he looked like a big pink sausage.

"Sure you are not going to have a cardiac Jimmy Dean?" I said obviously less than thrilled at the surprise visit.

"Why don't you take a shower to cool off. You are looking a bit rough," James said bringing him some water.

"Not to mention you smell a bit ripe," Ed added not too diplomatically.

"You take a shower while I head out to the package store to get some supplies for the evening," James added.

I gave James a look that told him I was not happy. I went into my room. I laid down on the bed. How did he ride all the way from Pennsylvania? In his condition. My thoughts drifted.

I remembered him teaching me to ride a bike. Pushing me down the driveway. Telling me he was right behind me. Hearing his laugh, behind me alright, at the top of the driveway! Crashing into the telephone pole across the street. Picking me up. Telling me to "get back on the horse that threw you."

I thought of him teaching me to drive. Drunk. Him that is. Passing out with a quart of beer between his legs as I tooled around the industrial center parking lots, grinding gears on the Ting, waking him up by slamming on the breaks. Hearing him startled say, "Easy on the clutch, easy on the clutch."

I must of fallen asleep.

When I woke it was dark.

I went out into the living room. James was messing with the stereo. Mole and Ed were out in the kitchen. I heard them talking.

James turned and seeing me, grabbed my arm and pulled me into the bedroom.

"You will not believe this Steve. When I went out to get some beer I bought your old man a bottle of vodka."

I gave him a look.

"I know. I shouldn't have done it. I know how he is with the hard stuff sometimes. But I figured he just pedaled all the way from Philly, give him a little treat," James continued. "Weirdest thing. I made him a screwdriver and he took it. That was two hours ago."

I interrupted "What's so weird about that? Sounds like just another day in paradise for Mole."

Pulling me back out into the living room, James said "I'll show you what's weird." He pointed to the coffee table. There, sitting in a small puddle of condensation was a full screwdriver.

"He did not even touch it. Either he is off the hard stuff or the bike ride kicked his ass so bad he can't drink. What do you think of that?"

"How's he acting?" I asked skeptically.

"Well he had a couple of beers with us. I really haven't paid much attention. He has been hanging with Ed a lot," James answered.

"I'm getting a shower. Mind making me a vodka and ice tea? Can't beat the bastard might as well join him. The mental patient did just ride his rickety old ten speed all the way here."

I slapped James on the back and went into the bathroom.

When I was finished, I walked into my bedroom. James was sitting on the edge of my bed.

"I'm sorry," he said.

"Sorry for what? Forgetting my cocktail?" I said and pulled on my pants.

"I fucked up."

"James, it's no big deal I'll get a drink when I come out."

"He drank it all."

"What?" I glanced out at the coffee table. The drink was still there. It had not been touched.

"There isn't any vodka. He fucking drank a quart in two hours," James said, sounding like he was reading from the *Guinness Book of World Records.*

Who knows maybe he was.

"He's passed out in Ed's room," he added, shaking his head.

I wanted to walk in Ed's room and strangle him.

I wanted to walk out. Just leave.

Instead, I started drinking. Granted it was only beer, Mole had made sure of that. Still I didn't learn from him, at least not the right lesson anyway.

I sat at the table and looked at the empty bottle. He hadn't touch the mixed drink but he snuck the whole bottle of Kamchatka right under my friends' noses.

He was worse than ever.

"Everyone has a cross to bear," Ed said, trying to say something to comfort me.

"At least you still have a dad. Look at me and your cousin here. Our pops are dead. We don't have anyone."

"Yea, at least you have a dad," James seconded, although he didn't sound like he wanted to trade with me.

"He's not so bad," Ed added.

"Compared to what?" I asked.

I was suddenly tired again.

"A drunk dad is better than no dad," Ed said

"Is it Ed? Is it?"

James did not say a word. Ed just got up and got us all more beers. My friends never did answer me.

//

The next day I went to work as usual. Everyone was still passed out when I left. My head hurt a little. I chalked it up to the cheap beer we were drinking due to our limited funds. It had nothing to do with the fact that I drank ten.

I drove to Ocean City and tried not to think.

Thankfully that day I was working at a beachfront house. Between looking at the ocean from a third story view and looking at the teenage girls sunning themselves on the beach, both the hangover and the day passed quickly.

I bet breaking rocks is bearable at the beach.

We finished the job early.

I drove back to Sea Isle City slowly. I was in no rush to hang with my father. For that matter I was in no rush to hang with my friends. All day I had time to think about it. My friends were part of the problem. They liked Mole. They thought it was cool for him to hang out with them. Shit, James was the one who bought him the vodka. With my money even!

Instead of the Garden State Parkway, I took Ocean Drive.

The slow road.

I tried to convince myself I wanted to take in the sights.

I wasn't very successful.

Toward Townsend's Inlet my mood changed. I was at the beach for the summer. I had a job. I was not involved in that nightmare of a relationship anymore.

Yea, Mole had crashed my good time, but at least he had gotten all his drinking out of the way early, without any damage to property or reputations.

Life was good, I thought as I turned up our street and headed toward the bay.

That's when I saw them.

Ed and Mole on top of the Coast Guard Station. Both were nude and obviously on something. They were drinking and shouting to James who was at the water's edge.

I pulled in the driveway.

"What the fuck now?" I shouted to James.

Mole and Ed waved like naked sightseers from the top of the building.

"I don't know how they got up there," James said excitedly. "The good news is they are not drunk and it was not your dad's idea."

I waited for the other shoe to drop.

Instead Ed did.

He dove from the perch and splashed into the bay. His wave caused the floating dock to bounce loudly against the moorings

He climbed out dripping.

"It's great. The whole thing has been dredged for the Coast Guard boats, so it is pretty deep. Your dad is one crazy bastard. He was the first one to jump. Did you know a marine can jump from any height?" he said in amazement.

"He hasn't been drinking?" I asked unsure where Mole would get the balls to jump without the liquid courage.

"No. We didn't have any money for booze. Only had a couple of beers. Told him we would have to wait for you to get home. We did a couple of lines of Meth though. That got us going," he said proudly. Then seeing my face, he added, "It was okay that I gave him some speed wasn't it?"

First a quart of vodka, now some methamphetamine.

"Yea, it no big deal," I said sarcastically.

I got back in the car. As I did Mole jumped off. "Geronimo!" he yelled.

"How fucking original!" I shouted as I pulled back out.

"You going to get some beer?" Ed asked oblivious to my disgust.

He had already started to climb up the gutter that led to the roof.

I drove off, my cousin looking at me as I viewed him out the side mirror.

I turned my attention back to the road.

A Sea Isle cop was coming the other way. His overhead flashers were on but thankfully no siren.

I turned around.

I pulled in the driveway again. Neither Mole nor Ed were anywhere around.

James was at the dock talking to the policeman. As I approached, Ed and Mole came out of the apartment. Thankfully they both were wearing clothes. Shorts and tee shirts. Ed even had flip flops.

"Is there a problem officer?" Ed asked. I took one look at his grinding jaw and I realized that having two guys high on speed was not who you wanted talking to an officer of the law.

I intervened.

"Officer can I speak with you?" I motioned toward his squad car.

The cop looked almost relieved.

"Certainly. Someone has some explaining to do," he said, eyeing Mole up and down. "You three stay on the dock, don't be walking off."

He walked to the back of the car. I followed him.

"I got a report of two individuals indecently exposing themselves and trespassing on the Coast Guard facility," he said. He managed to sound both angry and bored, in a way I have heard imitated over the years by many people in positions of authority.

"Officer . . ." I looked for his name on his badge. "Officer Kennedy, sir I can explain . . ." I began.

"How did I know you were going to say that?" he said, now sounding more angry than bored.

"Sir, Those two gentleman did dive off the roof of the Coast Guard building, but only the porch and not the second floor. And they did not expose themselves, I assure you," I began, I felt the bullshit flowing within me. "They did it once and only once on a dare. When the older gentleman, my father by the way, dove, his bathing shorts were pulled off on impact. Unfortunately an old guy and his wife who were crabbing must have seen it and assumed they were skinny dipping. They were not."

I looked over at Mole and Ed, they were smoking on the dock. They appeared to be having a grand old time.

"That son, is still trespassing. And it's a federal building too."

The cop took off his hat and rubbed his hair. Like the other famous Kennedy's he had a large mane of premature gray. He looked desperate to be bailed out of this situation.

I was ready to be his savior.

"Officer Kennedy, sir can I let you in on what's really going on here?" I said, although I didn't really know what that was.

"My father rode his bike all the way from Philly last night because my mother left him," I blurted out like I was confessing my sins. "Twenty two years of marriage and she ditches him. He was blindsided. We all were," I said warming to the story.

"He certainly has not been a box of chocolates all these years, but he doesn't deserve this."

As I said it, I thought yes he does deserve my mother leaving him, and more.

I continued. "My friends were trying to cheer him up while I was at work. Now that I'm home I will make sure it does not happen again."

I finished and pointed, "Look, there is his beat up bike. Two flats and he got splashed by a tractor trailer on the way. Can you believe it?"

I hoped he could.

Time passes very slowly when you are bullshitting a cop. We stood there for what seemed minutes.

Looking relieved to have an out, Kennedy finally said "Since the complaining witnesses do not seem to have stuck around and the station is unmanned on week days, I guess I could let them go with a warning," he paused and pulled out a cigarette, "This time."

I reached in my pocket for my lighter, felt my one hitter filled with pot and came out empty handed. "Sorry officer, no light. But thank you so much for the break. I appreciate it. I will try and get him home soon."

I gave the thumbs up to James who had come back out and sat by the front door. He smiled and shook his head. He walked over to the dock as the cop pulled out.

"What did you tell him Steve?" Ed said not believing his good fortune.

He reminded me of the guy in the movie *Trainspotting* at his job interview, all jittery and nervous. Mole looked the same.

"That meth looks like a good time," I said just to let Mole know I knew.

He looked at Ed, who looked away.

"I gave him a variation of the truth. Just exaggerated the reasons," I answered.

"Don't bother me with details. Isn't that what you say Mole you fucking asshole?" I continued.

I went in the house.

Later, we sat around our dock drinking beer and barbequing burgers and dogs. Of course Ed and Mole were not eating. They were certainly drinking though.

"Unfucking believable!" Ed said for the thirtieth time that night. "You are the undisputed heavyweight champion of bullshit. You talked that cop out of arresting us. We were screwed . . . but we were saved." he said pretending to bow down in front of me.

It was old the second time he said it.

James added, "You know you should become a lawyer. That was some F. Lee Bailey shit if there ever was."

He too, toasted me.

"You couldn't make acne on Clarence Darrow's ass. Or barely a blemish on F. Lee's butt. Perhaps a pimple on a public defender' posterior, is more likely."

It was Mole. He was drunk, speeding and nasty.

I saved him once tonight I was not saving him again.

"Yea wise ass. You are big with words. Always turning the clever phrase. But aside from wowing your drop out buddies where has language taken you?"

I didn't wait for an answer.

"To the basement of Hygrade meats. Shoveling fat!

Oh excuse me, an Assistant Manager Of the Protein Byproduct Removal Unit.

I gave you the job and the title—drunk boy. Why are you here anyway? No one invited you. All you are good for is fucking up my good time. You were lucky one of us could talk today," I finished.

I was now standing a foot away from Mole's face. I had no clue where my friends were.

"You puss gut college boy," Mole drawled.

He seemed to be weighing his options.

"I brought you in to this world I can take you out of it." he slurred. It didn't sound cute like when Bill Cosby said it in his stand up. Mole meant it.

He stood up to face me. He spit.

The disgusting lunger hit me in the eye.

I instinctively pushed him hard. He lost his balance, regained it, then squared off in front of me again. His drunk fighting stance reminded me of his favorite boxer Gypsy Joe Harris. Like Harris he bent over and squinted up at me. Unlike Harris who was blind in one eye Mole was just blind drunk.

"Hit me pussy, you don't have the guts." he hissed.

"That's it, you piece of shit!" I yelled and clocked him as hard as I could in the head.

"Ahh!" I screamed. Mole did not make a sound. He fell to one knee. He grabbed his right eye.

I looked at my hand. The bone stuck up through the skin. I began to panic.

"You had enough mother fucker?" I said trying to bluff him into quitting.

He had not seen my hand. He was too busy with his eye. The blood was now gushing.

"I'm just getting started," he said menacingly. He rose up off his knee and started circling me on the dock.

I began to paw at him with my right hand. It was a joke. I had no right hand. I felt like Frank Burns from the old TV show *Mash* trying to throw a football.

"Get the hell away from me before I kill you asshole," I said now sounding desperate. I looked at James for help.

"Come on you two. You want the cops to come back? It looks like you did a number on your hand Steve and Mr. Mo your eye is blowing up good."

He signaled to Ed to help break it up.

"Come on Mole," Ed said soothingly.

"Don't touch me," Mole pushed him away. A bloody handprint was now on Ed's shirt.

Ed looked down at his shirt. I saw a flash of anger in his eye then it passed.

"Fine. But at least take a look at that eye. You might need stitches or at least an ice pack," he tried again.

Mole brushed by him and went in the house.

I looked at James. "I broke my hand." I said. I felt sick to my stomach.

"Great. Just what I feel like doing. Driving you both back to Delaware County. Let's go before you go in shock or something. I got a couple of Percocets in my glove box." He looked at my swollen hand. "Lets get ice on it and a ace bandage."

Glancing back at the house he added, "I hope you didn't blind the prick. You got a funny way of getting rid of someone. Couldn't just ask him leave, could you?"

We drove home on the Atlantic City Expressway. We must have been a sight. An old Chevy Nova with a bike tied to the roof. One guy with an ice pack on his swollen head, looking a little like the Elephant Man. Next to him Quad Ed engaged in a nonstop banter. Brought on no doubt by the craziness of the situation as well as the fading meth high. In the right corner wearing the blue jean trunks and sporting a hand that also looked like the Elephant Man's was me.

I was sick to my stomach and slept some of the way, but I remember feeling like a school kid who had been told to stand in the corner after fighting on the playground.

With the exception of Ed no one spoke. Poor James just fiddled with the stereo the whole way.

Thank God my mother was not home when we pulled in to Glenolden.

Mole did not want to go to the hospital. I had no choice. We dropped him off, and headed to Taylor Hospital.

I suffered a compound fracture of my fourth metacarpal. A boxers' break I was told. They pinned it and put me in a cast. My painting and papering career was over. Despite the cliché, there are no one armed paperhangers.

I got back to the shore on weekends but did not get the full summer at the beach.

At least I didn't have to stick around and deal with the fallout. My mother was very Switzerland about it—Neutral. Her party line was; she wasn't there so she could not say who was to blame.

I was pissed at the time. I mean I told her the whole story. Mole couldn't even remember the whole story. Plus, I had James talk to her too. Still she stayed on the fence. I understand now. She had to live with him. I could run back to college.

That's what I did. Cast and all.

Back at school before the regular classes started, the cast was no big deal. My coworkers at the admissions office seem to buy my excuse that I hurt it loading carpet at my family's carpet company. This was a complicated double lie. Not only did I not hurt my hand unloading a truck. The carpet company, was not my family's it was my uncle's. It was getting hard to keep track of my lies if any one at school was keeping tabs.

Only one person did. The office secretary.

She told me once the summer before, out of the blue, that her dad was a nasty drunk growing up. I remember I looked at her like I had been shot. I didn't say anything but she knew. She always treated me special after that. I really liked her, but I never told her anything.

Now with the cast covering up the boxing break, I felt like Hester Prynne carrying around the Scarlet Letter 'A'. Only mine didn't stand for adultery, it was alcoholic or son of an alcoholic.

It was the same.

One punch.

One punch and I was right back to where I was before the trip and the World Series Of Birding.

Chapter 39

On Bars, passing them
and being behind them

Again I tried to focus on school. The only people I told the truth to were my friends from home like Triangle head and at school, Dan Barley. Neither one could believe I took on my old man. They both thought it was great. Fucked up of course, but great just the same.

Once again school saved me. This time I didn't go home for anyone or anything.

Thankfully, poor Larose never told me a thing about Mole. My sister would just say I was lucky to be away, then tell me she missed me. Looking back, I wonder if she thought it was odd I always asked her if dad hit her.

Thankfully he did not.

Not coming home paid off. Without the distractions I had my best year ever. It flew by. The trip seemed like centuries ago.

Beans' death a distant memory.

I was graduating.

I had a three point one and good LSAT scores. I would be able to get in either Villanova if I got the money or Temple if I did not. Either way I was sitting pretty. I needed only to make it through the graduation ceremony.

That was the easy part. Right?

Not when you had the Mole to contend with.

I called my mother. She made small talk. I cut the crap.

"Is he going?" I asked.

The line got silent.

"Mom you still there? Well?"

"He says since he didn't get to see his sister graduate then you are kind of the first Molineux to graduate from college. He wants to see it."

"No way."

"I will keep an eye on him," she said.

"Like you kept an eye on him at my district wrestling tournament, when he showed up bombed wearing the Sherlock Holmes hat, cursing and acting out the match on the side of the mat. He had to be dragged out, remember?

Or the way you controlled him at Paul's wedding when he drank all the vodka before the bar even opened, danced that god forsaken nightmare Joe Cocker thing and then picked a fight with Paul?

Should I continue?"

She hesitated then said, "He is so proud of you. This is the closest he can get to sharing your success. Let him go."

She was always a pushover.

I was not.

Without thinking I said, "I'm not going. Don't bother. There are fifteen hundred of us anyway. It really doesn't mean shit to me. It is the piece of paper I need. They can mail it. You can come to my law school graduation."

I hung up.

I never went to my graduation. I'm sure it broke my mother's heart but she understood. It was the same reason she never took him to any work functions.

I'd like to say the reason I did not go was because of Mole, but really I didn't feel like it anyway.

Instead, I went out partying with my buddies. I celebrated like Mole would have if he had the chance.

I hated him for the drinking, but it was okay for me.

That's how it went. After our fight, who am I kidding, after I punched him and fractured my hand, things were never the same. I kept him at arm's length. If I felt like I was getting soft I just looked at the scar.

I had all the reminders I needed.

I played a subconscious cat and mouse game. If he wanted in, I wanted out. If he showed up, I left. Oh, don't get me wrong, we saw each other, and we talked, but it wasn't the same.

Small talk, and books were our only discussions. Ones I should read, ones I already did.

I went to law school.

When he found out, he told me I was a sell out.

Even though I lived less than a mile from my parent's house I saw him only a couple of times each year. If he showed up at my place (always unannounced) I would pawn him off on my roommate.

When it came to visiting my mother, most of the time I would call before I went. If he answered I would make small talk then hang up. I would skip the visit. Usually, I would meet my sister and mother at my grandmother's or my aunt and uncle's.

Suitcase and Josh would occasionally call. Sometimes they would stop over. Once or twice we even went out for beers. They would joke and they would drink. On rare occasions they would even mention birding.

We never went again.

They seemed tired and old even though they were not even fifty. After a few beers they would get around to the 'Mole issue' as Josh called it. They'd ask me why I didn't see him. They'd ask me what was my problem. Once, Suitcase asked me why I didn't just apologize to him.

Instead of getting angry, instead of trying to explain his worsening alcoholism, I asked "Why don't you two hang out with him anymore?"

Suitcase mumbled something about family commitments to his nephew. He looked to Josh. "And Josh here is back with his wife . . ." he said trying to jumpstart Josh into backing him.

Josh understood.

"Touche Stevie," he said.

They knew Mole was no longer a serious drinker with a birding problem, he was non-functioning alcoholic.

He stubbed out his cigarette. "Let's leave the boy alone, he's got law books to read." He gathered up his money off the bar, and hugged me goodbye. Suitcase did the same. "He loves you," he said.

They walked toward the door.

I can't say I enjoyed this family arrangement. Can't say I didn't miss my father. I certainly would have liked to have seen more of my sister and mother, but that's the way it was.

I still kept tabs of course.

Larose told me Mole didn't work any more. She supported the family with her shipyard job. She told me Mole barely drove because of so many accidents, and possibly a DUI.

His health was going too. He apparently had seizures once in a while caused by the drinking. Although Larose said he claimed he had epilepsy.

I tried to make her laugh by telling her that he always had epilepsy it was called dancing. I'd remind her of his drunk Joe Cocker shuffle or his semi-nude late night piano playing.

She didn't laugh.

"I'm getting a divorce," she told me one night shortly after I graduated from Temple Law School. She had made the graduation. Mole had not.

"It is about time.," I said.

I meant it.

"I can help you. I will be practicing soon," I boasted.

I knew nothing about divorce law.

"How screwed up. After all that time begging you to do it, you go and do it on your own, without any influence by me. Did you tell him yet?"

"I'm telling him tonight. Your sister is at a friend's. I told her yesterday"

I could sense fear and elation in my mother's voice.

"Good luck. Call me if he is trouble," I said hoping I wouldn't get a call.

"He's always been trouble," she answered. "I will call you if something comes up." She hung up.

No call came.

Curious, the next day I called her.

"So? Did you tell him?" I began.

"Yes I told him," she said.

"Well, what did he say?"

I must of sounded like a house wife gossiping about someone down the street or the latest soap opera.

I was not ready for the answer.

"He started to cry."

"Really? The old bastard started to cry?" I said. I suddenly felt like a piece of bleached cat shit.

"He cried at the kitchen table for two hours then he left. He took my car too," she said a sound of worry in her voice.

"Are you concerned for the car or for the Mole?" I asked trying to joke.

"Don't be funny Steve. I have a bad feeling about this. Call me if you hear from him."

"You do the same."

I hung up.

I had a bad felling as well.

I called Suitcase and Josh. They had not seen him. I called the Halfway Tavern. The bartender said he was there last night but he had not seen him yet today. I left a number to call if he came in.

He did not call.

Judge Narkin did. Two days later.

"Steve, this is your Uncle Tom. Tom Narkin," he said sounding like a James Bond greeting if it was written by Harriet Beetcher Stowe.

"Judge Narkin," I answered. Now that I was waiting bar exam results I didn't dare call him Uncle Tom. From now on it was Judge Narkin.

"What's up your honor?"

"What's up your honor? How about how are you Uncle Tom?" he said then laughed. He had a laugh like hyena on magic mushrooms.

"What's so funny sir?" I asked.

"A couple of things. First stop being so stiff. Just because you will be a lawyer soon doesn't mean you need to be so formal. I am still your uncle. I just happen to be the judge of Collingdale as well."

Of course he had to remind me. Judges always do.

"Secondly, and I don't know how funny you will think this is but I locked up your father last night for drunk driving, resisting arrest, speeding, running a stop sign, well three stop signs actually and public drunkenness."

"Is he okay?" I asked. The announcement had not sunk in.

"Oh he is fine. He's as pissed as a hornet in my holding cell. Keeps screaming about a conflict of interest because I am his uncle. You know I am your great uncle by marriage," he digressed.

Like I needed a review of my family tree at this point.

"Sir, isn't it a conflict of interest?" I interrupted.

I might have been a new lawyer but it sounded like a textbook case to me.

"HaaaaaaaaaAHhhhaaaaaaa!" Judge Narkin let loose that laugh again.

"Conflict of interest? There is no conflict of interest. Why . . . what would you like for you dad most of all?" he asked. He didn't wait for my answer. "For your dad to get some help. Get himself straightened out." He paused, "And your mother? What about her? Of course. She would like him to get sober. Stop drinking. Get clean.

Me? Well you know I like your dad. But enough is enough. He needs to straighten up before we are burying him. I been hoping for the chance to save him for years.

So you see. There is no conflict of interest. We all have the same interest. Helping Mole, and I aim to do it," he finished and laughed that crazy laugh one more time.

"I will call my mother and be down with some bail money," I said, amazed at not only the man's twisted logic but also the fact he was a judge.

I thought Mole was crazy?

"Don't bother. I am setting bail at two hundred fifty thousand dollars-straight. Not even posting your house will get him out. Tell your mom this is the best thing that ever happened to her and to him.

Good night nephew. Good luck with the bar exam."

"I already took it," I answered.

He had already hung up.

Unbelievable. Mole locked up by his own Uncle. Keeping him on a quarter of a million dollars bail. I couldn't make this shit up. Only in Delaware county.

I called my mom, then Mole's friend Dan Erickson.

Larose blamed herself.

Dan thought it was funny, but a violation of Mole's rights none the less.

After a week and a number of calls to Dan's lawyer friends, we were nowhere. Judge Narkin had succeeded in cutting off all the angles. If Mole filed a bail reduction petition, the judge would dismiss the drunk driving and find him guilty of the lesser charge of public drunkenness. He could give him a three month sentence on that charge. If he did not file a bail petition, he would only get a weekend in jail on the DUI but he would have to wait four months for the trial to begin.

Four month's in jail.

I had to hand it to my uncle, he was pretty slick. He was serious this time.

Two weeks went by. I went to see Mole a couple of times. It was pretty weird going in to a prison as a newly minted lawyer to see your father who has the same name.

It made for some raised eyebrows and awkward conversations.

"You got to spring me," Mole said the second time I went. "I can't take it. The screws are driving me crazy. The turnkeys won't give me anything to read and the doc won't give me my meds."

"Easy there Jimmy Cagney. What's with the jailhouse lingo. You sound like public enemy number one," I joked.

"I'm not kidding. I will do whatever you want. You're a lawyer, get me out of here."

"I'll see what I can do," I lied. I hadn't a clue what to do.

"This place sucks. No books. Only a couple of magazines. I'm going crazy. These kids stay up all night and sleep all day. I can't even understand what they are saying let alone have an intelligent conversation. If you ever get busted commit a federal offense. At least that way you do your time in a federal penitentiary. Best library system in the world-those federal pens."

"I'll keep that in mind Mole."

Later, his friend Dan gave me the idea.

"Put him in a rehab," he told me over coffee at his office in Philly.

I was interviewing with the District Attorney's office down the street.

"It has to be better than Delaware County Jail, and he might actually benefit from a program. It helped me," he said draining his fourth cup of coffee.

Dan had not had a drink since shortly after he woke up under my Christmas tree years before. He was still buddies with Mole, just not drinking buddies.

"Do you think Judge Narkin will go for it?" I asked, not so sure he would. In fact I was beginning to think Narkin was enjoying my old man's predicament.

"Sure he will. Trust me, he has to be sweating the judicial disciplinary board getting wind of this act. It is a clear breach of ethics to preside over your own relative's case. Although usually the problem is a lenient sentence or charges going away, not the other way around. Certainly not the hammer he is laying down on your dad."

It was worth a try.

Dan was right. My uncle seemed relieved to have an out.

"A rehab, huh? I assume an inpatient?" he said closing the model train magazine he had been reading. "I would only consider an inpatient program. The same length as the jail stay," he paused, no doubt now considering my family's lack of funds. "On second thought he stays only long enough to complete the program. Then he is free to go.

Deal?"

I nodded.

"Oh and one more thing. You, and only you, are responsible for picking him up and delivering him to the facility. If he leaves before he graduates or whatever you call it, he goes back to jail and does the whole three months. Plus an additional three."

"When can I get him?"

"When you get him a bed date. Here take this list of rehabilitation facilities I hand out to defendants." He took a two page paper from a beat up coffee stained manila folder on his credenza.

Narkin looked at me than said seriously, "You know Steve being a good lawyer isn't always about winning. It's about helping your clients. You are helping your client today."

"He is my dad," I said and got up to leave.

Narkin smiled, then said "I represent only one client. My family. Tom Hagan said that. Robert Duvall, *The Godfather Part One* . . . See ya, Tom Hagan."

He let loose that crazy cackle again.

He was still laughing as I left his office.

My mother made the actual arrangements. Mole was on her government medical benefits, so Mole was cash on the hoof. It was amazing, if we did not mention insurance, there was never any space at any of the places we called. Once we mentioned coverage, government health insurance no less, everyone wanted him.

The message? If you are poor you have to stay drunk.

Claremont Drug and Alcohol Clinic agreed to take him for their thirty day program. Three to five days in detox. The rest spent in intensive inpatient rehabilitation. We had a bed date.

Narkin faxed the paperwork to the county. I was free to get him.

//

He walked out after what seemed hours. Getting out of jail happens a lot slower than getting in. I saw him go through the last gate from the main building. He was wearing prison issue browns. He wore a wrist band, that he pulled and bit at in an effort to remove it.

I got out of the car and waved. He smiled quickly, then the smile left his face. He looked around self consciously, then bee lined for the car.

Some inmates who were outside tending to the grounds, yelled to him.

"The Professor has been sprung!"

"See you around old head."

"Free at last. Free at last. Thank God Mole is free at last!"

A group of Hispanic prisoners shouted out something in Spanish.

Mole smiled then waved. In a big show to his new audience he threw the torn wrist band in the air. He then got down on his hands and knees and kissed the ground.

The inmates cheered.

"Get up off the ground. Who do you think you are Nelson Mandela? You did three weeks in county. Not even twenty days," I said sarcastically.

I admit it was pretty funny though.

"You don't even speak Spanish how are you friends with those guys?"

Picking himself up Mole said, "Everyone laughs and cries in the same language."

"Come on Brubaker let's get you some clothes before our next adventure," I said taking the manila folder he carried and opening the car door for him.

"Thank you son."

He took my hand and smiled as we pulled out.

I took him to K-Mart and bought him some clothes. He threw the prison issue jumpsuit in the dumpster behind the mall. Seagulls screamed and protested the interruption of their lunch.

We both smiled. I thought of our time in Cape May. I also thought of the fat factory.

"I'm sorry for embarrassing you, being that you are practicing criminal law in this county," he said after changing and getting some drive through at McDonalds.

"No big deal, Mole. I'm just glad you are finally getting some help," I said.

He sighed, "Don't remind me. People should only get help is they ask for it. I never asked for it."

I ignored the comment.

He looked out the window. "Anyway it is a beautiful day. The sky never looked so good. It seems like years since I've seen it."

He rolled down the window. The smell of fall and burning leaves filled the car.

"Twenty days there, Bird Man of Alcatrez. You only did twenty days," I reminded him.

"It felt like years." He paused. "I don't know why the caged bird sings. I certainly didn't. Speaking of which, how about some music. Any Creedence?"

I handed him a CD.

"Make do with The Band."

As we approached the Clermont Clinic, he apologized.

It was simple and direct.

He apologized for causing so much pain. He said he had no idea what was going to happen but he said he was going to try hard not to hurt us anymore. He asked me to apologize for him to my mother and sister as well.

I walked him to the admissions office where he was greeted by a thirty something counselor. She was an attractive dirty blond with a painfully tight ponytail. She was wearing a long sundress even though it was fall. She had a tattoo on her neck that said 'Laugh.' I wondered if that meant the obvious or if it short for her name. Her name tag said Laughlin. I didn't ask.

"Thank you very much for dropping off . . ." she hesitated, wrestling with the pronunciation of our name "Mr. Mo-line-ux" she finally tried, butchering it like my clients always did.

"Molineux" I corrected. "It's French."

She continued, getting the name right the second time. "Mr. Molineux is in good hands. He will be able to write you but not phone you. He will be able to have visitors in a few weeks," now switching to automatic pilot.

Mole seemed to like her looks. He looked at me and whispered, "Maybe the old man will land one while he's doin his time."

"You are undergoing rehabilitation Mr. Molineux, not doing time. And I am married, thank you. Follow me," she said.

She closed her admission file and shuffled Mole off.

"See you soon, Mole."

I turned and walked out.

I was now in my late twenties. Mole had been a heavy drinker for as long as I could remember. He had been a nonfunctioning alcoholic for a few years now. This was the first time, I could remember, he had been sober for this long. It was also the first time he had ever been in any treatment program.

He was not happy about either.

Despite this, he stuck with the program.

The month went by quickly. Truthfully, it was nice not having him around. I went out frequently with both my sister and my mom. We got together with my fiancée and her young son a lot and acted like a normal family. Whatever that is.

We did not talk about Mole or his rehab much. It felt like, if we did, we would jinx him or maybe we were afraid talking about him would jinx us. When my mother and I did talk it was apparent that with her pending divorce she did not want anything to do with him.

He would be my cross to bear.

As a result of this new reality, I took steps to set him up as best I could. I filed for Social Security Disability benefits. Believe it or not, his alcoholism, combined with a generous doctor's report suggesting bi-polar disorder qualified him for a monthly check from Uncle Sam.

This blew my mind.

I had a client who was an automobile mechanic. He lost an arm in an accident. Doctors were unable to reattach it. He could not get Social Security Disability. Mole on the other hand was an alcoholic, he could get benefits.

Lucky for Mole. Lucky for me.

I also got him an apartment in Darby, near where Seconds Flat used to stand.

I told him these developments when he could take calls. He didn't say much. Instead he wrote me. Two letters a week, sometimes three. I threw most of them away, however I found one in his social security file I kept at the time.

Sat. November 6.

Dear Steve-

Pumpkin pieces littered this morning's cycling streets. Blink an eye it'll be turkey carcasses. Blink both eyes and excommunicated Xmas trees either wrapped in dark plastic shrouds or waiting for cremation will be there.

Now, there's an opening paragraph deserving of Poe, what? But to the inexplicable contrary, me spirits are the opposite. It's probably your old axiom 'turn shit to fertilizer', but today is Saturday and aside from two meetings it's a free day. Hope you enjoyed your weekend. I was supposed to get a weekend pass. However a moronic bureaucracy prevented me from joining you. That's a polite way of phrasing it. Actually that imbecile, obese and cretinous counselor had the audacious gall to say that she'd never granted her permission for a weekend pass when the signed pass was right in front of her. "And you're not angry?" she asked.

"I'm disappointed, naturally, for a brief moment, but I put it in perspective. Two 18 year old drug addicts were shot across the street last night. Then there is the matter of earthquakes, famine, etc."

"Yes but that's not you. It's not good to smother your anger." And so on. She dragged it out for an hour.

A humorous aside—the other day during a small group meeting. I was reading aloud a long interpretation of Step 4 from the 12 steps of alcoholics anonymous. Of course no one pays a tad of attention, but just to test it—I improvised a little spice to the droning monologue. "A good recovering alcoholic will resolve to begin his day by constructively selling narcotics to preschoolers, shoot up with horse and crack, then, after anally raping an assortment of nuns, will hold-up a liquor store. A hit and run should put a closure to a productive morning."

No one blinked an eye. The monitoring counselor was engrossed in reviewing old photos. Two inmates, or I should

374   STEPHEN MOLINEUX

say patients were in a med induced la-la, and the rest were in
the suburbs of somewhere. This group of 15—odd said good
by to a very pregnant 19 year old heroin addict, yesterday.
When it was my turn I just gave her 2 bucks toward Pampers.
Actions speak louder than bull.

Another 22 year old Chester female crack head was kicked
out—she came in to a 10:00 meeting with her eyes so spaced
she looked like Mrs. Neil Armstrong.

I give serious thought to pulling a David Jansen act, and
while a fugitive's freedom is not one I crave, it has a better
flavor than the one I taste here.

But beggars can't be boozers (to change the saying) yet I
am reluctant to pen an articulate pleading to Judge Narkin.
This will begin my third week here, plus twenty slammer
days. Although animosity is a port I refuse to dock my boat
at, I can't help the thought that my sentence for drinking was
imposed by a man that has never had a drink. That my time
behind bars (of both sorts) was dictated by a man who has
never spent a day behind either. But this is but a very passing
thought. As Roethke put it "Reason, that dreary shed—that
hutch for grubby school boys, . . . my heart knows a different
tune."

The river this morning was flowing calmly, a gaggle of
mallards was led by a big white goose. He looked like an albino
General Custer duck. Mathew Brady's Polaroid band playing
the Civil War Rag. I wish I'd never read Tom Sullivan.

Love

Mole—Hugs to my girls

I read it to my mom and my sister. Larose just shook her head.
"What a waste of an intellect. Typical daddy. Better and smarter than
everyone," she said dismissively.

"I don't think that. He's trying to make the best of a shitty situation.
At least he still has his sense of humor, I think he might be okay when
he gets out," I said then pointed to my sister's shirtsleeve "Maddie how
did you get that on your shirt?"

When she looked down I flicked flicked her nose.

"Ha, made you look!"

"I don't even know what the heck daddy is talking about half the time. He is so weird."

She punched me on the arm. I exaggerated her power.

"Oww!" I yelled.

"Both of you knock it off," Larose said. A mother's work is never done.

"Let's hope this helps your father. Nothing else has" she murmured.

I noticed she folded the letter neatly then gave it back to me.

Chapter 40

How Mole rehashed the rehab

Mole was discharged successfully from Clermont inpatient rehabilitation program after thirty days. He then spent another month in a halfway house. He got sober and he got healthy. He really did not have a choice. Judge Narkin made sure of that.

He continued to write me regularly. Funny and tragic stories of the addicts and the alkies. He told me about a psychiatrist with an alcohol and coke problem who refused to acknowlege that he was anything but a treating physician and not a patient receiving drug addiction rehabilitation. Mole claimed the good doctor some how had a beer truck make a delivery to the halfway house. He was kicked out of the program as a result.

I wish I kept the letter.

His stories were always part fact and part fiction. They were always entertaining. Aren't those the best kind of stories?

He told me heartbreaking tales of doomed young addicts with no chance at all of making it. From his letters it was clear Mole cared about all of them very deeply. It was clear he wanted to help them, care for them, educate them and comfort them.

He was trying.

It was also obvious he realized the futility of the whole thing.

He wanted out.

I convinced Narkin to put him on a house arrest for the final thirty days.

He did good for about six months.

He didn't drink, at least not around me. He worked out. No longer driving, he rode his bike around town. Once in a while he would ride to my house a few towns over from Darby. He would show up unannounced and play with my soon to be stepson. He would drink coffee and flirt awkwardly with my fiancee.

This went on for a few months. Then he realized my mom was not coming back. In quick order, the divorce went through and the Glenolden house was sold.

He got a chunk of change and a divorce decree.

He started drinking again. He was just looking for a reason. With the divorce, he found one. If it wasn't the divorce it would have been something else.

He became a regular at the usual haunts. Cookies Pub. The Halfway Tavern. The Blue Moon. Even Dixons the 'black bar.' He would switch them up depending on who he owed money to, or what type of drunk he was into at the time.

Eagles fans during football season. Marine Corps veterans and bikers, especially around the Fourth of July and Memorial Day weekend.

Sometimes he would even see Josh and Suitcase. Most of the time it was a coincidence. Drinking in the same bar, occasional get togethers at George Conchon's house, helping out when Suitcase moved his sister, or borrowing or lending money to Josh. Other than that, they rarely did anything together anymore. Never went back to the Series as far as I know. No more birding trips.

Except for those occasional visits on his bike, Mole did not see me. Oh, don't get me wrong, it was not that dramatic. I saw him, I just did not deal with him when he was drunk. Since he was now always drunk again, I did not really spend time with him.

He would show up at my law office once in a while. He would ask for a loan or seek legal help for his new cast of characters he hung out with at his apartment in Darby.

The place was a one room efficiency in a brick building sandwiched between two autobody shops. It got so hot in the summer Mole called it the 'pizza oven flop house.'

Most of the men he spent time with now were on their last legs. Crack Mack who smoked the rock. His old friend Doc from the fire company who was now a full blown alcoholic. Charlie Hazel the trash man who was a little slow.

They would sit outside his place smoking, drinking and shooting the shit. They were all on disability, or comp, or section 8 housing or welfare.

Mole was the friend that always had a light or a smoke or an extra buck for a hot pocket from the Wawa market up the corner. He kept them warm in winter, and always shared his booze. He was also the one who explained everything to them. Changes in their benefits, the small print in their leases, or even a big word in the newspaper.

As I said, he would stop by once in a while because he was also the guy with the son who was a lawyer. "Mole's son can fix it," I heard all too frequently in the waiting room of my office. I took care of public drunkenness and disorderly conduct citations. Landlord/ tenant cases and changes in their government benefits. I tried to help Mole and whoever he brought with him.

During this time I noticed Mole seemed not have a care in the world. Although he had lost his wife and to a large extent his family (he really didn't talk that much with my sister either) I never once heard him complain.

When I discussed this with his friend Dan, he had an interesting take.

"Your old man is like a Buddist. He doesn't want for too many things. He tries to keep a positive outlook and always looks at the bright side. As long as he has a good book, his typewriter, and something to drink he will be okay. He has no stress, no responsibilities and he is so pickled from drinking he will probably out live us all," he told me one day after I saw him outside the courthouse in Philadelphia.

Mole's mind may have been content with his lot in life but his body was not. The drinking and smoking were taking their toll. His health was getting progressively worse. His seizures were increasing. He would not tell me, but he was hospitalized a few times a year because of them.

He became even more reclusive. I saw less and less of him.

He had no car, so he continued to ride his bike around town. Unfortunately, as his health deteriorated he could no longer ride as far. I would see him once in a while pedaling or more likely walking his old beat up ten speed with the milk crate bungee corded to the back. He would be dressed in all sorts of 'Salvation Army chic' as he called it. He lost so much weight and wore so many second hand clothes I began to call him 'Layers.'

He took it all in stride.

His favorite look was a old and dirty three piece white suit. He would show up unannounced at my house to deliver fresh produce or stolen library books he thought I might like. He looked like a dirty ghost in a matching fedora. My wife called him "a disco bum." She made me promise not to tell him. I thought he looked more like Tom Wolfe as a street person.

The Government would not trust him to receive his monthly disability check. He had me draw up papers to allow Josh to receive it for him. When I asked him why not have the check sent to me? He told me "Neither you nor Uncle Sam are my parents giving me my allowance. It is my money. I paid into it, I earned it. At least Josh will give me **my** money to spend as I please. No bull shit . . . I may be a sinking ship but I'm still sailing."

That lasted two months before he showed back up at my door.

"That thieving bastard Josh stole my money. Why did you let him be the trustee?" he screamed. His breath smelled like one of those frogs you used to dissect in high school science class.

I became the receiver of his disability checks.

The government required that I submit a quarterly report providing an itemized breakdown of all Mole's purchases. It was designed to insure that the person entitled to the disability was not only receiving the money but was also not blowing it on drugs and alcohol.

Mole refused to cooperate.

"I don't need to tell you or Big Brother what I am doing with my money," he complained when I asked him to keep track.

I was never going to be able to dole the funds out to him responsibly. Instead I just started endorsing the checks over to him at our monthly meetings.

When it came to submitting the form I typed in, 'Recipient is uncooperative. Refuses to provide accounting to trustee. Undersigned requests assistance.'

When this did not elicit a response, I wrote on the next one, 'Recipient is drinking up every dime of disability benefits with cheap vodka.'

Still no response.

Finally, in desperation I wrote on the last quarter's report, 'Patient now drinking and smoking crack on the Government's nickel. Trustee unable to do anything about it. Trustee is thinking of the old adage, can't beat em join em. Please advise.'

Uncle Sam never responded except to keep sending me the money.

Late stage alcoholism is no walk in the park. Unless you are being rolled through on a gurney bed, in an adult diaper, then I guess it is a walk in the park.

It always cracks me up when I see movies that purport to show you the **real** depiction of an alcoholic. Flicks like a *When a Man Loves a Women,* where America's sweet heart Meg Ryan plays the alcoholic soccer mom. Despite her crippling drinking problem she still can handle her close up. The climatic scene to illustrate her reaching rock bottom is her drunkenly falling out of a rowboat on vacation, only to be saved by her increasingly frustrated but still adoring husband.

Please!

How about a real version, where Meg Ryan loses her teeth from neglect. Where the blood vessels in her face start bursting with such regularity that she sounds like a bowl of Rice Crispies after the milk is poured. Where she wrecks cars with her kids in the back with no safety seat. Where her stomach distends like some malnourished kid on a Save Haiti commercial. Where her adoring husband drops her as soon as he finds her cuddled with another rummy she met at a AA meeting.

Nothing beats my personal favorite Hollywood portrayal of alcoholism—*Leaving Las Vegas.* Nicolas Cage plays alcoholic business executive intent on drinking himself to death. We never know why. On the way, he still manages to keep all of his perfect pearly white choppers and never once shits or pisses himself on his way down. He even manages to get the girl. A hard drinking whore who has perfect hair and skin too. She keeps them both although her ass is sacrificed for the good of the story.

Quick. The Academy Awards are calling.

Hollywood can't show you the real thing, because to do so would send audiences flocking to the exit doors. Hollywood is, after all, selling dreams not nightmares.

Alcoholism is a nightmare.

Mole, like Hollywood, spared me most of the gory details. I saw him each month when he came for his check. At first the decline was relatively slight. A missing tooth, an unexplained shiner, a limp,or a gauze pad on his arm to hide the bruises from the intravenous tube marks he got in the hospital.

After a while I had to deliver the checks to him. He would meet me outside and talk cheerfully about my stepson or my wife.

He would never complain.

He would never let me in, either his apartment, or his life.

Truthfully, I didn't really want to.

Soon, he didn't always answer the door. I started to have to go inside.

It was worse. Buckets of bloody puke next to the bed. Sores that wouldn't heal. The jars of urine by his bed. The soiled garments around his room. Toenail clippings in his pockets because he couldn't make it to the trash can.

Still he would not go to the hospital or let me take him out of his place.

When he did finally get taken to the hospital, it was his friend Mack who called the ambulance.

"I didn't want to betray him, Steve but I was worried he might die in that pizza oven," Mack had explained to me at my law office a day after Mole was taken by ambulance to Fitzgerald Hospital.

It could not have happened at a worse time. My wife was at another hospital for her own surgery.

I went to see Mole.

The hospital was a couple of miles from my law office. It was a run down place that mirrored it's neighborhood.

It did not always look this way. In its time it was a top notch hospital run by the Sisters of Mercy an order of nuns that put quality care as their first order in their service to Christ.

The sisters had left along time ago. The Catholics always seem to abandon the ones who need them the most. Fitzgerald Mercy, like other inner city Catholic Hospitals had joined the urban Catholic Schools in a mass exodus to the suburbs. The caring had left along with them.

The doctor met me in the hallway. He was an intern, probably still in medical school. He was younger than me. Probably not shaving yet I thought as I walked past him to my father's room.

"He is pretty banged up. Do you know he has a severe drinking problem?" he said as he reviewed his clip board and avoided looking me in the eye.

"You don't say. No I did not know that," I said trying hard to be as sarcastic as possible. "Where is he? Is he going to be okay?" I continued, annoyed by the impersonal and borderline negligent care provided to poor people in United States hospitals.

I walked past him and entered the room.

Mole was awake and smiling.

"Sorry old chap. I had a wee bit of a fall," he said in his best Monty Python accent.

Sure enough he had a large cut over his eye that had been stitched up roughly. It was swollen and bruised.

"That is the least of your problems Mr. Molineux," the young doctor interrupted, now fiddling with the IV tubes. "You need to start taking better care of yourself. It starts with quitting drinking and smoking," he added.

"Doctor, I might as well stop breathing too," Mole said.

"If you don't stop now, believe me you will sir," he said then walked out.

I stood at the foot of the bed reading Mole's chart.

"They might as well write down what you don't have, it would be easier," I said amazed that the guy with this chart was still sucking air.

"It would certainly be a shorter list," Mole said. He let out a small laugh, coughed, then grimaced and grabbed his side.

After a minute he said, "I'm sorry. I know your own wife is in for surgery today. You shouldn't have come. I will be fine."

"No big deal. She is okay just having a little procedure." I said. "What about you? What are we going to do about you?"

"I'm not your problem. I will be fine" he said. He began to reach for his cigarettes on the table.

"You can't smoke in here! You can't smoke at all."

He pulled his hand back,then folded them in his lap.

After a bit, he said, "What shall we talk about?"

"Do you want me to get you a bed in an assisted living facility?" I asked.

"I don't want to talk about that. I'm fine. I have my own place. I plan on going back to it," he sighed. "Let's talk about birds. I heard there is a peregrine falcon nesting on a window ledge at this very hospital. The nurses told me you can see it from the intensive care ward," Mole said with new energy. "I told them thanks but no thanks. I'll skip the intensive care. Although I would love to see that bird up close."

He tried to avoid the subject of long term care for the rest of the visit. Finally, I did get him to agree to the assisted living on a temporary basis.

"Only until I feel better," he insisted. "Anything is better than this place."

I spent the next three hours meeting with social workers and doctors. I filled out applications, waivers, releases and authorizations. I reviewed assignment of benefits forms and patient disclosures. All designed to get Mole into a nicer place.

"Is this worth it doctor?" I asked after hour two.

"Absolutely. If your father wants to change his lifestyle. If he stops drinking. If he stops smoking. If he takes his medications and eats right. If he goes into this assisted living facility, no doubt he can live a few more years."

"If he does not?" I asked.

"Six months. Tops." He said with absolutely no feeling at all.

"Helluva bed side manner, Doc," I said smiling at how impersonal it all seemed.

"You asked. Besides, your father beat himself up. He did this to himself."

I ignored the obvious.

"What if Mole leaves before the bed is available?" I asked, knowing my father's history with being told what to do.

"He isn't going anywhere. He is near death. He couldn't walk a hundred yards. Plus he has no transportation," the doctor said putting the paperwork into a folder.

"Good. None of his friends have any cars either, and his place is three miles away. Guess we will be okay. I need to get my wife."

My wife!

I had completely forgot. I needed to pick her up from Riddle hospital. It was thirty minutes from Fitzgerald Mercy. I was already an hour late.

I ran out.

Later at Riddle, I explained to my groggy wife that I needed to fill out paperwork to put Mole in hospice. She was not happy, but realized that with assisted living he would no longer be my problem. She forgave my tardiness.

The next day I called the hospital to check on Mole and his transfer to the assisted living place.

"Mr. Molineux is no longer a patient. He left the facility last night."

"So he is now at St. James Manor?" I asked assuming he had gone to rehab.

"No, Mr. Molineux left against doctor's advice. We have no additional information to provide." The receptionist hung up.

No way. He couldn't walk a hundred yards.

I called his place.

He picked up on the first ring.

"Hello son. Sorry I didn't let you know. I had enough of that place. No one gets better in a hospital . . . I feel better already."

"How did you get home?"

"I walked. The old ankle express. How else?"

"Son of a bitch. What about all that work I did to get you in St. James?"

"I told you I didn't want it. I told you I wanted to come home. Those places are not for me. Don't worry I feel fine. I will stop drinking and take my medicine. I promise." Then, laughing he said "I intend to live forever or die trying."

I didn't dare tell my wife. Later when he called to talk to her son, I told her he had been discharged. He was better.

She did not seem thrilled.

Six months went by. I saw him on his bike. He didn't stop but gave me a wave and a smile. He didn't look great, but he looked a lot better than before.

So much for medical predictions.

Aside from that chance sighting I had not seen him. Neither had my sister. None of us had talked to him.

It was my wife who suggested we have him over.

I picked him up on a sunny Sunday afternoon. He had poorman's luggage-

Plastic Acme bags filled with used gifts. Not re-gifts. Used gifts. Stolen library books, a charcoal drawing of Dylan Thomas or Brendan Behan I can't remember which, and a Whitman's Sampler that had obviously been sampled.

He seemed excited and nervous. Aside from needing a shower he didn't look to bad. He had ditched the Tom Wolfe look in favor for jeans and a flannel. Of course he had on his usual thermal underwear, even though it was spring time.

He was sober.

He showed me the books on the car ride.

"I got Christopher a book on sharks and a book on Greek myths. The Atlantic City library won't miss them," he said smiling.

When I did not respond he said "Don't worry I gave them a donation in the form of a ten dollar Caesar's Palace chip I found on the board walk."

"So you are back to making shore trips. That's great," I said trying to make conversation. He wasn't the only one who was nervous.

Later at the house, he ate the chicken dinner my wife made like he was a crocodile coming off lent. He apologized for wolfing it down but he did the same with seconds. He would not stop complimenting my wife on her cooking and our home.

Her son Christoher sat transfixed by this odd man at the table.

"You are my step dad's dad, not my pop-pop," Chris said after his ice cream.

"What should I call you?"

"Mole" said Mole.

"Dad, Chris should call you Mr. Molineux," I said looking to my wife for her approval.

"If he wants Chris to call him Mole than let him," she said.

Mole, sensing my uneasiness with the use of his nickname said, "If you want you can call me Pop-Pop Mole."

"No. I think I will call you Mole," Chris said sealing the deal.

"Mole it is." He looked at me and smiled. He was happy that my wife had invited him and he was happy that I did not get my way.

We finished dinner.

Afterwards he insisted on cleaning the table. He refused to use the dishwasher instead washing every dish by hand. My wife could not talk him out of it. She was not allowed to help either.

Later Mole overheard Chris ask me, "Will you read to me tonight Steve?"

Before I could answer, he said, "I am Steve too. How about I read to you tonight?"

"Ok Mole. What story?" Chris answered, happy to have a choice of readers for once.

"I was thinking I could read you some Greek myths. I brought you a book of stories along with the Shark book."

Chris had found Mole's 'gift bag'. The shark book was already a favorite. Never mind the library card in the back.

Chris grabbed the bag of books and brought it over to Mole.

"What is a Greek myth?" He asked.

"Don't worry I will explain it to you later," Mole said, pulling the book out and handing it to Chris.

We fixed him a nice spare bedroom, but he would have none of it. He wanted to sleep in the basement, he didn't care that it was not finished. It was cold and damp and it felt like a cave

He insisted, "I will be fine. You have an old couch down there. With a pillow and a sleeping bag I will be fine. It is still better than my hovel."

We put Chris up to bed around eight. Mole helped tuck the boy in then pulled out the book on Greek Mythology. He looked at me, then to the boy. When I didn't leave he said, not so politely, "I am reading to Christopher, not you. I think I can handle it. I used to read to you when you were little."

I got the message and went down to the living room with my wife.

"They okay up there?" she asked.

"He says he has it under control," I answered. "He wanted to read to him alone."

Seeing that Mole was upstairs, she asked, "What's with him in the basement? I wish he would stay in the spare bedroom."

"He is a social retard. He is uncomfortable around people. Plus, he thinks he is imposing on us. Let him go. One less bed to make," I said.

After a little while had passed, I went upstairs to use the bathroom. Okay, maybe I went up to spy a little. I was interested in how Chris was taking to the old man.

I listened outside the door. I heard Mole's voice. It was surprisingly tender. He was really in his element. I could hear him changing his tone and inflection. He was using different voices for different characters. He was reading from the story of Prometheus.

" . . . Prometheus gave man fire. He taught men in earnest. He showed them how to cook, how to keep themselves warm; how to make bricks and burn pottery, how to make metal and make tools. Men no longer lived in caves, they now lived in houses. Prometheus taught men to write and to do math. In fact he taught them the beginnings of all the arts, and he gave them one blessing above the others. Before Prometheus, men knew of the future, they saw trouble and death coming upon them and they could do nothing to help it, so they were always miserable. But Prometheus took away from men all knowledge of the future. In its place he put in their hearts blind hopes, which saw nothing, but made them to be always happy. He gathered together all the evil things in the world, hatred and war and pains and sickness and he put them all in a big bottle—a huge jar that he sealed up and gave to his brother . . ."

I went back downstairs. My wife was on the computer.

"Look up Prometheus on the internet, would you?" I asked.

"Who?" she asked.

"The Greek myth. Mole is reading a story to Chris. It is probably over the kid's head but he sounded like he was listening."

We both looked it up.

Wikipedia's definition said—A Titan from Greek mythology. He stole fire from Zeus and gave it to man . . . Later Zeus punished him by chaining him to a great rock on the side of a mountain, where an eagle (some say a vulture) devoured his liver each day. At night the liver would regenerate and the next day the eagle would eat it all over again . . . . This went on for thirty years until Hercules saved the Titan by killing the eagle and breaking the chains that bound Prometheus.

I finished reading and looked at my wife.

"Do you think this story is appropriate for Chris?" she asked.

"I will go and talk to him," I said and started back up the steps.

I walked in. Chris was sitting up on the bed intently listening to Mole's story. Mole looked up and said "We were just wrapping up one of my favorites *Prometheus* and then I was going to start *Icaros*, the boy who made bird wings and flew too close to the sun.

"One story a night Mole. Those are our rules."

I bent down to kiss Chris.

"Come on Steve. One more please? Mole told me about the eagle that ate the Titan's liver up," Chris pleaded.

If Prometheus was too much for him you would have never known it.

"I know all about it. Not tonight Chris." I flashed Mole a look. "Icaros is a good one. A man who can fly like a bird. Perhaps a much better story for a kid," I said to Mole as I answered Chris.

"Maybe another time, young man. I will leave the book here. Thank you for letting me read to you. Books are a wonderful gift. I hope you always enjoy reading them. Good night."

He got up and walked out with me.

As soon as I shut the door I jumped on him.

"Don't you think that story is a little harsh for a young kid? How did he handle the torture scenes? Why that story anyway?"

He looked at me and smiled, "Relax. He was fine. You know I love language. Words can be beautiful, but to a kid, words don't matter. It's the voice, and the story. Kids can sense the feeling from the tone of your voice. That boy is a smart one. He knew I was telling him a scary story, he didn't know what it all meant but by the tone of my voice, he knew it was okay for me to tell it. It was okay for him to listen. He trusted me with the story, all by the sound of my voice.

As for the story, it has always been a favorite of mine, like Icaros and his wax wings."

"You don't see the irony in you telling a story about a guy who has his liver chewed up by a bird?" I asked.

"Nah! You think too much. It is just a story that's all. You know what Brendan Behan said when a critic asked him what was the message of his plays? He said, 'Message? What do I look like, a fookin postman?' Next time I will read *Where the Wild Things Are*. You will probably find some hidden meaning about me telling that one as well." He laughed and hugged me. "Thanks for letting me come over. Thanks for letting me read to him. I'm turning in now. See you in the morning."

He walked down the stairs to the basement.

He was gone the next morning before I got up. A note explaining he had walked to the bus stop and thanking my wife was next to his coffee mug.

Later my wife noticed our parakeet had been turned loose. She saw it at the feeder in the backyard. I told her Mole did not like to see things kept locked away, but that he probably let it outside by accident. I didn't tell her that he also took all my booze. I guess he didn't like to see that locked away either.

Let the eagle starve I thought, maybe Mole's wax wings weren't melted yet.

Chapter 41

How Mole gave me a drunk parrot and
I got another phone call

I guess I didn't know what to expect. I mean Mole did call me. Early on a Sunday Morning. Fourth of July. My father was worse than a pack of Jehovah Witnesses with the way he could wake you early on a weekend.

I was in the Blockbuster Video Store. I reluctantly answered the phone even though the caller ID let me know it was Mole calling from his Pizza Oven Flop House.

I had not heard from him since his visit.

A voice at the other end let me know it wasn't my dad, it was the local judge Tom Narkin.

What was he doing at Mole's?

The answer came jarringly quick.

"Steve they found your father, he died last night," Narkin said matter of factly. Oddly, I felt nothing. I glanced down at the movie in my hand—*Punch Drunk Love.*

The title oh so fitting, this news of his death.

Born on Halloween, died on Fourth of July. Bastard robbed me of two holidays I thought as my mind wandered.

"What do I need to do?" I found myself asking. It was as though I were handling someone else's problem.

"Nothing . . . . Are you sure? . . . You had him taken for an autopsy . . . Do you suspect foul play? . . . Of course not . . . I was joking Uncle Tom. You identified him for me . . . thank you. Can you take care of the burial and tell my mom and sister too? . . . That was a joke as well Tom . . . Where is your sense of humor? . . . Tell the landlord I will be down tomorrow. Tell the coroner to call Griffin funeral home for me. I will be over tomorrow Judge Narkin."

I hung up.

I checked out from the rental, (which would also have been an appropriate title for Mole's final act) and left the store. The drive home was a blur. When I got there no one was around.

I don't remember what I did the rest of that day. I must have made calls. I must have made arrangements. I remember my mom burst into tears even though she had been divorced for a long time and had not seen him in a year. I do remember my wife took my stepson out to the fireworks. I insisted.

I remember I wanted a drink.

I remember I did not have one.

I awoke the next day with crusty and leaking eyes that itched and dripped like poison ivy on a cub scout's knee. It was as though God had forced my eyes to cry the tears and feel the pain that so far had eluded me. I had finally come down with the pink eye Chris had picked up along with passing his deepwater test at our swim club.

I took the trash out, then climbed into my wife's minivan. Suprisingly, the van not the Judge's call jarred me into the realization of Mole's death and my own middle age mortality.

I began the drive down to Mole's flop house. I settled in behind an old man who stopped at the curb to pick up his ancient wife. She made her way gingerly toward the passenger door with a walker that looked like a human scaffolding.

We are all in need of refurbishing, I thought, our exteriors crumbling.

As the old man started back down the road, I noticed his bumper sticker;

Retired—No worries, No hurries.

I had both.

My impatience must have been obvious because seeing me he immediately slowed down even more. He glared at me out his rearview mirror.

The old drive slowly because they know they are approaching the end of the road. They think by slowing down and puttering on they can prolong their life.

As though they control anything.

The man kept glancing back at me through his rearview mirrors, obsessed with what is behind him, looking back. The past is all he has, I thought.

Teenagers speed by-never glancing back in their rearview—their whole life is in front of them, and they are anxious to get there. Their road goes on forever.

I wondered if Mole ever looked in the rearview.

The times I was with him he always seemed to be in the present. But how could I know, I had not with him in a long time.

"Mole rode a bike," I muttered to myself as I passed the geezer when the road widened.

Would I have to see the body? I didn't want to take this ride, let alone have to see my father dead.

The coroner told me on the phone it looked like a heart attack although the official cause would not be available for a few days. The funeral home would get the body afterwards.

I parked around the corner and walked up main street to Mole's place. Mole wasn't the only thing that died in Darby. The once vibrant main street was now a dirty deserted shell.

I remembered my parents taking me here as a kid. New gym shorts and teeshirts from the Big Store. Dress pants from Bennetts. Slightly irregular sneakers from Cain's Department store. I didn't care—after all they were Converse All Stars, white high—tops! Afterwards a cheeseburger and a chocolate soda from the counter in the back of Woolworths.

Now they were all gone. Mole too. Boarded up or torn down or just plain old dead.

I passed the welfare office where, at Mole's request, I had helped his buddies so many times.

As I passed it and approached his apartment, an old Chinese women who still scratched out a living running a pizza shop on the corner approached me. She had tears in her eyes as she handed me a pizza. "I so sorry. Mr. Mole nice man. He look out for me. He take care of my bird feeders. I miss him."

She stood nodding and mumbling to herself as I turned the key in the lock. I left the pie on the steps.

I braced myself for the smell and entered.

The place was dark. The smell of death was everywhere but not as overpowering as I thought it would be. I fumbled with the curtain, then the window. I let in both the light and the fresh air.

The place was a disaster. I couldn't tell if it was ransacked by the police and paramedics, or if he lived this way.

I settled on the latter.

I went back outside to let the place air out and to collect my thoughts. I was met at the door by Crack—head Mack.

"Sorry about your dad, Mr. Molineux. It's a shame. I tried to get him to take it easy. It was hot Sunday and all," he began. "We were all hanging out down at the picnic table by the creek. We were drinking a bit. Mole said he wasn't feeling too good. He chalked it up to the heat. I tried to get him to cool off in the creek, but he said he would be okay in the shade.

Later, the guys started to argue about something stupid. We were pretty drunk. Your dad was drinking, but not like us. Anyway we were getting pretty loud and some of the guys started shoving and cursing. Anyway last I see of your dad, he says 'If this was to be my last day on earth, the last thing I would want to do is sit here listening to you assholes arguing about nothing. I've had enough. I'm going up to watch the birds in Miss Chen's feeder.' That was the last I seen of him. Doc found him when he went over to see if Mole wanted to go to the parade the next day. He died in his sleep," he finished. He stood, uncomfortably staring at his shoes at the bottom of the steps.

"Thanks Mack. I appreciate the information. Thanks for being my father's friend. Now if you will excuse me, I would like to be alone. I have to go through his things."

"Mr. Molineux any chance you could see me through with a couple of bucks?" Mack asked still staring at the ground.

No wonder he wasn't leaving. He was hitting me up! I couldn't believe it.

I gave him five bucks and the pizza. Any man that can hit up a son a day after his dad died must really need the money.

He took the money and the food and left.

I went back to the room.

I stared at the bed where Mole died. I looked at the pictures pinned on his wall. My law school graduation, my wedding, my sister's graduation, an article about me in the paper. I realized he had not been present for any of these events.

He wasn't invited.

What a waste.

I sat in a chair and tried to cry.

Nothing.

I started to throw the mounds of junk into a trash can. There was nothing but junk. As I loaded up the garbage I saw a package. It was crudely wrapped in newspapers and acme bags but definitely a Mole used present.

I picked it up and looked it over.

There, barely visible, despite being written in red ink, was a name tag—Happy Birthday Stephen Dean.

My birthday was not for another six months. What was on this crazy bastard's mind that he was putting together a homemade present six months before my birthday?

There, in my dead father's one room flop house in a dead town I opened the present. In typical Mole fashion it was a hodge podge of things. He had put a lot of thought into this one, I thought.

First I pulled out the now old pair of Bushnell Binoculars. The second pair we had won at the World Series of Birding. Next was the other copy of the Big Day Big Stay Award. It was old and yellow, but I could still make out the signatures of all the birders. At the bottom of the package was a book. It was dusty and stained but I recognized it immediately—*The Birds of North America*. The old Swarthmore College library book Mole had stolen years ago! The same book he used to teach me the birds that I would identify with Beans on that crazy wonderful trip. It was old and reeked of mildew but it was the best present I could ever receive.

The tears that had so far eluded me, now came flowing.

That sentimental bastard. He had looked in the rearview after all.

The trip was our best time together. Our last time together. With his 'used gifts' he was giving that time back to me.

I looked at the empty wrapper. There was one more thing. A drawing and a poem, with a note.

> Dear Stephen Dean—Happy Birthday! No card but I wrote a nonsense poem for you—hope you get a small smile out of it.
>
>   Love+ many, many more-
>   Pop-pa Mole

The poem and the picture were titled 'Polly'. The drawing was a parrot in a cage. The cage was shaped like a bottle. This is the poem.

Polly

I had a parrot/ and she could talk
She talked and talked/ Oh how she talked
She talked until/ one day I squawked
I said shut up bird/ give me some peace
Polly said; I own this cage/ I have a lease
Well I'll kick you out/ you can sue
But I do warn/ my cat has eyes for you
Why that old Tom/couldn't catch a mouse
He's got one eye/ and you're a souse
Why if I'm a souse/ then you're a sot
For I put gin in your water pot
I know you do/ Polly's not dumb
But don't you know/ that parrots like rum?
So rum to Polly/ I did give
To shut her up/ so that I could live
Now me Polly slept day and night
Worst of all how she snored
But without her talk/ I soon grew bored
I'm knocking off Polly, dear
All of your rum/ most of your beer
No! No! No!/ Not this day
I'll not join the bird AA
Yes you will for you're a pie-eyed parrot/a soak/and sot
Nah, not me/ I'm just a boozy old bird that drinks a lot
You're a tippler and a toppler/ you get tipsy/ you get sozzled
I do agree with thee/ that I do have a capacity for bibacity
But for you to think/ you can halt me drink
I say Boss/ Fook your audacity.

I laughed. Birding and boozing on his mind to the end. He was a crazy bastard. Although in hindsight it seemed the alcohol that once gave him happiness, that once let him escape and fly away had trapped him long ago.

Caged him like Polly.

Maybe on that last day, the birds in his neighbor's feeder gave him back a little of that joy. Maybe they helped him escape once more.

I closed up his room.

I carried his gifts with me.

There was nothing else for me. I had what he wanted me to have.

I paid Mack and the boys to clean the place.

I never went back again.

///

The next day I picked up his ashes from the funeral home. They came in a cardboard box like a mail order book. I put them in my car trunk.

Chris told his friends I had a mole in my trunk. The kids asked me what it looked like, did it bite, and how did it breath?

I carried the ashes around for a while while I thought about what to do with them.

When my wife brought Mole to the pool I knew it was time to get rid of the box.

One day shortly after he died, Christopher, remembering that Mole was in the trunk, worried he would get too hot. My wife not wanting to upset her son, dutifully retrieved the box of ashes from the trunk and put them on the pool blanket.

When I heard, "I brought Mole to the pool today," that night at the dinner table.

I knew it was time.

The drive to Cape May took longer than I remembered. The pine barrens were no longer pine nor barren. Housing developments and industrial buildings took their place. Thankfully, the cement ship looked the same. Oh, it was a little more beaten up than I remembered, but it was still there. So were the Cape May Diamonds. They sparkled and shone as Mole might say like ice in a scotch glass. I picked up some of the polished pieces of quartz for Chris and put them in my pocket.

I left most of Mole's ashes there that day. It is where I was able to be with him so many years ago. It was only fitting that I would give him back to the place. Maybe, like the cement ship, he will always be there.

I didn't give him all back though. After all, I needed a birding partner. At least until my kids get old enough to join me. I placed the rest of his ashes in a cocktail shaker and buried the whole damn thing under the bird bath in my back yard. Right next to the feeders.

I have a patch of woods in the back of my house. There are some wild cats back there, but I shoo them off when they hang out by the feeders. A little stream runs through the back too. Birds like to hang out here. I have hedges on the side and I usually get a family of cardinals nesting there each summer. I have a family of bluebirds in the bird house I built with Chris. They are back for the third year in a row. There is a loud and boisterous cat bird that hangs out in front of my house. He seems to have shown up just about the time I buried Mole. He is always around although I can't figure out exactly where he lives.

It is a good spot—for the birds and for me.

Beans and Mole and Suitcase and Josh would like it.

I'm sitting here typing and looking out my back window. The birds are going crazy for the bacon fat I mixed in their seed this morning. My beer is ice cold and the frost from the bottle is leaving a wet ring on my writing. A green buzz of a humming bird is all around the window feeder. I turn down the Creedence and reach for my old Bushnell binoculars.

The End

Breinigsville, PA USA
04 May 2010
237360BV00002B/2/P